PIVOT

Also by Laura Lexx

Klopp Actually

Laura Lexx

Pivot

TWO
ROADS

First published in Great Britain in 2022 by Two Roads
An Imprint of John Murray Press
An Hachette UK company

1

Copyright © Laura Lexx 2022

A CIP catalogue record for this title is available from the British Library

Hardback ISBN 978 1 529 34824 8
Trade Paperback ISBN 978 1 529 34825 5
eBook ISBN 978 1 529 34827 9

Typeset in Monotype Sabon MT by Manipal Technologies Limited

Printed and bound in Great Britain by Clays Ltd, Elcograf S.p.A.

John Murray policy is to use papers that are natural, renewable and recyclable
products and made from wood grown in sustainable forests. The logging and
manufacturing processes are expected to conform to the environmental regulations
of the country of origin.

Two Roads
Carmelite House
50 Victoria Embankment
London EC4Y 0DZ

www.tworoadsbooks.com

This one is for my friends.

I

The sea was not expecting to be hit full force with a golf club. To be fair to Jackie though, she hadn't been expecting to throw it either. Well, technically, at the point where she was standing on the beach staring at the sea and holding a golf club, with the encouraging words of Ros in her ear, by then she was half expecting to throw it. But not really. Jackie wasn't the golf-club-throwing type. She'd barely ever looked at these golf clubs before Ros had loaded them into the boot.

They were long, and heavier than she'd expected. Didn't golf last all day?

'Golf lasts for hours,' she said absently to Ros. 'How the hell do you lug these around all day without dying?'

'Caddies,' said Ros, looking up from removing furry covers from the lumpy clubs.

'Is that them?' Jackie nodded at the little golf sock things.

'No – these are . . . well, do you know I don't know what these are? Some sort of warmers?'

'Why would you want the clubs to be warm?'

'I don't know. Maybe it makes the ball go further?'

'So, what's a golf caddy?' Jackie shook her head, losing their thread. This was a common side effect of talking to Ros.

'It's the person who carries your clubs around for you so you don't get tired. Like a servant.'

'Lord, no wonder it's so popular with men. Someone else doing the hard work while you swan around pretending you're the dog's bollocks.' Jackie launched another iron hard out to sea and heard the splash as the lengthy pole slapped the surface of the dark water. The lights of Brighton stretched out along the coast and she felt tears pricking at the corners of her eyes again. 'Have you ever played?' she asked Ros, determined to keep talking rather than crying. Was this really happening?

'Me? Golf? Oh, for goodness sake Jackie no, of course I haven't. Jesus, you've known me forty years, Jack, at what point did you think I was sneaking off for my illicit golf habit? No. No. I've enough entitled men in my life at the office; I don't need ones loose in the wild with sticks trying to get their grubby little balls into unassuming holes. Pure phallic, golf is! Dicks and balls and don't think I haven't noticed, Jackie Douglas, that the only bit of the grass they're interested in is the neatly trimmed bit. One-track bloody ponies men are! No, it's not for me – not golf, not football, not nothing. Nothing doing, Jackie love. I've not played a sport since I was forced to by a nun and I shall never, either. I tell you, it was lucky those nuns already had sticks up their arses or I'd have happily put my hockey one there and asked Sister Mary what she was moaning about because *it's only a stitch, gel.*'

Jackie never felt like she had a choice over laughing at Ros. Ros seeped through the cracks of whatever Jackie was feeling and tucked herself in to help. Jackie started to laugh and felt that familiar runaway train feeling as she lost control of the laughter. Soon she was laughing so hard she could barely organise the muscles in her torso to suck in enough air to keep her alive. The proximity of exhaustion made the laughter thrilling and intense.

The lights of various hotels, clubs, pubs and cars reflected off Ros's glasses as she huffed and puffed. Ros put on a mighty performance – her tone ranging from secretive as if this was just for Jackie, all the way up to full McKellen at the National. Bawling and yelling and attracting odd looks from loved-up couples passing by to experience the cosy romance of Brighton's quirkiness. The laughter reached the peak of the roller coaster's track. She looked at her friend, standing here in the cold, performing like a wind-up monkey trying to keep her from the descent. She broke.

Jackie crumpled onto the pebbles and felt all the air beat out of her lungs in one movement. She honked. There was no other word for it, and if she hadn't been so distracted by the absolute physical painfulness of her sobs, she might have wished she were a more dainty crier. As it was, all that was in her mind was the wish for this not to be happening. For them not to be there. For Ros to not need to be dancing about shouting to distract her.

'Come here, Jack. Come on.' Ros slid down to her knees and scooped Jackie's head against her chest. 'Come on now, love. Come on. Get it out.' She stroked Jackie's hair off her soaking face. 'Oh, go on fecker, feck off!' she suddenly shouted, making Jackie jump. 'You never seen two old bats crying on the beach before? You've not lived. Get gone – go on before I do for you.'

Jackie laughed again through her tears and slipped a hand into Ros's coat to hold her friend tight round the waist. 'Ros, I don't want this,' she sobbed, the unnatural tightness of her throat already aching up to her ears, 'I don't want this. What did I do wrong?'

'You?!' Ros screeched. 'You didn't do anything wrong, Jackie! Don't you dare!'

'I feel like such an idiot.' And she did. Jackie had never felt stupider in her entire life: stupid for not knowing, stupid for believing she was enough for someone, and stupid for knowing she'd take him right back now if he asked her to.

'I just stood there looking at his suitcase asking if he had a business trip. It didn't even occur to me that he might be leaving me. Who do I think I am, bloody Heidi Klum?'

'Actually, I think she's divorced now too.'

'It's so embarrassing.'

'I don't know. *Hello!* magazine said it was pretty mutual.' Ros casually flicked a tear off the end of Jackie's nose.

'Stop making me laugh.' giggled Jackie. 'I'm trying to be heartbroken.'

'Oh, well – I'm not going to stop you doing that if you need to, but you can't be my best friend and not be laughing now, can you? It's all I'm good for.'

'You're good for a cuddle.'

'Yes, but that's a secret between you, me and approximately eighty per cent of the British Army circa 1981 to 1989.'

Jackie snorted and wiped away a rather gratuitous bubble of mucus that was making a dive for freedom with her amusement. 'I feel so stupid,' she said, giving in to the bass note of her emotions.

'Don't you dare let him make you feel stupid, Jackie Douglas.' Ros switched on her authoritarian tone again. 'It's him who should feel stupid. What kind of an idiot leaves my best friend for some bint with half a brain?'

'We don't know that she's got half a brain,' said Jackie mildly, feeling that particular bout of tears glide to a halt. She gave in to the delightful calm that comes in the lull between heartbreaks. Her back muscles sagged down into Ros. 'She might be extremely clever.'

'Is she? What does she do?'

'I don't know.' Jackie realised as she said it. 'I didn't ask. I didn't ask anything. Is that strange?'

'I don't know,' Ros admitted, 'I can't even begin to put myself in a mile of your shoes. I've no idea what I'd do if my partner left me.'

'Not something you have to worry about,' Jackie said drily, 'Pinot Grigio doesn't often wander off.'

Ros laughed. 'There's my girl. She's in there – I knew it. I reckon he's gone all stereotypical midlife crisis talks. Got himself a bimbo airhead with legs that spread like an eagle.'

'A what?' Jackie pulled up short in her laughter.

'An eagle. A spread eagle.'

Jackie laughed, and slipped off Ros to lie back on the cold pebbles. Her waterproof jacket crunched against stone as she laughed and coughed and looked up at the black night sky. The moment of release brought with it the next wave of misery and unbidden tears. It was like contractions, Jackie thought, through a tight stomach and more waves of hot tears pouring down the sides of her head and burrowing, ticklishly, into her hairline.

'What am I going to do, Ros?' she choked, barely able to get the words out past the panic.

'Whatever you want, my love,' Ros said, snuggling down into the stones next to her. 'What do you want?'

'I want what I had,' Jackie managed to utter, squashing the tears back in and breathing out deep cooling breaths between words. 'I want to be happily fat, old and married to a man I barely notice. I want to be a normal, boring grandma and grandpa who live up the road arguing over inconsequential rubbish. I want what I had; I was happy. Why wasn't he?' The sound disappeared into a higher pitch than Jackie could wrangle into words.

'I'm so sorry Jack.' Ros reached across and took Jackie's icy hand, squeezing it into her own, 'I'm so, so sorry. I don't know why anyone would leave you. You're the queen of my world. I'd get it all back for you if I could, Jack. I'll get you anything you want. You want to throw some more clubs?'

Jackie shook her head, letting her body just rack with the sobs that were passing less painfully now.

'Do you mind if I throw one then?' Ros asked, slyly. 'Look, I know it's your break-up and all and it's unfair of me to ask, but I really fecking hate the bastard too right now and I'd give any-thing to throw one of his bastard clubs in the sea.'

Jackie barked out a laugh and nodded. 'Go for it, throw them all.' She stayed lying flat out on the pebbles while Ros stood up swiftly and made her way over to the idle golf bag. She selected an iron and pulled it out, standing in her own approximation of a golf stand and swinging it testingly.

Laura Lexx

Ros swung the iron high over her head and then suddenly let go with a loud, gasping exclamation. 'Ow! Oh! Oh, the bastard! Oh, he's hurting me from beyond the metaphorical grave!'

Jackie pulled herself up on her elbows, laughing again at the figure of Ros hopping about in the dark clutching her shoulder. An iron was speared in the pebbles about eight feet from where Ros was dancing. 'What have you done?' Jackie called across over the washing of the sea.

'It got me!' howled Ros, somehow limping and hopping while also holding her shoulder. 'He's haunting them to spite me!'

'He's not dead!' Jackie insisted through her laughter.

'Not yet! More's the pity party!' called Ros.

Jackie lay back on the stones and decided to laugh until the next wave of tears came. Maybe she didn't have a husband any more, but she had Ros – and that was pretty good.

2

When she'd got up that morning, there wasn't a bit of Jackie that thought she was going to end the day crying on the beach with golf clubs scattered across the surf like discarded firework sticks. If you'd pressed her, she couldn't have one hundred per cent ruled it out; Ros was her best friend after all, and when Ros was your best friend there was always a chance you were going to end your day doing something slightly unexpected. Ros liked wine. Not too much wine – she just liked wine. And to be fair: wine really liked her too. A glass or so of wine and Ros had the best ideas; ideas that she would make you see through to the end. A few sips and she'd be telling you an anecdote so entertaining and engrossing that it wasn't until the end of the story that you realised you were actually there when the event happened and didn't recognise it because of the extra colours she added to the narrative. She only had to uncork the bottle and settle you into a booth at the Hawk and she'd have a sixth sense on what you needed and how to help you out. Ros was a chaotic, competent angel and Jackie had never met anyone like her.

They'd been best friends since they'd bumped into each other at university. Fate, life and A level results had brought them together. Jackie was studying nursing, as she'd known she would from childhood when she'd first triaged her dolls and happily taken the rap for shredding a pillowcase to make bandages. Ros was attempting to study everything by changing her subjects with the seasons. They met in the library as Ros slammed a book shut on another subject and possible life choice. Someone had shushed her and Ros's outburst back made Jackie snort so embarrassingly she left soon after Ros, who Jackie had found slumped outside the library pretending to smoke and looking sulkily at the view of Canterbury below them.

Jackie had accepted a cigarette, which she too held until it burned down, taking the minimum number of puffs she thought she could get away with. Ros grumped about how boring her English course was, and Jackie listened, saying she was sorry for Ros but was heartily enjoying her own nursing course. This led to Ros switching her subjects and lasting almost a month at wanting to be a nurse before making an attempt at maths. Nursing didn't last for Ros, but Jackie did. Jackie never quite got her head round what it was Ros liked about her, but then Ros wasn't the type to look a friend in the eye and say, 'You're just the kindest person I've ever met, and I want to keep you.'

Jackie, a shy and nervous rule-follower, was absolutely entranced by Ros's ability to speak to adults like they were fallible.

'But aren't you scared of getting into trouble?' Jackie had asked, trying to simultaneously look at Ros and her own shoes so as to seem appealing without being too pushy.

'What would I get into trouble for?' Ros seemed genuinely baffled, and amused.

'Well, for speaking back to them?'

'That's what speaking is,' Ros said, blankly. 'They say something, and I say something back, no?'

'But. . .' Jackie didn't have much of a rebuttal. That was what conversations were, she supposed. Just not any that she'd ever had with a grown-up. In her experience you got told something by an adult, and you nodded and then did whatever it was they had suggested. 'Yeah, I suppose so. They don't put in your reports that you answer them back?' *Lippy* was a word Jackie was very nervous of since a Mrs Harris had used it on her once at primary school. She'd never really recovered from the shame, and never wanted it used again.

'Sometimes.' Ros shrugged. 'But Mam and Dad just ask me what happened and then we talk about it.'

With that sentence, Jackie's world was blown wide open. The thought of a parent reading a school report and then asking for your take was insane. She knew right there and then that this Rosalyn Mackie needed to stay in her life for good.

When she'd got up that morning, she'd thought the day was mainly going to revolve around a shoe rack. Oh, the giddy life of the retiree. Jackie realised with equal parts smugness and alarm that she was actually quite enthusiastic about the thought of going to get a shoe rack. Was this what life had boiled down to? Enthusiasm about a shoe rack? But, on the other hand, wasn't it great that nothing so awful had happened in her life that her main concern was which shoe rack to choose? She'd made a cup of tea and a slice of toast and stared out of the window, through the diamond lead and into the neat, tidy garden. The leaves needed raking. She'd do that later, when she got back. As long as traffic wasn't too snarled up on the back roads from town. Maybe it wasn't sensible to go to town? She could go to Dunelm. That was a good idea. Dunelm was always nice, and it should be quiet on a Tuesday in term-time. She hadn't even bothered asking Steve if he wanted to come; she knew his answer would be some sort of joke where the set-up was Things I'd Rather Do and the punchline a variation on A Sharp Stick and My Balls.

Dunelm had indeed been nice and quiet, with a wide range of suitable shoe racks.

Oak or pine? xx

she had messaged Ros to get an opinion.

For your coffin? Jesus what a way to tell me.

Haha. Don't be daft. For the shoe rack! xx

> Christ you might as well make it a coffin if this is what your life has come to.

Jackie had smiled and muttered, 'Cheeky mare.'

> What a cheek you have :P Not my fault if I had the good sense to retire while I'm still young enough to enjoy . . . DunElm on a Tuesday. OK, you got me. Hawk tonight? xx

She closed the leather case protecting her phone and tucked it back into her handbag, knowing Ros's reply would always be in the affirmative. She'd chosen the pine. No sense splashing out on oak for something down there on the floor – save the money for proper furniture. A nice young man had even helped her carry it out to the car – Jackie had absolutely no issue turning on a bit of the older-lady charm when she didn't feel like carrying heavy things. She hoped the karma from this behaviour wouldn't come back and bite her on the arse when she genuinely did need things carrying. Sixty wasn't too far in the distance.

Her silver Ford Mondeo pulled back into the double drive-way alongside Steve's black one, and after pulling up the hand-brake, Jackie paused, seeing the front door wide open, propped so by a small suitcase. Her throat contracted immediately, giving her a dry sensation from ear to ear and making stinging tears appear in her eyes at the pain. She yanked the keys out of the ignition and clambered out of the car, the shoe rack lying forgotten in the boot.

'Steve?' called Jackie, stepping into the hallway and looking down at the suitcase. An overnight bag hadn't meant good things in their house over the last few years.

There was the sound of shuffling about from upstairs. 'Steve?' Jackie called out again, leaning a trembling hand out to hold the bottom of the banister and steady herself. 'You going some-where?' She tried to make her tone sound light and carefree, but the panic was overwhelming.

Steve's head appeared from the landing, looking down towards Jackie in the hall. 'Jack! You're home!'

'Are you all right?' Jackie nodded her head at the suitcase and the open door, 'You're not . . .? You've not had news, have you?' She watched Steve's face for signs that he was lying, hiding the truth from her. He didn't look pale. Had he been losing weight recently? Not that she'd noticed. So, had it not happened, or had she just not noticed it?

Steve came down the stairs slowly, carrying his suit wrapped up in the Hugo Boss bag. 'Do you want a cup of tea?'

Jackie felt her temper flare. 'Steve, stop it, you're scaring me – are you going back into hospital? What's going on?'

'No, Christ no, no. Nothing like that. No, I'm fine. Jack, come and sit in the lounge with me.'

Jackie allowed herself to be led by the elbow to their immaculate sitting room. The powder-blue sofas sat in a perfect right angle round the creamy silver rug. Jackie sat on one. Steve took the other. They looked at each other across the polished wooden coffee table. Steve calmly explained to Jackie that he had met someone else and was ending their thirty-something-year marriage to go and live with that someone else. Jackie listened, understanding and also not understanding. She heard every word and processed every word, and then at the end of each sentence her understanding of the universe snapped back to exactly where it had been before Steve started speaking and she felt it tilting and reeling as she understood and processed all over again. Steve was moving out; right here and now. This was a shame for many reasons; she'd already got two chicken breasts out defrosting for dinner and now she only needed one. Also, she loved him with everything she had in her and he loved someone else and was leaving her alone. Who was going to set up the Sky Box and cuddle her to sleep at night?

'Jackie, I'm so sorry,' Steve finished, looking at his feet. Jackie looked at him again, feeling her stomach lurch as she thought of him walking out of the front door. He'd be leaving here sad, but then turning up at this other woman's house and it would be an exciting day one for them. Like when the boys had left for university: all that turmoil at this end and then fizzy excitement at the other.

'So, you're not going to live here any more?' she said quietly.

'No,' he said, and it amazed Jackie that nothing else changed in the world except the way she felt. The colour didn't drain out of the room, the sun didn't blot out and no one ran screaming into the street to beat their chest and wail at the sky. She was surprised by how normally her thoughts were running too. The pain and the sadness and the shock were all so very physical, which was leaving her mind empty to ask herself questions like, *Am I doing this right? Should I be shouting? I don't often shout, am I wasting a legitimate opportunity to shout?* She felt numb, which she liked, because she'd read other people talking about situations like this and numb came up sometimes. Shock. She must be in shock; that's why the chicken breast was annoying her so much. Perhaps Ros could come round and have the other one? Before they went to the Hawk. Would they still go to the Hawk now that Steve was leaving her? What was the etiquette? Is it like mourning? Jackie didn't have many good black clothes; she preferred navy blue. 'Are you OK, Jack?' Steve said gently, reaching a hand out across the box of tissues and taking Jackie's. She felt his thumb rubbing on hers and suddenly felt like she was going to be sick.

'I am,' she said, pulling her hand away stiffly and hoping that breaking the contact between them would stop the queasiness. 'Are you off now?' She didn't mean to sound blunt or brutal, but she didn't really know what else to say. She couldn't deal with him leaving until he was gone.

'Yeah, just needed to grab my suit. I'll, er, I'll pop it in the car and then . . . Jackie . . .' He ran out of steam and sat looking at her. Was their living room always this quiet?

She'd stayed sat there while he got his remaining bits together. She heard the slam of the car boot from outside and then the shuffle of his shoes in the hall. Oh, that was a good point: that shoe rack was far too big now just for one person's shoes. His face appeared in the living room doorway.

'I'll see you then, Jack,' he said, softly, drumming his fingers lightly on the wooden frame as he did when he was uncomfortable.

'See you,' Jackie uttered, with a dry throat, nodding. He left. The front door closed, and the tears started. Jackie sat as the day ran away with itself, the sun set, and the warmth vanished, and she got colder and hungrier just sitting there on the powder-blue sofa with no one on the other one. No one ate either chicken breast.

Eventually the cavalry turned up in the form of Ros, who could only abide leaving so many voicemails before she had to turn up and check that you were eating OK. She took Jackie to the beach.

3

'Michael offered to fly over.' Jackie swallowed a mouthful of sandwich and looked up at her son, Leon. He was sitting hunched on the bench, in turn watching his own daughter, Freya, jump in puddles.

'Michael offered to fly?' He raised a mocking eyebrow.

'Offered being the operative word.' Jackie smiled. Her eco-conscious younger son was off saving the world one beetle at a time. He'd not been on a plane since she and Steve had been in charge of the travel arrangements, pre-whichever wide-eyed girlfriend it was that had made him swear never to do it again. The girlfriend was long gone but his steadfast romance with the planet and a minimal carbon footprint remained. She'd been quite overwhelmed when he'd offered to fly in and look after her. He'd missed his grandfather's funeral rather than get on a plane; she must have sounded awful on the phone.

'How is he? All right?' Leon and Michael weren't particularly close: brotherly affection at Christmas but thus far, very different people.

'Yes, I think so.' Jackie sighed, and opened her mouth to pass on to Leon news of Michael, and then found herself a bit stumped for words. She had listened. She really had listened to every single word. And actually, when she'd been on the phone, all the words had made sense, but it was when she tried to explain it to anyone else afterwards that she found the details of Michael's life shifting behind fog. It wasn't that she wasn't proud of him or interested, it was just all very far removed from things she knew about and so became hard to follow sometimes.

Leon was infinitely more understandable to her. She knew about being married and raising children; she didn't fully understand why washing powder was responsible for global warming or how milk was worse than driving. Obviously, she found it worrying, and of interest that she could do small things to make a difference, but overall, it felt like something for scientists and businesses to fix. She consoled herself with believing she'd made a whole boy, well, man now, who was out fixing things and that must be partly down to her.

'I think I'm still in his bad books,' Leon grumped, 'Freya, back this way please.' He raised his voice to caution Freya across the tarmac as she staunchly ignored all the brightly coloured play equipment and followed a trail of dirty puddles.

'For not adopting?' When Leon and his husband had first announced they were having children, Michael had been over the moon, assuming they were going to adopt. Unfortunately, the words *the last thing the planet needs is more humans* had already left his mouth before Leon and David had managed to get out 'surrogate' and the details of their upcoming family. The half-full flutes of fizz had been the loudest thing in the room in the silence that followed. Jackie had escaped as quickly as possible to go and fuss something in the kitchen that definitely hadn't really needed fussing.

Jackie remembered with a pang the exact view through the kitchen window from the sink as she'd rinsed mugs. The same garden as now, but younger. Five years' less growth on it. It had looked really bright that morning and she'd been half-looking at it when Steve's forehead nestled into the back of her neck. 'I'm going to be a grandpa,' he'd said, and she'd felt his tears slipping ticklishly down her skin. She'd turned round and sprayed foam from the washing-up all over both of them and they laughed as they hugged and both cried, listening to the stilted conversation filter in from the living room. In all the Michael grumping and backtracking, and the David stiffening, and the Leon sighing, they'd managed to slightly gloss over the momentous thing that had just happened. The new bit they had started.

Jesus but weren't you supposed to break up and get divorced before you had pivotal life moments like that? Didn't you leave someone for a better person *before* you both became grandparents together in the middle of a beautiful, argumentative afternoon? In the cold light of adultery Jackie suddenly wondered if Steve's tears hadn't been as happy as she'd assumed. Was that the beginning of his discontent with life? He wanted to go back to the days before being married to a grandma?

'No. No, I think Freya forced him to forgive us by being so damned adorable.' Leon broke in on her technicolour reverie with his somewhat gloomy monotone. 'It's the godforsaken new build he can't get over.'

'Ah, yes. I'd forgotten that.' Jackie smiled wanly, pushing thoughts of Steve away and replacing them with the reality of her frighteningly headstrong younger son. Once Freya was mobile, Leon and David had needed a garden for her and had moved from their chic town-centre flat into a new development behind the sports centre. While Michael was extremely fond of Freya, and professed to be saving the planet for her and her ilk, he was not about to sacrifice green land for her exercise yard and had read Leon the riot act for moving into a development that had come at the loss of some important newt habitat. Privately, Jackie thought the South Downs were probably big enough to have many more newts, what harm could Leon's house do?

The trouble with trying to persuade Michael to calm down about things like that was that he genuinely seemed to see no version of his future where a house or children happened to him. He wasn't doing adventures in the adventure years before the real-life activities of domesticity happened to him, as Jackie had previously perceived it. This was his life.

Leon twitched on the bench, watching Freya and fighting his body's insistence that he swoop in to avoid a fall. She tripped, and Leon and Jackie both hesitated to see the outcome. There was an infinite pause and then she scooped herself off the ground mercifully tear-free. Whatever this slightly bouncy underfoot stuff was they put in parks these days, it was better than the tarmac of her childhood.

'I was thinking, perhaps I could have Freya a couple of mornings a week, to give you and David a bit of a respite from nursery bills?' Jackie tried to sound light and jokey with it, so that Leon wouldn't hear the ribbon of desperation.

'Oh, thanks Mum,' Leon rubbed her hand gently, 'that's so lovely, but to be honest, now she's at school two mornings a week, it only gives her one nursery afternoon and I don't want to take her away from the friends she has there because they won't all be going to the same school. Thank you though – if we're stuck, we'll absolutely call you. I feel like I'm barely seeing her myself!'

'That only gets worse as they get older, trust me.' She meant it as a joke but the pained look in Leon's eyes didn't reassure Jackie that she'd nailed the tone.

'I'm sorry Mum, I am trying to be there for you. It's just with . . .' He trailed off lamely, but she could easily fill in the gaps.

'Oh, I know, I didn't mean that as a dig, I didn't. Honestly. I've been there, I get it: kid, husband, job, house and suddenly a week has gone by, and you haven't done anything except the basics. I know. I know you'd be there if I called.'

He rubbed her hand again and smiled a smile that turned into a groan. 'And, like the arsehole son I am, I do actually have to go now. Freya has gymnastics at four. I love you, Mum.'

She stood up so he couldn't do something patronising like kiss the top of her head and make her feel like a little old lady. 'Gymnastics! How lovely. Let me know if she has any shows coming up: I'd love to come and support her.' I'd love to do anything, she thought.

He assured her he would and after an enormous squashy hug with a puddle-covered Freya, the two of them made their way back to the big shiny people-carrier parked next to Jackie's car. She dawdled her way across the playground. A perfectly enclosed safe haven of playing. She'd not been here in a long time; probably some sort of Scout parade in the adjoining playing field that she and Steve would have watched when the boys were at school. They'd been down here every five minutes back then, or so it had felt. There was always a sports day or a thing or a something and at the time it had all felt so . . . so much to get through. Every week was a slog that she had to achieve to get through to the next bit when it would all calm down. She thought of Leon and his guilt at the business of his life and remembered it with a visceral ache. The friends that had vanished without a trace without either party noticing as the nappies heaped up around an ever more cluttered calendar. Thank goodness Ros hadn't had children or she might have lost her too. All those busy weeks she had just needed to get through to get to the quiet bit and suddenly here she was, with endless quiet. What she wouldn't give for a Scout parade now. She shut the wire gate with a clang behind her and left the ghosts to their proud smiles.

4

Jackie woke up. Annoyingly, she kept doing this. Every day without fail, no matter how hard she tried to just stay asleep, she would always find herself awake at six a.m. gazing in horror at the day ahead and wondering what on earth she was going to fill it with. God, what she wouldn't have done to have been this awake and alert at six a.m. when the boys were toddlers; that would have been great. No dry eyes filled with grit making it impossible to smile and nod along with whatever nonsense they were chirruping at her. Back then she'd have given her front teeth to have lain in bed until ten a.m.; she could have slept for Britain. Now that she could, something propelled her body to wake at six every morning and just listen to the silence descend.

Jackie rolled over and looked at the flat, empty left side of the bed. She was a very still sleeper, and so every morning she awoke to this cartoon of divorce whereby Steve's side of the bed lay ludicrously neat and flat and empty. She stroked the wrinkles out of the linen duvet cover to make it a perfect white sheet of fabric and then punched down into it, causing a soft crater.

She swung her feet down out of the bed, onto the floor and into her slippers before standing up. She pulled on one corner of the duvet and dragged the whole thing off the bed to slump down the stairs after her: the saddest bridal train you've ever seen.

The thing about daytime TV is the people making it really know what they're doing. They really get you to stick around and watch it. Jackie lay on the sofa under the duvet and stared at the screen across the room. A skinny male presenter in a suit with a stupidly skinny tie was kneeling on a TV set talking to a young lad in a tracksuit.

'Marriage is a lifelong commitment, you half-brain!' he bellowed at the boy.

'No, it isn't,' said Jackie, scooping more Philadelphia out of the pot and into her mouth. Poor lad, getting screamed at like that on national television. It wasn't his fault his wife was too stupid and ugly to hold his attention. At least he'd had the decency to leave her while she was young and could get with somebody else. The young lad was shuffling his trainers nervously and trying to avoid eye contact with the shouty suity man. This pantomime played out every morning at this time in between the one where the fleece people failed to sell ugly clocks and the posh swingers didn't choose any of the nice houses. Jackie didn't like any of the shows, but they stopped it being silent and they went nicely with Philadelphia.

Her phone buzzed on the coffee table, and she craned her neck forward to see the screen. Ros calling. Jackie slouched back into the sofa and wriggled her bum to see exactly how far down between the sofa cushions she could get if she really tried. The landline beeped with a piercing noise that made Jackie squeak and she looked around the room for the handset. It was buried under a several-day-old burger wrapper. Jackie wiped some grease off the buttons before looking at the screen. Ros again.

'Go away Ros,' she muttered to herself. 'I'm trying to die of shame – leave me alone.' She busied the call and turned up the volume on the trial-by-classism. She only got to hear a few more choice reprimands before a banging on the window startled her. Ros's face was peering in through the glass and looked horrified at what she saw.

'Jackie Douglas, what on earth does this look like? Get up and answer the door, you soggy cow. I can't believe you have me here in a flower bed banging on your window like I'm some sort of drug lord. What are you doing?'

Jackie pulled herself up in shock and smoothed her fluffed-up hair. She creaked her knees to standing and hurried to the front door. Ros stood on the step in an immaculate suit with her head tipped to one side.

'I'm so sorry to bother you,' Ros said in her most polite voice, 'I don't normally do things like this but I'm looking for my best friend Jackie Douglas? She used to live here and keep the place really neat and stuff. I'm not sure what you've done with her, but I'd like her back if possible?'

'Ha ha,' Jackie said without mirth. 'Get in the house, you're letting all my spinster vibes out into the neighbourhood. You'll do a number on the house prices.'

Ros followed her into the living room and surveyed the detritus with an open mouth.

'Oh, don't look at it like that,' Jackie snapped. 'It's not that bad.'

'Jackie . . .' said Ros, and swung an arm helplessly round the room. Jackie followed the arc of her hand with her gaze and looked at the living room. OK, maybe it was that bad. Crisp packets and takeaway wrappers littered every surface. There were mugs and glasses, plates and bowls all over the coffee table, the floor and the sofa. Jumpers and blankets and the duvet lay lifeless in a bulky heap on the sofa and the dust on every hard surface could take an essay being inscribed into it.

'OK, maybe it is that bad. But I'm wallowing,' Jackie whined, flumping down heavily onto the blanket mountain on the sofa.

'And I'm very here for your wallowing, Jack. I love that you've needed a wallow. I'm not the girl to tell you to get down the gym and get on Tinder.'

'What's Tinder?'

'See? Way too soon for that. Mustn't jump the gunge. I just want to lightly suggest . . . maybe a walk? Or even just a wash? It wasn't shampoo that left you, you know.'

'I can't go outside,' Jackie said, looking out through the glass and into the treacherous outside world. 'I can't face anybody.

Besides, there's nothing I need that I can't get some helpful young man on a scooter to bring me.'

'See if he can't spot you a bit of dignity with your chow mein.' Ros raised an eyebrow at the congealing goop on the dinner plate by Jackie's feet.

'I know it looks bad, but isn't this what you're meant to do? For the first week?'

'Jackie, it's been six.'

'Months? That went quick.'

'Don't sass me. Six weeks you've Uncle Festered.'

'Has it really?' Jackie wouldn't admit it to Ros, but she felt stunned. Nearly two months? That couldn't be right. God, all those years she had moaned about having periods but at least they gave you some sort of indication of the slow progression of time. Six weeks? Six weeks of DNA tests and terrible fathers, awful ceramic mermaid statues and four bedrooms with and without conservatories. Her skin started to itch at the thought of it. 'I suppose I lost track of time.' She felt tears welling up, and then an angry frustrated wave followed it. She was so sick of crying.

'I know, love, and listen – no one is going to be more support-ive than me of anything you want to do to get through this. You know that, don't you? But . . . you can't do this for ever. I miss you. I'm like a sailor with an urge; you can't do everything in a text message.' Ros looked deeply into Jackie's eyes, blinking at her twice. 'I really miss you.'

Jackie let the tears slip over the barricade of her lower lashes. 'Here I go again!' She laughed, indicating them falling.

'Ah you rainy-day blanket. Listen, I've got to get back to work. I just wanted to check you're still alive.'

Jackie held a hand over her mouth and puffed out some air. 'Still breathing.' She smiled. 'Just about.'

'Good, you keep doing that, and I'll work on getting the rest of you sorted,' Ros said, standing up to leave. As she did so a crumpled piece of paper pushed its way out of the top of her jacket pocket. She huffed crossly and grabbed it up.

'What's that?' asked Jackie, amused by Ros's annoyance.

'Oh, some stupid work initiative thing. Suddenly we're responsible for whether or not the parasites that work for us get heart disease and so we have to provide initiatives for them to not go to an early grave. I just wanted a law firm, that's all I wanted. So, I hired lawyers, and other staff, because I wanted them to do legal work for me. Never in any of these proceedings did any of us turn to each other and say *hey, how's about being my mam and my personal trainer while you're at it?* I don't know why they can't come to work on the time I'm paying them and then go to the gym in their own hours, but it seems they can't and now the government . . .'

Jackie held up her arms in submission. Once Ros had uttered the word government there was a tirade coming that Jackie would probably not follow, nor necessarily agree with her on. Ros sighed and blew her fringe up in the air. 'So each senior staffer had to choose a sport and offer provision for anyone who wants to take it up.' She handed the piece of paper over to Jackie, who looked down at it.

'And you chose NETBALL?' she almost shrieked. 'Good God, I'd forgotten that game existed. Why would you choose netball? Nobody wants to play netball!'

'That's what I thought!' squealed Ros. 'I thought, nobody will want to play this weird backwards game. It has four thousand rules, no one has done it since primary school – I'll stick some flyers up and they'll get ignored in favour of ultimate Frisbee – what is ultimate Frisbee?' Jackie shrugged. 'But noooo. The idiot members of my firm couldn't wait to get their bibs and play netball, apparently. Just my lucky charm.'

Jackie laughed at Ros's annoyance. It felt strange and good. 'You don't have to play, do you?' She chuckled.

'Lord no,' said Ros. 'I mean – probably I'm meant to or something but listen, it's my firm, so I'll just have to have meetings whenever they would have been expecting me to be jumping about under a net. Give me strength.' She threw the piece of paper dramatically over her shoulder and sashayed out of the room. 'Put that in the recycling with the rest of your baggage, would you?' she called back. 'Actually, no: landfill for the baggage. I don't want to be drinking out of a water bottle one day and find it's your reincarnated troubles.'

Jackie saw Ros out, although Ros declined a hug on hygiene grounds. Jackie mooched back into the living room. It was an absolute bomb site. If someone had invented a bomb filled with crockery and high-sodium-content foods. Ros had been the spellbreaker she needed. Time for a wash.

There was a knock at the door and Jackie headed back towards it with a grin. 'I haven't quite had time to strip off for my shower yet, love—' She stopped talking immediately as she opened the door to see Steve. He looked up, shocked at her words. 'Oh!' she yelped.

'Hi,' he said, swallowing. 'Who were you expecting?'

'No one. None of your business. What are you doing here?' Jackie's heart was racing. She'd had no contact with him since the day he'd walked out; she realised he'd almost been dead in her imaginings of him and now here he was back on the doorstep in his familiar leather jacket. Was he coming back to her?

'I just came back to grab a few things.' He shifted awkwardly. 'I have tried to call ahead to warn you but there's been no answer on the phone.'

'No,' she said, thinking of the blinking red light on the machine, 'I've been busy. Help yourself to what you need. I must just pop up and have a shower.' She cringed as she walked back past the door to the lounge, imagining him seeing her little dank cave of delivered shame.

He was out in the garage when she came back down, hair washed and feeling about three stone lighter with all the grime washed off her. She hurriedly scooped up the worst-offending items from the lounge and crammed them into various bins and the dishwasher. The fridge smelled like something had died in there, but she could deal with that later. She hurried into the living room and sat on her hands, hating every second of feeling so awkward and on edge in her own home. Steve appeared at the back door.

'You've not seen my golf clubs, have you?' he called through.

Jackie froze. 'Er no, no, I've not seen them.' She couldn't possibly have seen them – they were in the sea, about fifteen miles away, just off Brighton beach.

'They were in the garage?' Steve called. 'I can't see them now.'

Jackie shrugged, and then realised he couldn't see her and so the pantomime was largely pointless. 'Sorry Steve, I've not seen them. I've not been out there.' That wasn't technically a lie – it was Ros who had gone into the garage to get them, and she hadn't been able to see them particularly well because it had been dark at the beach.

'It's just, I have a big game on Friday, that's all,' Steve whined from the back door, and Jackie's temper snapped.

'I don't know what you want me to do about that. I don't know where they are.' There was a silence between them as he looked at her.

'Are you all right?' he asked calmly and Jackie could almost hear the blood vessels popping in her eyeballs as she tried to restrain herself from screeching at him.

5

'AM I ALL RIGHT? Am I all right, he had the audacity to waltz back into my house and ask me six weeks after walking out on me to go and live with the woman he's been having an affair with! Am I all right? That's what he asks? He's got the nerve to stand there in the doorway looking at me with his head on one side wondering why I'm angry with him! Looking at me with that STUPID EXPRESSION like *Why are you overreacting Jack? Jack it was a mild enough question, I just want to know where my golf clubs are?* Looking at me like I'm the problem! No, Steve! No, Steve, I am not all right – don't you dare ask me whether I'm all right when you're here looking for golf clubs instead of an apology. How could he possibly be wanting to play golf? Golf? What even is golf? I hate golf. I hate him. Oh, I miss him.'

She would scream all of this at Ros later across their favourite booth near the fireplace in the Hawk. There in the kitchen, though, she sat frozen, staring icily at him.

'I'm fine,' was all she managed. He hesitated, an entire marriage between them on the worktop. He swallowed.

'OK.' He nodded and turned to head back out to the garage.

'Steve?' The word lurched up her throat and landed on the back of her tongue, threatening to choke her if she didn't let it out after him.

'Yeah?' He turned back, one hand casually on the door frame, looking like he owned the place. She supposed, technically, he still did.

'What's her name?'

'Didn't I—'

'No. No, you didn't.'

'Michelle. It's Michelle.'

'OK.' Jackie turned and went up to the bathroom. The only lockable door in the house. She sat on the closed lid of the toilet and waited for the intense stomach ache to pass; her ears followed his noises round the house and garden, and she felt like she didn't let a breath out until she heard his car leaving the driveway thirty minutes later.

Ros handed her another glass of wine. 'Ah fuck him,' she said, 'fuck him and fuck her too.'

Jay, the barmaid, dropped off another full bottle to the table and smiled wryly at their conversation. It was nice to have the pair of them back. She had got quite used to the presence of Ros and Jackie over the previous year since she'd started work at the Hawk. They were friendly, and less predisposed to stare at her breasts than most of the other regulars. Apart from their insistence at sitting at a table for eight, no matter how busy the pub, they were model customers. 'Who are we mad at?'

'Jackie's husband,' Ros said, only slurring slightly.

'Soon to be ex,' said Jackie, looking up dolefully from where her chin was slumped on her folded arms.

Ros's eyes opened wide. 'That's the spirit, Jack! Yes! And we want to start thinking about that happening as quickly as possible because you only have six months from finding out about the affair to filing for divorce if you want to use the affair as . . .'

Jackie groaned into her elbow and flopped a hand about blindly to find the wine bottle. Jay helpfully lifted it before she spilled it and refilled the glasses. 'Stop talking about divorce!' Jackie mumbled. 'I don't like the word.'

'But you just ought to be thinking about it, that's all . . . I want you to be safe.'

'I'll be fine,' Jackie moped. 'We're not going to argue about it, are we? It's Steve.'

'My mum's boyfriend is going through a divorce,' Jay chipped in, perching her bum on the end of the leather seat. 'It seems complicated.'

'See?' Jackie pouted at Ros. 'It's complicated.'

'Only when people like me want it to be so we can bill you more.' Ros swatted the excuses away. 'What's the house worth? Can you draw down equity from that if you start to struggle without Steve's wage coming in?'

'Oh . . .' Jackie hated talk like this; it made her want to bury her head in literal sand. 'I don't know, Ros! I don't know! I'm not good at things like this like you are . . . Steve did it all.'

This made Ros grumble, 'Exactly. This is what I'm worried about. You need to get your eggs in a row out of the basket or you'll end up working on the supermarket checkout. What's your pension?'

'Don't say the "p" word!' Jackie all but shrieked; she hated it. 'It's only been two months.' Jackie sat up straight and tried to look like she was ending the conversation. 'That means I have four more before whatever this deadline is you're on about. I'll sort it. I'm just not ready.'

'Fine. But don't think I'll be as understanding as you are about infidelity if I find you've cheated on me and gone off with another lawyer.' Ros arched an eyebrow and managed to get a giggle out of Jackie.

'I promise you are the only one for me.' Jackie nodded solemnly, and then turned to wink at Jay. 'I certainly couldn't handle more.'

'You two aren't about to get all handsy are you? I have enough couples to boot out of the toilets on the weekends; I don't want it from my supposed classy regulars on a weekday!' Jay laughed.

'Classy?!' Ros and Jackie both said it at the same time and then laughed.

'Jack, I've never been called classy before!' Ros scrambled in her bag for a pen. 'I must have you write it down, Jay, as a Mento.'

'Memento, Ros,' Jackie corrected. 'Mento is a mint.'

'I know what I mean, I just don't always say the words.'

'You two are barmy. I'm not sure I should be leaving this wine with you here.' Jay jokingly retracted the bottle slightly, but Ros's hand shot out and grabbed it. 'Oof, nothing wrong with your reflexes!'

'Listen, Jay, I like you – so I'm going to say this very carefully,' Jackie warned. 'Don't you come between this woman and her wine. You won't like her.' Jay left the bottle on the table and then retreated, holding both her arms up in the air in surrender.

'Your divorce,' Ros continued, closing one eye so she could focus on Jackie, 'won't take a second. I'll have everything you want from him in a heartbeat and you won't have to do a thing.'

'I don't want anything from him,' Jackie said glumly.

'Not yet – that's because you're still heartbroken. But once you're angry there'll be loads of things. There always are. At least the house anyway.'

'I don't know if I need the house.'

'I'll have it!' Jay piped up from her position behind the bar. She grinned cheekily at Ros and Jackie. 'I mean, if it's going spare. About the only chance I'll get to be a homeowner is if someone's giving them away.'

'Don't be ridiculous! You're going places,' Ros yelled far too loudly across the pub. A couple of holidaymakers trying to enjoy a quaint, cosy date in a traditional rural pub looked over at the mild inconvenience to their ambience.

'Oh, look down again ya grockles,' Ros called over at them and they hastily shuffled their chairs in embarrassment.

'Shhhhhh!' giggled Jackie, letting the swirling effects of the alcohol carry her into laughter.

'You're going places,' Ros repeated, slopping more wine into the two heavily lipstick-marked glasses on the table.

'I've already been places and had to come back,' Jay said, smiling a smile that stopped obstinately at the cheeks, where she couldn't convince her eyes it was funny.

'You'll get going again. It's just a setback,' Jackie said kindly. She didn't like seeing Jay down. She was a local girl who had left to go to university and then got a job in London before losing it in a round of redundancies. From the little Jackie knew, it was some sort of charity coordinator position she wanted, and they were few and far between even in a booming economy. She'd had to move back in with her mum and the few months everyone had predicted it would be had now stretched into eighteen.

'Setback is right,' Jay groaned. 'I can't believe I'm back in the room I had as a teenager, in the job I had as a teenager but with way more debt.'

'Look on the bright side,' Jackie tried. 'At least your mum had space for you . . .?'

'Oh don't,' Jay groaned even louder and wandered back to their table so she could stop disturbing the tourists. 'I feel so guilty that I've ended up hating being there. I wish my mum was one of those lame, lonely women that are desperate for company so my coming back could actually be a godsend. But she'd never been happier: properly settled down in a relationship with someone who actually seems to be nice to her for a change, and then there's me; her lumpy failure of a daughter in the spare room ruining it. That's why I'm working every shift I can.'

'Have you not got friends round here?' Ros asked. 'Get out and party – make the most of that waist while you've got it.'

'Nah, all my friends moved away when I did. The only people left are the people who never left and . . . well, let's just say I left for a reason.' Jay looked morose and Jackie felt guilty for depressing her.

'I'm sorry, love.' Jackie tried to think of words of comfort but her mouth failed her. She was saved by a family of four coming and wanting dinner. Jay sprang up and back to the bar with a cheery smile pasted on and showed them to a table.

Ros tutted at the children. 'Children shouldn't be allowed. So where did you tell him they were?' she asked.

'The children?'

'The golf clubs.'

'Oh,' Jackie giggled again, 'I didn't. I just said I hadn't seen them. They might be in France by now!' They descended into fits of giggles at the thought of Steve's clubs on the bottom of the ocean, making friends with fish and sewage alike. 'I don't feel a bit guilty.' Jackie sniffed. 'Except, you know, in an environmental way.' She imagined the look on Michael's face if he'd known what she'd done to his fragile ocean.

'And neither should you!' Ros bellowed, again drawing glances from the cross tourists. Ros waved a hand at them. 'I'll pay for your next drinks if you stop looking at me every time I'm obnoxiously loud and drunk,' she shouted to them and they looked down at the table, humiliated to have had their obvious tutting acknowledged and disregarded.

'I don't know why the fact it was golf clubs he came back for annoyed me so much,' Jackie mused, swirling a finger through her wine. 'It just felt so . . . so annoying. You know? *So annoying.*'

'Golf is annoying. Stupid golf. My shoulder still hurts, you know.'

Jackie snorted. 'That wasn't from golf though. That was from throwing golf clubs.'

'True. Maybe we should play golf? See what the appeal is? Why men go crazy for the damn game?'

'Absolutely,' Jackie mumbled into her glass of wine. 'We'll go tomorrow!'

6

It was a huge mystery to Jackie exactly how and when the doorbell had been installed inside her head. She didn't remember requesting a doorbell inside her head, or letting contractors in for the work to be carried out, but here she was lying in bed with a full doorbell ringing inside her skull. As she woke further, she realised that perhaps it wasn't a doorbell inside her head, but just the regular doorbell amplified massively by white-wine dehydration. Could dehydration do that? Was hydration there to shield your senses from the full onslaught of the world? These questions were far too big to fit in her brain alongside the persistent doorbell.

The pillow was staunchly refusing to do anything to stop the pain from striking through her eyes, no matter how hard she pushed it into her temples and ears. Jackie fervently wished the noise would end by any means necessary; she didn't even particularly care if that meant her death needed to be brought about to make it so. In fact, if she could die quickly here in the bed and things went quiet it would be far better than living the rest of a full and healthy life with the fear of these noises happening again hanging over her.

Eventually, it occurred to Jackie that the doorbell was ringing because someone was ringing it. Someone was very intensely ringing it and not taking no for an answer. It couldn't be the emergency services because they would have broken the door down by now to get in. So, it had to be Ros.

Jackie flung the duvet back off herself and put her feet on the floor angrily. The jolt of contact with carpet-covered floorboards sent a nauseous wave up through her legs and into her stomach. Her eyeballs scraped drily against their dusty sockets and she sat frozen for a moment waiting for the world to right itself. It looked like her bedroom, but it really felt like a pirate ship.

Gingerly, Jackie wrapped her dressing gown round herself, taking care not to put too much pressure on her very volatile stomach region. She descended the staircase as floatily as she could, feeling the clammy suction of her palms against the banister as she held on to it for dear life.

'Someone better be dead and it better be you,' she shouted angrily, undoing the chain and pulling back the front door. Ros stood on the doorstep, looking fresh and polished in the early-morning light.

'My God, no. I think it's you,' Ros said, looking shell-shocked. 'What on earth's happened?'

'You. You have happened. Why are you leaning on my doorbell like a debt collector with an itch?'

'Is that a phrase?'

'Pot, kettle. Ros, I can't feel my knees, I can't do etymology now.'

'Go and sit down, I'll put your black kettle on.' Ros bustled past Jackie and into the kitchen. Jackie stood still, staring out of the open door. 'Close the door!' called Ros over her shoulder and Jackie obediently closed the door before following Ros into the kitchen and pulling up a stool at the breakfast bar.

'What time is it?' Jackie yawned.

'Six forty,' Ros said perkily, and Jackie nearly vomited on the words' impact.

'Six forty?!' she shrieked, 'What the hell are you doing here at six forty?'

'Well, it would have been six thirty if you'd answered the door when I first got here.' Ros was looking indignant, and Jackie blinked at her in confusion.

'But that would have been ten minutes worse?' Jackie said. Her mouth was so dry. The first time in months she'd been a) hung-over and b) asleep past six a.m. and Ros picked that day to take leave of her senses.

'We said six thirty so we could get a game in before my eleven a.m. meeting?' Ros was looking perplexed.

'A game?' Jackie tried to sort her memories of the night before, but they were all marinated in fog and bad decisions, and she couldn't jumble them into any more than a vague sense of being in the pub and laughing.

'Golf! You're really behaving like you were only born out of the stupid tree yesterday and you hit all the branches on the way down. Are you all right?' Jackie realised she had been silently mouthing the word golf over and over, trying to work some moisture into the desert that had previously been her mouth.

'Golf,' she whispered, shell-shocked. 'We said we'd play golf. We did. I remember now. I just don't remember the part where we were serious.'

'I'm always serious,' Ros said briskly, turning back to the kettle to make the tea. 'Besides, I've never played golf before, and I'm here now, so go and get dressed. I'll make you some breakfast.'

'Please make it both wet and absorbent,' Jackie said, wondering how she could feel so desperate for water and also want something that could soak up this ocean of inner sloshing. She nodded to herself and headed upstairs and then immediately regretted yet another decision because nodding was making the hall/pirate ship flail about on the foundations/waves.

7

From the moment she stepped into the foyer of the golf club Jackie was fairly sure she wasn't going to like golf. The people all smelled like new plastic and gave Ros and Jackie glances as if they knew they hadn't played before.

'They probably do,' said Ros. 'They probably all know each other really well. We'll soon be one of them.' But looking at the gold jewellery dripping off half the men in the club, Jackie wasn't sure she wanted to know them.

'Why are they all here so early?' Jackie was astounded.

'Retired, I suppose? Or fitting it in before work. Same as us. See? We're fitting in already. We are two fish firmly in the water.' Ros strode over to the receptionist and began to book them in. 'Nine holes or eighteen?' she called over to Jackie, who shrugged helplessly. Eighteen sounded like a lot, but she didn't want to be a party pooper as Ros was clearly going out of her way to be nice. 'I went for nine,' said Ros, coming back over, 'as the receptionist seemed to think eighteen was an all-day thing and I cannot miss that meeting at eleven or Adrian will have my gutters for garters.'

Nine holes or not, Ros was always destined to miss that meeting.

'Golf is awful!' she screamed at full volume and Jackie noticed with alarm that several golfers in the near – and far – distance turned their heads to see what was wrong. Jackie waved pathetically to indicate that everything was OK. Ros was not wrong: golf was awful. 'It's a terribly long walk and then instead of anything good at the end of each bit of *walking* you just have to do a gross little job getting an obnoxious ball into a hole that's clearly far too small, using a stick that is not fit for purpose. What on earth is fun about this?'

Jackie was very used to being the more measured one in their friendship, often finding the positives where Ros found some sort of hilarious rant. Golf was obstinately not providing much ammunition for her to wax lyrical about.

'The view is nice,' she tried lamely, but her stomach was rumbling so much that she was finding it hard not to see the trees as broccoli and the sheep in the distance as delicious little marshmallow-covered lamb chops.

'The view could be a photograph,' stropped Ros. 'It doesn't need me out here freezing my tits off wandering between flags – I mean flags, I ask you; could you find a game more invented by white men who like conquering things and drinking whisky? – here I am wandering between flags, and by Jesus it's been four hours and we are doing the SHORT VERSION of the "game".' She held the word game between her front teeth, refusing to allow it all the lip action it deserved.

'I did suggest we leave after hole two.' Jackie knocked her ball with the club again and it petulantly ran around the rim of the hole, managing to finish over a foot away from it for the third time.

'You know I can't quit things once I'm doing them. Anyway, speaking of terrible white men . . .'

Jackie couldn't help but laugh even though she felt her insides curling at the thought of where this was going. 'Yes?' She bent the word round a corner to try to indicate to Ros how tentative she was on this subject.

'Divorcing Steve.' It was unclear whether Ros understood the signal but, even if she did, she did nothing to cushion the blow.

'Oof. OK.' Jackie held her breath.

'Now, obviously I'm happy to handle it for you, but I'm also happy to strong-arm some people into doing it practically free. Whose name is the house in?'

Jackie felt panic rippling up her arms, 'Oh, I don't know . . . I don't know about the house. Didn't we talk about this last night? Does it all really need to be done now? I don't even know if we'll get divorced. It seems like a lot, doesn't it? A whole divorce?'

Ros pivoted neatly on her heels and stared at Jackie. 'You're not going to be thinking of taking him back, are you?' Her eyes pincered, Jackie felt the panic increase; what if she did?

'No, no, I'm not thinking of taking him back. Certainly not at the moment, anyway. I just . . . I hate all this legal stuff. We were married for so long, I'm sure we can separate amicably. Maybe we don't even need a divorce.'

'What if he wants to marry this other woman?' Ros really wasn't pulling any punches.

'Well . . . yes, I suppose. Oh, I don't know, Ros. It's all such a tummy ache and I'm scared about it all.'

Ros nodded and forced a smile. 'Righto, I'll drop it for now. But give it a thought, would you? Now, hurry up and hit the ball so we can go home. This is painful.'

Jackie reached down and picked the ball up, then dropped it into the hole from above and immediately squatted down to scoop it out again. 'There. Happy now?'

Ros nodded, her sense of completion satisfied. 'Very. Now let's leave this place and never speak of it again. I'm madder too because I was chuffed with us for getting rid of Steve's sticks and being meanies and now I realise that by depriving him of golf we've actually done him a favour. Practically an intervention, it was. I'm spitting.'

'Come on, let's get you some lunch.' Jackie guided Ros back through the foyer and delicately explained to the receptionist that no, nothing was actually wrong with their experience other than the concept of golf. She reassured the poor girl several times that no, Ros was not going to sue and that even if she did sue it would be the inventors of the game of golf and it would take her at least a week to track them down. The receptionist could not or would not see the funny side, so Jackie practically pushed Ros out of the sliding doors and into the car.

In the silence of the car Ros settled down a bit. 'Well there's no point in me heading to the office now, most of the day is gone.'

'Ros, it's noon.'

'I said what I said. Hawk?'

Jackie laughed and nodded and they headed to their local, where they slid into their usual booth and rested their aching feet.

8

Jay wandered over, pleased to have a friendly distraction from the tedium of afternoons behind the bar in a rural pub. Sometimes it was hard to believe from the quietness of the Hawk how close they were to Brighton, and really only just an hour outside of London. Not to mention Horsham and other towns within a shortish drive. The village seemed to just squeeze by in between, feeling more like deepest darkest Devon than flashy, money-filled Sussex. Jay missed the hustle of London.

When she'd first been forced to leave after the job hunt stretched on too long for her to maintain the rent on her flat, she'd convinced herself she'd be in and out all the time. What's forty miles? But sometimes, when an evening shift stretched on in the pub with only the same stories from the regulars to sustain her, she felt like she was on a different planet to the traffic-filled entertainment hub she'd grown to love. She shook off the boredom and padded over to Jackie and Ros, who she liked and who would help pass the dead afternoon between food services. 'What can I get you?' she asked, joining them on the leather bench seat.

'My morning back?' Ros groaned, slipping her feet out of her shoes and pulling them up underneath her to stretch out her aching leg muscles.

'What have you been doing?' Jay asked, pulling a stray leaf out of Ros's hair.

'Golf,' said Jackie, and a burst of laughter expelled itself from Jay's mouth before she could stop herself.

'Why?' She laughed. 'Sorry. I'm being presumptuous. Do you play golf?'

'We don't, no. This morning was our first attempt and it was . . . er, not a success,' Jackie said diplomatically.

'It was not our fault though!' Ros declared, slamming the menu down on the table. 'I'll have an open prawn sandwich and an open bottle of wine please, Jay. No, the failure of golf had nothing to do with us or the energy we put into it – I blame the game entirely. Have you ever played Operation? With the wee naked man who needs a lot of surgery? It's like that but massive, and opposites, and outside, and there's not even the buzzer to make it interesting. Extremely awful. I cannot believe people play it. I really can't believe anyone watches it. Lord it was awful. Awful!'

'I must admit, I've never seen the appeal. The men who come in here after golf are always the worst and they never tip. I prefer the rugby lads. Jackie, you eating?' Jay stood up to head back to the bar and process the order.

'Oh, yeah – I'll have the same sandwich but a tea please.'

'Don't be boring!' Ros exclaimed, but Jackie couldn't be persuaded to take any more of the liquid that had given her morning such a brittle feeling. She confirmed her tea order with Jay and then settled back into the comfy seat as Jay disappeared back to the bar. Jackie stared into space, feeling peaceful and enjoying the feeling of having done some exercise. No matter how terrible the overall experience had been, she had to admit she did feel better for having woken her legs up a bit and stretched. Ros was saying something, and Jackie tuned back in to reality to try to hear what she was saying. Ros was swiping intently down her phone screen and muttering to herself, 'They seem to play at weekends.'

'What are you talking about?' Jackie asked, wishing she'd ordered some water with her tea to get a head start on the rehydrating she felt she'd be doing for the rest of her life.

'Rugby,' Ros said, staring at her as if she was being extremely stupid.

'Rugby?' Jackie said, feeling as if she was being extremely stupid.

'Yes, weren't you listening? Jay just mentioned that the rugby lads were much nicer, and seeing as golf has been such a disaster and the one golfer we know isn't very nice either, I think maybe rugby will be our game?'

Jackie didn't even know where to begin with Ros's declaration. She found herself distracted, dwelling on Ros's earlier anger at Steve on the golf course. It felt so odd to hear it right out there in the open like that. She knew Steve and Ros had never exactly been best friends, but that was fine. They'd always got along all right when they'd needed to and then Jackie had enjoyed having Ros in her own separate little bubble outside the house. Hearing Ros openly criticise him in such a blasé way rammed it home for Jackie that the split was real. This was how people spoke about people you were no longer with – not people you had a good chance of getting back together with. Did she even want to get back together with him?

She imagined Steve walking in right now and declaring that he had ended it with the other woman, with Michelle, and begging her to take him back. Would she do it? Could she do it? Could she just forget what he'd done and enjoy his company in the same way again? Her body told her she could. That gentle trembling of feeling alone that seemed to permanently be there just below her skin begged her to go back to what was familiar. Her mind was smarter though and played her scenes of the two of them awkwardly living together, playing out a veneer of a life with every intimacy they had had destroyed by his infidelity and lies and. . . lack of love. What was she going to do?

'Jackie!' Ros's voice cut into Jackie's panicked daydream. What on earth was she even getting so worried about, trying to solve a conundrum like that when it wasn't even happening?

'Sorry, what? I was miles away.' Jackie focused back in on the screen Ros was showing her.

'I was saying, there's a game on Saturday if you want to go?'

'A game?'

'Of rugby!' Ros almost screamed it, clocking Jackie playfully on the head with one hand.

'You want to go and watch a rugby match? On Saturday?' Jackie knew she was risking another cuff from Ros, but she felt she very carefully needed to make sure she hadn't missed anything from Ros's latest hare-brained scheme or who knew what she was letting herself in for.

'Ooh, I'll come!' Jay said excitedly, popping the tea and milk down in front of Jackie. Jackie noticed that Jay's cheeks turned an adorable shade of pink as she spoke and she took half a hesitant step back and then looked at them. 'I mean, sorry, can I come?'

'Of course you may.' Ros nodded. 'I'll book us three tickets.' She went back to prodding at her phone screen while Jackie fell into her tea as though it were the Holy Grail.

'Exciting! Let me just check the rota!' Jay skipped off back towards the kitchen.

'But why though?' said Jackie, resurfacing from the steaming cup of repair. 'Why do you want to go and see a rugby match?'

'Because golf was a disaster.' Ros looked at Jackie with such a blank expression that Jackie felt she was going to have to replay the entire day to see what she had missed that was earning her this kind of treatment.

'So? Let's just never play, speak of or think about golf again. Why do we need to go to a rugby game?'

'Because you need to do something, Jack, and it needs to be something new. You can't just mope around your house feeling sorry yourself – you need hobbies.'

'I have hobbies!' Jackie said desperately, racking her brains for an answer to the question she knew was coming.

'What? What hobbies do you have?'

'I have—'

'Don't you dare say your grandchild,' Ros interrupted, 'She is not a hobby. She's a person who's not ready to be interesting yet.'

Jackie's mouth fell closed. There was no use arguing with Ros on the subject of Freya; it was like trying to explain to a normal person that you just loved paint rollers or something equally banal. Ros was capable of looking at children without the magical lens other people saw that made children phenomenal. Jackie had learned not to try to enthuse her when the boys were small. Ros had been the port where Jackie wasn't predominantly a mum, and it hadn't really mattered in the sea of baby groups. Anyway, Jackie liked spending time with Freya but technically Ros was right. It wasn't a hobby. What were her hobbies?

'I watch TV,' she said lamely, feeling more pathetic with every second that passed.

'Everyone watches TV, it's not a hobby, it's a thing you do when you're too tired to do anything else.'

'Well, what are your hobbies?' Jackie protested, thanking Jay for the delicious-looking sandwiches that had just arrived in front of them.

'I don't have any either. That's the point. We're two sad old biddies who have nothing in our lives except each other and that's going to change.'

'You have a job,' Jackie pointed out, glumly poking prawns around her plate.

'I do. But a job isn't a hobby, same as you have a family and I don't, but a family isn't a hobby either. We're getting a hobby, and so is Jay here.'

'Jay doesn't want to hang out with us,' Jackie said through a mouthful of prawns and lettuce. 'She's young and cool.'

Jay laughed loudly from her position behind the bar. 'Oh yeah, I'm super-cool me. Here I am at twenty-eight living back with my mother in my childhood bedroom with thirty grand of debt and the job I had at eighteen. I am living the actual dream.'

The three women looked at each other and laughed, each feeling a peculiar mixture of disastrous and supported.

'OK Jay, you're in our sad biddies club. And our first trip is to the rugby. I'll book some tickets.' With that, Ros looked back down at her phone and jabbed a finger at the basket button, smearing Marie Rose right across the screen.

9

The crowd roared with enthusiasm, a meaty sound reverberating around the stands. It was an incredible sight, that many people all moving in unison as they reacted to the players. The mass of people moved like an animal, in synch with each other. Except for three people.

As the crowd roared, Ros screamed in surprise, causing Jackie to slosh yet more of her pint down her legs and across her trainers. Jay fell into another fit of laughter and the three of them sat down to gather themselves.

'What are they roaring about?' Ros shouted over the din. 'Was that a score?'

'I don't think so,' said Jackie, peering at the pitch in confusion. 'They're still in the middle. The score poles are at the sides, aren't they?'

'Does the pile mean something? Can you score from in a pile?' Ros flicked through the match day programme again, wiping her own pint off the front cover, 'They should put the rules in this or it isn't fair.'

Jay felt her lungs and stomach bursting from being unable to suck oxygen into them for so long. She thought she'd probably never seen anything funnier than Ros and Jackie trying to consume a rugby match.

They'd arrived plenty early enough to find their seats and start getting warmed up with the crowd. At first, everything had been dandy – they'd made their way to the bar along with many, many of the other spectators and felt enthusiastic about what lay ahead. The problems had come when they reached the front of the queue.

'What Sauvignons do you have?' Ros had asked, and got a blank look back from the barmaid stood behind the pumps.

'I'm sorry?'

'What Sauvignons do you have?' Ros repeated, trying to peer round her to the fridges; then, clocking the blank expression on the barmaid's face, she downgraded her request. 'White wines?'

'Oh!' The barmaid smiled cheerily. 'Yes, we have white wine.'

Ros nodded patiently, painting on a frustrated smile. 'Yes, what kind?'

'Um . . . bottled?' The barmaid was looking behind her at the fridges in increasing confusion. She was obviously trying to be helpful and finding very little in her surroundings to assist with this.

'I don't think they have a wide variety, Ros,' said Jay, feeling for the poor woman just doing her job. 'It seems like more of a beer situation.'

Ros's eyes had sprung wide with enthusiasm. 'Of course! Silly me! We should have beers to have the full experience! Three beers please!' she called to the now happier-looking barmaid. Jay took over the conversation of deciding exactly which lagers they would have, so as not to give the poor barmaid a nosebleed at Ros's ineptitude. She also managed to talk Ros out of speaking to a manager over the issue of plastic cups. Jackie, meanwhile, stood contentedly by, trying to smile in a friendly manner at the barmaid and keep out the way of the groups of men and families making their way to seats around them. There was such a jolly atmosphere – not at all aggressive as she'd feared. She'd only ever seen snippets of rugby on the television, and in her mind she'd sort of assumed that she'd be going to a stadium like that. In actual fact, the local ground was much smaller (of course it was, Jackie – get a grip) and had a wonderful, ramshackle, cosy feel to it.

She felt a small pang that neither of her boys had been sporty; Leon liked his computer games and Michael never stuck to anything before the planet. 'I wish my boys had been sporty,' she mused to Ros. 'Then I could have done this sort of thing in my life.'

'You can do it now,' Ros stated obviously.

'Yes, I know, but if the boys had needed to come to training it would have been . . . part of the . . . oh you know, part of back-then life?' Jackie couldn't quite find the words she wanted to explain.

'The main part?' Ros said drily, and Jackie picked up on a hint of mild disapproval from her.

'Well . . . my main part. Maybe. Oh, I don't know.'

'Just because you're doing it now with friends doesn't make it any less your life, Jack.' Ros turned away to collect the full pints from Jay and Jackie was left feeling like she'd been hurtful, in a way she couldn't quite put her finger on.

They settled into their seats, each gripping their chilled pint and a burger, and prepared for the game. This was where it really came unstuck. The game was absolutely indecipherable.

'Why are they throwing it away from their score sticks?' Ros asked, peering at the pitch like an old woman doing needlework. 'The red ones are going left but they keep throwing it right.'

'They can't throw the ball forward,' said Jay, helpfully, trying to remember the few rules she had gleaned from serving pints in the Hawk and flirting with rugby players at university.

'Why not?' said Jackie, mildly, wiping ketchup off her sleeve. 'It seems very impractical.'

'I don't know, it's just one of the rules.' Jay shrugged.

'Pushing over seems to be a big deal,' said Ros, sagely. 'I can get on starboard with that – it seems quite therapeutic.'

Then with no warning the crowd roared in unison at something completely unnoticeable to any of the three women. Ros shrieked in surprise and Jackie sent the majority of her pint in a tidal wave across what remained of her burger.

'What on earth was that?' Jackie asked, looking in alarm at the pitch for any sign of progress made by either team.

'Absolutely no idea,' said Ros, 'but they all really went for it, didn't they? Jay?'

Jay shrugged and shook her head – there seemed to be a throw-in happening but she couldn't tell you why or what that meant.

The three of them knuckled down to watch more intently, but even with their focus entirely on the pitch the next roar from the crowd caught them equally by surprise and the remainder of Jackie's pint hit her shoes.

'But we were watching!' Ros shouted in exasperation, flinging her programme down on the sodden floor. 'How can we have been watching and yet still have absolutely no idea what was going on?'

Jackie laughed. 'God, is all sport only enjoyable after you're an expert? This is impossible.'

'Maybe more beer would help?' Jay suggested, and disappeared to the bar to get the next round in.

After the second beer, their toes felt a bit warmer, and they gave up trying to read the match and just read the crowd instead.

'Oh, that was a good one! Even that guy got up!' Jackie shrieked with excitement, pointing to a man across from them who so far hadn't cheered anything but had mysteriously cheered very heartily at a man sprinting ten feet and having his legs pulled out from under him.

'Yes! I think they like it when the mean-looking ones get involved – that seems to be a good thing!' Ros was making notes in the margin of her programme.

'I take it you've not been to a game before?' A voice next to Jackie chimed in with their discussion and Jackie turned to notice the jewellery-laden woman to her right. She looked like she'd been rolled in glue and pushed through the gift shop for one of the teams.

Jackie smiled shyly, 'No, we're new. How could you possibly tell!' The woman laughed and Jackie threw caution to the wind and decided that she liked her. So there, lack of impulsivity! 'Are you here on your own?' There was an empty chair beside the woman.

'Oh,' she waved a hand in the direction of the chair and wiggled her eyebrows, 'no, my husband is here but he spends most of the game near the bar with the "chaps".' She got so much emotion into the word chaps that Jackie felt sure she must have been to stage school. Her accent was posh; maybe she'd even been to a private school. Was there such a thing as private stage school?

'Oh, you poor thing, well, join in with us. I'm Jackie and this is Ros and Jay.' The other two waved down the line.

'I'm Claire. Nice to meet you. What's made you give rugby a try then? Excuse the pun.'

Jackie wasn't at all sure what the pun was supposed to have been, but she laughed anyway to be nice. 'Well,' the beer was infusing in her brain, 'my husband cheated on me and left me so I'm trying to do new things.' She expected Claire to laugh awkwardly and turn away, but Claire let out a ringing cackle and rubbed Jackie's leg fondly.

'First affair? Don't sweat it. He'll be back. If he's waited until this late in the game to cheat, then he obviously loves you. My husband seems to have a different one on the go every year. I just can't be arsed to get mad about it any more.'

Jackie was dumbfounded. If she'd been Roger Rabbit her jaw would have clunked down into the floor in surprise. She was aware that over her shoulder Ros and Jay were also listening in intently while trying to pretend they were still focused on the game.

'So, you . . . you just . . .?' Jackie couldn't think of any polite way to ask the questions she had floating round in her head. There was something about this woman's – well, for want of a less wanky word, energy – that she was already beginning to really like. But the idea of just letting your husband cheat on you? This was like something from the Renaissance or one of those other corset eras. Luckily, Claire saw Jackie's gaping mouth and just laughed.

'I know, I know. Too much? Sorry! I figured you were a too-much-info woman too. My sister is always telling me I give away so much info it's amazing no one's nicked my identity. I say who'd want it?! You must think I'm an absolute madwoman: sitting here telling strangers that I just let my husband have affairs!'

'No, not at all . . .' Jackie started, but as ever Ros's mouth was quicker.

'Absolutely I do!' she stated, staring at Claire without blinking. 'I think you're mad as a box of frogs. What you doing staying with a cheating rat?'

Claire laughed again. Jackie wondered if she was a lot drunker than she seemed.

'It just works for us . . . I don't know. I used to get angry and upset and insecure but then . . . well, to be honest I spent a lot of money on expensive therapy. His money, I should add. I'm not wasting my own cash on problems he's caused. And, anyway, through a lot of thinking about it I realised: he could be married to anyone and he'd still want change. He doesn't keep any of these twentysomethings for long, so they're disposable, not better than me. They don't stick around; I do. So that's the insecurity dealt with: even a perfect-looking twenty-two-year-old can't keep his attention for more than a year, so would anyone?' At this point, Jackie wasn't even sure if the rugby match was still going on. This was like the best Netflix drama she'd ever seen, happening live right in front of her eyes. She thanked several gods she didn't believe in for the placement of herself and Claire in the ticket allocation. Claire continued: 'Then I started thinking about my marriage and I realised, I like it. I like our life, our friends, our home, our pets . . . I like it all. If he stopped seeing other people he'd be around more and he'd want more from me. I don't think I want that. So, I had to come to the conclusion that I just like things how they are.'

Jay, Jackie and Ros looked like three statues. Jay was the first to break the reverie; she shook her head and blinked rapidly, smiling at Claire. 'Gosh. I've never heard anyone sort of talk like that. Does he know you know?'

'He knows that I'm not stupid and that I don't ask.'

'And you're sure you wouldn't just prefer to be single?' Ros was struggling to get her head round the concept of not finding this deeply undermining. Ros was pretty used to being the trail-blazer in any group of women because she was in her fifties, a business owner, happily childless and single.

Claire just shrugged. 'Maybe I would, but I'm certainly never sad enough to want to try it.'

Jackie was quiet, wondering whether if, on that shoe rack day, Steve had told her of the affair and not left she would have happily let him have two families. Obviously she knew the answer straight away: no. No, he couldn't be disappearing off and being with someone else because that wasn't fair, was it? She tried to make her thoughts as crystal as she could before she said them out loud to Claire. 'Do you have affairs too?' she said shyly.

Claire shook her head, not taking her eyes off the game, which seemed to have reached another crescendo 'No. No, I did think about it a few years back but honestly, trying to find someone was a lot of admin.'

'So . . .' Jackie reassembled her thoughts again. 'So, your husband has affairs and all this other life and . . . you don't? Isn't that . . . I mean, don't you feel like it's unfair?'

Claire took her gaze off the pitch and cocked her head to one side, looking at Jackie. 'Well, he has affairs, but I'm not doing nothing. I go on holidays with my friends and work and do projects and do all sorts of things . . . just not sex with other people. I can't be bothered to show a man under thirty what good sex is!'

Ros and Claire both laughed.

'Amen!' said Jay, laughing.

'See, Jackie? There's life beyond being a stay-at-home wife.' Ros turned back to Claire. 'Jackie is in the process of divorcing her particular swine. I like you, Claire' – Ros nodded to confirm her decision – 'We're going to be friends. I'll go and get more drinks.'

Ros squashed past Jackie and Jay moved up to take Ros's seat. 'Are you all right?' she asked quietly, noticing Jackie's retreat into herself.

'Yeah . . . yeah.' Jackie tried to nod.

'I'm sorry,' Claire offered, suddenly looking worried. 'I hope I haven't upset you?' She looked genuinely concerned and Jackie felt a rush of warmth towards this new woman.

'No, no not at all . . . it's just, I was sitting here thinking, as you were talking: if Steve hadn't left, if he'd just said he loved this woman and wanted to be with both of us, would I have let him? And then I was thinking: no, because it would have left a big hole in my life whenever he was off with her. Which then . . . well, it made it really obvious that I didn't really do anything other than be in that marriage. Everything I did, every hobby, every minute of the day was tied in to the two of us. No offence, Claire, but my instant reaction to what you said was *You're mad as a hatter.*'

Claire laughed again and nodded. 'Probably!'

Jackie continued, 'But, are you? Why's it any less mad to sink everything you're doing into one person? Why didn't I have any hobbies? What was I doing with my life?' Jackie felt embarrassingly close to tears and prayed that Ros would get back soon with the beer so she could bury her face in the cup and pretend she was invisible.

Claire gave what Jackie had said some thought and then rubbed the back of her hand briskly but with affection in that way that posh people do, where it seems like they're scared too much physical contact will get them kicked out of *Debrett's*.

'Who knows, eh? Too late to change it now. All you can do is move forward and, given that you're here attempting to get into rugby and making friends with the stranger sat next to you, I'd say you're giving it a bloody good go. Good on you.'

Claire was good at pep talks. Jackie smiled and Ros reappeared clutching four pint cups of amber liquid.

Jackie gratefully settled back into her seat, feeling exhausted, exposed but supported. She and Claire moved on to topics less raw and exhilarating. Claire's life was parties and horses: not things Jackie did – or, she corrected her thoughts, not things she *used* to do – but now, who knew?

The afternoon descended into giggles and hiccups and as the match came to an end and a tall, handsome man called Claire away, Jackie found herself being presented with Claire's mobile.

'Put your number in here. I'm sorry you're . . . you know,' Claire's clipped tones were unable to emote directly, but she looked sad for Jackie. 'Well, let me take your number.'

Jackie clumsily thumbed in her number and then felt her own mobile buzzing in her pocket. 'Oh! Excuse me!' she said, 'I've got a call.'

Claire laughed. 'It's me! There, now you have my number too.'

They all said their goodbyes and Jackie's eyes gleamed.

'Look at you pulling!' Ros joked.

By the time Jackie's taxi turned into her driveway long after sunset, she was feeling more buoyant than she had since the day she chose a shoe rack.

Jackie pushed open the front door and froze. The light was on in the kitchen and she could hear the rattling of crockery.

10

She flinched, one foot in the hallway and the other unwilling to follow it and pull her into the house. There was definitely an intruder. She pushed her keys in between her fingers . . . and then hesitated, unsure of the purpose of poking keys through fingers. Was it for punching? If it was, she didn't feel very capable of punching, with or without keys. But possibly better to have them there just in case? She felt fragile and alone and wondered whether to go back outside and call someone for help. The police? Leon? Ros felt like probably the most capable in a fight. Before she could decide whether to move forward or backward, Steve's head appeared from round the kitchen door.

'Jackie! You're home!'

Jackie jumped with shock and felt her muscles sag with relief. The adrenaline rushed out of her, making her want to cry and hit him all at once.

'Are you all right?' he went on. 'You look like you've seen a ghost?'

'I didn't know who was in here.'

'Who did you think it was going to be? No one else has keys, do they?' Steve was jocular, upbeat, but Jackie could hear the thumping of her blood in her ears and she couldn't seem to reach the same level as him.

'It could have been burglars,' she all but whispered, her throat dry and the ghost of her fear leaving her feeling belittled.

'Oh, you poor thing – I didn't even think. Sorry. Would you like a cup of tea?' Steve disappeared back into the kitchen and Jackie heard the sound of the kettle going on. She dropped her

54

keys into the dish on the hall table, kicked off her shoes and placed them on the shoe rack and then walked slowly into the kitchen.

Steve was taking mugs out of the cupboard and he popped a tea bag into each one, whistling a little as he did. She thought, unbidden, of the first cup of tea he had made her in this kitchen. He'd had a lot more hair and they'd had a lot more boxes stacked around the room. They couldn't believe they'd bought such a big house and got moved in before the bump became Leon. Jackie felt sick. What was he doing here? It felt like a dream watching him back in the kitchen as if nothing had happened. Had she dreamt the last few months?

'What are you doing here?' she asked finally, and he turned round, giving her a surprised expression.

'I just came to get a few more bits – that's all right, isn't it? I thought you'd be in at this time on a Saturday, or I wouldn't have come. Where have you been?'

Jackie ignored his question. Goddamn him, he didn't have to know where she'd been; she could feel the beer sloshing around inside her and she wished she had a clearer head. 'What bits do you need?' she asked, keeping her voice tight and firm.

'Oh, it's OK, I've packed them up – they're in the car,' Steve said cheerily, and poured the water onto the tea bags. Jackie processed this information, her mind working far slower than she wanted.

'How long have you been here?'

'Couple of hours,' mumbled Steve, 'Like I said, I thought you'd be home so I didn't think it would be a problem.'

'Couple of hours?' Jackie felt suddenly invaded at the thought of him here, looking through her stuff. Being in her home. She tried to tell herself that was ridiculous; it was their home, or it had been. For decades they had shared it. Since they'd unpacked that first box with the kettle in and got started moving in. Why did the thought of him in it now make her skin feel cold? Would he go home now to Michelle and tell her things he'd seen? About how full the laundry basket was or whether the windows were clean? She shook her head to dispel the thoughts. He'd never noticed those things when he lived here, let alone now when he didn't.

Steve added milk to the tea and then picked up both mugs, 'Shall we sit comfy?' He left the kitchen to head to the living room and Jackie found herself following stupidly, unable to resist his cheery, normal tone. She thought about the last time he had suggested they go and sit together in the living room. Maybe he had another bombshell to drop? Maybe Michelle was pregnant? Maybe he was pregnant? She didn't let herself wonder if he was about to tell her he was coming back.

She sat down on the sofa and stared into her cup of tea, unable to think of a single thing she could say to him that didn't seem petty or odd. He drummed his fingers on the arm of the sofa.

'So where were you?' he asked. His tone was light and pleasant enough, but Jackie found herself unwilling to answer the question. She didn't know why but she didn't want him to know about the rugby. She wanted to have something that he couldn't touch, couldn't have.

'Just out with Ros,' she said nonchalantly.

'Not playing golf again?' He laughed, and her eyes sprang up to look at him.

'How did you know about that?'

'Marie told me down at the club.'

'Who's Marie?'

'The receptionist. I can't believe you and Ros played golf. Oh, I'd have paid thousands to watch that. What was your handicap?'

You— thought Jackie, and then swallowed the thought. *Take the high road.*

'No, we weren't playing golf. Actually . . .' She hesitated and then went for it. 'Actually we went to see a rugby match.'

'Rugby? Why?' Steve spluttered into his cup of tea.

'Why not?' Jackie responded sharply.

'I didn't know you liked rugby, that's all,' Steve said mildly.

'I didn't know you liked other women but here we are,' Jackie shot back, surprised at her anger. Beery Jackie seemed much more ready for a fight than the sleepy Jackie wine produced.

'OK, I suppose we're not at a point where we can do this yet,' Steve said, putting his cup of tea down on the coffee table and pushing his hands into the armchair to help him rise. 'What's this?' His hand had brushed against some paper, and he pulled it out from down the side of the armchair. He read it with a bemused smile on his face, 'Netball? What, are you trying out every sport?'

Jackie recognised the flyer from her work initiative that Ros had dropped. 'No, I'm not playing netball. Give it here.' She snatched the flyer off him and scrunched it into her pocket.

'I was going to say,' Steve was still laughing, 'I can't imagine you running around in a little skirt and a bib!'

Jackie stood in silence, wondering how he could be managing to hurt her on so many levels and yet be so utterly oblivious. She opened her mouth but couldn't think of anything to say; she just wanted him gone.

'Sorry, Jack, I didn't mean—'

'What would you have done if I hadn't come home?'

'Just gone back, why?'

'No, not tonight. When you left. You were packing, while I was out. Were you going to wait for me to come home?' Jackie's pulse was hot and noisy in her ears.

He looked at her guiltily. 'I had a note ready . . . I . . . I thought it might be easier.'

Jackie nodded. 'A note. Right. I need to go to bed, Steve. If you wouldn't mind?' She gestured towards the door. Steve raised his eyebrows and then huffed a little to cover his uncomfortableness. He shrugged his shoulders and slouched out towards the front door.

'And leave your key please,' she said, in a hurry, so she could get the words out before she changed her mind. 'I don't want another fright when I come home. Leave your key please.'

Steve opened his mouth to argue but Jackie straightened her back and held the banister to stop her hands trembling. He shut his mouth again and reached into his pocket. It seemed to take an age for him to wind the key off its metal circle, but finally it came off and he laid it on the sideboard. He smiled forlornly up at her and she forbade her body to feel any pity for him. A note.

I I

Jackie lay in her bed making her mind up. She wasn't going to do it. Was she? Golf was one thing; golf was a laugh with Ros. Well, the actual golf was terrible but being with Ros was funny.

She turned over heavily. Her feet and legs twitched and burned with furious unspent energy. She felt like she'd been downing caffeine. Her toes scrunched and flicked angrily.

Steve had really got under her skin. Made her feel stupid and old. Maybe he thought of her as stupid and old now he had a new young girlfriend? Although, he'd been with her for a long time, hadn't he? At least months. How many months? Long enough to move in together. So maybe he had thought of her as stupid and old for a long time?

What would Claire do? Jackie struggled to imagine Claire lying in bed feeling old and past it. Claire with her perfect hair that smelled of Elnett and Chanel. Had she done her hair just for the rugby or was that her standard look? She'd have to blow-dry it every day, surely? Did she share a bed with her husband? Did she, then, miss him when he wasn't there? Could she lie still when he got in, even if she knew where, or who, he had just come back from? Jackie couldn't imagine not cringing away from skin that had just been far too close to someone else's.

But when you didn't know . . . She shrank back into the bed sheets, wanting a way to cover up some more. Wanting a way to go back in time and cover herself up all those times she had been naked in front of Steve when he had come back from being with someone else.

Her eyes sprang back open again and stared into the darkness. They seemed completely unable to stay shut; the required weight wasn't in them to keep them down. Perhaps they were trying to stay extra alert now, in light of having missed so much over the last year? More than a year? Why hadn't she asked?

She turned over again and stared at the vague outlines of the curtains. She'd been so pleased when she'd got those – the pattern and the colour were just perfect for this room . . . Tears appeared across her far-too-open eyes as her opinion of herself sank to a new low. Of course he had left; why would you spend the rest of your life with someone who got that excited over curtains and shoe racks? She'd got boring. So boring.

Ros ran a company. Claire practically encouraged her husband to cheat so she could fit more things into her life. Jay felt like a failure in her twenties for having more in her life than Jackie had in her fifties. Why had she let being a wife be everything she was? Why hadn't she noticed?

The tears made the skin on her nose itch, and she dropped back onto her back and wiped them away angrily towards the pillow. Maybe she had got boring, but wasn't that to be expected? After the years of chemotherapy for Steve and then the slow progression towards him being healthy again, she had become more cautious. She'd got gentler with him, and with their lives. She didn't want to be too flamboyant, or pushy or busy. She'd got used to letting him take the lead with life and she had fitted in quietly so as to not put pressure on him. Curtains and shoe racks had been a gentle distraction: just quietly improving their nest ready for when things were normal again and they could enjoy it.

But when was that going to be? she thought, swapping her pillow out for the other side where it was cool and, more importantly, dry. It was two years since Steve got the good news that he was cancer-free. Why hadn't she got back into her usual life?

What was her usual life?

She'd taken early retirement when Steve got sick because . . . well, because he'd needed her and why not? She had a good retirement package and good savings. Why not take proper care of him and . . . she'd never said it out loud, but, make the most of their time together just in case. Just in case.

Then he'd got better, and she'd found days just easily filled themselves up with their sons and the house and Freya and . . . well, there were so many radio and television shows these days. What were her hobbies? Who was she? If someone came up to her at a party and said, 'Hi Jackie, what do you do?' she would have to honestly say nothing. No job, no interests, no husband . . . nothing. A grandma. That's it. Not that there was anything wrong with being a grandma, but that couldn't be all she was as a person. Just a related babysitter waiting to get a call.

Jackie didn't want to admit to herself how physically weak she'd felt stood in the hall listening to the sounds of an intruder in the kitchen. Obviously, if they'd been burgled while Steve lived here it wasn't like he was a prizefighter, but at least there were two of them. She couldn't help it; her primary mode was that being with someone, anyone, was better than being alone. She imagined the two empty spare rooms lying in their own darknesses next to hers. Perhaps she should move? Get somewhere smaller? Somewhere with a community? Fresh sweat rose to the surface of her skin at the realisation that what she was half-talking herself into was some sort of assisted living. She wasn't there yet. Perhaps she could get a lodger? A big, muscly lodger who made Steve incredibly jealous when he came over. But one she trusted. The muscles would have to be just for show. The lodger would need to not turn out to be a murderer: that was important.

She lay sweating in the darkness, willing the night to pass so she could get up and do something. Tomorrow she was going to do everything. All the things in the world. Every hobby, activity and fun-looking thing. She was going to do them all. And find a lodger who had never even thought about murdering. And this wasn't going to be like all those times she'd started a diet at eleven p.m. and failed by ten a.m. This was real.

Then, the thought occurred to her that people who lived alone with nothing to do the next day could do whatever they wanted with the night hours. Why lie here feeling hot and prickly when she could get up and do . . . anything. Make the most of it before she had the giant, muscly pacifist in the next room who she might disturb. She put her feet over the side of the bed experimentally, feeling peculiarly exposed and ridiculous. She glanced at the clock. Two a.m. Jackie pulled her feet back into the bed and lay down again. No, she wasn't going to get up and just wander round the house in the middle of the night like a ghost or a crazy person. It wasn't who she was.

She stared through the darkness at the ceiling again. 'OK,' she said out loud, hearing her voice in the dark room and feeling excited at the sound of it, out loud at two a.m., 'OK, you don't have to get up and wander about at two a.m., but you can either get up now or you can go to the netball session tomorrow. Those are your options, Jackie Douglas.'

There was nothing she wanted to do even if she did get up, so she decided to just stay where she was. Besides, netball was the safer option because it wasn't right now, and she could always talk herself out of it tomorrow. Netball is the new diet. She felt sleepiness creeping into her limbs and lay back, relaxed. There wasn't a single part of her that thought she would, or wanted to, play netball the next day, but oddly the thought of having something in her plans for tomorrow (even if she fully intended to cancel them, and they were only plans she had made with herself) made her go to sleep feeling content. Less stupid. Less pathetic.

12

Jackie woke up the next morning feeling motivated, alert: ready for the day. Netball was in the evening, and she was absolutely definitely going to go. Absolutely. So, just the day to get through first. No, not get through: to revel in. Yes, that was better, more positive thinking. She was going to fill the day with brilliant things and hobbies. Although, maybe that would be too much in a day? Maybe one new thing in a day was enough? Yes, probably. She didn't want to burn out on day one of being an Interesting Person™. So, she would go to netball in the evening and just do the essentials during the day.

The only issue was there was nothing essential to do that day. There were precious few essentials to do any day really. She rang Leon to see if Freya needed watching, but she was at school and was going to a play date afterwards, so she didn't even need collecting. It was a dead end on ways to feel useful. Maybe this was why mothers in jokes were always prodding for grandchildren; it was just quite simply something to do?

Her fingers kept itching to text someone and see if they wanted to come with her to the netball try-out. Not Ros, obviously. She didn't think she'd ever hear the end of Ros's laughter if she suggested that. But maybe Jay? Jackie was feeling incredibly fond towards Jay these days, and in some ways they were both in the same boat: both out of kilter with where they thought their lives would be at this point. Something in her kept stopping her reaching out for company though . . . she felt like she ought to be able to do it alone.

The netball session with Ros's colleagues started at seven p.m. at the Kingfisher Sports Centre, only a twenty-minute walk away. Jackie glanced at the clock all day, waiting for it to be time to leave, but it was always only three or four minutes later than the last time she'd looked. She sat in front of the TV, but the screen might as well have been made of lead for all that managed to get through it and into her brain.

It wasn't too late to change her mind and not go. Obviously, no one was going to make her go to this netball thing . . . no one even knew she was considering going. Except for Steve. Arrogant, arsehole Steve, she thought angrily. How dare he laugh and come in here being casual and normal around her? How dare he let himself into her house. All the sad rawness that had been left over from exposure to him the night before had been replaced by cold fury this morning as she boiled to be better than he thought she was. She shook her head, trying to calm down: no, Steve didn't know at all that she was considering going, Steve had just seen the piece of paper and she'd convinced herself of the rest of it. Goodness, all this time to think was exhausting; what had she thought about before Steve left? Because there must have been the same amount of time to think, but she didn't remember being this rattled all the time.

Going to netball would show him. Not that he'd ever find out she had gone; but she would know. She would have a hobby then: she'd know people that he didn't know; couldn't know. It was occurring to her more and more that she felt exposed by his knowledge of absolutely everything in her life. She didn't like that he would probably be able to pretty accurately guess what she was up to at any given time. When she tried to picture him now she found it nearly impossible. What was his life like with this Michelle? Did they go out for dinner? Stay in? Were they giggly? Had Steve put his things out in her house? Things that had used to be out here? Was his ship picture on the wall in a new house somewhere in this town? Perhaps she'd driven past the house, not knowing that one day Steve, her Steve, would be living there.

She shook herself out of the avalanche of thoughts and tried to focus back in on the television but there was nothing convincing about the acting, and she couldn't bring herself to try to work out what the plot was. Something about some vets being very good at their jobs and bad at their love lives.

She made herself some lunch and then noticed it was only 10.30.

'Predict me having lunch at ten thirty a.m., Steve,' she said victoriously into the silent kitchen and then ate the sandwich, already deciding she was going to have another one at proper lunchtime. The afternoon crawled by in an itching, irritating haze of not being able to focus on anything but not being able to enjoy relaxing either. She half-cleaned several rooms in the house and made a list of DIY jobs that she could do . . . but probably wouldn't. She started and stopped several films and even dug out her old sewing machine to see if she finally felt like being someone who made her own clothes. It turned out she didn't, but she left the sewing machine on the table just in case that day turned out to be tomorrow.

Eventually, and with petulant slowness, the clock inched its way to 6.30 p.m. and Jackie stared between it and the flyer for the netball session. She suddenly felt paralysed. There was no way she was going to go. She'd be mad to. She looked at the little bag of what she hoped were netball-suitable clothes she had got ready and imagined herself putting them away. That felt even sadder.

If she didn't go to netball then this was just an eleven p.m. diet after all. She wasn't an Interesting Person™ with hobbies, she was just a person who couldn't change. An image of the shoe rack floated into her head. Steve's inability to learn to put his shoes away had driven her crazy; why couldn't he make this little adjustment? Why couldn't he change? He couldn't put his shoes away and she couldn't be interesting, she couldn't get out of her comfortable little rut any more than he could tuck his shoes somewhere less tripable.

She could just go to the sports centre and watch, maybe? Was that a good compromise? Maybe trying to play a whole new running-around-type game by herself was too big a step for her first day as an Interesting Person™? The clock was ticking on. Bastard thing seemed to have sped up now she was trying to make her mind up whether or not to go. Where was this kind of pacing earlier when she had an entire day to fill?

She could just go down to the sports centre and watch people playing? Or just look at it. Yes. Obviously there wasn't time to walk now; she'd have to go in the car, but maybe that was better? Yes, that way if she did play she wouldn't be too worn out from the walk there. Not that she was intending to play.

13

Jackie's car navigated into the car park and neatly into a space. The headlights shut off with the engine. Then they immediately came back on again as Jackie's car lurched back into life, pulled forward out of the space and made its way towards the car park exit. As it reached the stopping point for the main road the bonnet suddenly swung back round again and headed back to the space it had just left.

'I must be mad,' Jackie said to the cold air, thinking that if anyone was watching CCTV of the car park right now they'd call the police. She parked up the car again and sat in the silence, feeling the chill from outside seeping into her arms and legs now that the car's heaters were turned off. She grabbed her little bag off the passenger seat and clutched it fearfully in her lap.

'Come on Douglas, you can do this. Just go in and have a see,' she muttered, almost rocking in her efforts to prise herself out of her seat and towards the sports centre. She opened the car door and took her first steps.

It was obviously her imagination, but the car park felt like jelly underneath her legs. A couple wandered past with tennis rackets slung casually over their shoulders. They were in skin-tight Lycra and the woman had her long hair pulled back tightly to her head with a sweatband pinning any stray hairs in place. The insecurity about how she was dressed hit Jackie like a freight train. Her grey joggers humiliated her with every loose inch of baggy material. It felt like her velvet scrunchie was flashing neon lights out from her head and around the car park. Her nerves flamed and an insistent panic alarm screamed on repeat in her mind for her to get back in the car. A bulging squashy mass of fear lurched up the back of her throat and brought with it scared tears. She stopped walking and stood trembling. A car beeped at her politely to move out of the space and she waved a hand in apology and moved onto the pavement outside the gym. She felt a wreck.

'No, I'm going home,' she muttered to herself.

'Oh good, if you do I can too.' The voice made Jackie start and her skin prickled hot at the surprise. She turned to see a woman squashing a cigarette butt under a battered old trainer and then struggling to bend down and pick it up. The effort of bending over left her breathless and red in the face but she squeezed her cheeks into a nervous smile in Jackie's direction. 'Sorry,' she mumbled, 'I didn't mean to listen in.'

Jackie shook her head hurriedly and returned the smile. 'No, not at all. I'm a bit nervous about going in. Are you here for the netball?'

'Yeah,' the woman said, although whether she was mainly talking to Jackie or to her own shoes would have been hard to decipher from a distance. Her posture was terrible; Jackie had never seen anybody try to fold themselves into their own stomach with shyness. The woman looked young, maybe Jay's age, but lacking any of the vigorous confidence. Like a twenty-something playing the part of a pensioner. 'Well, I thought I was probably going to go but now I'm here I feel a bit sick. I've never tried to do a social work thing before.'

'Are you from Mackie and Howard?'

The woman nodded. 'Yeah.'

'I'm Jackie.' Jackie extended a hand.

'I'm Annie.' Annie took it. It looked like a handshake but from Jackie's perspective it was much more of a hand-tremble. The poor girl, Jackie thought.

'Do you like netball?' Jackie asked, feeling better about the whole situation now someone else was nervous too.

'Yeah, I do. I know I don't look like I play, but . . .' Annie trailed off, waving a hand limply at her body, which, Jackie had to agree, was not that of a committed athlete. Not that Jackie was one to talk, she thought, feeling the cut of her knicker elastic bite insistently into her hip.

'I don't even work at the firm. I don't even know if I'm allowed to be there!' Jackie felt her shoulders loosen a little with the relief of talking to someone. 'I just found the flyer from my friend and . . . God, what am I doing here?' They both laughed, 'Shall we go in? Come on. Let's go together.' Jackie made a confident step towards the door. This felt better; she was always better at looking after other people than she was taking care of herself. If she went home then Annie wouldn't go and play, and Jackie wouldn't have it on her conscience to spoil someone else's good intentions. A small voice at the back of her mind reminded her that she now knew someone Steve didn't, and she liked what that small voice had to say.

The reception was sleek and shiny with mood lighting that seemed more conducive to sex than a team sport.

'This is fancier than I'd thought,' Jackie whispered to Annie as they padded through past the receptionist.

'It's had a refurb,' Annie whispered back. 'Costs an arm and a leg to be a member.'

Jackie was half-expecting champagne on a platter in the changing room but made do with the existence of communal hair straighteners. Perhaps she'd give them a go after the try-out, just for a laugh. Predict me straightening my hair, Steve, she thought victoriously and then wondered if it was a positive that her husband would never guess she was making an effort with her appearance. She was already fishing about in her purse for a pound coin when she realised the lockers just required her to create her own code in the lock keypad. She chose her bank PIN, hoping it'd be memorable, and put her towel and purse inside the little cloth bag into a locker before heading into the enormous gym hall.

It was chilly, and echoed. Jackie looked around, amazed at how little places like this had changed since she last stood in one wearing a bottle-green PE kit many decades ago. No matter how hotel-like the reception, there was no changing what was in this room. It was sadly playing courts rather than a fluffy robe and a king-sized bed. Her trainers squeaked on the rubbery flooring as she made her way across to the group of women warming up at the other end of the hall. Jackie was grateful to have Annie by her side as she walked. An involuntary shiver of insecurity passed across her shoulders and down her spine. She wasn't sure if it was the thin jumper or how young and athletic everyone looked compared to her. Her breasts felt conspicuously voluminous and bouncy in her used-to-be-white grey bra, and she couldn't help looking at everyone else's clever-looking strappy-downy type sports ensembles.

A few women were tossing balls to each other or having a go at shooting, but Jackie couldn't see any balls lying around anywhere and she felt too insecure to go and ask anyone if she could join, so she tried doing some stretching. She put her right foot out the front and tried to lean into it at an angle like she'd occasionally seen people do when pausing in their jogging. The second she leaned forward a searing pain shot down the back of her leg and she immediately stood straight up again, hoping no one could tell. It felt like she'd ripped the seam of her leg open. This couldn't be right? Jackie racked her brains for the last time she might have exercised and then she glumly concluded that even trying to think that intensely was probably more exercise than she'd done in a long time.

Jackie decided to ignore her legs for a bit and concentrate on something easier like arms. She swung them in loose circles forward and backward and felt comforted by the regularity of the crunching noises coming from her shoulders.

A whistle blew and every head flicked in the direction of a bouncy-looking woman in a perfect blue tracksuit.

'Jog on in girls!' she called cheerily and twenty high ponytails started flicking as their owners led them in the direction of the woman. Jackie bristled a little at being called a girl but still made her way obediently over. Her leg felt as if it was on fire, but she decided it was probably warming-up pains and ignored it. She nestled in beside Annie, who had offered shy smiles to some of her colleagues but still looked painfully awkward.

'My name is Judith,' said the whistle-woman, holding a ball still under one of her feet and looking round at the circle of faces. 'I'm running the "get to know you" session today and then I'll be coaching the upper tier once we've graded you.'

The word 'graded' had an immediate loosening effect on Jackie's bowels and she felt a mild washing machine-esque panic begin in her stomach. Everyone else seemed to be nodding though, so she just stood motionless, wishing she'd read the flyer more carefully. Stupid Steve getting her all wound up. The thought of Steve seeing her here attempting this was worse than the idea of being graded on her netball ability and Jackie wasn't entirely sure her feet were still connected to her legs.

Judith was still talking, and Jackie tried to force her ears to hear anything other than an alarmingly shrill siren. She tuned back into Judith just in time to hear, 'So, just get a couple of laps out and then we'll start some drills.'

The pack of wannabe netballers began to move instantly into a calm jog. Jackie swivelled on her heel to join them, and her leg began to shriek at her in protest straight away. Ignoring it just wasn't an option, but she didn't want to immediately stop running and play the 'I've hurt myself' card.

The whole thing was a nightmare. She tried to run without putting too much pressure on the hurt leg, but that just made the ankle of her good leg feel all grindy and sore. She tried swinging the leg out in odd circles so that she didn't have to bend it and that seemed to ease the pain a little. But then, as the frontrunners began lapping her down at the far end of the gym, she swung her leg out just in time to catch the foot of a passing runner and flick the woman to the floor. She went sprawling out across the gym, sliding an impressive distance on her shiny pink tracksuit. Jackie was mortified and immediately hobbled over to help the woman up.

'Are you OK?' she whispered, helping the woman to her feet.

'Yeah, yeah, I'm fine.' The woman didn't seem hurt, but she did seem a bit cross and suspicious, which Jackie thought was probably fair given what had just happened.

'I'm so sorry. I didn't do it on purpose,' Jackie said, immediately regretting her choice of words as they definitely made it sound a lot more like she had done it on purpose.

'I didn't think you had,' the woman stuttered back, even more suspicious now. She smiled tightly and then turned round to carry on running. Jackie hoped it was just her guilty imagination that made the woman's run seem slightly joltier and more lop-sided post-fall.

'Did you do it on purpose?' asked Annie from behind Jackie. She jumped out of her skin and turned round to face her.

'No! No of course I didn't!' Her face felt beetroot red and blazing hot.

'Oh, fair enough. Why were you running like that?' Annie cocked her head to one side, looking at Jackie's feet.

'It's . . . it's just how I run. Shall we get going again?' She began to limp in the direction of the flow of runners. There was less of a clump now as they had all naturally found their pace and spaced out around the edge of the hall. Annie shrugged and begrudgingly followed Jackie.

'I was quite enjoying the break, to be honest,' Annie huffed as she kept pace with Jackie.

'I know what you mean,' Jackie agreed, as yet another person loped gracefully past them. 'Is it a requirement of your firm to be a reincarnated gazelle?'

Annie snorted and then groaned. 'Don't make me laugh – this is hard enough as it is. I certainly missed any memo about gazelliness if there was one.'

Running was far worse than Jackie remembered. Just absolutely awful. When she'd thought about doing it, she'd imagined herself in the bodies of those people she often saw jogging past her house in the mornings. They looked light and carefree – focused on the road or their thoughts or their headphones or something. Jackie had forgotten quite how awful gravity made jogging. Everything that bounced up came crashing back down with each step. Her breasts pulped into her ribcage, pushing all the much-needed oxygen out just at the point she most wanted to suck it all in and keep hold of it. Every time her foot hit the floor it sent a message to her knees that they were old and dry and not supposed to be here. Her brain was macerating against the inside of her skull and the gym seemed to shake about around her vision. She glared at Judith; willing her to blow the damn whistle and make this agony end. Judith, completely unaware of the death wishes raining down upon her immaculate figure, was engrossed in a conversation with another woman and seemed to have no intention of releasing Jackie from the circular torture of laps.

'So, you . . . you play netball?' Jackie shot each word individually at Annie, praying the puffing wouldn't make the question undecipherable.

'I used to,' Annie replied, 'then I . . .' She paused, and Jackie assumed Annie was just as out of breath as she was, but then the pause lasted longer, and Jackie took her eyes off the floor in front of her and snuck a look at Annie. She looked sad.

'It's OK,' Jackie offered quickly. 'Sorry.'

'No, no . . . it's OK,' Annie was quick to respond this time, 'it's stupid. I just played for a team that wasn't very nice. That's all. So, I haven't played in a while. Also: I'm a goal shooter. We don't run as much.'

'I want to be that too then,' Jackie said, and they both offered out haggard laughs and turned back to the relentless slog of putting one foot in front of the other.

Minutes that felt like hours dragged their enormous behinds around the clock and Jackie was starting to wonder if lungs could actually pop. A small part of her brain was trying to tell her to embrace the fact she was doing something new, even if the new thing was awful.

Eventually the whistle blew and the running came to a stop. Her muscles flicked and twitched under her joggers like horses' ears flicking at flies. She made her way back to the group of women feeling like she was learning to walk all over again. Every breath in caught on the sticky branches she had seemingly just grown up the inside of her throat. No one else in the group, except Annie, who was as red as Jackie, seemed even mildly out of breath and Jackie wondered exactly how much younger than her they were. At least a millennium.

'Grab some water and stretch out for five,' Judith called in a sing-song voice that Jackie knew she would hear in her nightmares. Jackie decided not to take the risk of doing any more stretching; stretching was dangerous and bad for the body. She plonked her bottom onto the end of a bench and was alarmed to see the other end go swinging up into the air.

'What is this, a cartoon?' she muttered.

'Sorry?' said a woman, pouring water into her mouth from a high-tech-looking bottle.

'Oh nothing, sorry . . . I was just talking to myself,' Jackie said, her breath now under control enough that she could form words.

'Oh! No worries. I'm Cherie, hi!' The woman seemed friendly and offered a hand to Jackie. Jackie shook it and then quickly looked away so that the woman could wipe Jackie's sweat off her palm without seeming rude. 'What department are you in?'

Jackie's jaw motored without noise coming out. 'I'm . . . in the back office.'

Cherie laughed again. 'Funny! I'm in finance.'

Luckily Jackie was saved having to find out why the back office was funny by Judith calling them all back in. She chose a spot in the huddle next to Annie, where she felt a little safer. Annie felt about as close to an ally as she was likely to meet in this echoey hell hall.

'OK! We'll do a little drill. Two lines. One feeder line, pass in diagonals and then shooting, pop round to the back and come up again.'

This, miraculously, seemed to be more than enough information for everyone else and they sprang to life, forming two lines. Jackie scurried to keep up with Annie and tucked herself into the back of the line to watch what was going on and get a sense of what was expected of her before the ball hit her hands. For the millionth time she asked herself what she was doing here. This was horrendous. But if she hadn't been expecting this, what had she been expecting? A moment of clarity showed her that this was exactly what she'd been expecting; she'd just naively assumed she'd be someone else, someone better, when she was here.

The queue was moving up terrifyingly quickly as one line passed the ball swiftly to the other side, shot and then dashed away, leaving a new person at the head of the line to gather up the ball and pass it back, allowing the second line to shoot and dash away. It was like peeling a banana. A banana made of athletic women who were finding this fun. It was just the middle bit of collecting the ball and getting it to someone she needed to worry about. Never mind the shooting bit; plenty of people weren't getting the ball in the net.

Eventually she was next. She watched her opposite woman take a shot: the ball looped up into the air and then neatly settled itself into the docile hoop. Jackie scampered forward to retrieve the ball but miscalculated the speed the ball was moving at and managed to bring her foot down directly onto it, causing it to roll away under the pressure. Jackie met up with her old nemesis gravity and swooped backwards to the ground, breaking her fall using her coccyx. All the precious air she had managed to store up since the running stopped was forced out in one motion. She lay looking up at the bright strip lights, hoping vainly that there was a large fire breaking out elsewhere in the hall that was distracting all the other players. Annie's face appearing in her field of vision told her there was no fire. She was the fire.

'Are you all right?' Annie offered a hand.

A small part of Jackie wanted to just close her eyes and lie there. Really embrace becoming a floor. They could play around her. Perhaps Judith could turn it into some sort of drill? Unfortunately for Jackie, and more specifically Jackie's backside, the floor was very cold and she could instantly feel her back stiffening as it seeped through her muscles. She accepted Annie's hand and got to her feet, smiling to reassure the others she was fine.

'Butter feet,' she said, attempting a cheery sing-song voice.

'Don't worry about it!' called Judith, jogging over with perfect ponytail swishing. 'Happens to the best of us. Just take your shot and we'll carry on as we were – well done for getting back up.'

A nameless pair of leggings handed Jackie the ball and she stared at it, dumbstruck. Surely a fall like that was your ticket to just be allowed to sit out and whimper quietly for the rest of the session? Perhaps she could fake stomach cramps? That used to work at school. No one is forcing you to be here, a stern voice reminded her, and she batted it away with an image of Steve's head held to one side looking at her like she was an old dishcloth. He was probably somewhere playing squash with his perfect new girlfriend. God, she could be one of these other players. Jackie fought down the urge to shout the name Michelle and see if anyone responded.

'Jackie?' Judith was looking at her with concern now. Jackie blinked and tried to focus back on being in the room. 'Did you hit your head when you fell?'

Yet more blood found its way to Jackie's cheeks, and she was frankly astonished there was enough left elsewhere to be running vital organs. 'No, no,' she muttered, 'I'm fine.' She turned to face the hoop way up above her head. The other women had made a weight-on-one-leg kind of pose and then leaned into the shot. Jackie held the ball above her shoulder and settled it with both hands. There was the faintest feeling of familiarity in her muscles at this pose.

She pushed the ball away from her body and it sailed up towards the hoop, hitting the rim and bouncing away towards the other line. Not a net, but not at all a disaster either. Jackie jogged carefully back to the end of the line, happy to be out of the spotlight. Hopefully there would be long enough stood in line to get rid of this slightly chiselled feeling that had appeared in her shoulder blade.

The queue whipped along and Jackie found herself having to try to shoot three more times before Judith blew the whistle again and released them. None of her shots scored her any points but there were plenty of other people who didn't manage to score either, so Jackie didn't feel too terrible about it.

'OK.' Judith smiled round at them all. 'We'll break up into three teams now and have a few mini games just to get us back in the flow of it. Who has played in the last year?'

A few hands went up, including Annie's, and Judith split them across the three teams. She went through all the assembled women making sure that the experienced players were spread evenly. Jackie's disappointment at not being on Annie's team felt out of kilter with how long she had known her.

Jackie's team hid their disappointment at her joining them admirably. She smiled a half-apologetic face contortion at them and took the last bib left over from the small pile in their colour.

Wing defence. Damn. She had hoped that she'd have one of the obvious jobs with 'goal' or 'shooter' in the name. Wing defence was irritatingly vague: defend the wing. From what? The attacker, presumably, but how and where? What was a wing?

Luckily for Jackie, her team was the first to watch and she got a chance to see how the game went. It was much faster than she remembered from school. Or perhaps she had slowed down. The main job of the wing defence seemed to be to stand and wave in front of the wing attack and try to stop her being able to catch or throw the ball. That seemed doable.

When it was her time to play, Jackie dragged her ancient-feeling legs to the court and was annoyed to feel them trembling.

'I'm Liz!' said the opposing wing attack in a friendly voice, 'I've not played in a while so go easy!'

'I'm Jackie. And don't worry, I've not played since school,' said Jackie, feeling calmer at the friendliness of this woman.

'Gosh, that long?' said Liz, just as the whistle blew and she darted away to receive a pass from her team's centre. Their team had scored before Jackie had even worked out where Liz had gone.

The rest of the ten minutes went by in a blur of arms and bounces. The ball seemed to always be just out of reach or just over her head. Every time Jackie moved, she heard the whistle announcing she was on the wrong side of the wrong line. There were too many bloody lines, that was the problem. Perhaps a colour-coded floor would help?

Liz's team shuffled off the court and the other team came back on to play against Jackie. She felt weary. No, not weary: dead.

Libby was Jackie's new wing attack, and she was fast and light on her feet. Jackie felt increasingly frustrated at always being five paces behind her. The ball whizzed about the court and Jackie's team had largely worked out how to play without needing to bother her. Tears pushed dully at the back of her eyeballs, and she felt ludicrous. Just as she was about ready to give up, she saw the ball flying down the line towards Libby and stuck out a hand to interrupt it. It worked and the ball dribbled loosely onto the floor. Jackie reacted like a spring, darting forwards onto the ball and grabbing at it with both hands. She had just laid her hands on the rubbery surface when another pair of hands settled on it too. Jackie looked up to see Libby pulling at the ball. Later, Jackie would describe it to Ros as a red mist descending but actually, it was more like a very calm but physically angry pale-pink mist. As Libby pulled at the ball, Jackie yanked back. She was absolutely not going to lose this ball. Hadn't she lost enough? Husband, life, dignity? The ball was hers.

'Let go!' muttered Libby, pulling at the sphere.

'No. Fuck off,' Jackie muttered back, wrenching her arms and trying to curl her body over the ball to use her weight to wrest it away from Libby. Libby's eyes sprang wider at the expletive, but she didn't relinquish her grip. Jackie could vaguely hear Judith's whistle blowing but it didn't matter. This wasn't about the game any more. She needed to win this ball.

'It's our team's ball,' Libby panted in a staccato rhythm.

'I don't care.' Jackie didn't take her eyes off her grip. 'I want it.'

'Are you crazy?' Libby was still pulling.

'I genuinely don't know.'

The whistle was getting louder and more insistent.

'Let go!' Libby whined.

'No,' Jackie insisted.

'You mad old bitch.'

It was the word old that did it. It settled in Jackie's imagination, and she heard it in Steve's voice. Old. Old model. Traded in. Old wife. Old woman. Old. Jackie didn't let go of the ball. She pulled so hard and suddenly that Libby came flying towards her with the momentum. Jackie neatly sidestepped and Libby went flying, the skin of her cheek making an awful squeaking on the gym floor.

There was silence. Jackie stood, breathing hard and clutching the ball. Coming to her senses and looking at the astonished faces staring at her from all around.

'I'm going to go,' she muttered. Trying not to look at the spreadeagled Libby on the floor, she crossed the courts to the door and made her way to the changing rooms. She remembered her PIN on the second try and released her bag. It was only when she reached the car that she realised she was still holding the ball.

14

Something about noticing the ball in her hands broke the dam keeping the tears in Jackie's chest. She leaned her forehead against the cool wet metal of the car and cried. The feeling of a hand on her back made her jump out of her skin. She yelped and spun round, ready to defend her accidental theft of the ball. She was met not with an irate Judith though, but with a worried-looking Annie.

'Are you OK?'

'No.'

'OK.'

'Do they want their ball back?'

'Who cares. They can afford more. I'm pretty sure this whole sport initiative thing is just a tax break for the partners.'

Jackie wondered whether or not to pretend she didn't know Ros, but didn't have the mental energy to lie. 'Probably. Ros Mackie is my best friend. That's how I heard about the netball.'

'Oh! That's cool. I like Ros. She seems permanently angry at having accidentally started a firm.'

'Yes, I think she thought it would take care of itself a bit more. More Wild West and fewer HR meetings.' This made Annie laugh. 'Thank you for coming out to check on me. They must think I'm crazy.'

Annie delicately paused before responding and then fished around in her bag for a packet of cigarettes. 'Well, I'm not sure they'd beg for you to come back, but I wouldn't worry about it. They're an ambitious lot, the girls in there; it's a nice firm overall, but I think a lot of the people really looking for a career leg-up came tonight thinking Ros would be here and it might look good for future promotions.'

Jackie laughed out loud at that. 'Ros wouldn't play netball if her life depended on it!' The rainwater from where she was leaning on the car was beginning to soak through the bum of her jogging bottoms. 'Do you want to go to the pub?' she asked Annie shyly, feeling like she was asking her on a date. 'If . . . if you're not going back in, that is?'

Annie smiled. 'Oh! Yes, no, that would be really nice. I'll just put this out.' She stubbed out her barely started cigarette and moved round to the passenger side of the car.

'What should I do with this?' Jackie said, holding the ball out like a bomb.

'Take it.' Annie nodded. 'It can be your souvenir, and if you feel guilty just give it to Ros – she's technically the one paying for it.'

As they drove, a silence descended and Jackie wondered if she'd made a mistake inviting this perfect stranger to join her at the pub. She drove on autopilot to the Hawk, her brain trying desperately to think of things to say to Annie that weren't stupid or extremely obvious. The poor woman, Jackie thought, she must feel like she's been kidnapped.

The song on the radio changed and Annie reached out a hand to turn the volume up. 'Oh, I like this one!' she exclaimed and Jackie felt the panic subside. Good Lord, she was a nervous wreck. How had she gone from making a new friend to such worry in a few seconds? It was then she realised just how hungry she was.

They stepped into the Hawk and were immediately greeted by Ros's voice across the pub.

'Jackie! What are you wearing?! Plant pots?'

Jackie looked down to see if she was wearing a plant pot and as she'd expected, she was not. She looked up blankly at Ros, but Annie waved back at her and leaned in slightly to Jackie. 'That's what she calls me.'

'Why?' Jackie said, breathing out and heading over to Ros at their usual table.

'Oh, I have a lot of plants at my desk.'

'Right.'

Ros was standing up to greet them. 'I've been trying to call you, Jack, to see if you wanted to join me. Where have you been? How do you two know each other?'

'Hi Ros,' Annie greeted Ros, who smiled briskly in return and turned her attention back to Jackie. 'What can I get you to drink?'

This held Ros's attention and she picked up her nearly empty glass of wine from the table and smiled at Annie. 'Oh, another one of these please.'

Annie nodded and headed off to the bar and Jackie sat down in front of Ros to somehow explain what she had been up to that evening.

'What . . . what were you thinking?' Ros stared at her.

'I don't know. I don't know if I was thinking. I just . . . I don't know. It was Steve. He goaded me. He sort of laughed at the idea of me playing netball like it was this utterly ludicrous, ridiculous idea and I just wanted to prove him wrong. Oh God, it's even worse now that I know he wasn't wrong. Also, if anyone asks, I work in your back office. But say you've fired me.'

Ros stared at her, obviously not knowing quite where to start. 'Steve was wrong. You can play netball if you want to.'

Annie arrived back at the table and settled a new bottle down along with two new glasses. 'Was she good?' Ros asked Annie, switching quickly into analytical mode.

'Oh . . . no. No offence, Jackie,' Annie added quickly, ceasing eye contact immediately.

'Absolutely none taken. I was awful.'

'But you don't have to be good to play,' Annie said, attempting a glance up from the oak tabletop. 'You know, just, if you wanted to.'

Annie seemed like an extraordinarily shy woman and Jackie wondered, not for the first time, what drew her to a sport that seemed so violently spiteful.

Ros was nodding. 'You're right. I've always liked you Plant P— Annie?' She tested the name in her mouth, checking it was right. Annie nodded, a small upward turn at the corners of her mouth. 'Annie is right, Jackie, you just need to find the right team. You don't want to play with them. They're a bunch of haughty bitches.'

'Ros!' Jackie choked on her latest sip. 'You can't say that: they're *your* staff.'

Annie laughed raucously at that and then stopped herself, looking at Ros to check it wasn't a trap.

'But that's exactly how I know they're haughty bitches.' Ros maintained a wide-eyed, innocent look. 'That's exactly why we hire them. They're good lawyers – they're not good friends. Plant— Annie will back me up on this. Annie, exactly how many Mackie and Howard Christmas parties have you been to?'

'Oh none,' Annie confirmed. 'Horrible things.'

'Exactly. I hire people who are ambitious and business-minded and I have a good firm and I do not socialise with them because they don't make for good friends.'

'Well, you're a good friend, does that mean you're a terrible lawyer?' Jackie laughed and rubbed the back of Ros's hand fondly.

'No, it means I'm an old lawyer and I'm done with all that thinking I have to be an edgy ball-buster to get anywhere.'

'Don't say ball!' Jackie wailed, burying her head in her arms. 'I'm having flashbacks!'

Ros laughed and Jay, who had found a break in the constant loading and unloading of the glass-washer, arrived at the table just in time to catch the end of the sentence. 'Interesting night, was it?' she said, her teasing motivating a half-smile onto her face.

'Young Jackie here has been expanding her horizons,' Ros explained, making sure the wine glasses were full and even. 'Grab yourself a glass, come and join us and we'll tell you all, young Panda-one.'

'Paduan,' Jackie murmured on autopilot.

Jay laughed. 'Ah, you know I'd love to but if I'm not clearly visible behind the bar at all times the regulars start to get a bit twitchy that they might have to wait over fifteen seconds for a pint.' As Jay spoke, Lydia, of Mike and Lydia local fame, tottered over to the bar to get their next round in. Jay didn't even have to turn round; at the sound of the heels on flagstones she mouthed 'Gin and tonic and a pint of bitter when you get a minute, please Jay.' It was like watching a film where the sound and visuals were slightly out of synch. Jay's mouth was moving only fractionally out of time with those exact words coming out of Lydia's mouth. Ros and Jackie smiled and swallowed their laughter. Jay spun on her heels and headed back behind the bar.

'Poor girl,' muttered Ros. 'She's wasted here.'

'I'm wasted here,' Jackie burbled into more wine. Annie let out a very unattractive snort that made Jackie follow suit and Ros frown. A brainwave struck Jackie. 'Can you not get her a job at the firm?' she asked Ros.

'No,' Ros said, quickly. 'No, I don't mix business with friends. No offence, Annie.'

Annie raised both her hands quickly to show no offence. 'Oh none taken! I don't even mix my friendships with friends.'

This made Ros laugh and relent a little. 'All right, you're funny, Plant Pots, I'll put you on my "Maybe" list but I reserve the right to call you Plant Pots when I've had wine.'

'OK.'

Jackie knew the phrase 'heart goes out to' and in that moment, she felt like her heart physically pulled towards Annie. She knew it was all in her head, but she was conjuring a past full of bullying and being an outsider and she desperately wanted to squash her all up in a ball of love. And fix Jay too: get her a job and her flat back. Wine on an empty stomach was a bad idea.

'So, you're friends with the barmaid?' Annie asked, clearly unable to sit with the silence.

'Yes, that's Jay. I'm not sure on the details but the charity she was working for in London downsized and she was the last one in so the first one out and had to move back here and in with her mum. Grim. I think it was the recession or the, oh what was the funkier first recession called? The Credit Crunch. It might have been that one. Or was that too early? Did the second one have a nickname? It makes me glad to be retired and out of it all. I feel sorry for their generation.'

For reasons she wasn't quite certain about, Jackie found herself in tears. She looked about for a menu to try to flatten out some of this ridiculous emotional rollercoaster she'd accidentally boarded.

'Hey now, Jack, come on . . .' Ros cooed, 'she'll be all right . . . she's bound to have a grandparent somewhere in the dynasty that'll die and leave her a semi.'

'You all right, Jack?' Jay had reappeared with a notepad and a concerned face.

'I'm fine. Daft old bat. Can I order lots of chips please? With cheese. And a delicious sandwich.'

Annie doubled the order.

'These two are hungry,' Ros explained. 'They've been playing netball!'

'God, I haven't played netball since school. Awful game.' Jay slid onto the end of the booth's bench, keeping her eyes on the bar to check for customers. 'I was goal attack. Do you like netball, Jack?'

Jackie shook her head into the nose-blow she was currently performing. 'No, no, not at all.'

'So why . . .?' Jay looked from Ros to Jackie and back to Ros again as though expecting details of an elaborate prank to come pouring forth at any point.

'Because . . . because of Steve leaving,' Jackie said, feeling the rollercoaster lurch and push her away from tears and towards hysterical laughter.

'Right . . .' Jay looked confused. 'Did Steve . . . did Steve never let you play netball when you were together?' This made Jackie release a honk that a goose would write home about. Annie was looking between them, baffled.

'Oh God, no . . .' Jackie laughed, rubbing Jay's hand fondly. 'No, not at all. No, Steve never stopped me playing netball. I don't think he would even know what netball is. He just . . . he left me for someone else and I have been feeling . . . shabby and old. Very old and very shabby lately.' Jackie turned to Annie. 'Sorry, I'm what a therapist might call "going through some stuff" and you appear to have become collateral damage.' Jackie could feel the never-ending prickle of new tears starting behind her eyes, and the heavy leaden-ribcage sensation that meant more crying. 'I wanted to do something different. I wanted to go out and do something. Anything. He's gone and I'v . . . I've let everything go with him somehow. I didn't realise my entire life was about him, but I suppose it must have been because now he's gone I just don't know what to do with myself. It was stupid. I just . . . I just wanted to go somewhere and do something.'

'It's not stupid at all,' Ros chimed in, pulling her iPad out of her bag. 'I think it's amazing that you had the get-up-and-go to get and up and do that. If you want to play netball, you're going to play netball Jackie my girl.' She started furiously prodding at her iPad.

'Oh, no, I don't want to play netball . . . it really looked awful, I just—'

But Jackie was interrupted by Ros having found what she was looking for.

'Here we go! Local amateur netball league! This is what I've signed the work team up to, but anyone can form and enter a team – all you need is to fill in this.' Her eyes scanned the screen. 'Easy. Then pay a small subscription fee. Easy. Then have seven women ready to play in a couple of weeks! Easy: we already have four.'

Jay gripped the edge of the seat and began to scoot herself off back towards the bar. 'Oh no absolutely not. I am never playing netball again EVER. I'll have flashbacks to Laurel Taylor from school. What a bitch. I don't think I could even hold a ball without hearing her snooty name.'

Ros's hand caught the back of Jay's shirt and held on tight.

'Sorry love, you were here when the team was born so you don't have a choice: you're in.'

'Don't listen to her: you do what you like. I need a wee.' Jackie scooted past Jay on the bench seat, feeling every single muscle in her legs complain at the motion. She'd barely even run; how could she be feeling this stiff this quickly?

Reaching the bathrooms, she stared at herself in the mirror, seeing every wrinkle and every version of herself that had been and gone. An overwhelming sensation started behind her breasts and came up like a tsunami towards the back of her throat and her eyes. She squashed it down and concentrated on her own face, feeling the effects of the wine and the running on the stability of her legs. It was hard looking at her own face: it didn't look like her, it looked like an old version of her. The her she associated with was the her in pictures holding the baby boys; getting married; going on those fancy, exploratory holidays as a couple and a family. That was her. That had been the main part of her life. The main part of her. Now . . . now she was this.

By the time she had washed her hands and got back to the table Ros was putting the finishing finger-stabs to the form on her iPad.

'We just need a team name!' Ros declared triumphantly, beaming at Jackie. Jackie felt like an old flannel someone had found at the bottom of a bucket.

'Oh, Ros, you're not serious . . . we're not going to play netball.'

'Why not?' Ros looked at her, that same unblinking best-friend stare that had haunted Jackie through a lifetime. Through the main parts of her lifetime and into this . . . this limbo. This— Jackie shook her shoulders and snuggled into the Sauvignon Blanc for courage. No. She needed to snap out of this train of thought or things were going to be very rough. Why shouldn't she try to make this the main part of her life too? Sure, she'd raised the kids and finished working but that just meant she had more time to do fun things, didn't it? Sure, she had absolutely no idea what she actually thought was fun to do, but never mind. She'd find something. And here was Ros, tapping an iPad far too roughly on the table and suggesting netball, so, why not netball?

Jackie pushed away the obvious thought *not netball because netball is awful* and smiled up at Annie and Ros. 'Annie? You in?'

Annie beamed. 'If you'll have me?'

Jackie looked at Ros. 'What do you think?'

'OK.' Ros put on a fake stern face. 'But don't think this helps your promotional chances.'

Jackie laughed a bit more convincingly than Annie, but she was pretty sure that Annie was relaxing. Jackie looked at Ros. How many people got lucky enough to have a friend like this in their lives? Not enough. That was for sure.

'OK. Let's go,' she said, and felt herself strapping into the Ros's Hare-brained Scheme Express.

'Jay!' Ros called to Jay, back behind the bar. 'We're making a team and you're in!'

Jay laughed and shrugged a helpless what-you-going-to-do?

'So, we need a team name. We want it to be something celebratory but not too cringey,' Ros said.

'Divorcettes?' Jackie offered without much enthusiasm.

'No, too sad. And also, some of us had the good sense to never get married in the first place,' Ros said quickly, and then eyed Jackie to see if that was perhaps a little too far. Jackie was nose-deep in her wine so Ros carried on. 'Maybe something celebratory about you? Like, Better than Bimbo, or You May Take My Man But You'll Never Take My Netball. OK, so maybe the last one is a bit long, but you get my gist?'

Annie was looking between them, trying to keep up to speed with the tone and details without intruding.

'Yes!' Jay said excitedly, popping back over to the table with a bottle of celebratory prosecco. 'I like that idea . . . An Affair to Forget!' The enthusiasm from the two of them was glorious and warm and Jackie felt her abs contracting into sustained laughter. She'd be OK. 'What's something you won't miss?' Jay asked, hiccupping with excitement and fizz. 'Like, what's an upside to Steve being gone?'

Jackie thought. She'd been expecting to enjoy having more of the bed to sleep on but actually that just felt lonely. She had thought the expectation of not having to cook for someone would be nice, but it turned out cooking for one was miserable and often meant having to eat the same thing three days in a row to get through ingredients before they went off. A hint of an idea crept into her mind and before she'd even fully skim-read it, it was developing into a full smile on her face.

'Have you got something?' Ros's sharp eyes picked up on Jackie's grin. 'Come on.'

'The Hidden Skidmarks!' Jackie exclaimed, barely able to get the words out without laughing to herself.

'The what now?' Annie looked baffled.

'Whenever he had a clinker in his boxers, he would ball up the pair and hide them in a sock in the laundry basket so I wouldn't see them.' Jackie's laughter was bordering on hysteria.

'The dirty fecker!'

'He never just washed them himself, oh noooo, that was my job, but he was just about embarrassed enough to try and get them out of my direct sight. I'll never have to wash another pair of his shitty pants ever again!'

Ros had picked up her iPad and was typing away, smearing white wine across the screen as she went. 'The Hidden Skidmarks it is!'

15

Jackie awoke the next morning with an almost caricature hangover. The pillow was claustrophobically close to her head, looming against her face, and her cheeks burned at the touch. Sweat popped out of every pore on her forehead and throat and she groaned away from the warm cotton, searching desperately for a cool piece of pillowcase. Her mouth was alive with crawling, desiccated bugs and her stomach swashed about on a high tide of leftover wine. This was unbelievably awful. She lay on her back and tried to remember the last time she had woken up this hung-over pre-Steve's exodus. It seemed to be happening far too frequently now there was no face at home to curb her excesses with Ros. She remembered being hungover on holiday with Steve. But that had been a young hangover; they'd moaned and laughed about how bad they were feeling. They'd had sex. To think that had felt like a hang-over!

She pushed fond memories away, chastising her mind for pressing at them like tender bruises. She tried to concentrate on being comfortable right now. Her thoughts were continually interrupted by blank seconds of time where her body interrupted all higher processes to try desperately to alert her to one of the things she needed to stay alive.

Lying on her back was not working – the wine was trying to burrow back down through her spine to escape her screeching liver. She rolled over gently onto her side, hoping that the movement wouldn't be so intense that the world fell off its hinges. Just as she moved, someone started beating a large mallet against the inside of her skull. It was difficult to say how someone had got into her skull, or how they'd got small enough for that to be possible, but it remained true that someone seemed to be inside her head and beating their way out. She begged them silently to go back to sleep, but they were intent on it being morning.

Jackie righted herself and baulked at the feeling of two bottles of wine looking for purchase on her stomach lining. She swallowed hard and pushed down through the soles of her feet to force herself upright.

'Water,' she said out loud, and was amazed at the gravelly timbre of her voice. Impressive. Had they been shouting last night? Or, worse, singing? Oh God. As long as they'd done it near the pub and not on her street.

She manoeuvred slowly to the bathroom, not daring to look at how dehydrated a yellow she was producing. Water would fix it all.

She made her way down the stairs and was annoyed to hear the inner drummer starting up again as she reached the bottom. This time, though, the banging was a bit less internal and with a start she realised it was coming from the front door. Oh God, what a time for a burglar to be trying to get in. It was definitely a good idea to get a big muscly lodger. Perhaps a local bouncer who needed someone to cook for him. She was in no fit state to deal with an intruder now. But why would a burglar be knocking? And also, when was she in a fit state to deal with one? Perhaps she should take up a self-defence class? Would there be time with the netball? Oh God . . . netball.

As the memory of the netball team hit her full force she opened the door, to see a perky-looking Ros staring at her from the doorstep.

'Oh Ros, you have to stop doing this.'

'Are you all right?' Ros looked alarmed at the sight of Jackie. She should be alarmed, Jackie thought; I look awful.

'No. Not by any measure.' Jackie let the door swing open and turned to go into the kitchen and start fixing the many problems she had heaped on herself the night before. The kitchen felt impossibly complicated, with too many hard surfaces that were making sound bounce cruelly at her delicate head. She focused on the kettle and attempted to fill it with water to begin making tea. Ros eyed her speculatively and then pushed her bodily out of the way.

'I'll do it,' she said briskly, 'it's painful to watch you. Sit over there and check the posters.'

'Does me having a hangover summon you here ludicrously early, or does your presence on my doorstep give me a hangover? Posters?' Jackie slumped onto a bar stool and eyed the stack of papers Ros had dumped on the counter.

'Yes, to drum up interest in the netball team.' Ros looked at Jackie as though she were an alien in the body of the world's stupidest woman. 'I told you I'd get them printed when we said goodbye last night?'

Jackie blinked dry eyelids over drier eyeballs and tried to make sense of what she was looking at. 'But that was only eight hours ago? How have you already done this? It's . . .' She checked her watch to confirm she wasn't going mad, '. . . twenty past six? A.m.? In the morning?'

'So? I slept for five hours, printed these and then came here on my way to work. I don't need much sleep – very fortunate like that. Are there any typos?'

'Ros, I can't even tell if there are words on this sheet, let alone typos. I'll have to trust you already know there aren't since you've gone to the trouble of printing out this many.' She let the pages riffle through her thumb and fingers.

'Good girl. There are no typos. I'll leave those with you and you can get them up around the town on noticeboards and stuff. Call that Claire woman from the rugby too; she was great. I bet she'd be up for playing netball with us. I'll book the village hall as soon as they're open later – I've left a couple of messages and an email, but I'd like to speak to an actual person as soon as possible to make sure we can have it the times I've put on the poster.'

Jackie made a mental note to wish good fortune on the poor person who was left to deal with Ros's impatience. 'Wouldn't it have been safer to wait to print the posters until we know we can definitely get the hall?'

Ros gave her the stupid alien stare again. 'Well, I can't do that because I've already told the journalist that the try-out is at eleven?'

Jackie stared. 'Journalist . . .?'

'From the *Gazette*? Honestly, did you have a lobotomy when you got in last night?'

'Feels like it. Talk me through the journalist part of this debacle one more time . . .'

'Well, Pot Pl—' Ros pulled up at a raised eyebrow from Jackie. 'Sorry, Annie, was telling us all about how she hadn't had a great time playing netball with her other team because they were Blue Meanies, and then Jay cried because she missed how easy it was to make friends at uni and then you cried because . . . well, because that's what you do now, and then I had the brilliant idea to contact the *Gazette* and tell them all about our team and what a boost it was going to be for women in the community. Sarah-Beth from the *Gazette* loves it and there's even talk about a weekly column tracking our progress. It all ties in very nicely with the Save the Playing Courts thing that's going on.'

'It's been a maximum of eight hours,' Jackie repeated flatly.

'Three, if you don't count sleep. So, the world is watching, Jackie Douglas! We're going to be famous!'

Jackie tried to de-fuzz all the information she'd been given. 'So . . . we're a team, and we're in the paper, and . . . and what are the playing courts being saved from?'

'From being turned into a play park or something. You know, there's all those sheets up around trying to get people to care?'

'Wouldn't it be better if they were a play park? For the kids?'

'Oh probably. But, for a starter for tent, not everything has to be about children, and secondary, it gives mums something to do, doesn't it?'

'Mums have loads to do.'

'No, but I meant something interesting.' Ros settled a steaming mug in front of Jackie and lifted her chin with a cool hand. 'Now, I don't want an argument about this but underneath all those posters are some pamphlets. Close your mouth – I said I don't want an argument, I just wanted to drop round some bits and bobs so you could start reading up on the divorce proceedings, that's all. I said close your mouth; you can swear at me when I'm gone. As in, to work – not dead. I want you weeping when I'm dead. So, I'm going to work. Your jobs: drink this, eat something, wash, eat again because I assume you'll have thrown up whatever you ate, sip water and get these posters up in every place you can find. OK? Oh, I didn't put dress in that list. Please don't do any of the outdoor things in your pyjamas or the nuddy, OK? Or maybe do? We could have a special interest netball team.'

Jackie laughed and set all the wine inside her sloshing again. 'No thank you. The thought of playing netball is terrifying enough as it is – let alone doing it with tits and bits flying around all over the place.'

'Tits and Bits! That could have been a good team name. Maybe that'll be what the column is called!' Ros was collecting her handbag and heading back to the door while Jackie begged her synapses not to remind her of their own team name. She couldn't put a finger on what they'd settled on and she had a horrible feeling it was better that way.

16

After a shower, a teeth-cleaning and a good stare at a blank wall, Jackie finally found herself outside the house and heading down the road clutching the stack of flyers under her arm. She realised she didn't have much of an idea where to go and felt like a bit of a wally. The supermarket. That would be a decent start – did they still have that little board there advertising for odd-job people and babysitters and stuff? Maybe.

She felt a bit annoyed at Ros for sneaking the divorce leaflets into her house. Parallel to that was her annoyance at herself for feeling disloyal to Steve for having divorce papers in their house. She'd run her eyes over the preliminary information, but it was just a sea of impersonal words like 'client' and 'petition'. She and her lurching stomach had realised simultaneously that they knew very little about the process of divorce and that they preferred it that way. She'd had no idea there were only five acceptable reasons to ask for a divorce. Five? She could think of fifty without even trying very hard. One of the five was 'Desertion', a word that immediately made her think of a solider from the Crusades giving up on the good fight to go home. Had Steve 'deserted' her? Yes. But he'd also done the adultery one, which had led to the desertion, both of which combined to make Unreasonable Behaviour. Which one did she want to stand and tell a judge her husband had done to her? Would there even be a judge, or was she just thinking of *The Good Wife*?

Jackie shook her dry head and pushed thoughts of divorce away. She went back to feeling annoyed at Ros for putting it into her life, and for making her plod around the town putting up netball posters, and for giving her a hangover, and for introducing the concept of netball to her life in the first place. There was a lot to be annoyed at Ros about, it turned out.

Three supermarkets, a primary school and several parish noticeboards later Jackie was indulging in a full-fat hot chocolate in a coffee shop and wondering how on earth she was going to go about playing netball if her feet hurt this much just from walking around pinning up flyers.

She looked over at the parents spilling out of the school across the road with pushchairs and impatient children. It filled her with an odd sense of melancholy looking at them all in the middle of their lives. You're only in your fifties, she reminded herself sternly, trying desperately to shake off this insubstantiality that kept taking over.

The bell over the door dinged and Jackie looked up to see Steve entering. Her stomach lurched and she felt the wine go flying with the muscle pulse. This was not the time she wanted to see him. Should she lie and say she was meeting someone? Pretend she was on a date? Then maybe they could both ask for the 'Unreasonable Behaviour' thing and she wouldn't seem like such a sad sack?

Steve's eyes scanned the room. He looked different: his hair was shorter, a much younger cut. A fade? That was a phrase she'd heard. A tighter T-shirt than she was used to seeing him in too. He looked good. She felt a painful longing to bury her head on his shoulder as she had done a million times before. To have him rub the side of her head and tell her everything would be OK and then ruin the moment by moving her off before his leg went to sleep. Her eyes stung with tears. She groaned inwardly. Crying was bad for two reasons:

1. She didn't want Steve to see her sitting crying alone in here.
2. She was far too dehydrated to be losing any more bodily fluids.

Steve ordered his drink to take away and stood looking around the room as he waited. Jackie held her breath, waiting for the moment he would notice her and they would be forced to fake-smile and nod and have a terrible conversation. His eyes looked at her and then away. Then the barista called his name, he took his drink and went back to the familiar car she could see double-parked on the kerb outside.

She felt weightless; panic-stricken. He hadn't noticed her. Hadn't recognised her at all. The man she had had two children with, spent a lifetime's events beside. He could scan over her face in a coffee shop and not pick her out of a crowd after only a matter of weeks that were barely plural months apart. Her throat was dry and something sharp seemed lodged just where she wanted to swallow. Her hands felt too heavy to move and she couldn't remember which muscles she was supposed to use to get them to do anything anyway.

'Is anyone sitting here?' Jackie looked up to see a man looking at her and indicating the chair opposite. She tried to say no but her mouth was so dry her tongue wouldn't move as cleanly as she needed it to in order to make sound. 'Are you all right?' He leaned in towards her, clearly concerned. Jackie tried to move her tongue again, but it did seem very much to be glued to the roof of her mouth: the thought crossed her mind that she should phone science and ask them to study this because she must be quite the unique phenomenon right now. She blinked at the man, trying to communicate to him that she was simultaneously both a) fine and b) far too weird to sit opposite. 'I'll get you some water,' said the man, and turned back to the counter. Jackie felt a backdraught of heat rush up her cheeks. This was dangerous. She was already so dry: she might burst into flames.

He returned and settled a glass of water in front of her and then sat down without asking again. Jackie took a sip and felt the cool liquid flowing all round her hot, dry tongue and separating it from the pulsing heat of her mouth. 'Thank you,' she muttered, feeling hugely embarrassed.

'Not a worry.' His voice was gentle and deep. He looked about her age, maybe a few years older? She'd be playing his mum in a film though, Jackie thought bitterly, wishing she was wearing her good bra. Why did she only have one good bra?

'Not feeling well?' He raised an eyebrow at her and she smiled.

'Not the best morning,' she admitted. 'But I'm fine.'

'Sorry to hear that,' he said. 'Do you mind if I just sit here quietly? I can't quite bring myself to go any closer to the brood in the corner. If I ruin one more outfit with yoghurt splatters, I'll never come here again.'

Jackie laughed and felt the prickling sensation in her skin beginning to settle as she calmed. 'No problem at all.' She eyed the mums rearranging the tables to make a baby corner with full barricade of prams and toys.

'What do you do?' The man's voice broke into her thoughts again and she looked up, surprised at how easily her thoughts were wandering. How rude of her.

'Nothing!' She almost laughed like a madwoman and then caught herself just in time. 'I mean, I'm retired. You?'

'Same.' He nodded and smiled an easy smile. Jackie wondered if she thought he was handsome and couldn't answer that question. He might be, but it had been a long time since she'd wondered that about anyone other than the unattainable television creatures thirty years her junior.

'Hence the tracksuit?' she asked, then immediately regretted it in case it had come across as judgey rather than lighthearted like she'd meant it.

'Ha! I coach after-school rugby at the primary school round the back of my house. I'm heading there in a bit.' He looked embarrassed. 'I'm newly retired, you see. I feel like I need to be out doing something. Can't quite bring myself to admit it's just gardening from now on.'

Jackie found herself nodding along. 'I know exactly what you mean; when I retired it took me two years to give my scrubs away.'

'A doctor?' He took a sip of his coffee.

'Nurse.' Jackie flushed and braced herself for the usual slight dismissal people greeted nursing with.

'Even better,' he said, surprising her. 'My son is a nurse; I don't know how he does it. I've never seen a human being more exhausted than him at the end of a shift.'

'Yes, it's a lot. I have sons too. Two. Any grandchildren?' This was nice, Jackie realised. How long had it been since she merrily told someone new about her life? Someone who wasn't behind a till in Sainsbury's?

'No, no, not yet. Maybe not ever actually.' The man, and Jackie realised at this point she didn't know his name or whether it would now be considered too late to ask, had a lovely lightness to his conversation. He sounded honest but not too grave. 'I have just the one son and he . . . he is a late bloomer. He was a bit of a wild child, and it took him a while to find himself. He lives with me actually. We're digging him out of a bit of a financial hole.'

To Jackie's astonishment she found herself reading into his use of 'me'. 'He lives with me.' Not 'us'. So, he might be single? But then 'we're' digging him out of a hole? What did that mean? She felt her entire world shift on its axis at the realisation she was even considering this concept about a man.

'Blimey,' she stuttered. 'Well, you and he have done well to get him back on the go. It's not easy getting into nursing. He must be dedicated.'

'He's a good lad.' The conversation naturally fell into silence and Jackie felt an uncomfortableness creep into her side of the quiet. She shuffled the remaining netball flyers on the table.

'Well, I'd better get going. I've got to put all these flyers up round town or my best friend will kill me. It was nice to meet you.' She smiled and stood up.

'Pleasure to meet you too, I'm Duncan.'

'Jackie.'

'Nurse Jackie!' He grinned, and she smiled back. People often said that; as far as she knew it was a TV thing that she'd never got round to watching. She shook his proffered hand and enjoyed how soft the skin was. God, this was all so weird. 'Nice to meet you, Duncan.'

'Would you like me to put one of those up at the school?' he blurted suddenly, and indicated the flyers in Jackie's hand. 'They have a noticeboard, you see. Only if it's helpful.'

She looked down at them, suddenly embarrassed that they might be terrible flyers in some way she didn't know about *and* that he would he know she intended to play netball. But who cared if a stranger knew she was going to play netball?

She hesitated and then relaxed: oh, what harm could it do? She slid a few flyers out of the pile and handed them to him. 'What school is it?' she asked. 'I'm not stalking you; I just mean so that I don't end up trekking over there only to find you've beaten me to it.'

Duncan smiled and laughed. 'I understood. It's Willow Grove. We're not good at flirting, are we?' He took the flyers and neatened them on the table in front of him. Jackie lost all feeling in her legs at the mention of the word flirting. Her first instinct was to flatly deny she had been flirting, but then a creeping sense of mischief took over and she changed her mind.

'No, we're not, are we? Perhaps we need more practice?' She smiled and picked up her bag, gave him another smile and then left the coffee shop. She felt like the bravest woman on the planet.

Duncan sat at the table smiling to himself, running his thumb over the bottom of the flyer and the printed telephone number for one Jackie Douglas.

17

'So, Scottish heritage?' Ros was lying on her back on the stage in the village hall throwing Maltesers up in the air and catching them in her mouth. Jackie was privately very worried she was going to choke, but decided not to say anything for fear of getting an eye-roll from a perpetually teenage Ros. 'And coaches rugby . . . did you mention that you're a fan?'

'I wouldn't say going to one match in fifty-eight years counts as being a fan.'

'Well, it's a start.' Ros was so delighted at the idea of Jackie meeting Duncan, she could barely contain herself.

'I doubt I shall ever see him again. He was just a nice man who picked me up a bit after I saw Steve. That's all. I don't even know his surname.'

'No, but you know where he'll be on at least one afternoon a week . . .' Ros was relentless.

'Ros.' Jackie sat up and looked at her sternly. 'I am not going to go and hang out outside a primary school like a pervert in the hope of catching a glimpse of the boy I fancy.'

'Ha! So you did fancy him!' Ros jerked up and the inevitable happened as a stray Malteser caught itself on her tonsils. Jackie patted her on the back and got up to stretch her legs.

They had been sitting in the freezing village hall for half an hour waiting for people to turn up and try out for the Hidden Skidmarks. So far . . . it was not looking good. No one had turned up. At all. No one. Jackie was trying not to feel despondent and, to be honest, the Maltesers were helping. So was filling Ros in on the squiggly feelings that meeting Duncan had awoken in her. She felt like a schoolgirl: netball and boys? Weird.

'He could be Scottish. Didn't have the accent though, so it could just be middle-class parents. Leon was telling me there's a little boy in Freya's class called Horatio. I mean . . . Horatio?' Jackie lay back down again to stare up into the dusty rafters and shovel in some more Maltesers.

'Maybe his parents were pirates?' Ros said, and it was Jackie's turn to choke on a Malteser. She sat up, feeling guilty for eating lying down. Bad Grandma. 'Well, half an hour until our journalist friend turns up.' She reached in her bag and brought out a Thermos. 'Wine?'

Jackie groaned. 'Oh God, I'd forgotten about that. This is going to be so embarrassing. She'll be all like, *How was your try-out?* And we'll be like, *It was great! No one came!* And then she'll print a piece about what a sad old bat I am and Steve will read it to Michelle and they'll have a good laugh at us.'

'Stop catastrophising,' Ros snapped. 'It's not the end of the whirl if we don't get a good turnout today; it was very short notice. We will just find another way to collect people. The woman from the netball thing was thrilled we're starting a team. Apparently the more teams they have, the more they can show lots of use on the courts and stop them being bundled into spongey soft play for the new houses. She was practically squeaking when I told her about the *Gazette*. I think we're going to be quite the celebrities in the league.'

Ros's enthusiasm washed over Jackie, filling in the cracks that should have been filled with intense worry. 'You're right, I'm being far too serious about the whole thing. So, when no one shows up how else are we going to—'

She was interrupted by the opening of the door to the village hall. Jay came in looking flustered. 'Sorry I'm late!' she called, and then looked around at the empty space. 'Where is everyone?'

Jackie looked around too. 'Oh blimey, they must have scarpered.' This made Ros cackle. 'No one came, Jay, it's been a bit of a let-down.'

Jay put her hands on her hips and scowled at Jackie and Ros. 'So, you two are just lying about eating chocolate?'

Ros and Jackie looked at each other and shrugged. 'Yes. We were just about to open the wine,' Ros said.

'Come on, up you get, let's do some passing practice.' Jay grabbed a ball and jogged into the centre of the room.

Ros looked appalled. 'Why?' she said, sounding genuinely baffled. 'We're already on the team – we don't need to try out.'

'No, but we do need to be good.' Jay threw the ball at Ros, who squealed and dived back down onto the floor.

'That was rude!' she squeaked, looking appalled at Jay.

'Why do we need to be good?' Jackie was struggling to keep up. 'If there's no team we don't have to go through with it.'

'We'll get a team,' Jay said determinedly, fishing the ball out from behind the heavy velvet curtain at the back of the stage. As she pulled the curtain back Jackie caught a glimpse of the castle set and memories flooded in of all the school plays she had sat through Michael and Leon performing in. Tears caught her by surprise at the memory of Steve on that stage as a panto dame. Surely that was the weirdest thing that could make her cry? Luckily, she was distracted from memory lane by Jay continuing her angry pep talk. 'We're doing this. I'm a twenty-eight-year-old bartender who lives with her mother. If I don't have playing netball with two lushes who drink in my pub then I have precisely nothing. I need this.'

Jay came to the end of her outburst and Jackie stood, shellshocked, looking at her. 'Well, OK then. Let's do this.' For some reason, things are easier to do when they are for someone else. She stood up and put her hands out in front ready to catch the ball, immediately feeling like a proper lemon. Ros joined them on the floor, and they began to throw the ball between them.

The vast majority of the balls went flying off past them and into dusty corners full of long-forgotten Brownie craft detritus. Only Jay seemed able to predict whereabouts the ball was going to come and put her hands in the right place.

'How the hell are you doing that?' Ros exclaimed finally.

'I'm keeping my eyes open.' Jay laughed, and Jackie laughed too, feeling loose and relaxed for the first time in weeks.

She checked her watch: 11.40 a.m. 'Shall we call it a day?'

'Yes, absolutely.' Ros was practically already in the pub. 'Let's go away from this dark horrible place and listen to more stories about Jackie's new boyfriend.'

'Jackie's what?' Jay moved her head in the sort of speedy move that would leave Jackie aching for a week if she tried it.

Jackie was spared having to explain by the door flying open again. This time two small children came racing in, followed by the back of a woman who appeared to be dragging an enormous pram. Ros looked disgustedly at the children but was prevented from speaking by the woman calling over her shoulder as she jiggled the pram to try to get it through the too-small frame. 'Horatio! Delilah! Shoes off! Sit down quietly on the mat! I'm so sorry everyone – things just got a bit hectic this morning . . . oh for goodness sake, what is this pram stuck on? Jesus—' She yanked it hard and came springing in through the door. She wheeled it around to face the hall. 'Oh.' She stopped dead, looking at Jackie and Ros. 'You're not playgroup?'

'We're not,' Ros responded bluntly. 'We're really not.'

'We're netball.' Jackie smiled, remembering those frazzled days of preschoolers all too well.

'Oh crikey, I'm so sorry to interrupt. Horatio, Delilah – shoes back on. Come on.' She began to reverse the pram back out of the door and then looked up again, confused. 'How did you get the hall?'

Jackie's face creased in confusion. 'We just booked it?'

'But playgroup is always here at eleven thirty on weekdays . . . they didn't mention it was cancelled?'

'It's Saturday,' Jay and Jackie said in unison and the woman's face dropped in horror.

'Oh my God! Is it? No wonder Luke didn't want to go to school! Horatio, Delilah, GET YOUR SHOES ON NOW, we have to go and get Luke. Oh my God.'

The family whirlwind left through the door and left the three wannabe netballers standing in silence looking at one another.

'Horatio!' Jackie half-whispered to Ros, eyebrows in her hair-line.

'What a mess,' said Ros.

And the door came flying back open.

'Hang on, sorry, did you say you were netball?' The woman pushed her overgrown blond fringe out of her eyes and looked at them despairingly.

'Yes,' Jackie said, and smiled kindly. 'At least, we're trying to be.'

'Can anyone join? Children?'

'No children,' Ros said sharply, looking suspiciously at the mischievous faces of Horatio and Delilah as they peered round their mother.

'Yes, any adults can play,' Jackie said gently, trying to calm Ros's deep fear of children.

'Oh, can I sign up? I haven't played since school but I'd love to do . . . well, anything that's not this.' She indicated the pram and the children, who were now pulling each other's hair.

Jackie grinned. 'Of course. I'm Jackie.'

'Kath,' said Kath, 'Here's my number. Now, I've got to go and find my son . . .'

She was back out of the hall before any of them had really processed what had happened. Jackie shook her head, smiling at the memories of raising small children. She looked up at Ros, expecting to see a curled lip and vague disgust at someone living such a chaotic life, but Ros was beaming.

'Five people!' she exclaimed happily and threw the ball in the vague direction of Jay. 'Now see how impressed that journalist is going to be with us.'

Jackie groaned again. Some sort of internal self-preservation mechanism in her was managing to wipe all memory of the journalist every time she stopped being mentioned. 'What time is she coming?'

'Any minute,' Ros said. 'Let's pick the ball up again and start doing the throws so she'll be more impressed when she comes in.'

'She might actually be more impressed with our ability if we're not doing it, to be honest,' Jackie muttered, but joined in gallantly.

They continued passing the ball between them and a few minutes later Jackie heard the door open again behind her. She was just passing to Jay as she heard it; the ball left her hands, but Jay was staring at the door behind Jackie and didn't react at all to the ball coming towards her. It hit her square in the side of the head, knocking her straight to the floor. Jackie swivelled to see what she had been staring at. It was a neat-looking blond woman coming in the door. Jackie swivelled back round and dashed over to help a dazed-looking Jay back up to her feet.

'Are you all right?' she asked.

'Uh, yeah, what's she doing here?' Jay glared at the woman in the doorway.

'I don't know . . . who is she?' The woman didn't look familiar and wasn't dressed as if she was here to get sweatily into netball.

'I'm Laurel Taylor,' said the official-looking woman, 'I'm here from the *Gazette*.'

Jay stopped trying to get up and went limp. 'You are kidding me.'

'Who is she?' Jackie hissed, taking advantage of the seconds they had while Ros crossed the room towards Laurel to check Jay was OK.

'I went to school with her,' was all Jay could manage.

Ros escorted Laurel over to where Jackie had managed to get Jay to her feet and brush her down a little bit. Ros's mouth opened to make introductions, but Laurel was faster: her neat, drawn-on eyebrows shot up to her perfect fringe.

'Planet Janet!'

18

'We can just tell her we've changed our minds about the column,' Jackie insisted, desperate to get a smile back on Jay's face. They were seated around their usual table in the Hawk and Jay looked as downcast as a person could look.

'No, then how's that going to look? She'll know it's because I asked for it.' Jay groaned.

'So what?' said Jackie. 'It's not like you have to see her again if we don't work with her.'

'I bet I would. I bet I'd start bumping into her everywhere I went. I bet she still hangs around with all the old crowd. She'll be in a WhatsApp group with them now, telling them that Planet Janet is back and a dropout. Oh God. Of all the people in the world, why her? Why Laurel fucking Taylor? As if I wasn't feeling shitty enough at being back here, with barely a job, living with Mum, now the one thing I've found to cheer myself up has Laurel Taylor attached to it.' Jay looked like she was going to cry.

'Oh Jay . . . oh we're so sorry.' Jackie used the plural to try to get Ros to look sympathetic instead of confused.

'So . . .' Ros began, 'your name is Janet?'

She sounded so perplexed that she actually managed to make Jay smile.

'Yes. Jay is short for Janet. And planet rhymes with Janet and I also happened to be large as a teenager. Alchemy for the blond, stick-thin bitch who bullies you.'

That seemed to settle Ros's mind and she was able to focus again on the problem at hand. 'OK, well, as I see it we have two options. One: we tell Laurel Fucking Taylor that we aren't interested in working with the *Gazette* for moral reasons. Two: we move forward with working with her and we go on to be the best damn team anyone has ever seen so she is incredibly jealous of everything to do with your life. Which do you want to do?'

Jay squinted at Ros. 'So you're saying there's no beat her to death and dispose of the body option?'

'Jay!' Jackie exclaimed, and then felt prudish.

'I'm joking . . . obviously.'

Ros laughed. 'I only offer that service in really exceptional circumstances. Let me get to know her a short minute and if she's as bad as you say she is then she'll be shagging the fishes before you can say Open *Sesame Street*.'

Jackie could see Jay trying to work out what Ros meant and decided to take over. 'Look, Jay, this netball team is meant to be fun, and if her presence will ruin it then we just tell her to bug off. And that's fine.'

Ros eyed Jackie. 'But if we don't have a team, that's one fewer team, and then it's all the more likely that the courts get closed down and there'll be a lot of disappointed people.'

Jackie eyed Ros right back. 'Don't you try and guilt-trip me there, Ros Mackie. We only just found out the courts were even in danger of being built on – no, I only just even remembered the courts existed last week, so don't start trying to make it so that I'll feel bad if I'm not instrumental in saving them.'

'But you would feel bad . . .' Ros persisted with a sly smile, pushing all the right buttons to tangle Jackie up.

'No.' Jackie stuck her chin in the air to try to hide how effective Ros's tactic was. 'No, I don't care. It's supposed to be fun and if it isn't fun for all of us we're not doing it, so, you just say the word if you want out, Jay.'

Jay was looking a bit chirpier after watching the sparky exchange between Jackie and Ros. 'No, do you know what, I'd like to show her how great I am these days. She was giving it the simpering smirk earlier in the hall, acting like she's still Little

Miss Popular, well, you know what: she's the one who has never left here, she doesn't have a degree or my life experience. I'll show her. I'm not sad lonely little Planet any more. I'm me.'

'That's the spirit! You show her! I'll show Steve too! Ros, who are you showing?' Jackie raised a glass, smiling.

'The whole world,' Ros said mock seriously, 'I always am.' They toasted and sipped their drinks. As Jackie sat there basking in the camaraderie, a thought occurred to her and she spat it out before she could think it through further and change her mind.

'Jay, if it's feeling a bit weird being back at your mum's . . . I'd happily have you stay a few nights with me. You know. If you need a different four walls. I've been thinking of getting a lodger.' She decided to edit out the part where her lodger was a burglar deterrent.

Ros spluttered on her drink and Jay looked wide-eyed at Jackie. 'What?'

'It wouldn't have to be a big deal. It's just, you've mentioned a few times you're not that happy at home with your mum and her boyfriend, and I've been feeling a bit rattly in the house all by myself. I have two spare rooms . . . you could stay any time you wanted. Only if you wanted. No pressure. But . . .' Jackie suddenly felt very exposed and like a mad old bat. Why on earth would Jay want to stay with her? 'Well, the offer's there.'

Jay was beaming. 'Oh Jackie! That's such a lovely offer. Do you know what – a break from home would be quite nice. We could have, like, a sleepover?'

'Oh! Yes, yes! That would be lots of fun. But no pressure. But if you think it would be nice. You know, up to you.'

'Yeah, OK.' There was a slight pause while they both navigated the awkwardness of having put themselves out there.

'Right, well,' Ros had an oddly businesslike expression on her face, 'if we're going to be such a good netball team that we make Laurel Taylor spit feathers then we're going to need to know the rules.'

'We're also still a player short . . . and that's even if Claire says yes,' Jackie tried to point out.

'For sure.' Ros waved the complaint away and began digging around for her iPad. 'Someone will turn up . . . and also, would you please ring Claire? What are you waiting for? Now, Jay, fetch another bottle while I fire up the modem and dust off the handbook . . .'

Jay did as she was told, and they settled in to try to get the fundamentals of netball firmly under their belts.

Sixty minutes later it was not going particularly smoothly.

'So, centre does all the running around but can't go in the interesting bits?' Ros looked distinctly unimpressed with the concept. By now they had a sketched-out drawing of the lines of a netball court in front of them to try to help them visualise what the game was like.

Jay sighed. 'Yes, if you want to see the scoring bits as the interesting bits then I suppose that's accurate.' She had been exceptionally patient, Jackie thought, talking Ros through all the rules and explaining over and over again that all the rules needed to be learned even though there were so many and some of them were indeed stupid.

'In my experience centres always lose their virginities first, if that helps?' Jackie offered, feeling the warm jacket of wine cuddling her pleasantly. Jay laughed but Ros just arched an eyebrow.

'That ship sailed many a moon ago I'm afraid,' she tutted.

'Full of seamen.' Jay couldn't help herself and Jackie and Jay descended into helpless giggles. Ros remained unmoved, poring over the pieces of paper on the table.

'OK,' she finally said, sternly, trying and failing to get Jackie and Jay to concentrate. 'So let's say . . . I'll play goal defence because I'm tall and she only has a small box to run around in. Jay . . . you said you're good at shooting too, so you go goal attack?'

Jay nodded through her snorts.

'Jackie . . . why don't you be one of these pointless side ones as you're not feeling as confident? These wing guys? They seem like backups. Maybe Claire can be the defence one.'

Jay opened her mouth to correct Ros's assertions and then obviously decided against it. Ros continued, 'Annie is a blast at goal shooting; so, she's shoed in for that, so then all we need is a slutty runner for centre. We can find that before next week.'

The laughter drained out of Jackie immediately. 'Next week?' she yelped.

'Yes.' Ros had the decency to sound a little embarrassed. 'Did I not say?'

'You know you didn't, Rosalyn.'

'Don't call me Rosalyn unless you're a nun and I have your permission to hate you. Yes, I got an email yesterday to say that our first match-up is next week, so . . . we'll see how it goes, shall we?'

'What if we don't have enough people?' Jackie gestured at the stick person with a C on the court sketch.

'Then the courts will become a block of flats, and everyone will blame you.' Ros stuck her tongue out at Jackie's oh-so-serious reaction.

'Laurel Taylor was the centre when I played at school,' Jay said, staring into space. 'I can't believe I'm nearly thirty and still having to deal with Laurel Taylor. She was such a bitch about me, telling everyone how up myself I was. I bet she's already telling everyone we went to school with how I've already failed and come back.'

'You haven't failed.' Jackie grabbed both of Jay's hands protectively and looked her deep in the eyes. 'Don't say that. You lost a job and that's terrible, but it doesn't reflect on you, it's the times. You'll get another one.'

'I dunno.' Jay's eyes were looking a little sparkly around the edges as she tried to avoid Jackie's supportive eye contact. 'I'm nearly at the end of my twenties. It's getting a bit late . . .' She didn't get to finish her sentence before Ros and Jackie were in hysterics.

'Are you kidding me?! I've got stretch marks older than you!' Ros exclaimed, trying desperately to suck in air between hoots.

'Oh Jay, I know twenty-eight feels late now but it's nothing. It's NOTHING.'

'I own my own my law firm.' Ros looked deep at Jay. 'Do you know when I qualified?'

'No . . .?' Jay said meekly, sniffing through her trembly nose.

'When I was thirty-one. I felt ancient studying with all those kids a decade younger than me, but I finished up and look where I am now. The Queen of lawyers. You have time.'

Jay looked despondently at the tabletop. 'I just feel like a bit of a failure.'

Jackie could see the tears layering up over Jay's green eyes. 'I think we all do sometimes,' she said warmly, feeling extremely maternal towards the other woman. 'I'm fifty-eight and single and jobless and my only hobby is this netball team. I feel like a bit of a failure too.'

Ros managed to break the mood almost immediately. 'I don't,' she said, before swishing down the remainder of her wine. 'If I ever feel like something's gone off, I sort it. I change it. You can't fail if you're still doing it; you just haven't finished yet. That's my approach.'

Jackie shook her head at her bulletproof friend and smiled apologetically at Jay. Some people just didn't have baggage. Lucky Ros.

'Let's have that sleepover,' Jay said, and nodded.

Jackie squeaked, 'Really?!' Jay wasn't exactly the muscled-up hunk she'd thought she needed but it was better than a silent empty house.

'Really.' Jay smiled.

Jackie beamed. Ros also smiled, but a little thinly, and Jackie made a mental note to ask her if she disapproved. 'Look, we're all in a weird place . . . except Ros,' she added before Ros could butt in, 'who has her entire life together without a single issue, but: we're a team now. Literally. If we stick together, we can get through this bit.'

19

As the week passed Jackie found herself feeling increasingly worried about where they were going to find players in time for the game. Her thoughts beat cyclically round the same points of panic: it began with worry about not having enough players; then it moved on to an apathy as she remembered it was just a team for a sport she didn't even particularly want to play; then it found a spiky worry that if she didn't get a team it would be a death sentence for the courts; which could only be sanded down by trying to persuade herself it wasn't her responsibility; and then she settled on a deep dread that without netball and a vague of idea of helping save the courts she didn't really have any responsibilities. So, she resolved again to find a team and the cycle was back to its spring.

She found herself at the checkout in Sainsbury's, watching the cashier's hand passing groceries across the bleeper. Fast hands. Would it be weird to ask her to play? Probably. Jackie was chatty at the checkout: always had been. It was in her DNA to talk to any stranger she stopped next to and just show them what a nice person she was. How people stood there in silence and let someone work for them without trying to befriend them she didn't know at all.

The day of the first match was looming and she could feel the pressure mounting to fill the gap in their team. She was sure that Laurel Taylor's piece on local netball, possibly featuring their team, would be not much more than a column buried twenty pages into the local paper. Even though she knew that, somehow it kept morphing into a front-page hatchet job declaring her a failure who couldn't even find six people to join a team. She could picture Steve reading it to Michelle over breakfast in their silk robes. At the point at which her imagination moved them into Buckingham Palace, she would usually manage to shake the worry off and get back to reality, but then the cycle would begin all over again the next time she saw a particularly tall woman reach something off a shelf.

As well as posting the flyers up in all the places that felt legal and like they would attract the kind of attention she wanted, Jackie had also made a concerted effort to learn the internet. Jay had showed her how to join local groups on Facebook and other websites and she'd set about trying to attract women to their netball team via engaging-sounding posts. So far, she had been sent one photo of a penis and scrolled through a lot of comments about how most women had hung up their netball bibs happily at the end of school and never felt inclined to play again. Personally, Jackie thought they were probably right; the more reading she did about the game the stupider it sounded.

Eventually Jackie had got up the courage to call Claire, the rugby woman. Surely asking a woman she had already met would be a bit easier than finding a whole brand new one? She'd made a cup of tea, sat on the sofa, moved to the other sofa and then scrolled through to Claire's number in her mobile.

'Hello Claire! Claire, hi! Hi, Claire, I don't know if you remember me . . . Claire, hi, it's me Jackie from the rugby . . .' She tried out all the different versions of the phone call she could think of into the quiet air of the living room. 'Sod it,' she said eventually, failing to find the perfect beginning, and just hit call.

'Claire speaking.' The posh voice answered almost straight away.

'Hello, this is Jackie speaking,' Jackie said, and then rolled her eyes at herself. 'Sorry, hello Claire – it's Jackie. The woman

from the rugby. The woman without a husband any more.'
She'd meant it as a joke, but it didn't come out right. She'd
swear anyone listening would think this was her first conversation.

'Sorry, I went through a tunnel, say that again?' Claire's voice
reappeared in Jackie's ear. Jackie thanked the god of dialogue
that she had a second opportunity.

'Claire, hi, can you hear me now? It's Jackie, Jackie Douglas.
We met at the rugby match the other day.' Much better.

'Yes, I know, darling – your name came up on my phone when
you rang. Is everything all right? You sound very anxious.' Claire
sounded so poised. Jackie pictured her in a convertible, swinging round the sort of Italian mountains that made the *Top Gear*
boys sweat.

'Yes, yes, I'm all fine. Listen, I was just calling because, and
feel free to say no it sounds awful—'

'You're selling it, Jackie . . .'

Jackie gave a hint of a laugh through her nerves. 'Well, me
and Ros and Jay, who you also met, we're starting a netball team,
and we wondered if you had any interest in a bit of casual, very
casual, local netball?'

'God, well, I wasn't expecting that. Get out of my arse! Sorry,
bloody drivers. Er, netball . . .? That's a thing I hadn't thought
about in many decades. Yeah, sure. Why not!'

Jackie had quickly given her the details and got off the phone
to let her carry on conquering the roads. She loved how Claire
seemed quite up for any adventure, and found herself more and
more comparing herself to this other woman. She didn't come
out favourably. She fervently wished she didn't have reserva-
tions about just about everything on Planet Earth. Her New
Life Resolution was to be more Claire: be more adventurous.
But even with Claire, and Kath the mum woman, they were still
a player short to make up even the basic squad. Ideally, they'd
have nine or ten so they could sub out when they got tired.

Given the fitness level of the team they'd probably end the first match wishing there were twenty of them.

She was so concerned with finding the missing players that she'd not even really had time to dwell on her upcoming smear test. Usually it sat on the calendar clouding up a whole morning and she managed to dread it for a full week. Jackie loathed dreading her smear test. After two babies and forty years of smears she was aware that they didn't hurt, but there was something so undignified about being bottomless on a bed. She hated the debate over socks on or off. The small talk. All of it. When it was looming she would mull for a week on ways to make the experience as smooth as possible. This time, however, suddenly it was Thursday and 10.10 a.m., and she was on her way.

The waiting room smelled like disinfectant and spider plants, and she sat, fidgeting, trying not to think about the indignity of getting changed behind a thin blue curtain. Socks on or off? What had she done last time? It felt odd to take them off, because it wasn't necessary for a cervical exam to be sockless. But it felt extremely strange leaving them on and having everything exposed except for your toes. How was she at this end of life and still didn't know how to waltz into circumstances like this and just occupy them?

The doctor called her through, and Jackie smiled tightly. At least she liked this doctor. Dr Hawkins went through all the usual blurb about whether or not Jackie would like a chaperone and what they were going to be up to today. Jackie nodded in all the right places and then disappeared behind the curtain. She decided socks off. So what if Dr Hawkins thought it was weird; it was how she felt most comfortable.

She pulled herself up onto the trolley and felt the rolled-out paper crunch under her exposed bottom. Please don't get stuck in there, she prayed fervently to the god of cervical humiliation.

'Ready!' she called out, and then immediately felt like a seductress from a 1940s film. She didn't want Dr Hawkins to think she was rushing her or impatient. 'Or, you know, whenever you want to,' she added, and then died without the sweet relief of actually dying.

Dr Hawkins pulled the curtain back and stepped in, taking care to be as professional with her eyeline as possible. She started unpackaging the bits and bobs that she needed for the job. 'So, what have you been up to today?' she asked, causally. Jackie knew she was just being distracted from the shoehorn that was about to be placed up her intimates but she decided to play along; it was basically the same as when she chatted to the Sainsbury's cashier.

'I've been trying to find players for a new amateur netball team we're starting,' she said, staring at the polystyrene tiles on the ceiling.

'Gosh! Netball. I haven't played in years. Are you good?' Dr Hawkins asked. Jackie went to answer and then heard the harsh tone of her mobile ringing. On instinct she turned her head to the screen of the phone, on the pile of folded clothes on the chair. She didn't recognise the number. 'Try to relax your muscles if you can,' Dr Hawkins reminded her gently, and Jackie complied; not remembering when she had tensed them.

'Sorry,' she mumbled.

'Not a problem, it's natural. So, netball, are you good?'

This made Jackie laugh, and it coincided with the speculum beginning its journey to the dusty bowels of her reproductive organs. It wasn't the best time to laugh, and the speculum shot back out again. Dr Hawkins looked up and Jackie flushed.

'Sorry,' she said, focusing on controlling her wayward muscles. At least she seemed to still have some decent muscle down there, she thought, that boded well for future dating. An image of the man, Duncan, from the coffee shop floated into her mind and she furiously tried to expel it to be fair to Dr Hawkins. You couldn't think of sex while someone was trying to smear you. She focused with all her might on the doctory surroundings. 'Try again. Um, netball, no, no we're not particularly good. It's just a bit of a laugh really.'

Dr Hawkins popped the speculum back in and this time Jackie managed to neither laugh, tense nor imagine more pleasurable things in its place.

'Did you play at school?' Jackie tried to keep her voice casual; this was just a job for Dr Hawkins, it wasn't a personal vagina, it was just a work vagina. Stay calm.

'Yes, goal shooter. I'm tall.' Dr Hawkins popped the . . . Jackie realised she wasn't sure what it was, the swab? Whatever it was that did the smearing, anyway, in up the speculum and Jackie felt the peculiar feeling of it sweeping about lightly. Not unpleasant, but not pleasant either. Pleasant neutral. But as pleasant neutral as it was, Jackie realised she might only have two or three of them left. Memories of lying in similar positions through two pregnancies floated across her mind and she felt a bit of a tug at her throat at all the things she was finished doing.

'Yes, yes you are tall.' Jackie was pretty sure her voice was too loud but the louder she talked the less she could think, so she forged forward. 'As I say, we need more players, if you wanted to play with us . . .?' Jackie let the question hang in the air, not sure if it was inappropriate to be propositioning someone as they removed plastic scaffolding from your genitals.

Dr Hawkins' mouth jerked, and Jackie watched in real time the doctor go from an automatic refusal to a confused acceptance. 'Yes,' she said eventually. 'Yes, why not?' She pulled the speculum gently out and smiled efficiently. 'All done. You should get a letter in the next ten days with the results. Shall I take a flyer for the netball? I'm not sure I'm allowed to just give you my details here, so I'll call later. Red tape safety stuff, you know how it is.'

'Bloody EU!' Jackie joked, and then wished she hadn't as Dr Hawkins just nodded and looked confused. 'Yes, well that's great. Here's a flyer. And then we never tell anyone about how we met.'

The turn of events had taken Jackie so by surprise that it wasn't until she was back on the pavement outside the surgery that she remembered the call she had missed. She pulled her phone out and hit redial in case it was Freya's nursery. A deep voice answered.

'Jackie?'

'Yes,' she said. 'Sorry, who is this?'

'It's Duncan. We met in the coffee shop a few days ago . . .' He sounded a bit apologetic for calling.

Jackie reeled. 'Oh! Hi! How did you get my number?'

'Sorry? Is it OK that I'm calling?'

I was just thinking about you while I got a smear test, Jackie thought but managed not to say. 'Yes, sure,' she said, aware that she didn't sound totally convincing.

'Your phone number was on the flyer for your netball team,' he explained. Jackie groaned inwardly. Yet another person who knew about the team. 'I don't want to seem like a weird stalker.'

'No, you don't! Seem like one, I mean.'

'I just, well, I'm too old to faff about pretending anything. I thought you were beautiful and nice, and I wondered if I could take you out for dinner?'

Jackie thought this might be the most romantic thing that had ever happened to her, and she wished it wasn't happening while she could still feel the remnants of cervical smear lubricant between her legs. It was so romantic she felt overwhelmed and guilty and then annoyed at feeling guilty.

'That would be so lovely. But I'm sorry. I'm not ready. I'm not quite there yet.' Her voice came out quietly as someone jostled past her on the street. She felt small and confused. Her refusal was instinctual: to just push the problem away. She pictured Dr Hawkins' face almost refusing the netball offer.

'I understand.' It was hard to tell over the phone, but it really sounded like he did. 'Perhaps we could stay in touch, as friends . . .?' He let it hang, leaving a door open for her.

'Yes, yes, I'd like that.' A start.

They hung up and Jackie stood in an emotional whirlwind on a quiet street.

20

Monday dawned and Jackie woke up with an ache in her stomach that she felt conscious of before she'd reached consciousness. To be fair, waking up and feeling confused and fearful had become the norm since Steve's walkout; but this morning, as the waking-up fog cleared, she began to realise that it wasn't loneliness and love grief that gripped her: it was nerves about the game.

The first match for the Skids, the name having been hastily adjusted when they had to tell Laurel Taylor what it was for the column, was the next day. Now that they had enough people, the realisation that she would actually have to play had moved up the triage list. It was like one of those clichéd nightmares about sitting an exam in the nude, except far worse because it was going to involve an audience and running.

Jackie mooched down to the kettle and found her phone on the worktop. An excitable voicemail from Ros, that needed listening to several times to make sense of, told her that she needed to be at the dreaded sports centre at six p.m. because Ros had booked a court for them to practise on and get some team bonding in. Jackie was thankful for the smell of toast to stop herself retching.

She was just about to place her phone back on the worktop and ignore the world again when it buzzed in her hand. The screen said Steve and she felt herself lurching back into that invisible position in the coffee shop all over again. He hadn't even seen her. Duncan had though. Why had she turned him down? Her thumb hovered over the button to cancel the call. No, what if it was something wrong with one of the boys? She answered it.

'Hello?'

'Jack! Thought you were never going to answer. What you up to?' Steve sounded bright and bubbly for so early in the morning.

'Nothing, nothing . . . just making breakfast.' Jackie's mouth felt dry. Why did she feel on the back foot? Like she was wrong somehow?

'Not disturbing an intimate morning, am I?' Was that a note of worry in Steve's voice? An image of Duncan sitting at the breakfast bar in a dressing gown shot suddenly to the front of Jackie's mind and she felt a guilty swirl join the other emotions circling her digestive system. Why had she answered this call? If something was wrong with the boys, they weren't going to call Steve before her. He could have left a voicemail; he liked notes.

'No. I'm just at home on my own.' What kind of dressing gown would Duncan even have? A silk one, surely?

'Oh, well – let me in then, I'll join you for a cuppa.' Jackie heard a rap at the front door and jumped out of her skin. She heard the line go dead on the call and paused in the kitchen for a moment, unsure what to do. She couldn't not let him in, could she? But she felt . . . exposed, here in her pyjamas. But that was ridiculous, they'd been married for decades – he'd seen her in pyjamas and much less and much worse a thousand times before. But, why was he here? After the way they'd left things last time. He couldn't think they'd be back on good terms already?

She pulled open the front door and Steve waved a brown bag at her. She assumed, from the greasy patches, that it was some sort of breakfast pastry and her treacherous stomach thanked him with a gurgle. To her horror, Steve's eyes flicked down to it with a smile and Jackie felt herself shrinking into a tiny, useless woman. She stepped backwards to let him into the hall and he strode towards the kitchen.

'Got much planned today?' he called back over his shoulder, and Jackie heard the kettle click on.

'No, not much,' she lied, unwilling to give him any details about her netball antics. He'd find out soon enough when *Panorama* ran their special into the events leading up to the world's most embarrassing spectacle.

'You need to get yourself a hobby, Jack.' He poured water into a mug.

Jackie bristled. 'Yes, probably. Did you need something?'

Steve sighed. 'I thought I should come round and make it normal for us to see each other. We've got to be able to be friends. We've got kids together. I know things are screwy, and it's entirely my fault, I'm owning that. But we have to move forward in a civil way and I think the only way to do that is for us to put the effort in right now, even though it's uncomfortable.'

She sighed too. He was probably right; but she just didn't want to be nice to him. Why, when there was a handsome man on the phone asking her out, did it make her feel loyal to Steve, but the sight of Steve made her want to throw things?

'What are you up to today?' She unstuck her tongue from the dry roof of her mouth and summoned the strength to talk to him.

'Turning the garage into an office.' His speech sprayed pastry over Jackie's immaculate countertops and she was annoyed at him, and then at herself. When did she become a sad old woman that needed a pristine kitchen to be happy? Maybe she always had been, but it was OK when you were married.

'That sounds good. Do you want the DIY stuff from the shed?' Now that they were talking it was easier, flowing. She felt herself relaxing a bit; but the memory of being invisible to him lurked behind their civility.

'Would you mind?' Steve smiled, and she melted. 'That'd be great. Save me going to B&Q to get new stuff. We're saving up for a holiday, me and Chelle.'

Jackie nodded, unable to speak as unbidden memories of all the holidays they had taken as a family came pouring over her defensive wall. 'That'll be great,' she managed, and then busied her mouth in the too-hot tea so she wouldn't have to say anything else. A little bit of her, the bit that had seen too many rom-com films, wanted to casually mention Duncan and pretend she had someone too – it would only be a half-pretend, after all – but she didn't.

As soon as she could she disappeared upstairs and dressed hurriedly. They loaded paint rollers and half-cans of colours into the boot of his car, each tin reminding her of a different redecoration that had signalled a new phase in their lives together. The whole time they were moving things she couldn't wait to see his car pulling out of the drive, but as the boot disappeared round the corner she felt hot tears springing down her face.

Jackie slipped herself down gently onto the front doorstep and let herself cry. Sod the neighbours. Sod anyone seeing her. This just hurt. A car turned into the cul-de-sac, and she wiped her nose quickly to not attract attention. She only looked up when a car door opened and she heard Steve calling, 'Sorry, I forgot the—' He caught sight of her tears and stopped. 'Jack! Are you all right? What happened?'

She stood up so quickly her vision didn't quite come with her in time. Both knees clicked loudly and she wobbled. Steve's hand was at her elbow. He guided her inside and she made a silent prayer that whoever was prolonging this agony would just hurry up and let her die. This was like an unending hangover made of memories.

Steve rattled around the house making sympathetic noises and cooing over Jackie while somehow managing absolutely nothing that made her feel better. He provided her with a hot cup of peppermint tea. She wondered where he'd even found the bags: she hated peppermint tea. Surely he knew that? And who was she keeping those bags for? She sat on the sofa, staring at the wall, wishing partly that he would leave and partly that he'd throw himself on the floor at her feet and wail about the mistake he had made and how much he wished he could come back. He did neither.

'Oh Jack, I'm sorry,' he said, sitting down on the edge of the armchair like the presenter of a particularly schmaltzy chat show, 'I should have known how hard you were finding this.' She nodded, dumbly. There was no strength in her to pretend he wasn't right. They sat in silence for a few seconds longer before Steve flattened both palms on his thighs and stood up. 'Look, I sort of need to go; Michelle is doing us a special dinner tonight. But I don't want to leave you if you're upset?' He rubbed Jackie's head softly, 'I hate that you're upset.' He knelt and their faces were level, and close in a way that was no longer OK. A little too close, and too still for too long. She held her breath.

'Jack. I'd better go. I'm sorry.' He headed for the front door. Jackie scanned the floor for the insides that she was sure were not in her any more.

21

'He does it on purpose, Jack!' Ros exploded, her voice echoing round the empty gym hall.

'Keep your voice down,' Jackie hissed, looking around at the imaginary crowds she was embarrassed in front of. 'No he doesn't: he's not like that. He just doesn't know how to navigate this any more than I do.'

Ros arched an eyebrow, but Jackie countered it with an intense frown. 'I don't need a telling-off from you.'

'It's not a telling-off,' Ros hissed. 'It's dire strait-talking from your best friend because you need to hear it. He pops up period-ically to check you're still upset and then swans back to his other woman knowing he's kept you hanging on and into him.'

'You're only seeing the worst in him,' Jackie complained.

'Why are you seeing only positives?'

'Because . . . because . . . if I give in and admit that he's awful then what was I doing with him? Why am I not already over him?' Jackie was more angrily frustrated than upset, and in a way that felt good, more manageable: 'If I had half a brain I'd have said yes to Duncan.' She bit her lip instantly, wishing she could squash that information back inside. She'd not told Ros about the phone call yet and the look of delighted glee on Ros's face reminded her why.

'Said yes?!' Ros's eyebrows shot up so fast it was a wonder they stayed on. 'Said yes to what? Seeing him? A date? God, you're not marrying him?'

'Yes Ros, he phoned me after a chance meeting in a cafe and asked me to be his geriatric bride. He asked me out for dinner.'

'But you didn't say yes?'

'No.'

'Why not?'

'I don't know. I didn't want to go. I felt guilty. I don't know how to date someone.'

'No one knows how to date people,' Jay said as she and Dr Hawkins sidled over, having given up pretending that shooting was more interesting than gossip. 'And anyone who does know how to date is not worth dating.'

'Offence taken,' pouted Ros.

'What apps are you on?'

'Jay, I am not on any dating apps,' Jackie said flatly.

'None at all?' It was Dr Hawkins' turn to sound surprised.

'No! I've only been single a short while . . .'

'At least three months . . .' Ros muttered under her breath.

'But apps are for young people,' Jackie protested.

'I'm on some.' All three women said it almost in synch and Jackie couldn't help but laugh out loud.

'Well, I'll get on them and see if I can date you lot, shall I? I don't need to be on an app. I can't even say yes when I get asked out in the real world, so what's the point in having more ways to turn down nice handsome men?'

'Do you regret saying no now?' Ros had hope again, which was bad news for Jackie.

'Maybe. Oh, look, I don't know. Let's do some netball, shall we?'

Jay and Dr Hawkins, who was slowly trying to persuade Jackie to call her Renee, a concept that she was struggling with, resumed their shooting practice. Jackie and Ros stood nearby and made some shapes with their bodies that they hoped people might mistake for stretching. Annie arrived, looking a little flustered, but soon calmed down when she realised that far from chastising her for her tardiness the team were thrilled to have an excuse to start late. Claire was at a wine-tasting event, and Kath had been unable to afford a babysitter for two nights in one week, but both had promised absolutely to be sure of the rules and to be there on time for the game the next day.

Annie, Jay, Renee, Ros and Jackie all found themselves stood in a small huddle and to Jackie's horror they were looking to her to begin the session. 'Right,' she said, and then didn't know what to do next so said it again: 'Right . . . well, thank you all for coming. I um . . .' She felt irritating tears spring up and was at a loss to explain them away. 'I'm very grateful to you all for being here.' She cleared her throat, trying to swallow down the uninvited lump. 'I have no idea how to play netball and no real idea of what this will be like, but whatever happens I hope we have a good time.'

'Well said!' said Ros, raising an arm in a cheer. The others merrily joined her and cheered too. They then went back to looking at Jackie, who realised they were expecting her to have an idea of what they needed to practise in the session. Jackie gave Ros a panicked look and Ros turned to Jay.

'Jay, you're probably the most experienced player, perhaps you could give us some pointers?'

'God, if Planet Janet is your best bet you really are screwed!'

Jackie flinched and turned round to see the journalist, Laurel Taylor, eyeing them through a scowl.

'Oh nutballs,' Ros muttered, 'I forgot she was coming. Hi Laurel.'

'Good evening.' Laurel offered a formal hand to shake, and Ros limply waggled it about a bit before dropping it. 'Don't mind me – I'll just be observing and making some notes.'

'Well . . .' Jackie raced around the corners of her mind looking for something useful to say or do, 'Go easy on us; we're here for fun, not to win.'

'Yes, because of your divorce isn't it?' If Laurel had tact, she hadn't brought it. Jackie absorbed the shot and smiled tightly.

'That's right. It's a sort of . . . new start kind of a team. I imagine you'll watch us tonight and decide it's far too small to bother your paper about.'

Laurel's eyes widened. 'Opposite actually! Human interest stories always go down much better. Heartbroken netball team is a much better column than just netball team. There's been such a noise about the courts being built on that the paper is keen to find stories connected to it.'

Jackie felt herself brighten internally. 'Oh, are people rallying round?' Perhaps it wouldn't be quite so essential to have a netball team. She was beginning to struggle with feeling like she was responsible somehow for keeping the courts going.

Laurel raised a well-designed eyebrow and rolled her eyes beneath it and its straight man companion. 'Oh, they always do . . . at first. They make a big outcry: *No, you must leave things exactly as they are: my children have memories there.*' She leaned hard and pathetically into memories as though they were an embarrassment to admit to. 'But then they sign a petition and consider it done. It's almost better when the petition fails because it gives them a coffee morning subject.' Her disdain for the type of woman Jackie had been, and would be still given half a chance, was palpable.

Jackie swallowed. 'Well,' she coordinated her defensive thoughts into something more mature than 'go fuck yourself', 'people are busy, Laurel. They do what they can.'

Laurel laughed lightly. 'I don't even see what the fuss is. The courts are gross and the plans for the new park are great. So it'll be slightly smaller to fit in a couple of new houses? It'll still be better.'

'Some people like old grotty things,' Jackie mumbled. She felt suddenly twinned with the ancient courts; why should people get to upgrade them to a pair of shiny new swings just because they'd got a bit run-down? Jay rubbed Jackie's arm and Jackie smiled at her. Jay's face was focused on Laurel's and Jackie could swear the daggers being stared were nigh on visible. She squeezed Jay's arm back and switched her voice into a bright, twinkly tone. 'Shall we begin?'

'Yes, we need to make the most of this hall.' Ros grimaced. 'It's costing an armour and a leg to hire.'

Jay nodded a little over enthusiastically and began showing them some ways to make their throwing and catching more accurate. Jay kept throwing glances at Laurel and Jackie felt awful that what had been meant as a nice escape had become torture.

Jay was a good teacher though, and she relaxed them all into practising via fun little games. Jackie found she was a lot better when she wasn't strung taut as a piano string with nerves about what people thought of her. The hour flew by with gales of laughter and some improvements on all sides. Annie really was a great shot and Jay wasn't bad. Renee, Ros and Jackie were extremely awful but by the time they called it a day even they were managing to get the ball to bounce off the hoop rather than just flying past wildly. There were long periods of time where Jackie even managed to forget about the scribbling pencil on the side bench noting everything down.

They gathered at the end of the training session and in that moment Jackie had a fleeting feeling of confidence about the game the next day. She made her way over to where Ros was speaking to Laurel Taylor.

'No, wrong again,' Laurel was saying, her heavily mascaraed eyes wide and bright, 'the paper doesn't see the point in competing with nationals on news, so they love stuff like this. I pitched it as a weekly column following your progress and—'

'So, you'll be here every week?' Jay interrupted sharply.

Laurel didn't bat an eyelid. 'I will, Janet, yes, it's my job. I realise it's not a high-flying London University type job like yours. . . was, but it's still my job.'

'I didn't go to London University,' Jay snapped.

'Well, sorry I don't even know the proper terms for universities.' The two women stared at each other, and Jackie watched in fascination. Laurel's anger was coolly detached: years of masking her emotions to imitate strength. Jay was less good at it and her anger boiled through her skin.

'Shall we go to the Hawk?' Jackie interrupted, hooking an arm into Jay's and looking round the other team members.

'I won't join you,' Laurel said primly. 'I think it's best if I preserve professional boundaries.'

There was a silence in which no one present quite knew how to respond. Jackie thought she could see silent laughter bubbling under ~~Dr Hawkins'~~ Renee's T-shirt.

'No problem,' Ros eventually managed. 'We shall see you at tomorrow's game. Unless there's a local UFO or some such.'

Laurel Taylor clacked her way off across the hall and the rest of them gathered up their stuff and cleared out of the hall, into their cars and off to the Hawk. Jackie took Jay in her car, feeling desperately sorry for her that Laurel was now mixed up in their escapism.

'Honestly, we can tell Ros to give her the boot.' Jackie glanced across from the driver's seat.

'Oh no, it's fine. I don't want to give her the satisfaction of knowing she upsets me. I just thought things couldn't get any worse: being back in my old room, in Mum's house with Mum all loved up, and now my school bully is back too. I must have been awful in another life to deserve this.' Jay tacked an unconvincing laugh on the end and Jackie smiled sadly.

'You and your mum get on OK though, don't you?'

Jay thought about it. 'Yeah. . .? I mean, I think as well as two grown women used to their own space can when they go back to living together. She's not great at recognising I'm an adult, and all I do is feel under her feet. I'm glad we're off to the pub now so I don't have to go back and spoil her anniversary dinner. Please say you'll stay out until midnight with me so I don't have to hear them shagging?'

This time Jay actually did laugh genuinely, and Jackie joined in, simultaneously checking her blind spot on the big roundabout near the pub. 'Why don't you stay over at mine tonight? Keep out of your mum's hair completely? I've got the spare room. I can drop you back in the morning.'

Jay stopped laughing, but carried on smiling. 'Oh. . . I. . .' Jackie could feel her on the verge of declining and then there was a pause. 'Actually, yes – that would be so nice to have a night away. Are you sure you wouldn't mind?'

'Of course not! It'll give me one night this year when I'm not lying half-awake listening for someone breaking in!'

'Our first sleepover! I'll text Mum now.'

Jay finished with her phone just as they pulled into the Hawk car park and saw Renee and Ros getting out of their cars.

The whole team piled into the usual booth and wine was nestled into coolers. Jackie took the opportunity in the bustle of settling down to whisper harshly to Ros: 'You shouldn't have let Laurel Taylor stay – it's not fair on Jay.'

'Sorry, wouldn't want to upset your new best friend,' Ros huffed, keeping her voice out of range of Jay.

'I knew you were feeling pernickety about that!' Jackie shook her head, disappointed.

Ros's sharp eyes glanced up at Jay. 'Do you want me to give your Laurel the heave-ho, Jay? Just let me know and I will.'

Jay blushed furiously as the conversation screeched to a halt and everyone looked at her. Jackie could happily have clocked Ros and her usual lack of tact over the head with. . . well, something hard.

'It's fine, really.' Jay tried to make her face look less apparently miserable. 'We're grown women. I'm sure we can learn to play nice.'

Jackie reached a hand across the table to Jay to offer solace. 'You really don't have to though if you don't want to. The whole point of this team was a bit of a distraction from people we don't like.'

'It would be nice to win occasionally though. . .' Ros muttered.

'No, honestly. . . I'd like to rise above her. We're not at school any more.'

'You shouldn't have invited her! You're a bloody meddler, Ros Mackie!' Jackie said.

'I am not a meddler! I didn't know anyone would know her; I was just trying to get us. . .' Ros was the wide-eyed picture of innocence. Renee and Annie buried themselves in their drinks to avoid the conflict.

'Yes? Finish that sentence. What on earth were you thinking getting a journalist to write about our little netball team would achieve other than utter humiliation?'

Ros's jaw bounced loosely. 'Motivation,' she finally landed on, then nodded, pleased with herself.

'Motivation?' Jackie shot back sceptically.

'Yes – now we have a reason to have to carry on playing if we don't want Little Miss Bitchy to write that we're terrible quitters.' Ros laid a sly look sideways and continued, 'Besides, we don't want to be responsible for the courts getting built on, do we?'

'Oh good.' Jackie was warming to the fracas now. 'So, to make this little experiment more fun you've made it so I might be humiliated in front of the ex I am trying to forget about, and Jay is now being observed by her bully? And don't get me started on trying to guilt-trip me about the courts—'

'It's OK, really,' Jay interrupted before Ros could parry. 'Don't you two fall out over it for goodness sake. I can certainly cope with playing netball near Laurel Taylor once a week. And we'll all do our best to make it a success so Steve is never opening his paper to a description of our failure.'

'That's the spirit!' Ros brightened immediately, and Jackie dismissed the notion that she might ever learn a lesson about her behaviour. 'Now all we have to do,' Ros continued, 'is learn to play netball!'

'Is that all? We're going to need a bigger bottle.' Jackie wiggled the nearly empty bottle on the table and Jay immediately hopped up out of her seat to grab another from behind the bar. Jackie took the opportunity to attempt to talk to Ros again. 'I'm serious, Ros, you need to think about Jay's feelings a bit. She's going through a rough patch and this team is meant to be an escape, not a chore.'

'Ah she's young – she's fine.' Ros couldn't meet Jackie's eye.

'Ros, I'm serious. You don't need to apologise or anything, but you do need to be different moving forward, OK?'

'Sure, whatever. Can't upset your new pet now, can we.' She turned her attention brusquely back to the table. 'OK, I got some information on netball to make sure we know all of the rules. So, these lines on the floor: they're important and each person can only go in certain bits of the court. They all have to start in the two end thirds, except the centre; the centre starts the game from the circle in the middle and has to throw it to someone else within three seconds and that person needs to be in the middle third.'

'So, they have to throw it to the other centre?' Jackie's face scrunched.

'Hmmmm. . . well, yes, the centre is the only other person in that third. Unless, no, I think your team has to quickly dash in? Well, that seems stupid, why not just start in there?' Ros was poring over the rules, her face squinting at her iPad, reading glasses eternally forgotten in the bottom of her bag.

Jay returned with a bottle and it was gratefully received. They topped up their glasses and continued trying to decipher the rules.

22

'Everyone has a landing foot and that's the foot you can't move,' Ros read loudly, slurring excessively on every consonant that wasn't nailed to the floor.

'Oh my God, it never ends,' Jackie murmured into her sleeves, feeling all sloshy at the excess wine. 'Which foot is your landing foot?'

'Whichever one you landed on.' Ros looked at her like she was being deliberately stupid. 'The other one is the pivoting foot.'

'Where am I going to be that I'm going to be landing all the time? I'm not typically an airborne kind of a woman,' Renee asked, looking genuinely concerned that there might be some kind of flying aspect to the game. At this, Jay snorted with laughter and then had to deal with the wine she had sucked into her respiratory system.

'It's just for when you're jumping to get the ball, or if you catch it while you're running,' Annie supplied helpfully. She had a rosy edge to her cheeks and had been constantly in a fit of giggles about the lack of understanding her future teammates were showing in the game. It felt like this might be the first time she'd ever felt confident enough in a group to admit superiority on a subject. She looked comfortable, and that wasn't something Jackie had thought about Annie before.

'Yes.' Ros nodded as though she'd already known this fact. 'It's for all the landing off all the jumping you'll be doing.'

'I don't think I will be jumping, Ros; my knees are over fifty years old.' Netball was sounding worse and worse to Jackie with every new rule. And netball seemed to have an abundance of rules.

'It's OK. I don't jump. I don't like to be off the ground. I like the ground. The ground is my friend.' Annie was slipping down the leather seat, getting ever closer to her best buddy the floor. Jay hooked an arm through hers, still laughing, and did her best to keep her propped up.

'It's all right for you two!' Jackie waved a sloppy arm at Renee and Annie. 'You're tall! You're that sweetcorn bloke! What am I supposed to do?'

'You'll have to just stretch.' Ros waved a hand at Jackie's complaints.

'So, if I'm not landing, how do I know which foot I'm allowed to move?' This game was clear as mud.

'Erm. . .' Ros pored over the rules, 'Well. . . maybe you can choose?'

Jay was in hysterics now, clutching at her abs with both hands and trying to massage the pain away. 'Oh my God, stop it you two. . . stop it.'

'Are you all right, Jay?' Jackie asked, genuinely concerned at the red, airless glow on Jay's skin. She seemed to be completely unable to breathe in.

'You really don't know how to play netball, do you? Like, I mean, you *really* don't?' Her speech came in breathless bursts between convulsions of laughter. Jackie and Ros both looked at her, perplexed.

'No,' said Jackie. 'No, we told you we didn't. Why is it funny?'

'I just. . . I don't know, I assumed when you decided to start a netball team completely of your own volition that you had some, even extremely minor, experience or interest in netball. Why else would two people suddenly randomly decide they were going to play netball?' Jay's voice was getting squeakier as the ridiculousness of the situation took over.

'Well, we. . . we're getting back at Steve, aren't we? You were there when we came up with the plan,' Ros supplied, jaw stuttering at the attempt to justify their actions. If she thought this sentence would calm Jay down, she was wrong. Not only did it cause Jay to emit a gratuitously porcine snort, but it set Jackie off on an immediate waterfall of heavy laughter.

'You're getting. . . back at Steve.' Tears poured out of Jay. 'I'd forgotten that bit!'

'He knows less about netball than we do!' Jackie squealed. 'Oh my God, what have we done? Set up a team to spite someone who's barely heard of the thing we're doing! Oh my goodness. . . and we're not even telling him we're doing it!'

'Who is Steve?' Renee asked, squinting at the conversation to decipher it. This caused paroxysms of laughter to spasm through Jay and Jackie.

'Steve is my ex-husband who left me quite unceremoniously and so to spite him I am playing a game he has never heard of! That's why I'm here!' Jackie panted through her little speech, her eyes streaming with happy, ridiculous tears.

'And I'm here because I'm seeing out my twenties single and jobless, unless you count serving pints in here, which my university emphatically does not consider to be a good use of my very expensive degree. So, I am playing netball to give myself one night of the week where I'm not back living at my mother's house watching her and her boyfriend snogging and giggling,' Jay said.

'Snogging!' Jackie shrieked, causing several other pub visitors to throw unimpressed looks her way. 'I haven't heard the word snogging in years! Oh Jay. . . sod the sleepover, why don't you just move in with me permanently? I don't snog anyone!'

Jay laughed. 'OK! I'll move in with you but the second you start bringing dates home and snogging them I'm outta there!' They laughed again.

Renee raised a glass, her hand shaking a little as she nervously made herself the centre of attention. 'My turn. I've lived here seventeen years and never once joined in on a single thing because I'm always too scared someone will want to show me a weird mole or a rash on my day off. You might just be my first friends in the village.' They cheersed her announcement and then turned to look at Annie, who looked surprised at the attention.

'Oh, I actually want to play netball,' she said, and there was a millisecond where she looked worried that she'd said the wrong thing and then everyone laughed again and she relaxed. They sat enjoying the aftershock of intense laughter as it rippled and died away.

Ros sat totally unimpressed at the gales of laughter coming off her friends. 'Are you going to calm down now so we can get back to these rules? We haven't even started on how far you're allowed to throw the ball and who is allowed to score yet. . .' Unfortunately for Ros, this sentence was like pouring petrol on the remnants of a fire and before she could look back down at the rules a fresh barrage of squawking laughter came out of her teammates. She had to make do with reading the rules herself while the others amused themselves with gasping laughs and attempts to repeat bits of how to play back at her.

23

The ground felt awfully hard. When they'd practised in the gym the floor had been soft and almost springy under Jackie's trainers, but the outdoor netball court they were imminently to be playing on was extremely hard. Too hard. Suspiciously hard. And not smooth either. What would happen if someone fell over? This felt too dangerous.

Even thinking that made Jackie feel guilty, though. . . she was feeling very at one with the courts. Somehow in her head, the playground had become Michelle's idea. The faceless witch who had stolen her life was plotting to smooth the hard concrete and replace it with her perfect new bright, bouncy floor technology. She had to remain faithful to the courts; what was the point of saving them if not even the people saving them loved them?

There were so many rules floating about in Jackie's head; she probably didn't need to worry about playing a match safely because she was going to get sent off within five minutes for some sort of landing-foot sin. They'd never really got back on track with concentrating at the pub and Jackie sorely regretted that now they were gathered round the side of the court looking at the other team.

'I can't believe our first match is against these bitches.' Ros was glaring at the eight women limbering up on the other side of the court.

'Ros! You can't call them bitches; they're your staff.'

'They were mean to you. And you're my best friend. Staff are replaceable: you are permanent.'

'I dunno. . . Steve got rid of me, maybe it's your turn next?' It came out more woe-is-me than Jackie meant, and Ros didn't rise to the bait. Jackie had somehow managed to forget that there would be another team. She already felt so at home with her own team that she'd convinced herself not being good at netball would only lead to slight embarrassment in front of them. But here was a whole other team plus a referee.

'They have four spares too! Four spares! That's almost a second team!' Ros's head was steaming.

The referee blew a whistle to signal play would be starting soon and Jackie's tummy lurched. They headed over to the court, each adjusting the bib they had frantically pulled over their heads. Claire was managing to somehow still look glamorous in hers. Jackie felt like she was in a straitjacket. There was a big WD on it; Jackie had taken the role of wing defence again. It felt like the least obvious position, so hopefully it wouldn't be too clear that she had no idea what she was doing. She wasn't sure whether it was better to look like she didn't know what she was doing, or to seem like she knew exactly what she was doing but was just not in possession of a body that could achieve those goals.

Luckily for Jackie, the wing attack for the opposing team was not Libby, the woman she had previously bodily harmed. In fact, looking about, Jackie couldn't see Libby anywhere. Perhaps a scrap with a mad old bat like Jackie had been enough to put her off netball for ever? She smiled at the Not-Libby who was her opposing player and tried to give her I-Won't-Give-You-A-Bloody-Mouth vibes.

'I'm Kate,' the woman said briskly, 'Nice to meet you.'

'Jackie.' Jackie smiled. 'Have you been playing long?'

The whistle blew and Kate vanished. One minute she was standing next to Jackie, the next she was about five paces across the court and had the ball. How the hell had that happened so quickly? Jackie scampered after her and thought about waving her arms madly to intercept, but by the time she caught up the ball was already gone. It sailed through the air, back towards the centre player who had initially got it to Kate. Jackie watched in amazement as Jay leapt up just in front of the opposing centre and reached out a hand at full stretch to not only keep the ball away from the team but also clutch it into her own body. She landed lightly with one foot and then the other and then began a circling motion, moving her foot and looking for somewhere to pass the ball. It was slim pickings on options.

Ros was still stood where she had started the game. Kath was nearer but stood looking at her shoes, half bent over with her hands on her knees trying not to be sick. Claire was locked in her defensive box at the other end, Renee was being marked by a woman who definitely had more limbs than the legal limit allowed, and Annie was at the other end of the court waiting to take a shot.

'Jackie!' screamed Jay, and bobbed her head to the right. Jackie came to suddenly. Of course! She could be the one to try to catch it. She waved back at Jay and saw Jay's eyebrows shoot up in surprise. She bobbed her head backward to indicate Jackie should run nearer. Of course! Jackie started to jog and noticed Kate making her way back over to block the throw. Jackie threw her arms up in the air and planted her feet ready to catch.

The ball left Jay's hands just as the referee lifted a whistle to her lips to call her out on a time penalty. The ball sailed towards Jackie, arcing up into the air before smoothly declining. Jackie couldn't believe how accurate Jay's throw was: she was far better at the game than she'd let on. Jackie watched the ball coming towards her; she was going to catch it! She kept her eyes focused on the ball, ready to feel the rubber surface nestle itself into her waiting palms.

It hit her hands with a sharp, hard thump and Jackie squealed. The ball dribbled miserably back off her irritatingly non-stick fingers and hit the floor, where it was scooped up by Kate, who had reached Jackie's position without breaking a sweat.

'Jackie!' Ros was furious. 'You have to catch it!'

'It really hurt!'

'Toughen up!' Ros shot back.

'Easy for you to say! You haven't even moved yet!'

A whistle blew and it seemed the other team had scored.

Jackie was still just stood staring outraged at her bright pink palms. Between the cold air and the slap with the ball they felt like they were on fire. Surely not everyone could be catching throws like that? Was Jay a lot stronger than she looked?

The players were jogging back to their positions for the next centre throw. It was Jay's turn to throw the ball and Jackie felt relieved that everyone was facing the other way so it was unlikely to come to her. Jay flicked her foot out behind her and pushed the ball away with a neat jerk of her arms to Renee, who had managed to get away from the opposing goal defence marking her. The ball was just descending from its arc when the opposing centre leapt up in what looked to Jackie like a truly inhuman feat and intercepted the ball.

'She was like Wayne bloody Sleep!' Ros would later exclaim in the Hawk.

Now that the ball was in the hands of the other team the action quickly swivelled back in the direction of Jackie. Kate pelted for open ground and Jackie did her best to keep up. Kate caught the ball without interference from a panting Jackie and quickly moved it up the court towards the waiting goal attack. From there it sailed towards their goal shooter and despite Claire's best efforts to intervene, it made a perfect duck-dive into the inviting net.

Two–nil down, Jackie thought to herself sadly. She'd seen enough games of football over the back of Steve's head on a weekend to know that it took a spectacular team to come back from two–nil down.

To add insult to stinging palm-based injury, out of the corner of her eye Jackie saw Laurel Taylor sitting neatly on a bench scribbling notes in a tiny book. Jackie briefly wondered what she was writing and then realised she would know soon, as soon as the paper was published.

24

'Perhaps we should have watched a game before we played one?' Kath suggested. She looked traumatised. Disembowelled.

'It was so fast.' Renee was staring straight at the wall. 'I'm having flashbacks. I can't believe I honestly thought I was quite fit. I run ten kilometres a week. How is it possible to feel this broken?'

'When you're running in a straight line you're usually not interrupted by seven other people trying to ruin your day.' Claire's voice was a monotone. 'That was a *casual* game. I'd have popped the lot of them into the Olympics.'

'Didn't your babysitter need to get home by. . .?' Jay began helpfully to Kath.

'Sod the babysitter, I need this.' Kath was cupping a whisky.

'Thirty-three–nil,' Ros said wearily. The graze on her knee from a particularly inelegant tumble shone a vivid red in the warm glow of the pub's evening lighting. 'I think you're right, Claire, I think they must have been Olympians. That's what this was.' She nodded, fervently. 'Some sort of Olympic prank. Next week we will be up against a normal team of us sorts and everything will be normal again.'

Only Jackie looked unfazed by their defeat. 'Ros, they're your employees. You know they're not pros,' she reminded her.

Ros shrugged this explanation off. 'So, they're playing the long con?'

Annie shook her head. 'No, that kind of score is quite common in netball.'

'Oh well, I can't wait for next week.' Renee rolled her eyes drily.

Jackie thought about joking about Renee stealing them some painkillers from work, but didn't say it. She felt like it was important to Renee not to be the doctor when she was with them. Jackie was feeling jubilant and trying to squash it as it was the very opposite of how the rest of her team looked. 'This bit is good though!' She waved her wine at Renee and gestured round the circle.

'You know you can come here without the game, right?'

'Oh, they do!' Jay assured Renee.

'Well, thirty-three–nil or not, I'm still glad we played.' Renee put her lemonade down and smiled at it. 'Thank you for dragging me out of my comfy little rut.'

'It's our pleasure.' Jackie glowed on the inside. 'Someone poured concrete into my rut and I *had* to get out of it – at least you did it of your own accord.'

'You've made me feel very at home.' Renee's words came out quickly. 'I actually don't feel like a GP for once!'

Jackie felt vindicated for her earlier joke avoidance.

'I like you being on the team,' said Claire. 'You might be the only person I know who's seen more vaginas than my husband!' Claire laughed in a light, loose fashion. It made the whole group laugh and Jackie looked at her fascinated; was it an act? Was she genuinely this comfortable with her living arrangements?

'We should have an initiation!' Jay said suddenly.

'A what?' Kath turned to look at her.

'An initiation! For the team! They did them every year at uni. You go out and have a drink and do games and stuff. Like a bonding session. It gets messy, but it's fun.'

'I want to go on a night out.' Kath nodded emphatically and checked her watch again, no doubt wondering if the babysitter would have just left her children to it by now.

'Me too!' Jay enthused. 'I cannot spend another night in with *Family Guy* turned up over the background hum of heavy petting. It's just unreal how all over each other they are.'

'Hey! We old people deserve sex too!' Claire laughed.

'Not in front of your daughter you don't!'

'Yeah, all right, I'll drink to that,' Claire said, sipping her drink.

'I'll drink to it too.' Jackie joined in. 'But only because I'll agree with most things if there's a drink at the end of it.'

'So will you fill out some divorce papers if I put a G and T at the end of them?' Ros asked. Jackie felt blindsided by her bringing this up, even jokingly, in front of everyone and decided to ignore her by laughing it off. Luckily Claire picked up the momentum of the jocularity.

'Oh see, I'm the other way,' she said. 'I find I'm much more likely to agree to things after the drink!'

'Let me know when you've had enough to lend me the money to move out!' Jay giggled.

'This initiation is the best idea you've ever had.' Ros nodded. 'I have been sat here thinking, too, and we do need to have a lot of fun and an initiation sounds perfect for that. Should we perhaps also think about getting a coach?'

A few of them nodded and considered noncommittally, but the idea of an initiation was far more enticing than the thought of being told what to do and Ros's suggestion was washed away in a tide of enthusiasm for shots and drinking games. Jackie listened to the swirl of conversation around her and felt far, far too alive for a middle-aged woman who had just lost dramatically in an amateur netball game. Before she knew what was happening, tears were pouring down her cheeks.

'Jackie! Oh my goodness Jackie, come here, what's the matter? Are you OK? That last fall was a big one, have you broken something?' Ros whizzed into caring mode and began inspecting all the parts of Jackie that had the best chance of breaking.

Laughter burst out of Jackie through the tears, 'No, no. . . I'm fine. I'm really fine.'

'It's just hard to believe you because you're crying,' Renee said softly, smiling.

'She might be tired. My lot cry at anything when they're tired.'
Kath nodded.

'I'm not tired,' Jackie said, laughing and sobbing and sniffing.
'I mean, well, I am; I'm bloody knackered. I haven't run like that
in. . . ever. But, oh for goodness sake I don't know why I'm crying. I'm so happy. Is this endorphins?' She looked at Renee, who
shrugged.

'Could be.'

'I. . . I don't know. I don't know how to say it without sounding like a mad old bat. I just haven't had this in a long time. This
feeling of friends and things going on and feeling in control. I
know we lost—'

'By a LOT!' Jay raised her glass in a toast to their spectacular
failure.

'By a LOT!' they all chorused, and Jackie felt her heart pressing hard against her ribs; immensely painful and borne only of
an overwhelming feeling of happiness.

'We lost by a lot but. . . oh my goodness I am so grateful that
we played.'

'I don't know if you'll still feel like that once the review comes
out!' Ros muttered.

'Oh don't! Bloody Laurel fucking Taylor.' Jay slumped back
against the cushions.

'It's not going to be a review. . .' Kath countered. 'Maybe she'll
be really nice about how hard we tried?'

'She won't.'

'Honestly, I don't care,' Jackie declared. 'Whatever happens, can
we swear we'll see this season out? I know we won't all want to stick
to it afterwards, but. . . I'd rather every single one of my neighbours
read every week about how I laughed my way through losing thirty-
three–nil than Steve knew I'd failed to even have one hobby. And
we need to at least try to save the courts. Those poor shitty courts.'

Ros was beaming at her. 'You couldn't get me off your team if
you tried, Douglas, you know that!'

The others all chimed in with their agreements and then Jay stuck a hand into the centre of the table and they laughingly all added theirs to the pile.

'In for the season?' Jackie asked, snorting with laughter as she looked each one of them in the eye individually.

'In for the season!' they cried and at least one drink flew off the table in a wet shatter.

The conversation split off into little pockets of chatter and Ros took Jackie's hand under the table. 'I'm proud of you,' she said gently.

'Thank you. I couldn't, and wouldn't, have done it without you,' Jackie replied, resting her head on Ros's shoulder.

'Now listen, no pressure, but I did bring these for you to take home and read over just to familiarise. . .' Ros pulled a sheaf of papers out of her bag and laid them on the table next to Jackie. Jackie skimmed over the words on the front and felt her happiness draining away.

'Ros, I asked you not to push this. I'm not ready to think about the divorce yet.' She tried to push the forms back towards Ros, but Ros laid a hand firmly on top of hers.

'I'm not saying you have to file, or do anything, but you do have to just start thinking about it. That's all.'

'OK, but did you have to do this now? Did you have to spoil my happy night?'

'I didn't think it would spoil a night; it's just some information.'

'Yes, information about a divorce I don't want to get.' Jackie's voice was rising.

'I'm not the one divorcing you, Jack, I'm—'

'No, but you're pushing it.' The others were trying their best not to look at the argument unfolding.

'Because I'm trying to protect you and help you protect yourself,' Ros insisted.

'Yeah right,' Jackie snorted before she could stop herself. 'You love that I'm not with him any more.'

Ros sniffed and sighed. 'I'm going to ignore that because you're angry and white wine turns us all into our mothers. Take the papers or don't take the papers. I'm just trying to help.' She picked up her wine glass and dived too loudly into a conversation with Claire and Renee. Jackie sat stewing, unsure who was in the wrong and desperate not to look at the papers on the table.

Jay leaned in and whispered, 'You OK?'

'Oh. . . yeah. I'm fine.'

'I, er, I could stay over again tonight if you like. If you don't want to be on your own?' Jay's eyes flicked meaningfully to the papers. Jackie's heart soared.

'Oh! Well, if you want to? But don't feel you have to. . . I mean, I don't need babysitting or anything.'

'No! Not at all. . . it's nice being at yours.'

Jackie smiled and nodded and joined back in with the chat. One side of her heart couldn't help but focus on the papers she had tucked into her bag under the table. Now she had to think about a divorce, and apologise to Ros somehow.

25

Jackie bounced into netball practice the next week, absolutely delighted to dive back into chatter and laughter and the mayhem of all these new strangers' lives colliding into friendships. She couldn't wait to carry on bonding with the team; and, if she had to, to throw a ball around, perhaps even run a little. If she had to. She felt simultaneously exposed and cushioned. It was a little disorientating, but ultimately good.

Claire stalked into the gym reception as Jackie was arriving. She was kitted out head to foot in new athletic wear and Jackie's jaw dropped.

'Oh, stop it, you'll inflate my head.' Claire swatted her appraising gaze away with a calm ease.

'You look better than I did at my wedding!' Jackie tutted, and Claire twinkled with amusement and a little self-congratulatory pride.

'Speaking of which, I noticed you weren't that keen on the divorce papers coming out at the pub last week. Everything all right?' God, Claire could get to the point. Jackie held the door to the changing rooms open for her and sighed.

'No, it's all good. It's fine, really. Just new territory for me, and Ros is. . . Ros is being good pushing me to do it but it's hard. You know?'

Claire nodded. 'Yes, completely. Legal stuff and friendships rarely mix. Let me know if you want me to set you up with a different firm. Could be best not to have Ros handle it?'

Jackie felt a wave of loyalty to Ros pass through her. 'Oh. Oh no, I couldn't do that. Well, maybe you're right, maybe that would be easier. I'll have a think about it. Thanks Claire.'

They gathered up their water bottles and made their way to the main hall.

Jackie waved at Ros as she entered the room. Ros was stood talking to a man, but they were too far away for her to see who it was. It must be the gym manager. She popped her bottle by a bench at the side of the hall, and it was only when she got to a few feet away that she realised who it was Ros was stood by.

Jackie's cheeks burst into flame. She was sure she could feel a red colour physically race up from her neck to the top of her powdery cheeks like a thermometer racing for the sky.

How on earth had Ros found him?

'Jackie!' he said pleasantly, his eyes crinkling into a smile that Jackie found herself already beginning to enjoy. He looked surprised to see her, but there was no way he could have been as surprised as she was. Jackie tried to force her brain to work quickly: if he was surprised to see her then he wasn't here *for* her. That was good. Was it? She remembered she needed to reply just before the silence got rude.

'Duncan!' She tried to sound casual, but she was convinced there was a clipped tone to her voice that he might detect. Ros would certainly notice it.

'What a small world!' He laughed. 'I wondered if there was a chance it would be. . . but I thought no, how could it be? Are you on Ros's team?'

'Oh, it's Ros's team now, is it?' Jackie arched an eyebrow jokingly at Ros, who tapped a foot, still waiting to see how Jackie would react. Duncan laughed, not reading any of the tension between the two women.

'I pay for the hall hire. And it's not cheap,' Ros said, and sniffed to show she wasn't bothered by Jackie's comment. 'Do you two know each other. . .?'

Ros didn't fool Jackie for a second, but she decided to play along to save face in front of Duncan. 'Well, not really, we happened to meet in a coffee shop when I was putting flyers up for the try-outs,' Jackie stated, and then saw a flicker of disappoint-ment cross Duncan's face. His expression pumped oxygen across the dying embers of her cheek flames and sent them roaring back to top heat. Was that rude of her to play it all down? Would he think it a rejection? It would be weirder to also bring up the actual rejection. . . God, this was all so difficult.

'I was looking for a coach for the team, like I mentioned at the Hawk the other night,' Ros said, reading between the searing red lines and helping Jackie out, 'and after a bit of looking, I met Duncan.'

'Right.' Jackie continued to play along; she smiled at Duncan in what she hoped was a very friendly way. 'I thought rugby was your thing?' Insecurity immediately racked her – would he find it weird that she had remembered the detail? She backtracked to try to obscure her mistake: 'Or was it hockey? I can't remember.' She felt completely paralysed by an inability to behave in any of the myriad ways she'd always managed up until this moment.

'It was rugby. Good memory. Yes, I can't say I'm a genius with netball, but I have helped out at the school with supervising the netball training. Not coaching, mind, just another pair of eyes, so I know the basics. Ros said you probably needed help with the basics. And maybe some fitness training? I can definitely do that. You'll probably outgrow me pretty quickly. But, like I said at the coffee shop, I mean, not that you'll remember, but I'm pretty newly retired and. . . bored.'

He was rambling too! Jackie felt the muscles at the base of her back relax a little.

'Yes, yes we're beginners. Well, Annie is very good. And Jay is sporty but the rest of us, we're a bit of a. . .'

'You're beginners.' God, he was so nice and solid. Jackie wanted to sit and talk to him for hours. She'd always wondered as a teenager and young woman if you just put up with having to date old people as you got older, or if you learned to try to fancy people with wrinkled skin and old hair. Standing in front of Duncan she realised that, thankfully, the latter was true and it hadn't been that hard to learn.

Duncan's hair didn't have a pinch that wasn't strikingly silver, and she wished she could go back in time and tell her teenage self not to worry: one day someone wouldn't be able to pay you enough money to date a twenty-something. Jackie put highlights through her hair to keep her grey a bit more on the blond end of the spectrum. Steve had used Just for Men to keep his head of hair a solid brown. She'd never thought anything of it. She wondered whether Steve would ever let himself go grey. She realised she'd drifted off down a thought hole and came back to the present; she was determined not to start comparing Duncan and Steve.

She smiled forcibly brightly at Duncan, holding his eye contact as long as she could without melting. 'Welcome to the team.'

If Jackie had found playing netball hard before, it was damn near impossible to play it while under the scrutiny of someone that she may or may not have warm fuzzy feelings for. They practised throwing and catching, or 'passing and receiving' as Jackie was trying to remember to call it, and she felt like every nerve ending in her legs and arms was hooked up to a taser. She had no memory of how she used to stand, or look, or smile because she was so focused on doing it normally that all traces of normal had flung themselves out of her body.

When she landed a foot right, or managed to keep the treacherous, slippery ball in her arms, she couldn't help herself sliding a coy look over to Duncan to see if he had noticed. Invariably he had. Jackie couldn't work out if he really was paying her more attention than the others or if that was just what she wanted to believe because she had a crush.

Oh God, crush. What a word. That was a word she thought she'd left behind in her teenage years with those boy bands.

By the time practice was over Jackie felt like she needed two showers: a hot one to think about Duncan in, and then another one to wash off.

'So,' she said, addressing Duncan but keeping her face buried in her bag, 'do you think you'll be able to help us?'

'Oh, well, perhaps. . . I'll be honest – I don't think I've got much netball chops, but I think with Annie's help I can be a good pair of eyes watching as you train. And I'll be good for drilling.'

There was a choking sound behind her, and Jackie spun round to see Kath and Jay stifling snorts into their own gym bags.

'Grow up!' giggled Jay, forcing an elbow into Kath's ribs.

'Pub then?' Ros called out to the rest of the team. There were nods of assent from most people, but Renee shook her head.

'I'm sorry, I can't tonight. I'd say have one for me but. . . I'm not sure you need encouraging.' She waved before dashing off. Jackie was still watching Renee leave, and reeling from proximity to Duncan, when she heard her own voice saying she couldn't make it. She wasn't really sure why she said it and before she could even think of an excuse Ros was staring wide-eyed in dismay.

'We always go to the pub.' She was seconds away from stamping her feet, Jackie would swear.

'Well, I can't tonight. And I don't *always* go.' She tried to assert herself, a voice in her head telling her Duncan wouldn't like her if he thought she was always pickled.

'Yes, you do,' Jay and Ros said in unison, and Duncan smiled and looked down at his shoes.

'Well, I just can't tonight because of reasons. OK?' Jackie hadn't used this petulant a tone since she'd been fifteen and standing at the top of the stairs declaring she hadn't asked to be born because her parents wouldn't let her go to the cinema with her friends.

She picked up her bag and looked Ros defiantly in the eye. 'I'm sorry Ros, I just have a thing tomorrow. A grandchild-type thing.

It's important and I can't be squiffy-eyed for it.' To her surprise, Ros looked hurt.

'Oh, a grandchild thing. Well, I wouldn't know anything about that, would I? Not having had any and all. Ah well, you enjoy your early night and we non-grandparents will go and drink the bar dry. By the way, if you can get a look at those divorce papers this week I think that would be best.' She turned away to grab her bag, her movements hurt and jerky. Jackie didn't press it. She said her goodbyes to everyone, attempting a bit more fizzy eye contact with Duncan before she left.

The cool air outside the gym felt beautiful on her face, sliding the warmth off it and whisking it away into the night air. Jackie breathed in and felt herself let go her stomach muscles. How long had she been sucking her stomach in? She didn't have to wonder for long though, as the sound of Duncan's voice behind her seemed to make them involuntarily retreat back in again.

'Jackie?' he called, and she turned round, hoping her face looked serene and not wound up.

'Oh, hi Duncan!' she said, and then wondered if that was trying a bit too hard to not try. This was exhausting. When was the last time she had cared how she said hello to Steve? She tried to block Steve out of her head and focus on Duncan. There was nothing to feel wrong or guilty about even if she did fancy Duncan. Which she definitely did and she definitely was not ready to admit yet. Or even admit she wasn't admitting it.

'I just wanted to say, I think I'm on to your friend Ros there. . .' He was either a bit twinkly or Jackie was a bit giddy. Maybe both.

Jackie didn't fully understand. Was he telling her liked Ros? 'Sorry, what do you mean?'

It was Duncan's turn to look uncertain. 'I. . . I mean, she's doing her very best to set us up, isn't she?'

'Oh. . . well, yes. Essentially yes. I'm very newly separated and Ros. . . well, I told her about you, so I suppose she's rather latched on to that.'

'I'm sorry. If I'd known you'd be here I wouldn't have agreed,' he said softly.

'No?'

'Actually that might be a lie.' He grinned, sheepishly. 'There was a big part of me that only said yes to that random woman's request for a netball coach in case you were here.' He laughed, and then forced his face into a more serious expression. 'But now I do know you're here, I think I will tell Ros I'm not the best for helping you with netball. I don't want to make your team awkward for you. Or come across like a stalker.'

'Oh, you didn't make it awkward. . .' she started, and then gave up. 'Yes, I think that's probably best.'

He smiled sadly and nodded. 'It was nice to see you again, Jackie. I hope you're coping OK, with the separation.' He smiled a smile that looked decisive and began to walk away from the glowing lights of the sports centre towards his car.

Jackie's pulse was a siren. 'Let's go for that drink.' She threw it across the tarmac before she could swallow it again. She watched her words bounce on the wet ground and hoped he'd scoop up the pass. She didn't know what she was doing. She thought of Renee's face when she'd nearly turned down the team, and then how happy she'd looked in the pub the week before. She wanted that. To start saying yes and see if it brought good things. She waited for the inevitable humiliation of having put herself out there. For him to get in his car and drive away and for her to always know she'd tried and he'd not actually wanted her. Why would he want her? This excruciating, humiliating half-second was why she didn't normally blurt things like that out. Why she had been safer not being anything adventurous.

And then he stopped, and to her immense relief, turned.

'I much prefer a drink to coaching. Where?'

'How about the White Hind?' she offered. 'Somewhere a bit different to the Hawk?' Ros and Jay were coming out of the gym, and Duncan caught Jackie's meaning instantly.

'Absolutely.' He nodded.

'Tomorrow night?'

He nodded and smiled widely. He looked so genuinely happy at the prospect of a date with her that Jackie could barely compute what he was seeing in this exchange. Tears threatened her eyelids and she nodded back and scuttled to her car before Ros could catch up with her and continue the argument she was in that she didn't understand. Her ears rang in the silence of the car. A date. For goodness sake.

26

Jackie swung the car into the driveway, feeling buoyant. Perhaps these were those elusive endorphins you were supposed to get from exercising? It could be, she told herself, wanting to deny that the good mood was entirely caused by Duncan and their proposed drink the next night.

She pulled up the handbrake and climbed out of the car. She might even have whistled if she'd been able to. Perhaps whistling would be the next thing she would conquer? She grabbed her bag off the passenger seat and locked the car.

'Jack?' A voice came out of the darkness on the front step.

'Jesus Christ!' Jackie fell back against the car, feeling for the solidity of the metal to support her.

'It's me, Jack. It's just me.' Steve stepped out of the shadow of the porch, and Jackie swallowed the acidic taste at the back of her mouth.

'Jesus *fucking* Christ Steve, what are you doing lurking in the shadows like that? You scared the devil out of me!' Jackie was furious. She glanced about at the neighbours' windows to check no lights were coming on from the disturbance. It wasn't late. It was only just gone ten. But that was late here, if you believed the 'polite' notes about noisy barbecues that sometimes came from number twenty-four.

'You took my key away; I couldn't get in.'

'You can't get into any of the other houses on the street either. . . because you don't live in those houses. And you don't live here.' Jackie's heart rate had begun to drop back to normal, but now the anger was helping it gain pace again. It felt good throwing words at Steve. She felt powerful instead of cowed.

'Where have you been?' Steve asked, waving her concerns away with his direct question.

'Out.' Jackie got movement back into her feet and walked past him to the front door.

'Well, I got that. Oh, come on Jack, don't be like that. I'm trying to be friendly.'

Jackie wheeled round. 'Don't be like that?!' she half-shouted and then caught herself as she saw a curtain twitch. 'My God, were you always this callous?'

'I just wanted to check you were OK. . . after, after last time.' Steve's voice had an unattractive whiny note in it and Jackie wanted to just get in the house and be rid of him, but she felt herself give in to the pressure not to be rude. She swallowed the sentence her mind was forming, telling him the only reason she had not been OK 'last time' was because he had turned up. Cursing herself silently for her weakness, she let him into the house.

On autopilot, she put the kettle on and set out two mugs with tea bags inside. She might be single, old and in a brave new world, but she was still British after all.

'So. . . good night?' Steve sat at the counter and drummed a finger lightly on the surface.

'Yes, thank you,' Jackie said stiffly. An image of Duncan stood in the car park flashed into her mind and she felt her stomach lurch at how far away that moment felt now she was in the kitchen with Steve like old times. She caught sight of the divorce papers sitting at the end of the worktop and felt a shot of strength at their existence.

'What were you up to?' Steve's eyes followed hers to the papers and away again. His tone was light, but it crumbled the last of Jackie's civility and she whirled round, wishing she had put the teaspoon down before she did so that she wasn't holding it as she unloaded on him.

'It's none of your business, Steve. I was out. Out getting on with my life. The life you walked out of because you didn't want to be here any more and yet, somehow, every time I come home, here you are, back in the house you didn't want to be in.'

'Don't be like this, Jackie. I want there to be a way we can be friends out of all this. We've got too much between us to just walk away and pretend none of it happened.'

'I'm not pretending none of it happened! I'm working out how to carry on now that *all* of it happened! Our marriage *and* you leaving me! It's impossible to pretend none of it happened because it's everywhere! I can't even have a drink without Ros showing divorce papers to me and telling me I should be getting on with it.' Jackie's blood was pounding in her ears, and she gripped the teaspoon like a talisman, looking back at the papers. Steve looked again too and then slowly pulled the pages across the worktop. He scanned the top page for a few seconds and then looked up at her.

'But what about me?' His voice was very small.

'What about you?' She kept her voice low and even. That question wasn't in any version of this conversation she had practised.

'I don't know.' He sagged. 'You're right. I'm sorry. I shouldn't be here. It's just. . . I don't know. I should go.' He made no move to go.

The teaspoon begged Jackie silently not to cave, but she felt her will dissolve. She'd spent too long being the caregiver not to care. 'What's happened?' She turned back round to the tea so that he wouldn't see her tears building. The disappointment she felt in herself was immense. A sea of resentment at her own lack of spine. It washed up against the wall at the back of her eyes, pushing all the achy stingy buttons.

'I miss you,' he said simply. She pictured him sat behind her examining the ends of his fingers the way he did when they had to talk about something serious that he was uncomfortable with. Three miscarriages and a remortgage had seen those fingers examined with forensic detail. 'I know. . . you're right, I left and I should stay. . . left. But if the Labour Party can't do it, how am I supposed to?'

She let his joke die softly in the silence of the kitchen. He sniffed a laugh to himself and then sighed, pushing the legal papers away from him 'Everything feels odd. Like I'm on temporary mode. Every time I drive *home*,' he emphasised the word to make it sound alien and wrong, 'it feels like I'm pretending somehow. Like I'm on a weird holiday. This feels like my home. You feel like my home.'

Jackie was frozen. Tea dripped off the sodden bag on the teaspoon to the worktop. She'd have to bleach the surface tomorrow to get the tannin off.

'I suppose that's natural. . .' She tried to get words of comfort out to him, but they dried in her mouth and stopped. The words felt like they needed an unnatural amount of air to push them through her throat. They didn't want to come out, that was what it was. How did her unformed words stick to their guns better than she did?

She heard him get off the chair and prayed he wouldn't come towards her, but whatever deity she temporarily believed in ignored her, and she felt Steve's hands on her waist. She sucked in breath at the feeling of being touched so intimately. The familiarity outweighed the anger and betrayal. It would be so easy to just melt back into him and go back to the way things were. She wouldn't have to try any more: try to be this exuberant, busy person. She could just be original-flavour Jackie who didn't know any better.

She let go the teaspoon and laid it gently on the counter before turning round to face Steve. He was close. So close she could smell a thousand micro-scents that smelled like her life.

'Do you still love me?' she asked, trying not to let her voice sound breathy, too Jessica Rabbit.

'Yes.' He looked at her intently and she believed him.

'Right.' She nodded and took in a breath. As she breathed in, she noticed her stomach: sitting proudly out above her trousers' waistline. 'Right,' she said again, to buy herself some time to ponder. Was it good that she wasn't sucking it in? She certainly felt more comfortable with Steve. Of course she did. You couldn't not after that long together. But was it a good or a bad sign that she'd subconsciously sucked it in around Duncan?

'If you say right again I'm going to have to kiss you,' Steve said with a smile and Jackie groaned at the cheesiness of it. She batted his shoulder with a hand to half-reprimand his silliness and then suddenly they were kissing. He pressed her lips gently but firmly and she felt electric, kissing him with a passion that hadn't existed between them in a long time. She felt her eyes shedding the tears that had built up and she kissed back gently and expressively, hoping that when she opened her eyes none of the last months would have happened. He left one final kiss on her lips and then pulled back, wiping a stray tear off her cheek with his thumb.

'Right,' she said, and then laughed, hearing how her nose had become runny from the tears.

'Right,' he said and his hands found hers.

'So. . . what does this mean?'

His eyes immediately flicked to the kitchen door, even as his hands squeezed hers giving her some comfort that those words weren't an enormous mistake.

'I just don't know, Jack,' he said softly, and she believed his uncertainty, 'I don't know. I feel like I owe it to Michelle to see. . . to see what we have but here, with you, this feels like me. This feels like home. I don't know.'

Jackie felt herself trembling and she pulled her hands out of Steve's. It felt like a light going out. His fingers made a slight grasp to keep her there, but her skin slid off his.

'I need you to go, then,' Jackie said quietly but firmly, trying to keep all emotion out of her voice. 'You are not being fair.

Or kind. To either of us, actually. Me or Michelle.' It was easier to do this if it was in pretence of protecting someone else's feelings.

His eyes were wide open, looking beseechingly at her. She could see Leon and Michael in his face, looking up sadly at her when she told them off as children. 'I didn't realise,' Steve said. 'I just thought. . . I thought you'd be fine. You have the house, and everything has pretty much carried on as normal for you, just without me. I didn't think you would struggle.'

Jackie reeled at that. 'You think just because I didn't physically move out everything stayed the same for me?' Was he stupid? But, was he stupid?

'Well. . .' Steve shook his head, looking like he was grappling with his thoughts.

'Are you stupid?' The words shot out of her mouth like they were greased, and he flinched.

'No need to be rude. I'm trying to open up to you here.' He backed away and Jackie wished she weren't so squashed up against the sideboard. She turned round to the half-finished tea and then picked up one cup and poured it down the sink. It was the best she could think of as a power move. Not quite what Meryl Streep would do in one of the many billion films Jackie had ever been very impressed with her in, but it was a start. 'What are you doing?' His whininess set her teeth on edge, and she consciously relaxed her jaw to ease the pressure and keep herself calm.

'You have absolutely no idea, do you? You think nothing much has happened to me because I've stayed in the house? You walked out on me, Steve! You left me! Completely out of the blue, you just left me! You wouldn't have even told me if the traffic had been twenty minutes worse. How do you think you have it worse than me?' She was gobsmacked, and also curious.

'I don't mean I have it worse than you. That's not what I mean, you're putting words in my mouth. It's not a competition for worst off anyway. I just meant like, not as much changed for you. . . I'm trying to work out living somewhere else, with someone else. . . not just Mich, but her family too, and it's hard. I feel like an imposter: I'm just transplanted into another house and another life. That's all. I'm not trying to say it's harder for me, I know what I did. I just, I just thought less was different for you because. . . because you're still here.'

'Then I don't think you have any idea of how much I made my life about us,' Jackie said, feeling hollow. Not so much scooped out as just suddenly rinsed. Like when you've been swimming in the sea for too long and when you get out you still feel the waves knocking. She picked up her faithful teaspoon, promising herself to always remember which spoon this was and treat it nicer than the others. She reached for the milk and stirred it into her tea. 'Everything I did was for some version of us. I let my entire life be about us, Steve. You leaving hasn't just meant I have one fewer person to talk to in a day: it's just undone everything I was.'

'Jackie, I. . .'

She felt strangely cold and distant. 'No, I'm not interested. This helps. Actually, this helps. I was struggling to understand how you could do this to me: the affair, the leaving. . . it didn't make sense with all we had. But if you thought we were just two people leading separate lives I understand it more. You didn't know how much of me was us. You weren't doing the same.' Jackie estimated she had a maximum of four more minutes before she was entirely consumed by the sort of sobs that won you an Oscar without you even needing to be Meryl Streep. She turned round and headed up the stairs. The sound of him calling after her didn't break her stride.

'Should I go?'

'I don't care,' she called back from the top of the stairs and then closed the door to the bedroom. She lay down on the bed, on top of the duvet cover, and waited for either the sound of the front door or the sobs to begin. The front door was first and she lay there waiting to be consumed, but the sobs never came. She felt frozen and blank. Somehow this was worse than his initial leaving. The tea went cold by the bed and when she woke in the morning, it followed Steve's cup down the kitchen sink.

27

Ros had flown round to the house as soon as traffic had, not so much allowed her, but been forced to acquiesce to her need to be with her best friend.

'You *kissed* him?' she screeched, before Jackie even had the door fully open.

'Shhhhhh!' Jackie hissed, her eyes searching the neighbours' houses for signs of the Neighbourhood Watch taking up arms against her. 'At least get in the house before you start treating me like a pariah.'

'If only you were a pariah! You might have eaten him instead of kissing him!'

Jackie paused. 'That's a piranha.'

'Same difference. You *kissed* him?' Ros demanded.

Jackie hurried Ros into the house and closed the front door firmly behind her. 'I wouldn't say I kissed him, but yes we kissed. A small amount of stupid kissing happened.'

'You're not taking him back?' Ros said it like a question but there was enough strength in her voice for Jackie to feel it like an instruction. She bristled.

'I might,' she said, wondering why on earth she'd said that when she had exactly no intention or opportunity to do so. 'It wouldn't be the end of the world if I did, would it?'

Ros's eyes flared. 'Jackie, don't you dare! You can't take back a man that's been cheating on you for all this time!'

'He didn't cheat on me for longer than he did cheat on me.' Something about Ros's insistence made Jackie fight the other side, for no reason she wanted to explore. She felt backed into a corner by Ros. She didn't want to be told what to do by anyone; even someone who loved her as much as Ros did.

'You're being ridiculous.' Ros flounced into the kitchen and threw her bag onto the table.

'You're the one who has run out of work to come here and find out about some kiss that barely means anything.'

'How can a kiss with your recently separated ex-husband barely mean anything?'

Jackie was impressed with the stamina in Ros's eyes. They could really go some time without blinking.

'Because it was just kissing.' Jackie was exasperated. Why did she have to explain herself? Wasn't she the victim in this? 'I have kissed Steve more times than. . . more times than I've done most things. Kissing him is as familiar as waving to someone. We were arguing, or maybe we weren't arguing. . . maybe that was when he was being sad. He'd just seen the divorce papers. I don't know but it was a bit heated and there was a little kiss. It didn't mean anything.'

Ros wasn't cooled. 'And then what?'

'And then we stopped kissing.' Jackie remembered what she'd said post-kiss and decided Ros didn't need to know.

'So, you don't want him back then?'

'No. Well. . .' No was what had come out of Jackie's mouth, but was it true? Or was it just because she wanted to seem like she didn't want him back to please Ros?

'Well. . .?' Ros wasn't letting it go. Jackie didn't like this. Wasn't a friend supposed to support you no matter what you chose? Even if what you chose was your lying soon-to-be-ex-husband?

'Well. . . no, I don't want him back under the current circumstances, but if there was a way to go back to having him the way it was before any of this happened then maybe I would choose that? That would be nice.' Ros looked hurt for reasons Jackie couldn't quite fathom. She thought fondly of the non-judgemental teaspoon who had briefly been her best friend last night. Perhaps spoons were better fodder for friendships than people? Hell, perhaps she could marry the spoon? No. It would only run away with a younger dish. Jackie smiled sadly at her tired brain-shambles and shook the thoughts away.

'I see,' was all Ros said.

'Would you like some tea?' Jackie felt tired. Far too tired to go on a date with a perfect stranger that evening. She would have to cancel.

'No, I've to get back to the office.' Ros was standing up.

'Oh, Ros, don't leave like this. I don't like it when we're cross with each other.'

'I'm not cross,' Ros said crossly. 'I just have a meeting. Where are you with that paperwork?'

'I'm nowhere,' she said, her lips tight. There was no way Ros thought this was going to calm things down between them.

'I'm not pushing, I just thought. . .'

'You just got a text from me telling you that Steve and I had kissed and the first thing you did was race round to help me fill out forms to divorce him?'

Ros flung her arms up in a good impression of an irate footballer. 'Yeah. So sue me. I don't want my best friend to be fucked over in a divorce by her scumbag ex.'

Jackie blazed, caught between hating confrontation and desperately wanting there to be someone in her life that she didn't lie down in front of.

Perhaps she could distract Ros with mention of the date with Duncan? No, she decided she didn't want to share that with Ros. She felt like Ros would be pro anything that kept her away from Steve but for the time being she just wanted it to stay a secret.

Ros's heels were loud in the hall as they headed back to the front door. Jackie had never noticed how clacky they were before but, she supposed, that was probably because they were usually always talking.

'Well, I'll see you then,' Jackie said, lamely.

'The Hawk tonight? Clear the air?'

That was as close to an apology as Jackie had ever got out of Ros. She wished she could say yes. 'I can't, I have. . . um, plans tonight.' Damn her brain for not thinking something up quicker.

'Oh. . .?' Ros was so good at letting a silence hang.

'I have a date.' Jackie begrudgingly gave away her secret.

Ros's eyes narrowed suspiciously. 'Not with Steve?'

Again, Jackie felt her hackles rising at Ros so blatantly giving her unsolicited opinion. 'So what if it is Steve? Not that it is. It's not Steve. But if it were, you somehow managed to be my best friend for the first thirty-four years of my marriage, so if we do decide to give it another go on the other side of all this then I hope you are still up for being there for me.' It was possibly the sharpest she had ever spoken to Ros and they both looked at each other, not sure to where to go from here.

'But you say it's not Steve? So. . . so it isn't Steve?'

'It's not Steve. It's Duncan. Which I can only assume you're thrilled about as it was you that sought him out and brought him in to the netball to get me to see him again. Happy now? You've got your way.'

Ros didn't have anything to say back to that and Jackie puffed her chest in her hollow victory.

28

Jackie's residual anger at Steve and Ros followed her all the way through into the evening and her date with Duncan. She'd been quite surprised to find herself excited to get ready, but the mood hangover made her impatient with her wardrobe and angry with her body in its clothes. When she sat down at her dressing table to apply make-up, she found herself angry all over again that her mascara was clumpy and the liquid eyeliner long since dried up. How long was it since she had put make-up on? She decided to just freshen up and go au naturel. Sod Duncan. If he couldn't fancy her as she was then he was a rat who didn't deserve her. She caught herself getting premeditatively angry with Duncan and forced herself back into a more reasonable place. He hadn't done anything wrong.

The trouble was, she didn't have a mental template for sitting opposite Duncan at dinner. She only had Steve's face to use and she was incredibly angry at that face, making it a terrible Duncan placeholder.

Jackie swung her car into a parking space outside the White Hind and sat for a moment in the post-engine silence. She'd driven so that wine had to be limited and she could keep a tighter grip on her mouth and behaviour. Everything felt very in flux, and she firmly wanted things back out of flux. What is flux? She shook her head and tried to focus.

Crossing the threshold into the restaurant of the pub, she felt a world of memories come racing up to greet her. This was where they'd come for dinner the night before Michael moved abroad. Leon sulking because he was nervous about missing his brother but didn't want to admit it. It had felt so momentous and exciting seeing him go, but she'd sat there thinking casual dinners like this with all four of them would be few and far between from now on. It had been a perfect evening. But no, actually, it hadn't been. . . because Steve had kept prattling on about Michael being such a real man now and she'd noticed it prickling Leon but hadn't said anything. She hadn't wanted to ruin the moment out loud, so she'd let it be ruined for Leon silently.

Duncan waved and stood to greet her. He'd picked a nice little spot by the fireplace, although it was nowhere near cold enough for them to have lit it.

'You look lovely,' Duncan said, smiling.

'Thank you.' Jackie smiled back, a bit prim and nervous. 'You look very fine yourself.' What was that as an opening line? It came out neither fluid and fifties-style Grace Kelly nor up-to-the-minute rapper. She flushed. 'Can I get you a drink?'

'Lovely, thank you. I'll have an ale.' He smiled and sat, and Jackie was relieved he hadn't pulled the man card and insisted on getting the first round. She ordered their drinks and brought them back to the table, wondering what on earth they were going to talk about.

'So, why netball?' he asked, solving her problem.

She blinked. 'It was an accident, really. Ros was organising a work team and she left a flyer at my house and then my ex-husband saw it and laughed at the idea of me playing and then Ros. . . Ros and I just sort of. . . decided to play. Our team really is the product of wine and spite.' She laughed at herself, and he smiled, and she felt herself relaxing.

'That's as good a reason as any! What an arsehole for laughing at you.'

'Yeah. . . kind of, I mean, this time last year I'd have just laughed and agreed with him, to be honest. What am I doing playing netball? I don't know the game, I'm not sure if I like it but I do like having a hobby. It feels like a new toy.'

'I took up surfing after my divorce.'

Jackie looked at Duncan's neat, stocky build.

'You didn't?' She just plain couldn't imagine him on a surfboard, and she swallowed her attempted laugh right down into the depths of her desire to not be Steve.

'I did!' He smiled and nodded confirmation. 'I wanted to do something so, so different to life before the divorce and I just thought, what have I never done and never wanted to do?'

'But why do something you'd never wanted to do?'

'To see if I'd actually never want to do it or whether I'd just never thought of myself doing it.'

'And?'

'Hated it. Awful, awful idea. The sea is very salty, and what isn't salt is something's faecal matter. The best way to be in the sea is to be in a very steady boat. Not a flat piece of nothing that's constantly trying to turf you into the salt and faecal matter. I kept it up for six months and then put all the gear in the garage and gave up on it.'

Jackie laughed and it felt nice. He was funny. That was good. It also made her instantly notice that she wasn't being funny; so what would be his reason for wanting to see her again? She poured a sip of wine onto the paranoia, hoping it would go the way of dampening not exacerbating.

'So, did you find something better than surfing?' she asked.

'I did. I found Crete.'

'Crete? Good work. Had we lost it?' He laughed and a small tally chart in her mind popped up with 1–1 on it, making her feel relaxed. She could be funny. She made Ros laugh all the time, just at her not with her. The wine left a note to tell her to apologise to Ros. She didn't want to be angry with Ros.

'I had somehow misplaced going abroad. I don't know how we let it slip but I think, we, me and my ex-wife, got so squabbly about everything towards the end that we just stopped doing anything that gave us more reasons to disagree. Going abroad was one of the big ones.'

'What would you squabble over?' Jackie thought back over holidays with her own family; there hadn't been much to argue over. She made all the decisions and Steve carried round a wallet full of euros paying for it. Teamwork.

'Where to go, what kind of accommodation, how long to stay for, where to eat out. . . anything and everything.' Duncan looked exhausted just thinking about it.

'Gosh, we never argued about anything like that. So you'd both be involved in deciding where you went?'

Duncan looked at her like she was mad. 'Of course. You weren't?'

'No.' Jackie thought on it; it had never seemed odd before, but now she thought of it why hadn't Steve had any input? 'No, I just planned it and packed and organised and then Steve. . . well, Steve came.'

'I'd have loved that. No arguments. Bliss! I didn't realise how much we'd stopped doing until we split up and then I could suddenly do all these things without having to bicker. That's when I bought the house in Crete.'

The divorce conversation was starting to make Jackie feel decidedly down and she jumped on the mention of the house to try to divert them both from ex-chat. It was probably the subject of a thousand blogs that you shouldn't spend a first date talking about previous partners if you had any intentions of a kiss at the end of it.

'You bought a house in Crete?' She suddenly wondered if there was a lot of money hidden away in this man's life. An unbidden image of Carmela Soprano jumped into her mind's eye.

'Yes, in Koutouloufari, about an hour out of Hersonissos. I just thought, why not eh? I like sun and gyros. Why not spend a few months of the year indulging in both ad nauseam?'

Jackie laughed and wondered if that was how you were supposed to pronounce gyros. If it was, she'd been doing it wrong all her life. 'How often do you go?'

'Whenever I like. It's my promise to myself: I don't have to go, but whenever I want to go I can. Why not?' He sipped his pint, looking relaxed.

'Gosh. How nice to be so carefree!' Jackie sipped her drink too and tried to mimic his relaxed pose.

'What would stop you doing it?' he asked, putting his drink down on the table.

'Stop me doing what?'

'Going to Crete?'

'I don't go to Crete. . .?' Jackie really had lost the thread of this conversation somewhere.

'No, I know.' He chuckled easily, 'But, what stops you, I mean? Sorry – I phrased that question confusingly.'

'Oh! Oh, I see! Oh, all sorts. . .' she said lamely, wondering what on earth she was going to produce as evidence. 'Grandkids. . . the netball team. Nothing.' She laughed and found refreshing honesty suddenly: 'Absolutely nothing would stop me. I'm just not brave enough!'

'Have you eaten?' he asked, and Jackie's eyes met his across the table and she felt exposed and a bit raw. She hoped he wasn't basing that question on the stomach gurgles she could hear herself. She felt excited but wary. Was this passion?

'No, let's have dinner.'

They ate, but the fact that it was edible was all Jackie really noticed. She felt like a video game of herself hitting all the motions of being on a date; none of it felt real. But, and this was the crucial part, it didn't feel bad either. There was no sickly feeling of wrongness pacing about the base of her chest telling her to flee.

When the cheque was argued over and paid, and the table cleared, they sat with no more excuses tying them to the meal.

'This was really nice,' Jackie admitted softly.

'Yes, it was,' Duncan agreed.

'Shall we do it again some time?'

'That would be exactly what I was hoping you would say.' He had a very contagious smile; it really used all of his face and seemed almost too joyous for such a solid-looking man. 'And before you worry, Jackie, I'm not expecting this to be anything other than seeing what happens. I don't mean to overstep, but, just. . . don't worry about anything other than where we're going to go to just do exactly this again.'

Jackie let out the breath that had been cowering under her ribcage. How had he known? More to the point, how had she stumbled out of a marriage and into a date this good? Dating hadn't been like this the last time she did it!

'I'll get my thinking cap on,' she said with a wink, and they stood to leave. He escorted her to her car and then as she turned, ready to negotiate the awkward moments at the end of the date, he kissed her. His hand lifted her chin gently from underneath and there was a moment when his eyes met hers, silently checking for permission. For all the money in all the Cayman bank accounts she couldn't have honestly said whether she nodded or not, but she felt like she was nodding; and then he placed the shortest, gentlest whisper of a kiss on her lips before pulling back.

'Thank you for a wonderful evening,' he said, stepping back to allow her to get into the car. She waved from behind the steering wheel and, before she left the car park, saw him in her mirror, still stood there, watching her leave.

The house and front porch were mercifully Steve-free when she arrived home and she floated up to bed feeling for all the world like she could be wanted.

29

It was a day of the boys. If they hadn't both been so equally infuriating in their own ways, it might have felt like the old days of raising them. Or perhaps they had been this equally infuriating in those days and she'd just sanded down the splinters of irritation in her memories of it.

Michael had phoned first.

'I'm so proud of you, Mum!' She'd heard his beam down the phone.

'You are?' she said, racking her brain for what she'd done that anyone would be proud of. Irrationally, the first thought through her mind was how well she had done on the date with Duncan. But, for starters Michael didn't know about that, and secondly, if he had, he probably wouldn't ring her to say she'd done it well.

'Yes! I read the article about you standing up to the building company and stopping them cramming more houses in. Amazing! You should have told me you were doing it. Those houses are little heat blocks – the concrete just pounds out CO_2. Not to mention what it does to the water table squashing so much into. . .'

She knew from experience she needed to cut him off before he started mentioning things he would forward to her. There was a guilty little folder in her email in-box of things that he had forwarded her that she needed to read one day in case he ever quizzed her. Luckily his attention span didn't stretch much further than the day he was on and the impending environmental disaster. Jackie always meant to care more, but it just felt like there were always earlier deadlines than the apocalypse.

'How did you find out about it?' she asked.

'I read the column in the *Gazette*.'

'How did you know about that?'

'I have a Google alert on your name.'

'A what now?'

'A Google alert. On your name. So whenever "Jackie Doug-las" appears new on the internet I get an email to tell me,' he explained simply.

'But I'm never on the internet.' What a bizarre thing to be able to do, she thought, shaking her head at the ways Michael would always manage to find to surprise her.

'No, I know. This is the first time I've ever got the alert and it's been you. I read the article – terrible grammar but really cool that you're doing it.'

Jackie made a mental note to tell Jay that Michael thought Laurel's grammar was terrible. Perhaps it would be the start of a romance between Jay and Michael, and he would finally come home and do something she understood. No. She told herself off silently: stop trying to wish your life on him. He's happier than you. 'Well, thank you darling. Is all OK with you?'

'Oh, yes,' he said vaguely. 'As well as it ever is.' He was always so jovially dismal, that was the most confusing thing about Michael. The cheerful pessimist. 'Listen, I've got to go – the bus is here. But, Mum, I'm dead proud of you.' Was that a slight northern accent he'd picked up? Where was he again?

'Oh. OK love. Well, thank you for calling. Let's have a proper chat soon, shall we?'

'Yes, by next week I should be somewhere with a landline so we can have a proper catch-up. Give my love to Aunty Ros. Love you Mum.'

The phone clicked off and her tiny whirlwind was gone. It was hard not to picture him dashing off as he had as a child: never with enough layers on and always too close to the road. He used to like padding along the white line of the kerb. For a moment she saw a memory of him doing it as they all walked home from primary school. She remembered detachedly thinking that it was a weird coincidence that, just as she was musing, *this is one of those picture-perfect moments that you think parenting will all be,* Michael wobbled on the kerb, horribly timed to coincide with a speeding Skoda. Steve had grabbed Michael's elbow just in time and wrenched him back onto the pavement and her heart had thrown itself so hard at her ribcage that she'd been sure it would bruise. Michael had cried from the shock and his tears forced Jackie's back into their box so she could be his mother. After that she told him off for walking on the kerb countless times, but would still often see him from the window, dawdling along in his own world, wobbling, near their world.

She was still stood by her phone thinking about Michael when it rang again. This time it was Leon.

'Is it Mother's Day?' she said, lightly.

'That's in March.' Leon articulated his frown. 'Are you all right?'

'Yes, yes – just being silly because I've just had Michael on the phone.'

'He all right?' Leon asked out of courtesy.

'Yes, fine I think. He saw the column about my netball team and just called to say he'd seen it.'

'Oh, right. Yes, that's why I was calling too.' Leon swallowed and Jackie sensed a hesitation in him. 'Are you part of this committee to block the park?'

'Uh, no. No, I'm not part of any committee?'

'Right,' Leon cleared his throat, uncomfortable with having the conversation, 'it's just the article made it seem like you were part of the groups trying to stop them putting the park in. We've spent a lot of time fundraising for that park and it'll be great for the children on our estate: for Freya.'

'Right, well, sorry love; I didn't know you had been doing that.'

'Did I not mention it the other week?'

His voice had an impatient note to it that made Jackie feel cornered, and she thought back to that day at the playground with Freya playing in the puddles, but her mind played her nothing except thoughts of being without Steve. 'I don't remember if you did. Sorry darling.' She wished she wasn't apologising, actually, but the word did seem to be coming out of her mouth. 'I didn't mean to jump into a campaign: I just happened to start playing netball and this whole thing came with it.'

'It's a bit embarrassing for me with some of the other parents at nursery.' He was curt.

'Oh. . . but one of our players is a mum at your nursery, so. . . so that should help?' She trailed off a bit lamely, but she didn't really know what to say. 'What is it you wanted, really, Leon?' She offered the question tentatively as though pushing it across a floor in a peace talk. 'Is this you asking me not to play on the team?'

'No, not at all, Mum. Don't be dramatic.' Leon sighed, and Jackie swallowed her impulse to tell him she hadn't been dramatic in the slightest. He could be so like his father sometimes: no coping mechanism for the complicated. 'I just. . . we really want the playground to go ahead.'

'I'd love you to have a playground, love, but. . . well, there needs to be somewhere to play netball too, doesn't there? And there are plenty of parks around here and only one court.'

'Yes, but you have to cross four lanes of roads to get to the nearest park from our house so a lot of the parents on the estate are really happy about having this one a bit nearer. It's for the children, you know.'

'I really do understand, darling, and it's not like I started the petition to save the courts, I just happened to start playing netball. I know the children need parks but, well, us grown-ups need somewhere too.' Was this a petty thing to say? She felt on very strange ground in this conversation. It felt like Leon expected her to be able to snap her fingers and give the go-ahead for the park if he asked her firmly enough.

'Right,' he said thinly.

'Leon, are you angry with me?' This was excruciating.

'No, Mum, I'm not angry. I'm frustrated with the whole situation, and it was just quite a surprise to see your name on the other side, that's all.'

This genuinely made Jackie laugh out loud, but Leon didn't join in on the other end. 'I'm not on the other side, love,' she said. 'I'm really just a casual netball player, and Ros got a journalist to write about us, and it's loosely connected to this netball courts thing, that I didn't really know you were involved in.'

'I did tell you the other week,' he complained.

'Leon, that was months ago, sweetheart, and I had just split up from your dad, so I wasn't really processing things. Perhaps if you'd rung me recently we'd have discussed it.' She heard the words pouring out like every mother who had ever been a punchline.

'I do try and text you, but you don't reply!'

'Leon, I don't want to have an argument. I'm sorry it was a surprise, but I don't think it's as big a deal as you're making out.'

'Sure, OK.' He sounded a bit sullen, but then she heard a big sigh and his voice cleared, 'Yeah, you're right. Sorry Mum – I'm glad you're still enjoying the netball. I'd better go, I've got to get Freya. I'll speak to you soon. Love you.'

'Love you too. Bye love.'

They hung up and Jackie breathed out. It wasn't like Leon to be stroppy. He must be stressed. She'd take him out for lunch soon. The last thing she needed was another complication. Perhaps she should walk away from the team? It was nothing but trouble. The problem was, she was really just starting to love it.

30

'Oh . . . oh! Oh bollocks, no wait: YES!'

The ball thwacked into Jackie's hands and for the first time she managed to hold on to it despite the stinging skin. The surprise caught her off guard and she turned to wave it at Ros: 'I caught it!' she called excitedly and Ros hopped about, thrilled. Jackie was seconds away from throwing it when the whistle blew.

'Footwork!' called the referee and Jackie looked around, startled.

'What did I do wrong?' she asked.

'You moved both your feet. That's a footwork offence.' The referee signalled to one of the opposing team to come over and take the ball.

'Oh, yes, but I was only showing Ros that I'd caught it. I put them back where they were before I went on to throw it.'

The referee cocked her head to one side as if talking to a young child. 'Well, that's just not how it works though. . .'

Laurel flounced over. 'For goodness sake. You need to start taking this seriously or I'm going to be a laughing stock writing about you.'

'Oh no,' Jay said sarcastically, having drifted over to protect Jackie from Laurel's acidity.

'What's that? If you've got something to say, then say it to my face.' Laurel squared off against Jay.

'If you don't want to write about us then don't. You know we're not very good: we're just doing it for a laugh,' Jay said evenly. The referee looked very uncomfortable in the middle of the showdown and Jackie tried to mouth an apology without any of her teammates seeing.

'Maybe I will!' Laurel pouted.

'Hey, calm down, maybe—' Jackie tried, but Jay interrupted her.

'No, you won't. You don't have anything else going on that you can write about. Besides which, you're having a great time lording it over me that you're a fancy journalist. So, stop threatening to go.' Jay looked unreasonably angry with Laurel.

'What makes you think I wouldn't? Just because you have nothing going on in your life and you have to play, doesn't mean I do. I could be writing about the train station expansion. . .'

'Oh, is that back on?' Kath said mildly, having wandered across to see what was going on. She'd conjured up a Flake from somewhere and Jackie was exceedingly jealous.

Laurel ignored her, and straightened her jacket. 'Why don't you go home to your mum and your *degree* and carry on thinking you're better than me?' The venom in her voice took Jackie quite by surprise. She knew there was bad blood between Jay and Laurel, but it was springing into flames a lot faster than she'd imagined.

'Are you kidding me? Get a grip!' Jay spat back, squaring up to Laurel. 'You're here *with your actual mother* and you're having a go at me for having moved back in with mine?' A lot of heads swung round to where Gail, Laurel's mother, was sitting in her Fiat Panda waiting for Laurel to finish.

'I have my own flat.' Laurel pouted.

'Because she bought it for you!' Jay flailed an arm angrily towards Gail, whose eyes were flicking from player to player as she clearly wondered if she ought to be getting out of the car.

'So what? I didn't waste all my money on swanning off somewhere to go to a fancy university so I could tell everyone I was better than them.'

'I have never told anyone I was better than them. I did though spend a lot of time at school being told I was shitter than everyone else, and I wonder whose fault that was?'

Everyone on the court was stood in silence staring at the screaming row happening over the centre circle. Jackie made eye contact with Ros, who just shrugged helplessly.

Luckily the referee was literally made for being in the middle of contests of wills like these and she blew her whistle loudly three times.

'Are we done here? There are other teams waiting for the court.' She raised an eyebrow, which made even Jackie quiver and feel guilty for misbehaviour she hadn't committed. She felt in that moment that, even at gunpoint, she couldn't have honestly said who she thought this team was helping. At least if the courts were a play park, children were meant to squabble there.

The ball was given to the opposing team, who scored within seconds, and they all headed back to their starting positions. 'It's good exercise all this walking back to where you started,' Jackie said jovially to her opposing player. The woman just smiled in a very humouring way and concentrated on her own centre, who was getting ready to begin the game again.

The ball flew from the centre's hands and Jay was quick off her mark, intercepting. She pivoted neatly on her foot and turned to face Claire, who was further up the court with her arms above her head.

'If you need!' called Claire, who was improving suspiciously quickly, and Jay cleanly shot the ball towards her. Claire caught it and pivoted incredibly efficiently to focus on Renee and Annie, who were waiting nearer the posts. Jackie was sure Claire must be having private training to have got this much better this quickly.

Renee was tall and managed to catch the ball with ease, but her pass to Annie never reached Annie's outstretched fingers. The goal defence for the opposing team was like some sort of sticky whippet: always in the right space and seeming to call the ball to her glue-filled hands like a shaman. Within moments the ball was at the complete opposite end of the court and sailing through the opposing team's net yet again.

'That was a close one! Best one we've done yet!' Jackie said cheerfully, trotting back to her position by the line. She felt a small, desperate lump of fleshy emotion at the back of her throat, urging her to make this team a team.

Laurel glared at her cheerfulness from the sideline and scribbled hard in her notepad. 'You know, if you want advice, you only have to ask,' she snapped.

Jackie's head jerked in her direction, surprised. The beginning of a thought sparked to life in her mind, but the whistle blew before she could follow the thread and she darted off to try to get involved with the ball.

The ball sailed towards Kath, who produced a fairly lazy attempt to reach it with a casual arm stuck out. She was nowhere near catching it and didn't seem particularly bothered. Her opposing player scooped it off the floor and soon they had scored again.

Play returned to the centre circle with the Skids' turn to start. Jay rocketed the ball to Jackie, but Jackie's fingers couldn't get a grip on it and it slipped through to the ground.

'You can't throw it that hard to these new players, Jay!' Laurel burst out from behind her notepad.

It was a spark to a dry brush and Jay whirled round: 'Fuck off, Laurel. You're not on the team.'

The referee blew the whistle and called Jay up for bad sportsmanship. It sounded like a made-up rule to Jackie, but Jay had sworn, so maybe it was real.

The opposing centre took the throw, but a fired-up Jay leapt assuredly and caught the ball. She spun quickly and fired the ball into a space that Jackie realised she was meant to be running into. She pushed off with her legs, determined to catch it in case Jay felt that missing the catch was Jackie choosing Laurel's side. She ran at full stretch, feeling her leg muscles making poses they had possibly never known they could do. The ends of her fingers raked the bubbly surface of the ball, and it stopped its flight out of court and dribbled to the floor, where Jackie scooped it up with an impressive lack of grace and hugged it into herself. Two catches in a game! She remembered how the first one had ended, and quickly looked up to see if one of her team was able to take a catch. Renee looked like she was struggling to get away from her opponent and Claire the same. Annie had got as far down the court as the rules would allow her, but it was nowhere near Jackie's throwing range. It would have to be Ros. Jackie lined up her arms and attempted to sail the ball in a high arc towards her. Unfortunately for the ball, Jackie, and Ros, the ball slipped and instead of sailing sort of dribbled across the court. The other team seemed so surprised that this was her pass that they didn't manage to intercept it.

Ros scooped up the ball and then seemed to develop a fairly major fear of it and so launched it like a grenade to a hand Renee had managed to get free.

Renee took a slap to the eye from a loose wave of her opponent's hand. 'Ow!' she cried, dropping the ball in surprise.

'Play through!' Laurel screamed in a rage, just as the opposing player apologised and the ref's whistle blew all at once.

'STOP GETTING INVOLVED!' Jay bellowed. The skin below her hairline was puce.

'Oh God, I'm so sorry!' the poor goal defence said, stooping over Renee to check she was OK.

'It's fine,' Renee said, through slightly gritted teeth, 'I don't use my eyes much anyway.' She was joking, but Jackie felt a weary note in it and her stomach lurched thinking that Renee might not want to play with them after this. It wasn't exactly the fun japes she had hoped it would be. Everything was fun except the netball.

'You really need to learn how to play through that sort of thing,' Laurel was insisting.

'No she doesn't,' Jay snapped, 'The ref blew the whistle. It's non-contact.'

'Yes, but she had the advantage . . .' Laurel pressed.

'You should be pleased, look at all this ammo you've got for your hatchet piece.'

'Hey now, Jay, it's OK,' Jackie whispered, appearing at Jay's side and edging her away.

'Oh, she gets so under my skin!' Jay seethed. 'I'm never like this usually.'

Jackie glared at Ros, who was hanging about nearby trying to look innocent. 'Yes, well, it's not your fault. She shouldn't really be here, but Ros can't keep her nose out of people's business.'

'I heard that! Excuse me for trying to get you a netball team to distract you. I was just wanting to be a friend. I'll not pick you up next time you're down, shall I?' Ros stalked off and Jackie felt instantly stomachless. Perhaps that had been a bit harsh, but she just wanted to cheer Jay up.

The rest of the game passed in a blur of nets for the other team. Jackie felt all at sea coming off the court. It felt like no one at all was having a good time, except possibly Kath, who just looked permanently cheerful about everything.

'Thanks for coming along.' The centre for the opposing team caught up with Jackie and breathlessly smiled at her. 'We're so grateful for the new teams. And bringing your journalist too: it's a real boon for us in keeping the courts.'

'Oh . . .' Jackie was very pleasantly surprised, but as the wave of happiness lapped up her shores and receded, it was followed by a wave of panic that if the team fell apart she would go back to being part of the problem. 'Oh, it's fine, we're loving it. I hope – I hope you do get to keep the courts. But, you know, there's always the sports centre.' She hoped she sounded fair and even.

'Yes, that's true. They're just four times the price, so I think a lot of teams would fade out. Still, it's looking good for proving good use here! See you next time.' She jogged off to her water bottle and Jackie trudged back, adrenaline from the game still flooding her heavy feet in a curious mix of energised exhaustion. She surveyed her court-saving team with a dubious eye.

Claire was re-gluing on the fingernails she was told to remove before each game, Ros was arguing furiously with the referee about why she felt it necessary to enforce all of the rules no matter the skill level of the team, and you could have cut the tension between Jay and Laurel with a spoon. Annie seemed to shrink as the tension rose, and Renee turned practically invisible to avoid conflict.

Only Kath looked chirpy. Jackie waved and Kath bounced over and linked arms. 'That was fun!' she said brightly, and Jackie was pleased to have someone cheerful on the team.

'Yes! I caught the ball twice. That feels like progress. I'm looking forward to the next game. I don't know about everyone else.' Jackie indicated the miserable team around her.

'Yes, it's a tad strained, isn't it? Feels like the aftermath of a particularly tense children's pass the parcel. Perhaps we ought to get that night out initiation thingy done sooner rather than later?'

'That might not be the worst idea. I hope the team is nice for people. I don't want people to feel like they have to play if they're not enjoying it.'

'What do you mean?'

Jackie squirmed. 'Oh, I don't know really . . . I'm just so aware of how much I want this team and I get worried that people are only sticking with it as a favour to help me out.'

'Well, that's ridiculous,' Kath huffed. 'For a start, most of us barely know you' – she held up a hand to stop Jackie's attempted interruption – 'I know it doesn't feel like that, but let's face it: we just met. And also, you're being a bit self-involved to think that. Most of us are playing because we're just as desperate for an escape as you are.'

Jackie inspected Kath's face. 'I don't know about that. Sure, you want a break from the kids every now and again but Claire and Renee . . . they—'

'They have their stuff. They're in exactly the same boat as a lot of us.'

'I'm not sure it's a boat, to be honest.' Jackie laughed. 'I think we might have been mis-sold a colander.'

'Yes, and why is the rescue tug made of netball?' Kath returned to her usual jollity.

'It's a very good question. Couldn't Steve have laughed at the idea of me eating a load of chocolate and lying very still?'

'There's nothing to stop us forming that team too. Honestly, Jackie, you have the weight of the world on your shoulders. Do you know how good this team has been for my marriage? It's so stupid but two nights a week where I'm out of the house; it's gold. I come home and Ron and I have missed each other. I have something to tell him other than what poos happened where and the plot from *Doctors*. I know you started the team for . . . reasons, but that's not why we're here. Or not why I'm here anyway.'

Jackie nodded. 'Yes, maybe you're right. Sorry. I'm being very self-centred. Let's do an initiation for this team as soon as possible: blow the cobwebs out a bit, and if that fails we'll start Maltesers Club'.

Kath smiled and nodded in agreement.

Jackie took advantage of the nice moment between them. 'By the way, the name Horatio . . .'

She didn't need to say any more. Kath groaned. 'Oh, don't. Look, Ron wanted Hercules and I thought by pretending I wanted Horatio he would realise what a ridiculous name Hercules was. I didn't realise he'd "agree" with me while I'm all out of it post-labour and somehow we'd end up with a little pirate. You can't even shorten it.'

They laughed their way back to the car park.

3 1

Jackie pulled her car into the cul-de-sac feeling heavy and tired, but not sad. However, the sight of a car in her driveway shook her thoughts and emotions like a snow globe. She couldn't quite make the car out clearly in the gloom of evening light. She couldn't cross her fingers and *drive,* so she squeezed her pelvic floor muscles instead and fervently hoped it wasn't Steve. It might have been the first time in the history of driving that a suburban homeowner hoped a perfect stranger had decided to use their drive.

She parked next to the car and breathed a sigh of relief at the blue paintwork: not Steve. She got out of her car, wondering if coming home to people lurking was a thing all single people coped with?

'Mum!' It was Leon.

'Hello you! What are you doing here?' she asked, leaning down to pick up her bag off the back seat and feeling her entire body seek revenge for the netball hell she had put it through.

'I thought I'd pop in and see you but you weren't in! Do you ever turn your mobile on? I stuck a note through the door and I was just about to leave. Where you been?'

Jackie wondered whether she wanted to mention the netball, given how their phone call had gone, but then decided she couldn't be bothered with the complication of lying. 'I've been playing netball,' she said, giving him a peck on the cheek. How did he get so tall?

'Oh, yeah, Dad thought it would be that.' Leon smiled and took her bag for her as she opened the front door and let them both in.

'Oh, you're speaking to him again are you?' she said, carefully. It was taking all her decades of mum training to try to simultaneously be the injured wife party and the neutral mum.

'Yes . . .' Leon didn't sound particularly comfortable with his decision, 'I hope you don't mind? He called round all droopy-faced and feeling sorry for himself and I didn't have the heart to carry on ignoring him.'

'Yes, he keeps doing that here.' Jackie laughed without a drop of humour.

'He's coming round here?' Leon was always quick to sharpen on perceived injustice. He was much more reserved than his younger sibling. Leon was very defensive where Michael was forward. Possibly Michael felt he could be braver knowing Leon was always there to stand up for him. Jackie liked that idea.

'Yes, once or twice. Hangdog expression, not knowing what to do with himself. He wanted to be the victim and I'm afraid I gave him fairly short shrift with it,' Jackie said, putting on the kettle on autopilot.

'He wants his head examining,' Leon seethed. 'I give him one more month before he's back, don't worry, Mum.'

Jackie froze. 'You think he'd come back?'

Leon was getting into a good rhythm with his anger, and Jackie let him. It was better than him being stiff with her about the playground debacle. 'Oh, definitely! Michael said he couldn't work out at all what him and Michelle were in it for. She seems to have her head together, nice house, nice daughter: Michael couldn't see at all why she'd want to be with Dad.'

Jackie's fingers felt tingly, 'Michael has met her?' Her voice sounded drier and less strong than she was trying for, and she cleared her throat to get it back to normal. Something about the liveliness of Leon made her feel a bit paler: a bit more like a cartoon old woman with adult sons who discussed what they would do if she ever had a fall.

'He didn't tell you? They had a Skype or a Zoom or whatnot. Some sort of excruciating-sounding quiz.' The wind left Leon's sails.

'No, no he didn't. It's not a problem or anything' – even Jackie wasn't convinced by her tone – 'Michelle is part of your dad's life now so of course you boys should meet her.' The kettle finally mercifully boiled but the sound vanishing just left a far more oppressive silence.

'I'm not going to meet her,' Leon declared, moving off the stool to get the milk. He never could sit still when he felt there were things needed doing. He got that from her. 'Not at all. It's confusing for Freya too. How do you explain it to children? Dad's embarrassing himself and it'll be better when he gets his head straight and gives up on this stupidity and puts things back to normal.'

'Normal? What if . . . what if I didn't want him back?' Jackie tested cautiously.

It pulled Leon up short. 'What do you mean?'

'Well, it's just . . . you know. It's been a lot. What if I didn't want to take him back, even if he did want to come back?'

Leon just stared. 'But what are you going to do if you don't?'

God, he looked like his dad sometimes.

'I could do anything.'

Leon grinned. 'Yeah, I know in theory you could do anything, Mum. You're a strong powerful goddess or whatever it is Aunty Ros makes you chant at yoga . . .'

'We don't do yoga any more. She fell out with the instructor.'

'How do you fall out with a yoga instructor? Aren't they the most relaxed people in the world?'

'This is Ros we're talking about.'

'True.' Leon nodded and began searching the cupboards. Jackie reached behind the big bag of tea bags and pulled out a packet of biscuits to toss his way. They made their way into the living room. Jackie hoped the change of scenery would change the subject with it, but Leon had other ideas.

'So, yes,' he said, through a mouthful of Hobnob, 'I know in theory you could do anything but, the thing is, and I mean this is in the nicest possible way, Mum . . .' Jackie braced herself for the painful bluntness of a thirty-something son. 'You're not going to do those things, are you? You're not going to sail the world or go to university or do all the things people make driftwood signs about.'

Jackie didn't like this. She leaned across to the lamp on the dresser in the corner and flicked it on. The room glowed warmer in its light, but she still felt uncomfortable. 'Well, no, I probably won't fling myself off a cliff on a bungee rope, but that doesn't mean I'm going to take your dad back after what he's done.'

'But then, bungee jumping aside, what are you going to do? Just . . . grow old on your own?'

'Well . . . I hadn't really thought that far ahead. I might meet someone . . .' Jackie decided to keep any word of her date with Duncan to herself. It was ridiculous to bring it up anyway. It was irrelevant.

'Yeah, you might. I dunno.' He crammed another biscuit into his mouth and Jackie was spirited back to his childhood suddenly. This slow-burn of a little boy who made her a mum. 'Sorry Mum. This is all coming out patronising. I'm just angry for you. And I'm sorry I was such a dick on the phone the other day. I don't know if I'd really processed everything happening, with you and Dad, and . . . well, I'm sorry.' Crumbs flickered across the carpet and Jackie wanted to squash him in a cuddly, giggly ball and read him a story.

'If your dad did want me back, and I did say no . . . what would you think of that?' There were a lot of ifs piling up.

Leon shrugged, the urgency of the conversation seeming to wear off the more sugar he got into his bloodstream. 'I dunno Mum, whatever makes you happy. I suppose . . . I suppose I don't really see Dad sticking to this. I think it's one of his fads. In my head, I think this is a pretty shit' – Jackie flinched at his swearing and then mentally told herself to grow up – 'year or so but, I dunno . . . I didn't really think about it as being a permanent thing.' They sat in silence for a second. A neighbours' headlights swung across the window and then settled. 'Are you allowed to be upset about your parents splitting up when you've moved out and have your own kid?' Leon half-laughed.

'Oh, I expect so, you're allowed to blame your parents for everything aren't you? I certainly did.'

'Yes, well, Grandpa was a nutter so you had a reason.'

Jackie leaned across and swatted at Leon playfully. 'I don't know, Leon. Your dad has made a bit of a fool out of me. Yes, and himself – I know,' she held up a hand to stop him inter-rupting, 'I admit, a lot of me thinks I would just let everything go back to normal for the chance of everything being easy and simple again but another bit of me just knows I wouldn't feel the same about him again. We had a little life and now he doesn't feel like the same person I had that life with. How would you feel if David did it to you?'

'Yeah, but that's different.' Leon blinked.

'Why?'

'Well, we're younger. You know, we're . . .' Leon considered, chewing his words carefully before placing them out in the living room, 'we're not like a "thing", you know? We're two people who love each other but we're not a set like you and Dad. You know? We're more . . . more individual.'

Jackie would have laughed if she hadn't thought it would hurt him. 'And do you think that's how Freya sees it?' She let the ques-tion hang for a second. 'Me and your dad are a unit to you, but to us we're just two people who fell in love and made it work, same as you and David. We're future you.'

'Oh God, please don't say I'm going to be Dad! He's ridiculous!'

'I don't know, he seems to have played a blinder. Get a depend-able wife to sort your life out for you and then trade her in for a hot new one as soon as you feel the need to spice things up.'

'He's such a cliché.'

Jackie shrugged. 'Is he? He clearly wasn't happy. Better to go, I think, than keep pottering along unhappy.' Hearing the words come out of her mouth made her wonder if she believed them. Or did you just say the right things regardless when you were trying to make your children feel better?

Leon looked instantly worried. 'Were you unhappy?'

'No, no not me. No, I wasn't. But I don't particularly know if I was happy either. I just was. I didn't wake up bubbling over with enthusiasm every morning, but – but I wasn't sad. Maybe your dad is just braver than me to walk away and see if there's something better than just fading away separately together?' This stumped Leon. He sat, looking at the lace curtains and slowly nodding. Jackie smiled at the sight of the gears turning in his head behind his eyes. He was an absolute open book, that boy. 'I don't want you to worry, love,' she said, taking his tea mug back to the kitchen, 'I'm fine. I'm playing netball, I've made some friends . . . I'm sorting myself out.'

Leon encircled her in a long-armed hug. Jackie always felt she would have loved a daughter but every time one of her, now enormous, sons wrapped her up in his arms, she knew she'd never change a thing about having them.

She showed Leon out, smiling and light with him so that he would leave without a heavy heart. She shut the front door and listened to his car pulling away. Gloom descended immediately with the weight of his words washing over her. It had all sounded so reasonable when she'd calmly explained it to Leon, but now he had gone and she was back to being a woman instead of a mum, and it was somehow far less reinforced. What was she going to do for the rest of her life?

32

'I'm a hundred per cent serious,' Jackie said, maintaining eye contact. The conversation with Leon had spurred her on to some big-change thinking. She'd made a list of all the things she didn't like about life now that Steve had gone. Top, number-one item: being alone. She hated flinching at every creak in the house, and having no one to tut to when the TV characters were irritating. It needed solving and she was going to show the men in her life that she was capable of change.

'I would need to pay rent,' Jay said, a million thoughts creating a hive behind her eyes.

Jackie nodded. 'You absolutely would. I would accept your rent. I've looked online this morning about what rooms are going for in shared households. I'll be accepting no more no less than just under the going rate – ah, be quiet – the house isn't on a public transport route, and you are coming into a house already pretty established as mine, so it isn't an equal split.' Jackie decided to be quiet about the fact that she intended to put half of Jay's rent aside into a deposit pot for her and present it back when Jay was ready to move out.

Jay chewed a fingernail. 'OK,' she said finally.

Jackie jumped. 'OK?'

'OK.'

Jackie squealed. That had been far easier than she'd imagined. Things generally were though: her imagination had managed to turn the whole negotiation into a scene from *Glengarry Glen Ross*. She composed her face and tried to look calmer. 'When would you like to move in?'

'Today?'

Jackie laughed, and then stopped laughing when she realised Jay was serious. 'Today!'

Jay's face softened. 'I mean, obviously not if you have plans but I finish at three after the lunch shift and theoretically could, so . . .'

'Of course I don't have plans. If there's no netball: I'm planless. Let's do it.'

'You're sure?'

'I'm sure. You're sure?'

'Oh God, so sure!'

'OK!'

Jackie left Jay behind the bar of the Hawk and headed home to take the last few bits and pieces out of the spare room. She vacuumed and dusted and wiped and prepped until there wasn't a speck of Steve's office to be seen.

She picked Jay up from the Hawk at three sharp and they drove over to Jay's mum's house to begin collecting her belongings.

'You're sure your mum doesn't mind?' Jackie asked. She was worried Jay's mum might feel like Jackie was encroaching on her territory or trying to steal her daughter.

'Mind? She's delighted! I'm just sad you won't get to see her. They're out tonight doing salsa or rumba or something else Mum saw on *Strictly* and wanted to learn. But maybe she could come over so you can properly meet sometime?'

'That would be great.'

The afternoon was sweaty and busy: Jackie's only complaint was she'd forgotten to put on her new Fitbit so did any of this exercise really count? It took three trips to move Jay's various boxes and bags across and by the time they were all piled into the spare room Jackie was exhausted.

They ordered a pizza and stared at the mountain of belongings that neither of them had the energy to unpack. Jackie's phone began piping a heavily unpleasant, beeping tune into the room and she plunged greasy fingers into her pocket to release it.

'Rosalyn, my love! What can I do for your fine self?' Jackie said through a mouth full of cheese and endorphins.

'You can get your butt here on time so I don't look like an old rhino sat here with a whole bottle all to myself.' Ros sounded cross.

Jackie's stomach lining wobbled. 'Oh God! We're meant to be at the Hawk tonight!' A stray bit of tomato sauce caught itself on the back of her throat and she coughed it out. Jay leaned over to pat her back, looking concerned.

'You forgot?' Ros's voice was chilled.

'No . . . well yes. Jay moved in with me today, see, so we've been lugging boxes and stuff and it was such a whirlwind decision that everything else has sort of popped out of my head.'

'Charming.' Clipped, dry. Jackie was not improving the situation. 'So, you'll be on your way now?'

Jackie swallowed the last belligerent lump of tomato and tried to imagine herself getting ready to go out in public now. 'Well, actually I'm sort of knackered and sweaty, to be honest, Ros . . . why don't you come over here and join us for pizza?'

'I've already got the wine in.' Ros stated.

'They'll let you take it; we've done it a million times. It's the Hawk.'

'Tell them it's for me!' Jay called from the armchair. Jackie winced; she wasn't sure why she knew, but she knew that Jay joining in would not soothe Ros.

'I'll just drink alone then. You enjoy your night with your new bestie.' Sniffy, short and utterly ignoring the solutions provided by Jay. The phone line cut off and Jackie slumped.

'Oh shit, have we upset her? God, I'm sorry.' Jay looked wide-eyed with worry at the abrupt end of the conversation.

'Oh, don't be silly. She'll come round. It's my fault – I completely forgot we'd go. I don't know why she's being like this though. It wasn't big plans. It was a bottle of wine in the Hawk: that's an almost everyday occurrence.'

Jackie fired off a text message to Ros, apologising again and inviting her over once more to share the pizza. She knew she wouldn't hear back, and she was right. Jay and Jackie attempted to watch a film but both of them were wrestling gritty, lazy eyelids before the first plot twist and they gave up and went to bed.

Jackie lay in the half-moments between consciousnesses, listening to the sounds of Jay getting ready for bed in the next room. She could half-pretend it was Steve, or Duncan, or a fifteen-year-old Michael going through an insomniac stage. Or she could not pretend and know it was her real-life housemate. She could absolutely change her life. Maybe she would bungee jump after all?

33

Jackie's phone buzzed harshly on the table while beeping in a high-pitched tone at the same time. She groaned. It had been doing that all morning and no matter how many options she tried she couldn't seem to turn off both the buzzing *and* the beeping. And inevitably she now seemed to have got it stuck on both.

Jackie had never been in a WhatsApp group before. Apparently it was the prime method of communication for large groups such as netball teams. Who was she to argue?

Usually there was just the odd update from Ros letting them know what time to arrive, or a condescending link from Laurel sending them an article on what was expected from a certain position on the court. Jackie was keeping them in a list that she was definitely going to get round to reading, after the list of things she needed to read from Michael. Every time the phone pinged with an update from Laurel, though, Jackie felt her theory solidifying: the girl was lonely. Jackie was absolutely sure of it. Lonely, and, unbelievably given her behaviour, jealous of Jay. Jackie got the impression that the column might mean an awful lot more to Laurel than she would ever let on: it was a lifeline for her to a new lease on life just as much as it was for the players. She'd not voiced any of this to Jay because she desperately wanted to discuss it with Ros first, but Ros wasn't returning any calls or messages. Jackie would need to go a-grovelling before she could be let back into the Mackie-loving fold.

Plans for the initiation were in full swing and this meant that the WhatsApp group was an incessant hive of activity. Hive was the right word, Jackie thought, as the phone almost buzzed itself off the table. The number of messages coming in made it feel like she had a pocket full of bees.

She just hadn't thought planning a night out could be this tricky; surely it was pick a day, pick a time, pick a restaurant: go. Apparently, a night out involving eight very different almost-strangers was much trickier. Not to mention the initiation elements.

Jay had suggested they meet at someone's house before they head out for 'pre-drinking'. Claire had offered up her house because the terrace had a superb view of the sunset. She'd then asked what canapés people would be interested in. Apart from the idea of drinking to prepare for going out drinking, Jackie was so far onboard. Then Kath had asked what they would be dressing up as and Jackie felt a sinking feeling. Support for the idea of fancy dress was not strong until Laurel declared she absolutely would not be in attendance if there was a costume and Jay threw herself full force behind the dressing-up contingent. Privately, Jay was also messaging Jackie from behind the bar asking why on earth Laurel was coming in the first place. Jackie didn't know how to put a sigh in a text message and so had just put something vague about Laurel trying to get a nice, rounded piece for the paper. She didn't say anything about her private ideas on Laurel just wanting to be part of the team but unable to ask.

There was a full three hours of pocket-buzzing while different themes were offered back and forward, and Laurel left and was instantly re-added to the group by Ros. Jackie wished she had the courage to leave the group but felt certain pressing that little exit button, which felt very aggressive, would only summon Ros to her doorstep with a disapproving stare. Perhaps she should leave and see if it did conjure a Ros she could apologise to? She didn't, just in case it only made things worse.

Eventually a compromise was reached where they would all come as sports stars. Laurel declared she would come as Anna Kournikova. Jay asked why a journalist not in the team needed to come in a costume at all. Laurel said the only thing stupider than being on a night out in fancy dress was being the only one on a night out not in fancy dress. Jackie smiled at the exchange, fondly remembering Michael and Leon in their early teenage years.

Jackie had hoped that nailing down the costume plans would be the end of it, but she was sorely disappointed. Talk then pivoted instantly into the initiation details. Jackie had naively assumed initiation was a loose term used interchangeably with 'casual bonding night'. She was wrong. Jay, Laurel, Kath and, surprisingly given how quiet she had been so far, Annie were extremely vocal about the need for a series of tests to make sure everyone was committed to the team.

The tests seemed to mainly revolve around the idea of drinking something disgusting in a manner likely to make it come out of your nose. This led to Claire investigating what colours were added to the drinks they were having to see if she would need to lay mats down to protect the marble on the terrace. This really didn't seem necessary; Jackie thought showing up to practice in the cold in sports clothing was enough proof she was committed.

The latest round of buzzing had all been around what club they would head to after the pre-drinks at Claire's. Kath didn't mind where it was as long as she could dance all night. Jackie had never heard of any of the places whizzing into the thread. Ros only wanted to go somewhere where they wouldn't make her drink out of a plastic cup. Laurel didn't want to go anywhere where she would be seen out with the team. Claire kept unhelpfully suggesting places where you had to be a member and to be a member you needed to have applied four years ago and have been born into old money. Renee had very carefully never acknowledged the existence of the accursed WhatsApp group and therefore everyone forgot her existence. Clever girl, Jackie thought.

The buzzing reached a point where she couldn't bear it any longer and she picked the phone up off the counter to deal with the latest batch of argumentative emojis. Her heart immediately began to race as she noticed in the lock screen list a message from Duncan nestled among the group chat. She unlocked the phone on the third attempt at the passcode and headed straight for Duncan's missive.

'It's casual, that's good. Well phrased; light but asking questions, so you know you can reply without him thinking you're weird.' Jay finished summarising the message and passed it on to Ros to have a look.

Jackie looked at Jay aghast. 'Why would he think I was being weird in replying? Are there messages you're not meant to reply to? Why would you message someone if you didn't want a reply?'

Jay smiled kindly. Ros put the phone down on the table and looked at Jackie like she was newly born from a convent. 'Well, because sometimes, Jack, you have a night with a potential lover and you realise they are not someone you ever want to have to put near your body again and so you send them the perfect closure message to let them know, without saying it, that you are done.'

'This is a thing people do?' Jackie looked from face to face.

'Well, yeah . . . it's better than ghosting.'

'What's ghosting?' Jackie asked, 'The thing with the pottery?'

Ros laughed and Jay looked blank. 'Ghosting is when you just stop replying to everything without any explanation at all. What's pottery got to do with ghosting?' Jay said.

'From the film? You know, *Ghost*?' said Jackie.

Jay shrugged. 'Never seen it.' The generation gap yawned wide.

'I knew she was too young for you.' Ros sniffed. Jackie picked up on the slight barbs but given that Ros had relented enough to come out for a light dinner with them, she decided to let them wash over her.

Jackie looked at her phone. 'So have I ghosted him because I haven't replied yet?' She didn't want him to think he'd been ghosted – or was a ghost? Or was she the ghost? 'God, this is all so confusing.'

'Welcome to my world. Dating sucks,' Jay grumbled.

'Not if you grip the reins firmly.' Ros pished their misery.

'So, I should reply then?'

'Yes!' chorused Jay and Ros.

'What do I say?' Jackie's stomach felt acidic and temperamental.

'What do you want to say?'

'I don't know.'

'Do you want to go out with him again?' Jay prodded.

'I don't know.'

'Oh, for goodness sake.' Ros's short temper got the better of her and she snatched the phone from Jackie and began typing.

'Don't you send that!' Jackie shrieked, flailing fingers at the phone Ros was holding just out of her reach.

Ros gave her a stink-eye and then rolled it. 'I won't send it. I'm just breaking you out of this little rut of indecision you're in.' She finished typing and handed the phone back to Jackie. 'There, how about that?'

Jackie read over the message. It was polite, inquisitive and nice. 'Yes, that looks good. How did you know how to say that?'

Ros stared at her like she was an alien. 'Because it's just human interaction, Jack, it's not rocket science. Just talk to him like a person, not your next potential marriage prospect.'

'All right, no need to get stroppy. I just haven't texted anyone new in a while. That's all. In fact . . . ever. Mobile phones weren't a thing when I met Steve.' Jackie felt quite defensive at Ros's hard-edged tone. There was only so much apologising she could do for daring to make a life choice without consulting her.

'That's because you've been in a rut. You got in a rut with Steve and didn't bother reaching out of it.'

'Oh, no, not a rut . . .' Jay murmured, feeling the change in the tone between the two of them.

'My marriage was a rut?' Jackie straightened.

Ros didn't blink. 'Well, yes.' Her mouth closed firmly, and Jackie felt anger rising up her skull. Ros was too good at saying what she thought and then sitting in silence.

'Pack it in, Ros,' Jackie muttered, unsure what to say back but fairly sure she didn't want to pull at this thread. Ros merely shrugged again, infuriatingly. Jackie forced a smile at Jay. 'Well, you two have been very helpful. Message sent. I'll report back if he replies.' As if on cue her phone buzzed on the table, and she looked down. 'Ah, well. There we go. Dinner at the weekend.'

'Great!' Jay beamed.

'Great,' Ros repeated without the enthusiasm.

'What's the matter now? I thought you wanted me to go out with him?'

'I did.'

'Sorry, am I not dating right for you?'

'If you're going to go on a second date with him, you really ought to get those divorce papers sorted just in case he moves in. How are they going, by the way?'

Jackie stared at her. 'Ros, I love you, but stop it. I'm going to go; I feel like I need a night's rest to prepare myself for this initiation.' She forced an overly positive tone to cover Ros's grumps. She started to gather her bag and coat and smiled at Jay, who nodded in response.

'I'm going to stay for another glass,' Ros declared, and then looked petulantly up at them as though disappointed they were leaving her.

'Oh . . . OK love. If that's what you want to do.' Jackie smiled.

'It is.' Ros sniffed.

'Ros, is there something you want to talk about? Are you OK?' Jackie relented, wishing she didn't feel the need to be the bigger person and ask.

Ros held eye contact. 'Yes. Why wouldn't I be?'

Jackie swallowed a sigh. 'I don't know. You just seem tense.' Jay shifted uncomfortably on her heels.

'I'm fine, I suppose.'

Jackie was a patient woman but dealing with Ros in this mood was like dealing with a toddler too tired to eat and too hungry to sleep. 'OK, well that's good then. Enjoy your drink and we'll see you tomorrow for the initiation.' She smiled brightly and falsely and spun on her heel. Jay gave Ros a weak wave and followed.

'What was that about?' Jay asked as they climbed into Jackie's car outside.

'Oh, heaven knows. She's got the sulks about something. It'll blow over, knowing Ros. She'll be fine by tomorrow.' She didn't want to talk about the feeling of a widening crack between her and Ros.

They pulled out of the car park and onto the main road snaking home. Driving home with Jay was lovely. Jackie hadn't realised how tense she had got about the thought of unexpected visitors being at the house when she arrived home. But being with Jay made her feel protected. The ongoing low-level fighting with Ros was tiring her out and she felt good with the chattery, buoyant Jay in the passenger seat keeping the mood light.

Jackie pulled into her street and felt her stomach roll over at the sight of Steve's car in the driveway. For goodness sake. This time though she had backup.

'What's he doing here?' For a split second, Jackie honestly thought she had said it. But it was Jay. Jackie blinked at her. The realisation of what was coming manifested itself in her consciousness before she physically thought the words that explained it to herself. A veil of whining calm settled itself on her and she parked the car gently.

Jay was her usual self; she clambered out of the car and turned to face Steve: 'Everything all right? Mum OK?'

Jackie got out of the driver's seat with legs full of peanut butter.

'Jackie,' Jay said, 'this is Mum's boyfriend Steven; Steven, this is Jackie who I'm living with.'

Jackie and Steve looked at each other across the cars. 'Steven,' Jackie said, quietly, feeling it sit uncomfortably in her idea of him.

'Oh Jesus,' Steve said, 'I thought it was probably too wild a coincidence . . . When Jay joined a team I thought, ah there's loads of teams round here probably. I talked myself out of it. What are the chances? But then Chelle said Jay had moved in with a Jackie from netball and I . . .'

'You know each other?' Jay's brain worked quicker than her mouth and Jackie could see her working it out before she'd finished saying the first half: 'Steve/Steven. Oh my Jesus fucking Christ.' She spun on her heel. 'Jackie, I'm so sorry. I'm so, so sorry. I didn't realise AT ALL. This is mad.'

Jackie gaped at her. 'What are you sorry for?'

But Jay's mind was obviously still whirring. 'But wait—you only split up a few months ago and Mum and Steven have been? But he was cheating on you . . . so . . .' She looked at Steve. 'So you were with Mum while you were still with Jackie? You creepy fucking . . . Mum was the other woman? Wait till I tell her. Oh my God, this is going to kill her.'

'Jay, come on—' Steve started, but Jay was livid. Jackie thought the only thing that could make things worse for him would be if Laurel turned up and took his side.

'No! You cheating, scuzzy, gross old bastard. I knew there was something I didn't like about you but I . . . I can't believe you would do this to Mum. And Jackie.' She was seething.

'Don't be so stupid, Jay, there's nothing your mum doesn't know about.' Steve tossed it casually across the driveway and Jackie was reminded of the way he argued. Unpleasantly disconnected. So hard to rail against when you were emotional, like she was. What he said worked and Jay stumbled into a shell-shocked stutter.

'What?'

Steve rubbed his eyes and glanced at Jackie. 'Should we go inside?'

Jackie felt like a bystander in her own life, watching this unfold between Jay and Steve, 'Er, no. No, I don't think so. Let's just keep the volume down and wrap this up quickly.' Wrap this up quickly? What was wrong with her? All thoughts of a nice early night before the initiation had gone up in smoke. She'd be churning this all night . . . Michelle, Chelle, Jay's mum. Would Jay want to move out?

'Your mum knew about Jackie the whole time. I've never lied to her.' Steve held eye contact with Jay. 'You can ask her.'

'Mum wouldn't do that.' Jay's lip was wobbling, and Jackie watched her bite it down to keep it still.

'She didn't do anything wrong,' Steve consoled. 'But she did know. Jay, I'd never lie to your mum.'

Jackie shifted uncomfortably. How was she not even the main character in her own divorce? 'Did you need something Steve?' she asked, wanting him gone so the shrapnel could settle and she could see where she stood in this new view of her life. She'd been so happy at the thought of Jay living with her.

'I just . . . I am so tired of all the lies and confusion. I wanted to see if I was right in suspecting you two knew each other. That's all. I'm sorry. I didn't want to cause any issues.'

'Of course you didn't,' Jackie said, exhausted. 'You just can't help yourself.' She unlocked the front door and stepped inside, turning on the doorstep to look at Jay. 'You coming in, Jay? Tea?'

Jay looked up at her. She looked forlorn. Little shining eyes full of confused, hurt tears sat above burning red cheeks. 'You're still OK with me being here?'

Jackie could have burst. She dashed back down the step and across the few feet of distance. 'Of course I am, you dafty. Come on, get inside. Steve – we, um, we will maybe need to talk about this another time?' She ushered Jay inside and shut the door. There was seemingly no end to the havoc Steve could wreak. No matter what she did, or how she thought she had moved on, he would be round with a hammer to take the shine off it.

Weariness settled on Jackie in the silence of the hall. The frostiness of Ros, the explosion from Steve. She looked at the shoe rack and yearned for the day when that had been her biggest drama. Jay hovered awkwardly.

'Tea?' Jackie offered again, not knowing what else to do.

'Jackie, honestly, I can go. This is so weird.'

'No, no. I don't want you to. Unless you want to? I don't want you to be uncomfortable.'

There was a pause that neither of them could deny was uncomfortable.

'No, look, I'll stay tonight, but maybe we are going to need to rethink this?' Jay smiled sadly.

'Probably,' Jackie admitted. '. . . Tea?'

34

Clothes were scattered over every surface and several different types of powder were smeared across the kitchen counters. None of the dodgy powders; Jackie had checked several times to make sure they were all just make-up detritus. If she had thought the hall was annoyingly full of shoes when she lived with Steve, then she had had her eyes opened by the situation now evolving as they got ready to go for the initiation night out.

She picked up her phone off the dressing table and fired off a reply to Duncan's latest text. In a bid to squash thoughts of Steve and Michelle from her mind, she had been engaging in a bit of back and forth with Duncan all day. It was nice, and distracting. He was funny. She told him she was ready to go out and would speak to him tomorrow.

Picture please!

he shot back instantly. She laughed, and then switched her camera into the selfie mode Jay had showed her. The light was too dim and the camera too poor for the photo to be any good. Not to mention the chins; she'd have to get Jay to show her the good angles again.

Have you forgotten what I look like?!

she sent back, and felt the fizzing excitement of flirting take over her stomach. The sound of different fizzing then caught her attention.

'I thought we were going to Claire's for the pre-drinking?' Jackie called through from the bathroom as she heard another bottle of prosecco popping open downstairs.

'We are!' Jay called back. 'This isn't pre-drinking. We're just having a bottle as we get ready.'

Jackie had made a resolution to pack the previous evening's Steve revelations firmly into a box until she was ready to deal with them. She desperately wanted to enjoy the initiation. Jay was having a harder time compartmentalising. She was alternating between apologising to Jackie for the affair, and disbelief that her mother would have partaken in a relationship in the full knowledge that her boyfriend was married. She reminded Jackie of Leon's naivety at the idea that older people were complicated, emotional beings. At some point she and Jay were going to have to acknowledge that they needed to make a decision about their living arrangements, but there was no reason for that day to be today.

'But that's the third bottle?' Jackie's complaint was ignored, and she heard raucous laughter coming from downstairs. Somehow, she had Renee and Kath here with her and Jay at the house getting ready to go to Claire's, which was the place they were going to get ready to go out. No wonder young people were always moody and confused. Life had got very confusing while she was on hiatus being a married mother and nurse. Ros had opted not to join them by pointedly ignoring Jackie's invitation.

Jackie looked at her reflection and decided that was as good as it was going to get. She looked nice. Underwhelming, she thought. But nice. She slipped on her shoes and headed downstairs.

'Oh, Jackie you look lovely!' Kath was slurring already from her position halfway off the stool.

'You do!' Jay crooned. 'Want me to do your make-up?'

'I'm wearing make-up,' Jackie said, putting a hand up to her face.

'Oh, it looks lovely!' Jay backtracked. She reddened immediately and the guilty look made Jackie wonder if Jay would be bothered about putting her foot in it had Steve not turned up in the driveway the night before. There was a quiet pressure on them.

'Are you?' Kath scrunched her eyes up and peered in closer to inspect Jackie's face.

'Well, mascara, yes,' Jackie said, sure that she blushed enough to not really need anything else anyway.

'Oh, yeah, well if that's all you want, you look beautiful. Sorry.' Jay handed her a flute of prosecco and Jackie fell into it gratefully to cover how exposed she suddenly felt with everyone inspecting her face. Jay turned back to Renee and began swiping an iridescent powder across her very fine cheekbones. Jackie gave it a good look and decided that it did look, really, very nice whatever Jay was doing to Renee.

'Oh, well, maybe I do want a bit of sparkle? You don't get initiated every night, do you?' Perhaps a nice make-up session would repair the bond beginning to grow between them.

'I'm so glad we didn't do costumes in the end.' There'd been a WhatsApp based U-turn at the eleventh hour that they were pretty much all grateful for. Kath breathed out a sigh of relief. 'It's so long since I wore something I felt good in.'

Kath really did look spectacular.

'You look amazing.' Jackie smiled, 'Did you buy it special?'

'No, I bought it for Ron's birthday last year but then Horatio got a stomach bug and we didn't go out in the end. We were going to go later but it never happened. You know how it is.'

'Oh, yes. I remember. Somehow months go by and you haven't been anywhere except the school gates!'

'Exactly!' Kath wailed. 'Don't get me wrong: I love my kids and I wouldn't go back and not have them for anything. And I can't even say no one warned me it would be like this – but bloody hell. Sometimes I think about breaking up with Ron just so I'd have some peace every other weekend!' Kath laughed and drained her glass.

'I don't know if I want kids,' Jay said, peering at the black lines above Renee's eyes to check they were even. They were. Jackie decided she might want some of those flicks too. Perhaps they would stop her eyes being too piggy. Or would the lines not work if you have this many crow's feet?

'I always knew I didn't,' said Renee, inspecting Jay's work in the mirror and smiling. 'God, it used to annoy me how many people would pop their head on one side and say *Oh you'll change your mind*.' Jackie, who had had half a mind to say that to Jay, with an added *if you meet the right man*, swallowed the thought immediately and sat back to burn in shame and watch a mind's-eye action replay of every time she had said that to someone in the past.

'That's so annoying, isn't it!' Jay agreed, beckoning Jackie over to the make-up chair.

'Completely.' Renee refilled their glasses with an elegant hand. 'I used to think, no one says that about any other massive life choices. I was thrilled when menopause kicked in and people had to shut up about it.'

'I'm dreading menopause,' Kath admitted. 'It's the next thing, I suppose.'

'It's not that bad,' Jackie said, trying to keep very still as Jay came at her with several very tickly brushes.

'Oh, it's not the physical side of it,' Kath said brightly. 'I've been pregnant with twins. Physical stuff doesn't worry me at all any more. No, it's the not being fertile any more. I like the option being open. If I want to have more babies I can, you know? I like being all mumsy. This feels like my prime form: I was a rubbish teenager and a loser in my twenties, but I like being a middle-aged mum. I'm comfy. I don't want to have to evolve again.'

'I know *exactly* what you mean,' Jackie said, her eyebrows shooting up and ruining Jay's art. 'That middle bit, that mum bit, the raising bit: that was everything I ever wanted to be. It's so strange that it's done and you just can't do it again. It's why I loved nursing so much: eternal mumming!'

'Oh, see I'm dreading my thirties!' said Jay. 'Not young enough to be a whippersnapper but I won't have done enough to match up with other people my age.'

Jackie tried to remember her thirties, but her memory of it blended with her twenties and forties. It had all been nursing schedules and raising the boys and endless driving backwards and forwards to different sporting events they were competing in. She'd loved it. Hadn't she?

Jay stepped away from her face. 'There,' she pronounced, pleased. She indicated Jackie should check out the finished look in the mirror. Jackie peered at her face. It certainly was shiny. But in very specific places that looked deliberate.

'Thank you,' she said, having no idea which regions she should comment on the most. The eyes were the most colourful bit. 'I love the eyes.'

Jay beamed. 'It's this new palette I got for Christmas from . . .' She pulled up short and her eyes flicked up to Jackie's in a panic. 'Oh God.'

Jackie filled in the blanks and tried to smile over the flutter of confusion in her stomach. 'From Steve?'

'Oh God Jackie, I didn't even think, I'm so sorry.'

'No, no, don't be daft . . . it's fine. It's fine.' It was fine, wasn't it? She looked at the palette, trying to imagine Steve choosing that. For Christmas. Had he bought Jay and Michelle their gifts at the same time as buying hers? If their anniversary was recent, they would already have been together months at that point. Had he known that Christmas would be their last together, or was he still unsure he would leave then? Christmas presents for the daughter seemed serious. The previous night's revelation had disturbed all the sediment of her post-break-up healing.

'Steve . . .?' Kath asked, trying to make sense of the awkward silence. Jay and Jackie looked at each other. What did you say?

'Steven. My mum's boyfriend,' Jay mumbled, unable to make eye contact with Jackie but not wanting to explain the situation further. Kath smiled, oblivious, but Jackie saw Renee look from Jay to Jackie and scrunch her eyes in concentration. Had she twigged? She was so smart.

'Do you like him?' Kath asked, oblivious.

'Yeah, he seems all right. I think Mum could do better. He tries a bit hard.' Jay let the sentences trip out of her mouth in a falsely bright, stalling staccato.

Jackie put down the mirror, forcing her voice to come out loud and strong to help Jay out of the quagmire. 'Well, I think I look like a million pounds, so you can thank Steven for the palette because it's definitely going to help me pull tonight. What a world!' She tried to laugh and it convinced Kath, but there must have been a quiver in her voice because Renee looked up and smiled in a sympathetic way; Jackie felt a silent hug come her way. 'Jay, show me how to do a good selfie. I want to send a picture to Duncan now I'm all made up.' A round of photos of all of them followed and Jackie sent the best one to Duncan, giggling to herself at how the bubbles had really taken over all her decision-making.

'Right,' Renee said, taking action, 'if we're all ready, let's go, shall we?' She raised her glass. 'To the Skids!'

'To the Skids!' they all crowed, then downed their drinks and headed out.

35

By the time they stumbled off Claire's terrace Jackie was pretty sure she was the drunkest she'd ever been in her life. Certainly the drunkest she'd been in a decade. The only time she'd ever felt so loose and carefree was on the gas and air that, if pressed, she'd have to admit she hadn't needed during Michael's birth.

She'd laughed so much she was pretty sure she had abs. At first she'd been fairly sure she wasn't going to have a good time as the pre-drinking (not to be confused with the getting-ready drinking that happened pre the pre-drinking) had begun with a game called I Have Never. The idea of the game was that you took it in turns to declare a thing, and every time you had done the thing declared you took a sip of your drink. Jackie had sat, eyes wide, watching the team drink while she stayed stoically sober in the reality of the very boring life she had apparently lived.

'Outside outside?!' she shrieked, watching Ros drink up an admission of yet more bedless sex.

Ros looked nonplussed. 'Of course. Haven't you?'

'No! Where did you do it?' Jackie leaned in, flabbergasted that she'd not been told this wild story.

'Lots of places,' Ros said, to gales of laughter from the others. 'The beach – not good. Gritty. A forest. All right, but I'd pick a less pine-needley one next time, or I'd go on top. You know that wine bar we like that just got the outdoor heaters?' she asked Jackie, who nodded. 'Well, you didn't hear it from me, but I might be the reason the owner wanted to put in outdoor heaters. I got my own back on that sandpit in the middle of the golf course too.'

'I can't believe I never knew about that!'

'Well, we don't really talk sex, do we?' Ros said, shrugging but looking uncomfortable.

'Well . . . no. But only because I wasn't having any and I assumed you were the same!' More laughter from the assembled team.

'Why would you assume I wasn't having sex just because you were trapped in a passionless marriage with the dullest man in the universe?'

This took the wind out of Jackie's sails, but Ros's tone was just light enough that she felt she couldn't voice her hurt. The others didn't see it, but Jackie knew from the sparkle of grit in Ros's eye that she'd put a little more weight behind the punch than totally necessary. Ros had fallen stroppier at the plans changing last-minute to getting ready at Jackie's. She felt slighted at not having been invited ahead of time and no matter how many times Jackie had explained it was unplanned, Ros hadn't thawed. Jackie hadn't even found a way to tell her yet about the Jay complication. She knew Ros would use it as an excuse to push the divorce again and, while Ros might be right, Jackie just didn't want to hear it. She had leafed through the paperwork briefly and the words and the formality of it all just felt so wrong.

Jackie fell quiet and the game carried on. She didn't drink for a threesome and she didn't want to know anyone's stories behind that one. Thankfully Kath, Annie and Jay were also sat out on that one, although Jackie noticed Renee taking a sneaky sip as Ros and Claire swapped raucous tales of their shenanigans.

Annie offered up that she had never been abroad. It was a choice, she assured them, even if it sounded more like a choice born of fear than anything else.

'Well, it's hard when you're single, isn't it? It's a lot of . . . stuff. Flights and languages and places I don't know. Just to be alone somewhere else. Sometimes I think I'll just book it and go, and then I freak out and I think: what if I waste my two weeks' annual leave on something more stressful than work?'

Jackie wondered quietly if she would have the confidence to go abroad alone. Probably not. She'd never thought about how single people holidayed.

'What about going away with friends or family?' Renee asked, genuinely curious.

'My family aren't really like that.'

No one pushed her on the mention of friends. There was a slight hush, the awkwardness of acknowledging someone's minor otherness, that none of them knew how to pass softly. Kath, ever the appeaser, swooped in with a warm tone and the declaration that next summer would see the Skids on tour, visiting somewhere hot with good food and better wine. Annie managed a small smile at the thought of abroad with people. They all cheered and the attention moved off Annie and on to Jackie.

'Oh no, I haven't thought of one yet!' She flapped.

'Ah, come on, you've had all round,' Ros chided. Jackie was beginning to get annoyed with the constant nit-picking from her. It was just low-level enough that if she snapped, she would be the arsehole, but she knew Ros well enough to know exactly how deliberate it all was.

'I know, but I was thinking about other people's ones. OK . . . um, OK, here's an easy one. I have never kissed a married man.' She laughed at her own joke. 'Except Steve, of course.' And then drank. Claire drank easily and then Kath drank too, and then, slowly, Ros raised her glass to her lips.

Jackie's glass slipped down from her own lips with barely a drop passing them.

'What?' Ros shrieked, defending herself against the attack of Jackie's gaze. Jackie couldn't believe her eyes.

'You've never been married!' It came out wobbly, the alcohol already fumbling Jackie's tongue.

'I know. So?' Ros was defiant and equally slurry. Jay tried to laugh to dispel the tension, but it failed fairly miserably.

'So . . . what married man have you kissed?' Jackie watched Ros decide how to play the rest of the conversation.

Ros wafted a hand casually and rolled her eyes. 'You remember Harry?'

Jackie racked her brains for a Harry. Ros didn't really date anyone long enough to bother introducing them to Jackie, so she didn't meet many of her men and she didn't remember much about them for long as it was pretty pointless. 'Harry . . . the builder?'

'That's right. With the arms.'

'So . . . he was married?' Jackie spoke cautiously, almost wanting to reverse back out of the route she had gone down but not sure how to now she was here.

'Yes.' Ros sniffed, trying to be carefree and failing.

'But, separated?' Jackie persisted.

'He talked about leaving her.'

A dam inside Jackie broke. 'Ros!'

'What?' Ros's eyes were screaming defiance at Jackie's interference. 'It was years ago anyway.'

Jackie stood up, unappeased. 'You had an affair?' Fury was licking the edges of her skin like flames. Jay looked like she wanted to melt into the terrace; her eyes shone with pain.

'No, I didn't. I wasn't married to anyone. I just dated a man.'

Jackie caught sight of Jay and wished she'd never picked this stupid subject. Tonight was meant to be about getting rid of all the friction, not exacerbating it. Why did every damn thing have to be so difficult and complicated?

Jackie could feel the others shifting feet and trying to find other places to look, especially Annie, who had now pushed her drink as far away from her as she could. Jackie found she couldn't calm down. 'But a married man! A man who had a wife!'

'So? Jackie, life isn't perfect. It's not like I ruined their marriage. Maybe I made it better. He had a good couple of months and as far as I know they're still together.'

Ros lit a cigarette and Jackie noticed her fingers trembling. She realised she was still standing up and sat down quickly. 'I just can't believe you would do this to me.'

Ros's head whipped around to face Jackie, but Claire intervened. 'Gosh, this game! It does stir some things up, doesn't it?! Perhaps it's time for a new game?'

'Good idea,' said Jackie, downing her drink and wishing it would soothe her pulsating cheeks, 'I'll just pop to the loo.'

'Second on the left.'

Jackie nodded wordlessly and headed into the house for a much-needed moment alone with her own reflection.

'You OK?' Kath caught her elbow.

'Oh, yeah . . . yes.' Jackie squeezed her hand and pulled away.

The next game involved them trying to pick up an ever-shrinking cornflakes box in their mouths without bending the various limbs they had evolved to aid such a process. The sights and shrieks of the team contorting into positions that allowed them to pick up the box eased Jackie back to laughter and she shook off the unease from the previous game.

The cornflake box was barely inches off the floor within twenty minutes and the team looked expectantly at Jackie.

'Your go!' Kath encouraged, while Claire got her phone ready to film Jackie's attempt.

'Then we have to order a cab!' Jay said, checking the time. 'Laurel has texted me four times to say she's waiting at the club.'

'Are you OK with that?'

Jay shrugged. 'It's fine.'

'No one told me not to invite her,' Ros said sulkily. Jackie rolled her eyes and made a valiant attempt to reach the box despite protesting bones and joints. She was barely an inch from the box, lips outstretched, emitting laughter from every pore, when her knees gave way and she collapsed full force on the box, crushing it and the game beneath her giggling body. The team piled on to help her out, laughing and snorting and spilling drinks as they went.

'I got it all on camera!' Claire declared merrily.

'Burn that phone,' Jackie laughingly grumbled, straightening her hair. She looked down at the crumpled remains of the box. 'Well, I've ended the game somewhat prematurely . . . to the club!'

36

The music was louder than Jackie could possibly have imagined. If she'd seen it in a TV show, she'd have argued vociferously that it was being ridiculously badly done because no one could stand music that loud in the real world.

The Skids had a booth in one corner of the club. Apparently it was a VIP booth but Jackie felt anything but important sitting squashed between Laurel and Renee, trying to join in with conversation but unable to hear a syllable. She smiled along with people's facial expressions and hoped she wasn't putting her foot in it anywhere by agreeing with the wrong thing. She felt approximately 1.4 billion years old. The fashion, the music, the look and feel of the place was like a different planet.

There was a shriek from the side of her and Jay and Laurel lurched themselves out of their seats. At first Jackie thought they were fighting, but then she realised that the joy of the particular song that had just started playing had temporarily united them and they were both attempting to reach the dance floor in the shortest possible time.

Jay actually scrambled over the table, causing Annie and Claire to send arms shooting out to right glasses, well, plastic glasses, that had gone flying. Kath laughed at their eagerness and followed them to the dance floor, which was apparently where you needed to be when this song played. Annie shrugged and followed with a shy smile. Jackie looked from Claire to Renee and then finally to Ros. Then she pulled herself out of the plush seat, annoyed that it took two jolts of her stomach muscles to lift herself out, and followed the others to the dance floor.

It was madness. Out under the lights with the bass rolling through her legs and feet. There were so many people on the dance floor that it was impossible not to dance as your body was pressed and jostled from each side. Laurel and Jay were enthusiastically singing and dancing along. They were even making eye contact with each other. The power this one song seemed to have! Jackie couldn't really make out many of the lyrics but it was loud and exciting. Something about snakes and everything having a bright side.

Kath had really thrown herself into moving. Jackie wouldn't necessarily describe it as dancing, but it looked joyous and perhaps that was the main point of dancing? Annie was a sight – it was the least self-conscious Jackie had ever seen her and she looked carefree and liberated there in what felt, to Jackie, like the least carefree place in the world.

'I don't know how you're dancing so free!' Jackie leaned into Annie's ear and shouted to her.

'It's the best place to do it!' Annie called back, laughing.

'What, right in the middle of everyone? I don't know, I'm so nervous people will laugh at me!' Jackie lamely flailed her hands, pulling her handbag further up her arm and stepping from side to side.

'But nobody's looking at you. That's what great about the dance floor. Look.'

Jackie did look and Annie was right. The dance floor was so packed that it was hard to make out what any individual was actually doing.

Jay was at Jackie's side all of a sudden. 'Here, put your bag down with ours!' she shouted, tugging at the strap on Jackie's shoulder.

'I can't! It's got my stuff in it!' Jackie clung to her safety strap.

'Put the important stuff in your bra, come on!' Jay reached into her dress and flashed a key and a debit card at Jackie, then put them back in, smiling. Jackie looked doubtfully at her handbag.

It was full of mints and all sorts of things. It wouldn't all fit in her bra. She began to sift through it and Jay intervened again, 'No, just the important stuff! Just the stuff that really can't get nicked.'

Jackie picked through the bag and removed her debit card and her keys. She felt doubtful but threw caution to the wind and put her bag into the pile with the others'.

'Not your phone?' Jay mouthed over the music.

Jackie looked at the bag, confused. 'No, no one's going to be calling me at this time.'

'But if it gets nicked . . .?' Jay looked baffled.

'People will call me on the landline.'

For some reason this caused Jay to burst into a wave of laughter and she grabbed Jackie's hands and began to make her dance. Jackie felt the self-consciousness begin to melt as she joined in with Jay's infectious smile and laughter. So what if she didn't know how to dance? Who cared!

A woman in hot pants came round with a tray of tiny drinks hung round her neck.

'Ooh, it must be the interval,' Jackie cried. 'Time for ice cream!'

Kath laughed, but Jay and Laurel looked baffled and then pulled their cards out.

'Shots!' Jay cried, but her eagerness faded at the sight of the scowl on Laurel's face. 'What?' Her hand went to her hip in immediate defensive posture.

'We don't need you to buy us all shots.' Laurel nodded her head towards Jay's bank card.

'We don't need you to buy them either.' Jay indicated Laurel's own bank card, clutched in her hand. The shots girl shifted her weight awkwardly.

'I can pay for them just as much as you can. I somehow managed to get a job even without A stars and a degree,' Laurel sniped. Jackie wondered if she could ask the DJ to put back on the magical song that had united them.

'Pay for them then. You have a better job than me. I don't know what your fucking problem is.' Jay slammed her card back into her bra and Laurel seemed thrown off balance by her lack of pushback. Without the stubbornness to push against, she quavered and then turned determinedly to the shots tray and began handing out small cups of spirits.

'What is it?' Jackie asked, giving it a cursory sniff.

'Doesn't matter! Shots!' Jay cried, taking a cup from Laurel without looking at her and raising her glass in a toast. The others joined in and downed their drinks. Jackie followed suit and it tasted like something she was more used to dispensing than drinking. Her eyes threatened to water and she stared up, blinking to get the tears to go away before anyone laughed at her. When she looked down, though, Laurel was just as misty-eyed-looking as she was and also trying desperately not to show it. Jackie's heart throbbed towards her in a bizarre warmth for this spiky, prim, distant girl who was all at once awful, insecure and awfully insecure.

Jackie danced and danced, feeling the alcohol and the anonymity massage strong fingers into her insecurities. After what felt like hours, the others signalled going back to the booth and Jackie readily agreed, hoping it would be OK to get a glass of water. The woman selling the shots was so good at her job that Jackie was very worried about both her bank balance and her actual balance.

Jackie collapsed into the booth, still laughing at Laurel trying to shake off some unwanted attention of the male variety. Jay and Annie snaked off to the bar to get them all drinks. Kath set her bag down in the booth and headed off to the toilets. She mentioned something about breaking a seal and Jackie fervently hoped it wasn't a drugs reference.

It wasn't until Jackie had settled down and stifled her laughter at Laurel's emergency disentanglement from the eager hands that she noticed the lack of conversation in the booth and looked about. Renee, Claire and Ros had company. Two men had joined them and looked surprised at their sudden appearance.

'Hi!' Jackie said, trying to simultaneously get her breath back and cover up the fact that she had lost it.

'Hello,' one of the men said. He was the slightly more handsome one, Jackie decided, although neither were brilliant. The other man had a bit less hair and for some reason Jackie assumed the overpowering scent of cologne was coming off him, even though in the close confines of the booth there was really no way to tell which it was.

'I'm Jackie,' said Jackie, shoving a hand across the table. Her motor skills were seriously unimpressive at this point in the alcohol intake.

'Careful,' Ros snapped, clutching at a glass that Jackie hadn't touched and that was empty anyway. Jackie looked at her in surprise and apologised. Ros nodded, not wanting to look grumpy in front of these new potential dates. 'This is James,' she said, pouting a little. Jackie swallowed down how much Ros was winding her up and smiled at James.

'Nice to meet you, James,' she said.

'The other one is Damon,' Renee said, sounding bored. 'He doesn't say much.' Then much quieter, 'Just drools.'

Jackie snorted and looked at Damon, who did appear to have morphed into a cartoon version of a man in love and was just staring at Claire. Claire looked like she would have Spider-Manned to the ceiling if she could have just to get away. Laurel had pulled her phone out and was steadfastly avoiding noticing the men existed.

'Nice to meet you both,' Jackie said in a friendly manner, and then shifted her body language to focus on Renee, who she felt needed the attention.

'James is a doctor!' Ros declared loudly.

'That's nice.' Jackie smiled.

'No, I'm a salesman—' James tried to correct her, but Ros shushed him.

'He's a handsome doctor.' Ros was very drunk.

'That's good, Ros.' Jackie smiled again, trying to assess what Ros wanted from her. It was certainly combat of some kind, that was for sure – but on what front?

'And if I want, I can take him home. Because. Because that's what I can do if I want to.'

James was looking less and less comfortable with that idea the more Ros talked, but Jackie didn't think for a minute that Ros wasn't ultimately correct.

'Do you want some water, maybe, Ros?' Claire tried to intervene in the odd battle that was brewing in Ros.

'No, I don't. I don't want water and I don't want her pity.' She folded her arms, petulantly. Jackie was stunned.

'What do you mean pity?' She looked in confusion from Renee to Claire and back to Ros.

'Ah forget it,' Ros said and turned a beaming smile back on James the not-doctor.

Jackie did try to forget it, and that was helped by the return of Jay and Annie from the bar with more drinks. The booth was now very crowded though, and all of them trying to sit there was uncomfortable. Kath returned from the bathroom, exclaiming loudly about the length of the queue.

'I used the men's in the end!' she shrieked. 'Them teenagers didn't know what hit them! Probably a crime or something but ah well: it would have been a worse one to piss myself in my good knickers.' There was nowhere for her to fit into the booth, and she hovered awkwardly at the end of the table. The atmosphere wasn't as good with James and Damon there and Claire looked like she would spontaneously combust if she had to slap Damon's hand down one more time. He kept attempting to stroke her cheek with the back of his hand. It was making Jackie's skin crawl just watching. At least Steve had left her and got into a relationship so he wasn't crawling nightclubs and making a fool of himself, she thought. Her blood ran cold instantly at the thought that post their relationship she was the one in a club making a fool of herself. She downed her drink and tried to push away the paranoia.

'Shall we go back to the dance floor?' she said, looking pointedly at Claire. Claire nodded vigorously and there was a chorus of 'Yes' from everyone except Ros.

'Rude,' Ros said, staring at Jackie.

Jackie blinked back at her. 'It's rude to go and dance with the team on the team initiation night?' Jackie spoke to her like she was a child; it would wind her up, Jackie knew, but she was behaving like a child so sod her. Jackie was good at dealing with children. Ros just pouted and made a show of talking at James again. She was so drunk she could barely focus on his face. He must be desperate, Jackie thought, and then wished she hadn't because she loved Ros a lot usually. Ros showed no signs of joining the rest of them. 'OK, well, have fun!' she said to Ros. 'We'll be just over there.' They headed back to the dance floor and left Ros with James and a heartbroken-looking Damon.

As the night got later the music got cheesier and cheesier, to the point where even Jackie could sing along to a few tracks. She danced and laughed and generally had the time of her life. It would have been perfect if not for the sight of Ros over her shoulder sitting fuming. Jackie had no idea what her problem was, but she got the feeling it was her fault. Ros sat staring at her dancing team, but every time she saw Jackie looking she poured herself all over James with sudden vigour. Is she trying to make me jealous? Jackie wondered, baffled. The woman was an enigma. An exhausting enigma.

Jackie pushed through the crowd to the toilets and entered a cloud of hairspray and perfume. A row of toilet-paper-strewn cubicles lined one wall, and a row of tight-dress-clad young women the other. They leaned in towards the brightly lit mirrors, adjusting smudged make-up and perfecting hair that didn't need perfecting. In one corner Jackie saw a pair of legs sticking out across the floor like a Barbie posed at a tea party. The legs' owner was sitting, shielded by a crouching friend mopping up tears. That'll hurt in the morning, Jackie thought, looking at the state of inebriation, but then, she was hardly one to talk. Jackie headed into a cubicle and appreciated the few minutes of isolation from bodies on all sides. She gave herself a moment to look again at the approving message from Duncan in response to her selfie.

As she emerged from the cubicle the sinks were far less crowded, and Jackie was surprised to see that the tearful pair on the floor in the corner were Jay and Laurel.

'Are you all right?' she said in alarm, looking at Laurel's weeping face. Jay looked up in surprise at Jackie's voice.

'What's happened?'

'I'm a bitch, apparently,' Laurel squawked, breaking into fresh sobs.

'We're dealing with some stuff,' Jay said, slightly more measured than Laurel, but with a definite wobble in her legs as she tried to maintain her squat.

'I can't believe you think I bullied you!' Laurel's eyes were barely focusing as she angled them on to Jay's face through the tears.

'You did!' Jay protested, at the same time as wiping at Laurel's streaming make-up with a wad of tissue. 'You were always so harsh and always undermining me. You and all your perfect friends . . . you made my life hell.'

'But you were the one all the teachers made such a constant fucking fuss of! I didn't think you really knew who I was,' Laurel muttered.

'Are you mad?' Jay's eyes were wide as they could be. 'You were the most popular girl in our year! Everyone worshipped you. Do you think it mattered that teachers liked me when none of the rest of you would stand near me?'

'It doesn't matter anyway, does it?' Laurel mumbled into her lap.

'What do you mean?' Jay sounded a bit exasperated. Jackie moved forward to help her a bit, but Jay waved a hand to keep her back. Jackie stopped.

'You still ended up back here showing off how great you are, didn't you? It wasn't enough that you spent all of school with all the teachers all over you getting you to uni, you then had to come back here and carry on rubbing my nose in it all. Why didn't you just stay away if you had it all going for you?'

Jay shook her head. 'Because I didn't have anything going for me, you nut job. I spent school being friends with dinner ladies because no one else wanted to be my friend, and then I ended up back here because I failed at my job and had to come back having failed.'

'So, being here is being a failure?' Laurel was beyond reasoning.

'No,' Jay said softly, 'Here is great. It just wasn't what I wanted.'

'Me neither,' Laurel hiccupped, and then launched herself into Jay in an enormous sloppy limby hug. Jay's ankles finally collapsed under her, and she fell back into Laurel, hugging back and laughing at the ridiculousness of it. 'No one ever wanted to see what I could do.'

Jackie left them to it, feeling very maternal and emotional at the possibility of reconciliation for the pair. She never could have believed one night could contain so much drama. Jay would be mortified come the morning to have argued so publicly. Jackie made her way back to the dance floor, where an Elvis remix was blaring into the crowd, and melted into the happy anonymity of the movement.

37

As it neared midnight Jackie began to pray someone would want to go home soon. Her feet were killing her and the underwire of her bra now felt like it was between her ribs. She didn't want to be the first one to tap out of the fun, but she also knew the alcohol was wearing off, and she couldn't drink more for fear of a week-long hangover. Luckily, Kath looked as if she was struggling too, and Jackie caught her attention across the circle of women. Without speaking, Kath nodded, then threw her arms up in the air.

'Girls! I'm sorry – I've got to get back for the babysitter. I'm going to have to call it a night.'

'I'll go with you!' Jackie said quickly.

'We'll all go,' Renee said, making Jackie think she must also have aching feet. 'Although I might need to stop for chips on the way.'

'Chips!' said Jay, loudly, making Annie laugh and nod. Jay and Laurel had progressed their drunken reconciliation to now gripping each other's hands and having feverishly deep conversations. The initiation had very much done the trick in bringing them together.

'Come on then, let's see if Ros is joining us.' Jackie raised an eyebrow at the others.

'She didn't even seem to like him that much,' said Claire, looking concerned about going back within touching distance of Damon.

'I don't know what's going on with her.' Jackie shook her head. They arrived at the booth and Ros looked at them all and then back at Jackie.

'We're going to go now,' Jackie said, trying to keep her voice even. 'We were thinking chips and then home?'

Ros sniffed, evidently making up her mind what her play was going to be. 'OK then,' was all she said. 'It was nice to meet you, James.' James looked gobsmacked and his mouth began to stutter open in surprise. 'Now don't start,' Ros snapped at him, 'I don't owe you shite. You've had my time just like I've had yours. It was nice to meet you.' She slipped her way round the other side of the booth and stood up on wobbly legs with the rest of the girls. Kath slipped an arm into hers to keep her upright.

The night air of the outside world was sharply cold. Laurel, who had come out without a coat, looked freezing but was declaring herself fine. They ducked into the nearest kebab shop and huddled on a table, each placing an order much bigger than the ones they had admitted to wanting on the walk there.

'So, you have a date tomorrow with Coach Duncan?' Claire teased Jackie.

'You don't!' Annie looked surprised. 'Oh I'm jealous, he's handsome.'

'He's far too old for you!' Jackie said in surprise.

'I like them old.' Annie giggled. 'Better taste.' Jackie's happiness flared at the effect the team was having on Annie's confidence.

'Well, you can't fault Duncan's taste!' Jay said, laughing and winking at Jackie.

'Coach Duncan!' Renee corrected. 'He worked hard for that title. You make sure you use it, Jack.'

'Oh, she'll use it,' said Ros, stuffing ketchup sachets into her handbag. 'She'll be Mrs Coach Duncan before you know it.'

Jackie whirled around, her temper snapping with Ros's puncture of her good mood. 'What is the matter with you?'

Ros squared up, obviously thrilled to finally be able to have a real argument without having to be the one to start it. 'Face it, Jackie, you're going to get all cosy with Duncan and go back to being boring and married and not interested in your friends any more.'

'Woah, cool it a bit, Ros . . .' Jay tried to soothe Ros with a hand on her arm, but she shook it off.

'You're the one who invited him to be a coach!' Jackie couldn't believe what she was hearing. 'You practically pushed us together.'

'Yeah, because I wanted you to finally wash Steve out of your hair, not settle down with the first man that came along!'

'Settle down!' People were staring now, but Jackie was too incensed to calm down and care. Surely the people who ran the place were used to bigger fights than this. At least neither of them had a knife. She wondered if anyone had checked to see if Ros had a knife. 'I'm just going on my second date, what on earth makes you think that's settling down?'

'Because I know you. I know all you want is to be comfortable and looked after by a man.'

Jackie already felt on the verge of tears but was absolutely determined not to cry until she got home and had biscuits. 'Oh well, sorry if I don't just want to jump from bed to bed pretending I don't give a damn that no one loves me.' It felt too harsh the second she heard it. She didn't mean it and the surroundings and the shouting made her feel cheap and ridiculous. How was her life a slanging match in a kebab shop?

'Like I want to be loved the way Steve loved you!' Ros sneered. 'You were some sort of brainwashed servant thinking that's as good as life gets. Then he decides to up and leave and you just pop out and find yourself a new one. I'd rather bed-hop and have you look down on me than be deluded.'

'You just want me single so that I have to be with you. You wanted to prise me off Steve and then keep me in your perpetual teenage existence.' Jackie was almost shrieking, and her hands were shaking with anger and an oddly exposed feeling. She hated this moment with every fibre of her being: more than

Steve's cancer diagnosis, more than Steve leaving her. If she could change one of those events, she'd throw Steve to the wolves and put her and Ros back to a time before this argument.

'Lamb kebab with extra pitta?' The man behind the counter must have known he wasn't going to get much response, but he valiantly tried anyway.

'My teenage existence? I own my own law firm, I own my own house, I live my life exactly how I want it. You have no job, you won't deal with your finances or your future – you won't even find out what you have to do to keep your house in case it's hard! How am I the teenager? You're useless.'

'I didn't know that was what you thought of me.' The wind had gone out of Jackie. She'd never been very good at arguing, especially with Ros, and her short supply of venom and the desire to spit it had run out. She turned sadly to the counter, feeling a hard meaty chunk in her throat, pressing on all sides. Jackie grabbed the nearest plastic bag to her and nodded thanks to the man. She was pretty sure it wasn't her food, but anything was going to taste like cardboard and between the argument and the efficiency of the shots girls she knew she was going to throw it up anyway.

The rest of the team hesitated, not knowing who to stick with. Then Jay followed Jackie, and Kath hovered momentarily before dashing out too. Laurel grabbed the food for her and Jay and followed close behind. Annie, Renee and Claire stood frozen to the floor with arms around a stock-still Ros. Jackie turned and looked back through the glass at Ros. She'd never seen her cry before.

38

None of it felt real. The heat on her skin; the view; the bed she had woken up in; the man she had woken up next to. None of it felt real. None of it could be real. She was Jackie Douglas who lived in a cul-de-sac. What was she doing in a villa in Crete with a man she barely knew? She was supposed to be on a rain-soaked netball court in England sorting things out with her best friend.

She took another sip of her coffee and looked at the sea. She didn't like coffee, not at all, not even a little bit, but drinking tea here just didn't seem right. She looked at her phone and briefly considered turning it on but wasn't sure whether a lack of communication from Ros or a worried voicemail from one of her sons would be worse. She pushed the phone away and looked back out to sea.

She'd woken up from the initiation with a pounding head and gritty eyes from crying. She'd tried to call Ros so many times that eventually Ros must have just switched her phone off, because the calls started going to directly to voicemail. There had been an awkward air in the house with Jay; that same slight tinge of politeness that had gilded every interaction between them since they had found out about Michelle and Steve(n). It had just been too much, and Jackie had been a hair's breadth away from cancelling her dinner with Duncan. But then she had decided she needed a reason to get out of the house.

She'd cried. Right there in the restaurant in front of him. Before the starter even arrived she had cried huge, dry sobs through her shoulders. She found herself telling him everything, even the soap-opera-style development about Steve's connection to Jay and the effect it had had on their arrangement. Along with the tears came stares from the other diners, but Duncan was unruffled.

'Let's get you out of it all then,' he said simply.

'What do you mean?' she snuffled.

'A holiday. Let's just get you a change of scenery.' His voice was so even and warm, she held his gaze across the empty table.

'I can't just up and leave.'

'Why not?' He leaned back to allow a server to dispense plates and thanked them politely before returning his gaze to Jackie.

'For so many reasons. Because this is our second date. Because I don't do things like that. Because I have to read the divorce papers and make up with Ros. Because if I leave then we don't have a netball team, and we barely have one as it is.'

'So what? I thought the netball was for you to make yourself happy?'

'It was, it is.' She struggled through the hiccupy sobs and the stares of other diners. 'But then, there's the save the courts thing, and if I leave the team, it's one less team and they are barely showing enough use as it is to save them. They'll build houses on them, and a new play park, and if they do that one son will be thrilled and the other will be angry because I've killed all the newts and it all feels like my responsibility.' She ground to a halt, having heard it all out loud and finding it at best ridiculous and at worst completely egomaniacal.

'So . . . the only thing between newt extinction and a play park is you not having a week's holiday?' He raised a bushy eyebrow and she laughed, hearing it through a less intensely guilt-ridden lens.

'Well, when you put it like that . . . yes. Yes, I could leave. But I shouldn't.'

'Why?' he persisted gently, and she didn't feel like he was persuading her, more genuinely asking. It was nice. Nice not to feel pushed, just asked.

'Well . . .' She struggled for an answer that was better than *I just never have before so I don't think I can* and failed to come up with one. She thought about how she would give Annie the confidence to have a holiday if she could. She blinked sticky eye-lashes and decided to just let the fantasy play out. 'Where would we go?'

'Crete,' he replied confidently and she remembered back to their first date and him mentioning his house there. His post-divorce gift to himself.

'I've never been to Crete,' she said, buying herself time while her head swam with the unfolding memories of him saying how difficult it had been to go anywhere with his ex-wife. A voice was telling her she therefore mustn't be difficult, while another voice that sounded suspiciously like Ros's was telling her to stand up for herself and do whatever she wanted to do. She was damned either way: either she was trying to please him or please Ros. Her eyes brimmed again, and she tried to clear her mind and work out what she wanted to do . . .

'I suppose it's very nice there, is it?' Her voice came out almost in a whisper.

'I think it's the best.' He smiled. She felt like he really under-stood how hard every decision ended up being for her. Immedi-ately she'd thought that, she wondered how much of her feelings about him were just projections of what she wanted him to be like. She barely, barely knew the man. But how did you get to know someone without letting them in? Thought after thought after endless ifs and buts marched incessantly through her cacophonous mind.

'And there are frequent flights?' She looked up from her untouched scallops and met his gaze.

And twenty-four hours later she was here. A wide-eyed Jay had nodded supportively and taken responsibility for the house while she was away, solemnly promising to water various ficuses. The flight was barely three hours, Jackie told herself all the way to the airport; if she needed to get back it was pretty much the same as being in Manchester. And then suddenly she was taking off, and watching clouds, and landing, and . . . here. It all felt too unreal, so she just kept looking out to sea for confirmation. It was such a different sea that it took a full ten minutes to remind her of Ros and golf clubs and that first excruciating night where she might have died if it hadn't been for Ros.

She stopped looking at the sea. She didn't want to think of Ros. Ros wouldn't speak to her and would probably only be angrier now that Jackie had disappeared to a foreign country with her new man at the drop of a hat. Perhaps Ros was right about her? Sod what Ros thought. It was nice to have an ocean between that problem and the sad, awkward living arrangement with Jay that was meant to have been such a godsend.

Duncan returned with delicious-looking pastry breakfasts, and he took her out for a stroll around the impossibly beautiful villages a little further down the hill from his house.

'If you go right down to the bottom you'll hit the high street,' he explained. 'And then you will be grateful for two things: one, that you're not in your twenties any more and two, that you do not work in a pub with British people in their twenties in it.'

Jackie laughed and was surprised at how easily it happened. Duncan really was very easy to be around. He slipped a hand into hers and she tried to hold back the flinch at the strangeness of it, but she somehow knew he felt it from the slight stiffening of his fingers. Her arm suddenly felt completely alien, held hostage by this other hand gripping it. She tried to relax. Why shouldn't they hold hands? She was staying with him, in a foreign country, they'd shared a bed, albeit without so much as a kiss, the night before . . . panic crept up her skin to her eyes and she pulled the hand away under the pretence of inspecting some olive-wood soap dishes on a stall outside a small shop.

'These are beautiful.' She held one up to show Duncan and he smiled and nodded.

'If you like olive wood, you've come to the right place,' he said. They continued to wander, chatting mindlessly about the sights and the smells. Duncan told her as much as he knew about the local life and she calmed. He didn't try to hold her hand again and she was grateful for that, as well as annoyed at herself for having been so frigid.

She enjoyed his company all afternoon, and into a dinner at his favourite local restaurant, run by an impossibly wonderful Cretan woman named Kate who Jackie fell instantly in love with. Her eyes twinkled and she seemed utterly delighted that the handsome Englishman up the hill had someone keeping him company at last. It wasn't until they were wandering in the warm, orange-scented air of the evening, making their way back to the house, that Jackie started to panic again. They had slept in the same bed the previous night, and while he hadn't pushed at all for anything to happen, could she be expected to be able to do that twice? Her brain was a whirlpool of thoughts chasing their own tails. Why shouldn't she be able to sleep without him coming on to her? Why was she already mentally accusing him of going for a fondle when he had so far been nothing but a perfect gentleman? Why was she so sure sex with him wasn't entirely what she wanted and needed to take her mind off things? Perhaps she did want to sleep with him, but on her own terms. Yes, that was it. And so far, he hadn't done anything to make her think any hypothetical sex on the horizon was not on her own terms. So what was the problem? God, she found herself exhausting. It was never failing to surprise her how many more thoughts there seemed to be in her mind since Steve had left. Surely she hadn't thought at this frantic a pace her entire life? Was marriage like a sedative? Perhaps Ros was right. She didn't want to be back thinking about Ros.

Duncan unlocked the door, and they entered the high-ceilinged living room where a beautiful orangey evening glow was bathing the sea-facing window. Something about the stone walls and floor made their movements sound loud and their lack of speech desperately quiet. Jackie checked her watch: she had about an hour to sort her head out before it was reasonably bed-time. There were two bedrooms in the villa, so she could sleep somewhere else. However, she had spent last night in Duncan's bed so if she asked to move would that be a nail in a coffin? Was that taking it slow or switching things off?

Duncan poured them both some wine and they moved out on to the balcony to sit and watch the remainder of the sun sink away.

'I can see why you fell in love with the place.'

'It's very peaceful. I feel like I can float about here. It's care-free,' he said lightly.

'Oh, well, I don't know about carefree but it's definitely. . . diet care.' Jackie laughed. 'My cares seem to be a bit stubborn.'

He looked at her worriedly. 'Do you wish you hadn't come?'

'No! No, not at all. . . I just haven't quite relaxed. I feel like I've left a big monster at Gatwick airport and it'll still be waiting for me when I get back.'

'At least if Ros is waiting for you at Gatwick she'll have to speak to you.' He topped up her wine and she laughed. 'Give yourself some time to just be. The sun and the lack of things to do will kick in soon and you'll have more time to think than you know what to do with. If you don't have a solution by the end of a month then there quite frankly can be no solution.'

Jackie just about managed to stop her eyes flaring wide at the mention of a month. Was he expecting her to stay that long? She couldn't stay that long. . . could she? She'd never gone a month without speaking to Ros. She couldn't ask Jay to look after her house for a whole month. And miss four games? The assessment on community usage of the courts was going on as she stood here gaping at Duncan in the middle of the Mediterranean. Would she have messed it all up for them if their team were out for that long? No, she couldn't let the girls down. She didn't want the courts built on. She wanted the team to play out the season together like they had promised to with their hands across the table in the Hawk. The sudden panic let her know that with immaculate clarity. It was nice, in a way. She would need to be back.

It occurred to her that she hadn't even looked at the return date on the ticket – he must have bought an open-ended return. Did such things exist? Or was there no return ticket as yet? Was she stranded? God, Ros would kill her for following a man to another country with no sense at all of her own safety or travel arrangements. The thought of Ros, and facing her, and going back to England, made her retreat back into herself all over again. Everything could wait. Except maybe the courts; they might end up gone – but who cared? They were just courts. Just old, sad courts that probably needed improving anyway.

'You look terrified, Jackie.' He was half joking, half inquisitive. 'If the thought of doing nothing but thinking is that bad, I have some crosswords around here somewhere. . .?' He acted out a farcical searching around him and she giggled.

'I'm more of a sudoku girl myself,' she quipped, trying to defrost, and he slapped his forehead in regret.

'Ah, well, I shall put you back on the next flight to a WHSmith then, shall I?' He was joking, but holding her eyes as if trying to give her an opportunity to talk if she needed to. She wanted things to be easy with him. No, she wanted things to be easy with her.

'Oh no, you don't get rid of me that easily,' she found herself saying. 'I'm getting in that pool tomorrow and there's nothing you can do to stop me.'

'I've got the linen sorted for the spare room, if you wanted to move in there tonight,' he offered tentatively. 'I'm sorry it wasn't ready when we got here last night.' She looked at him, under-standing the decision he was offering her.

They shared a bed that night and nothing more. Jackie lay, waiting for a hand or a whisper to try to instigate things, but as his breathing turned into more regulated sleep she began to slowly relax and the next thing she knew he was putting coffee on the stand next to her and she'd disappeared an entire night.

39

Each time Jackie woke up to the lofty ceiling and cool floor of the villa she found the worries about her life on English shores took a few minutes extra to properly penetrate. So what if she'd upset Ros by not being divorced in exactly the way Ros expected her to? So what if Jay's mum was Steve's girlfriend, it didn't change who Jay was, did it? So what if Leon's parent friends had to cross a road to get to a park? That's what crossings were for; they needed a netball court. She was sick of feeling guilty and responsible for every damn thing under the sun.

Duncan was a dream and seemed to know exactly how much to be around and how much to vanish to make her feel comfortable.

On her third day in Koutouloufari Jackie had switched on her mobile phone and, between text messages from her provider informing her of the extortionate post-Brexit cost of communication, she had an influx of messages from Jay, her sons – and Steve. He had had the audacity to ask her if she could orchestrate Jay forgiving Michelle for the affair. Jackie didn't even know where to begin with replying to that one and so had ignored it. This had only led to Steve texting again, and then calling, and then texting again to ask why there was an international dialling tone when he called her.

There was nothing from Ros. Jackie ached for contact but had absolutely promised herself she was not going to communicate again until there was some sort of response from Ros. It had to be a two-way street; the silent treatment just hardened Jackie's resolve to stay put and not give a shit. She had pored over every second of their argument (that she could remember) and had assured herself she was definitely only as bad as Ros.

She found herself seeking out Laurel Taylor's latest column on the netball team to check up on the game she had missed. She half wanted to feel still in the team, half wanted to convince herself that her absence wasn't a fatal problem for the rest of them.

Jackie was not particularly surprised to read that Laurel herself had volunteered to fill in for Jackie while she was away and, while they still had not had their first win, they seemed to have played marginally less embarrassingly.

Jackie pored over the words on the screen, devouring this new development. You could feel the crackle of enjoyment from Laurel at being the most experienced player on the team; she seemed to have invented for herself the role of team captain. Jackie couldn't help scouring the column for Ros's name but there was nothing. It was as free of Ros as her phone.

She ached to have her friend back. There was barely a walk or a meal or a sunset that she didn't think would be funnier with Ros in tow. Duncan was wonderful company; he was interesting, articulate, calm and funny. However, whenever Jackie thought about how great he was there was a barely formed 'but' in her mind. There was a two-dimensionality to being with him that she couldn't get past. He was funny and charming and kind and interesting, but. . . but he was missing something she couldn't put her finger on. She could picture Jay rolling her eyes dramatically if Jackie tried to describe it as she was feeling it: that he was a little too perfect. Too uncomplicated. But when your only comparison was a thirty-four-year marriage, wasn't every new man going to seem uncomplicated while the complications slowly revealed themselves? He seemed too good to be true, but of course he did; she was in paradise with him and she only knew about him a tenth of the things she knew about Steve. Of course, it was nice to be with him out here with great food and weather, but what about when it boiled down to domestic things? Was he the sort of man who showed an interest in helping you choose a shoe rack?

Crete was a dream. Duncan drove them out east to a town called Agios Nikolaos and they explored an abandoned leper colony and had lunch next to a big inlet of water that Jackie was assured occasionally attracted sea turtles. He drove them out west all the way across the island to a town called Chania that was made up of higgledy-piggledy avenues and close buildings with washing hanging out and plants and shutters all over the walls. A few days later he drove them due south across the hills and down hair-raising twisty-turny mountain passages and they emerged in a place called Matala. Probably the most breath-taking beach she had ever seen. Duncan told her stories about the cliffs next to the bay and how they had once been home to Bob Dylan and Joni Mitchell. Each time he drove them back to the trio of tiny villages where his villa was nestled, she decided afresh that he had picked the best spot to heal his heart.

She was having a great time, but she knew it was because she was refusing to think about things, rather than actually sorting her head out. This place was too perfect for that. . . she was aware of it all circling, and she was thinking about it, she just wasn't thinking anything through to the end. How could you solve the problems of wet, autumn Sussex when you were in timeless late-summer Crete?

On her tenth night they returned to Kate's restaurant just down the road and Jackie drank raspberry daiquiris under a ceiling of pink flowers and decided she'd never believe a life like this existed if she wasn't witnessing it. Impulsively she shot a hand out across the table and took Duncan's hand in hers. He looked up, surprised at the contact she had initiated.

'Having a nice time?' he said, sipping his own far less sweet cocktail that had made Jackie wince.

'I am,' she said, and meant it, 'I really am.' She took a deep breath and held his gaze across the table. 'Shall we go home?'

He caught her meaning on the warm breeze and nodded to Kate for the bill. Jackie's internal 'but' was circling from above like a falcon; swooping in to peck at her intentions for the night. She batted the potential problems on the horizon away and concentrated on the feel of Duncan's hand in hers as they made their way back to the house. It was cool inside compared to the Mediterranean evening. Jackie shivered and covered it by leaning in to kiss Duncan. He kissed her back and she led him to the bedroom, grateful again that there were no stairs for her to trip on. Villa was a much nicer word than bungalow, Jackie thought, and then tried to concentrate more on what she was doing.

They had shared a bed for over a week without touching once when they were beneath the thin sheet. Tonight, Jackie was going to change that. She was going to put the effervescent 'but' to bed, via putting Duncan to bed. No, not putting to bed: that made her think of Freya and being a grandma. Concentrate, Jackie, she told herself. She focused on Duncan's face as they lay down together kissing.

'Are you sure you want to?' he asked, slipping his arms out of his shirt and coming back to kiss her again.

'Yes,' she said, nodding to emphasise the point and pushing more unwelcome thoughts of her granddaughter away, 'I do.'

'I do too,' he said, smiling in an adorable way that made him look relieved and even more worthy of being the first new person she slept with in over thirty years. Then he broke away again. 'You don't owe me this, or anything. Promise you want to, you don't just feel you should? I should have offered you the spare room the first night instead of. . .' He looked uncertain of himself for the first time since she had met him, and her heart pulsed for his, wanting to soothe him and be kissed by him some more.

'Duncan,' she said firmly, gripping him round the waist, 'I want to have sex with you.' It was so much easier to say when it was to make him feel better, not convince herself.

And so she did. They did. And she concentrated. For the first time in years, she thought only about his skin on hers and the way she was moving and the way he responded. She didn't think about the pile of laundry in the corner or the state of the fridge in comparison to what they might want to eat the next day. She wasn't rolled off afterwards by a grateful but finished partner.

They both stayed awake afterwards, lying quiet and still and looking at one another.

'I like you,' Duncan whispered, smiling a bit sheepishly. Jackie blinked and brought his face more into focus.

'I like you too,' she said, and the 'but' circled so close she had to let it have its moment. 'I wasn't sure if I was going to. . . I mean, obviously I liked you straight away, but I wasn't sure if I was going to *like you* like you. God, is there a way to talk about any of this without sounding thirteen?'

Mercifully, Duncan laughed, 'Yes, I could feel you maybe felt like that. I hope I haven't pushed you. . .' The wrinkles between his eyebrows wrinkled with concern again.

'You haven't.' She reached out a thumb and smoothed them down, smiling and feeling her cheek burrow into the pillow as she did. 'I wanted this. With the argument with Ros, and Steve being so recent, and. . . well, everything else, I have been quite confused by how I could like your company but not want to do anything more about it. Does that make sense?' He nodded lightly and she continued, 'I have no roadmap for what to do with fancying you; the only thing I've ever done with those emotions is marry, move in and have children and. . . and I don't want to do those things with you.' She waited for him to flinch, but he just nodded again. 'Not at the moment anyway, and I wasn't sure if ever, but I also didn't want to say that in case it meant I had to stop seeing you at all.'

'I understand,' he said, shuffling to make himself more comfortable and patting the pillow down so they kept a clear view of each other across the bed. 'I don't really want to do any of those things either. Maybe one or two children but certainly not living together.' She laughed heartily and relaxed.

'OK,' she giggled along with him, 'Maybe some girls as we've both got boys, but let's not put a label on ourselves like girl-friend and boyfriend, OK?' He nodded and she felt words push-ing their way up her throat. Half of her wanted to swallow them down until she was sure what they were going to be, but the more impulsive part of her brain won out: 'I think I am going to *like* like you. You were shaping up to be a bit perfect; a bit unreal, but. . . I can't stop thinking about your worried little face con-cerned you were tricking me into bed with you. I think I'm going to *like* like you. I might already do. It's a relief to know you're not too steady.'

There was a silence from his side of the bed and she blinked, hoping she hadn't upset him. He opened his mouth, closed it again and then licked his lips. 'Little face?' he said, and it caught her so by surprise that she thought she was going to choke laugh-ing. When she had calmed down she lay looking at him, unable to keep the smile off her face. 'Seriously though,' he stroked her cheek with the back of his hand, 'I could cope with not being anyone special in your life, Jackie, but I couldn't cope with being someone who hurt you.' She felt tears press at the corners of her eyes and she tried to frown them into submission.

'I don't think you would hurt me,' she said honestly, 'I hope this is the beginning of everything coming round. Ros, Jay, the courts the everything. . .' She trailed off.

'Ros and Jay I understand,' he said. 'You can't honestly be too worried about those old playing courts though, can you?'

Jackie sighed and rolled onto her back to look at the ceiling. 'This is going to sound very stupid. . .' she began.

'Go on,' he teased.

'And I don't know the etiquette for not talking about your ex when you're in bed with your new. . . thing.'

'Thing now, is it?'

'Shut up. Whatever.'

'Just tell me?'

'I feel weird. No, you're right, I will completely live if some random playing courts get built on. But. . . I feel an affinity with them. Like, the courts are this funny old rubbish place that I've found something brilliant in. And they're old and battered like me, and there's nothing particularly brilliant or worth saving about them except why shouldn't they get to exist? Why does everything have to be new and shiny?'

'OK,' he said simply.

'This is where you tell me you're a multimillionaire and you'll buy them for me as a Christmas present.' Jackie rolled back on to her side to look at him.

'No can do I'm afraid, I spunked my fortune on the villa you're recuperating in.'

'Oh, don't say recuperating.'

'So you're not recovering?' He let his tone carry the euphemism.

'No, I'm good to go again if you are?' She matched him back.

'Oh, don't be ridiculous, I'm sixty-two.' He groaned and they both laughed into a comfortable silence.

It was only when she awoke completely unable to move her fingers that Jackie realised they had fallen asleep holding hands.

40

With the 'but' exorcised, Jackie managed to finally fully relax in Duncan's company. He had faults and complications and as they negotiated being together she saw them and liked him all the more for knowing them. Somehow another Cretan week breezed by and the finished crosswords piled up. She only really got to grips with the passing time when Jay sent her a link to the latest column by Laurel.

Jackie read with tears in her eyes all about how the Skids were teaming up with a local charity trying to get more women out of isolated lives. The story of the Skids had been noticed by the charity, who had got in touch to see if they had space on the team for other women. Ros had fobbed it off on to Jay, who had sprung into action like a woman possessed, from the sounds of things. Jackie had found the conversation bounced back and forth between her and Jay quite smoothly now they had something exciting to talk about. Jay had a fresh energy behind her, and Jackie could picture her behind the bar making notes on new ideas and ways they could help. It wasn't quite the level of charity work she'd been doing at her job before, but it was something.

Jackie felt a fierce pang of guilt for not being there. Interestingly, it was a pang she had not felt when reading the several texts from Leon about some emergency childcare woes with her gone. The Skids had been her salvation in a world that was blown apart by Steve and now here she was in another country with a different man, having fully abandoned them. When Ros had accused her of being intent on settling down with anyone it had felt ridiculous and obscene, but wasn't that exactly what she had done? She shook those gloomy thoughts away: no. She was going back; Duncan wasn't Steve; she deserved a holiday; not everything had to consume her life to the extent of all else: netball included.

> How was the game tonight? xx

She fired off another message to Jay and picked up the crossword she was half-heartedly doing. Her phone buzzed almost immediately though, and she gave up pretending she understood cryptic clues and opened the message.

> It was ok. No Ros so we were a player down, but we got over half their score so still a point on the board! x

Jackie's thumbs drafted several ghost replies in the air above her phone before settling on the screen with her response.

> That's great, well done!! Where was Ros? xx

Asking someone else the whereabouts of Ros felt like having someone else peg out her underwear on a washing line. She didn't even pretend to go back to the crossword but just sat scrolling through the last messages between her and Ros from the before times. Her thumbs twitched to shoot off a message asking if she was OK, but she stiffened her joints and refused to go begging for contact again. Mercifully, the phone buzzed with a new message from Jay before she lost control of her opposable digits once and for all.

> Dunno! She's been so quiet lately and left straight after the game last week so no one's really spoken to her. Annie says she's been at work most days. I've text but not had a response. Assuming you've still not heard from her. . .? X

For some spiteful reason, Jackie felt better that Ros wasn't speaking to any of the rest of the team either. She knew it was petty, but the fact that Ros wasn't cock-a-hoop let her know she wasn't the only one regretting her behaviour at the initiation. It was eerie though, Ros not being constantly there. Jackie felt with a pang all the times she had offloaded on her dependable friend and just assumed she never had problems because she didn't talk about them. It hadn't been intentional, but she had done it. But it wasn't that Ros didn't know she could tell her if she had problems, surely? If only Ros could be more open.

Probably still sulking. Leave her to stew. xx

It felt mean, and she knew it wasn't the response that best suited her but she sent it anyway. Why not be the hard-nosed one for a change? She was always the one seeing it from someone else's perspective. Her husband had cheated on her for nearly a year, and she'd never so much as screamed at him; the high ground was boring. On the other hand, was it fair to take it out on Ros that she hadn't taken it out on Steve. . .? Oh, sod the other hand. The other hand was always flapping about sticking its nose in where it wasn't wanted.

She reread the netball column and beamed at the photo of Kath stood with a single mother of three who had come along to watch and see if it was for her. What an outcome from a shitty end to her marriage. Perhaps the humiliation in the original try-outs was worth it? No. No, Jackie wasn't selfless enough to think she'd go through that again just so some women could make friends. Everyone had a limit. But the team was a good thing, and getting better. They'd found a decrepit old corner of the world and turned it into something good. Everything was good, except that she was here in Crete, not talking to Ros: the woman who forced it all to start.

'Shall we go to the beach?' she called through to Duncan, who was watching tennis in the next room. She heard the TV switch off immediately and footsteps padding through.

'I thought you'd never ask!' He smiled. They grabbed some bags and headed out to the car. Jackie eyed her phone by the book of crosswords and then decided to leave it here. She deserved a day without checking her phone for messages from Ros. They were stubbornly not arriving, so why wait for them?

They decided to make a proper day of it and return down south to Matala, the incredible secluded cove by the cliffs. They wandered over to a restaurant overlooking the water. It was on wooden boards and hovered out over the sea so that Jackie could see fish drifting about in the clear water beneath her toes. She ate a wonderful lunch in the shade, and then they headed down on to the sand to do some snorkelling. It was like being in a holiday catalogue: everything was so picture perfect. Especially the burgeoning tingly feeling of being with Duncan.

'My son has a new job,' Duncan blurted suddenly as they sat together on the sand, eyes on the horizon.

'Oh really? That's good! Is it?' Jackie scanned his face for clues. He didn't sound elated.

'Yes, oh yes. Oh, great for him. It's just, it's in Leeds. He's moving out.'

'Oh.' Jackie waited. A geyser of thoughts erupted. Would Duncan move too? Would he want her to move in now Stewart was moving out? Just wait, she told herself like a child, listen.

'Yeah.' Duncan sighed, 'Obviously I'm thrilled for him; he's really turned his life around. But I'll miss him. It's one more thing over, you know?'

She nodded; she really knew.

They sat together, watching an enormous sun settle at the back of the ocean, and didn't get up to drive home until every strand of pinky-purpley light had faded from the world around them. Duncan drove along the straighter, main roads and much to Jackie's surprise she nodded off and only woke when he turned up the sharp bend into the driveway.

'God I'm so sorry! How long have I been asleep?'

He laughed. 'Only about half an hour. Good nap?'

Jackie yawned. 'Yeah. Not as good as the really long one I'm going to have now though.'

'Oh, does that mean you're not hungry again? I had big plans for that pizza in the fridge.'

'Well, just because I'm not hungry doesn't mean I won't eat pizza,' she responded, enjoying herself. Looking down, she wondered when she had stopped sucking her stomach in. They threw the pizza in the oven and compromised by eating in bed.

'You know,' Jackie said through a mouthful of cheese and anchovies, 'People throw around the phrase *better than sex* but sometimes. . .' She raised the rest of her slice to the light fitting and smiled.

Duncan put on a look of faux outrage and immediately moved the box to the floor. 'Now you listen here, young lady,' he said, raising an eyebrow and turning to look at her leaning on one elbow, 'that is just not a phrase I will permit a house guest to use while currently in my bed.'

He whipped the slice of pizza out of her hand and threw it on the floor before moving in towards her. She cackled with laughter and the laughter soon turned to gasps as he began to massage her neck with soft and increasingly harder kisses. Over the course of the next half-hour he proved her wrong and she wondered what she could ever have thought was so good about pizza.

41

Jackie woke to another beautiful morning and several pizza crumbs embedded in the soft flesh of her upper arms. She jumped in the shower, stifling a laugh to herself about the previous night's antics. She thought it was probably the most perfect day and night she had had in decades. Why bother ever going home? Surely, with the extra women from the charity and the extra PR the courts would never get built on, and Michael's newts would be safe; and she could persuade Freya to take up netball and then even Leon couldn't be mad. Jay could keep her house; sod it, why not? Steve can pursue Jay in court for it if he wants half. And Ros . . . well, why should Jackie have to chase Ros to make up? Things worked both ways. Jackie could bury her head in the Cretan sand and stay here in this uncomplicated bubble for ever. She wouldn't, and she knew she wouldn't, but she would stay just a little bit longer and was determined not to feel guilty about it.

She brewed a coffee and gathered up her phone to go and let her hair dry naturally on the balcony. The roots were coming through rather urgently, but perhaps a bit more sun would help bleach them and put off the need for a hairdresser and hours in foil.

The lock screen on her phone was awash with notifications. Six missed calls from Steve. This was getting ridiculous. Just as she went to draft a stern message to him that she would edit down later to a mild reproof, her phone buzzed again with his name at the centre of the screen.

'Oh Steve for goodness sake, Jay and her mother are not my resp—'

'No, Jackie, it's Ros.'

42

If getting out to Crete was a blur, then getting back was a badly pixelated slow-motion nightmare. Duncan drove them to the airport, bought them tickets, got them seated and sat quietly beside her. She didn't even have the strength to smile at the irony of Ros being the reason she'd let a man completely organise her day.

Had she had longer before Steve called again the previous morning, she would have seen that behind his missed calls were fifteen from Jay. Text after text was piled into her abandoned phone begging for her attention while she'd been at the beach watching the sun go down. She thought she might be sick. There was an unswallowable lump of guilt forcing itself into every breath she took. This was why you didn't just walk away from everything; this was why not everyone could be selfish. The plane crawled through the sky.

Duncan had to remind Jackie to do up her seatbelt. His voice filtered through, and she blinked the patient but firm face of an insistent flight attendant into view. She fumbled the belt into position and then felt her body return to its state of frozen, numb tension. Her ears were blocked up, fuzzy like the worst hay fever day, and concurrently acutely tuned in to a high-pitched tinny whistle that changed frequency every time she thought she might get used to it.

They landed in grey, rainy, boxy Gatwick and Duncan drove them straight to the hospital. Ros looked tiny in the bed. Pale and drawn. Jackie was surprised to see Steve and a woman she assumed was Michelle by her bedside. For some reason this made her want to cry again but she wasn't sure if it was gratitude to him for being there, or worry for Ros that she was so ill she had let Steve into a room unharmed. Jackie was so focused on the sick person pretending to be Ros in the bed that she didn't even register the look on Steve's face when she walked in tanned, with Duncan in tow. In another world she and Ros would cackle about how jealous he looked. But Ros was pale and asleep and too still.

Jay leapt out of a plastic chair and ran to Jackie; her face a mess of puffy skin and black smudges from her trademark eyeliner.

'Oh Jackie!' was all she managed before she let out a day and a half of tension into Jackie's shoulders. Jackie brushed her hair and shushed her sobs without taking her eyes off Ros. Bad things didn't happen to Ros; Ros didn't get sick. Ros didn't even get hangovers. Ros was the one with no complications. Jackie felt a wringing in her stomach over all the times she had simplified Ros because it suited her to have an easy friend.

'And they're sure it's encephalitis?' Jackie hated being in hospitals out of uniform. Being on the other side was so difficult.

'Yes,' said Steve, 'viral encephalitis. Rare, I think. It causes the brain to swell, but they think she's going to be OK. I think they just about got to her in time.'

The words made Jackie want to vomit. She kept expecting the cast of *Holby City* to wander in and reassure her this was a dream. 'Right,' she managed, and then went back to staring at Ros while Duncan asked some more questions that she couldn't comprehend. Her brain was playing her a horror film of Ros lying alone in her apartment with a migraine that got worse and worse until the fits started and no one was there to help her. Her employees knew better than to question her not being in the office, her family lived four hundred miles away and Jackie had been in Crete. If it hadn't been for Jay . . . Jackie pulled Jay in tighter to her, not noticing the uncomfortable glances from Michelle at their proximity. 'Has she been awake?' Jackie croaked.

'A little bit,' Jay snuffled into Jackie's damp shoulder. 'She's not very with it. Apparently it's common to lose your memory with this but . . . but maybe not permanently. She's not really recognised us yet.'

Duncan returned with tea she hadn't realised he'd left for, and introduced himself to Michelle and Steve.

'Lovely to meet you.' Steve offered a weak smile. 'We'll get off and leave you to it. You can't have more than four visitors and the nurses are Nazis about it.' He attempted a laugh, and while the joke fell flat to everyone except Michelle, Jackie was disproportionately grateful that he was still capable of making someone happy. Steve felt like nothing while Ros needed her. She wondered how there had ever been other priorities.

She sat in the bedside chair that Jay had vacated and took Ros's hand. It was cold and felt bony. Ros had always been thin, but now she looked like a person perfectly cast to play a hospital patient extra. There was a flicker behind Ros's eyelids as Jackie stroked the back of her hand and looked hopefully for signs of waking up, but there was nothing. There was nothing for hours.

Jay left around dinner time and Jackie called Ros's family, once she had recharged Ros's BlackBerry and dug out their numbers from behind the passcode that only she and Ros knew. For some reason that detail made her cry more than anything else. Jackie slept in the plastic chair, waking to more news and updates from the doctors that made sense to her on a nursing level but not in relation to her best friend.

Duncan went home and despite everything he said about it making sense for her to come too, she ignored him and stayed. The room was quiet except for the machines that had replaced the tinnitus. She was amazed at how unboring worrying could be; when was the last time she had just sat in a chair and done nothing for this long without getting itchy feet? Texts came and went from Leon and Michael, Steve, Renee and the rest of the

Skids. Jackie didn't have much to reply. Just endless 'X's and 'Will Do's and 'Thank you's.

Nurses came and went, and Jackie hoped that she'd been as comforting as they were when this had been her job. She was grateful to have worked here; she wasn't entirely sure she'd be allowed to stay around the clock if there weren't a few faces who recognised her. Hours, minutes, seconds and a day bumbled around each other in time soup. Jackie just sat and was and waited.

'Have they gone?' It came so suddenly out of nowhere that Jackie couldn't for the life of her remember what she had been thinking about before Ros spoke and knocked all the thoughts into the weeds. Her head spun to look at Ros so fast her spine emitted a loud clunk, and she shot a hand up to soothe it.

'Ros!' she squeaked, immediately bursting into tears, and then, trying to get hold of herself: 'Has who gone?'

'The others.' Ros licked dry lips, speaking with closed eyes and deep breaths.

'Yes, there's no one here but me, love.' Jackie wanted to shuffle closer but didn't want to move in case it upset the balance that was Ros being awake.

'I don't like Steve,' Ros said, and Jackie let out a noisy, honking seal noise that was all the relief in her body taking the form of a very unattractive laugh.

'I know you don't. I know you don't. Neither do I. Well, that's not true, I'll always have a soft spot for him. But I don't really like him any more. I love you though, Ros. I'm so sorry. I love you so much.'

'That's good,' said Ros, and then lay still, eyes still closed, lips still pale and cracked.

Jackie thought she had gone back to sleep. She let the tears fall uninhibited from eyes that were glued on Ros. All the conclusions that had been impossible to find in Crete had been found for her in this. Sitting, with a numbed, cold bottom, on the hard plastic chair, she wondered how she'd ever thought her choices were about netball or Duncan, the courts or newts, Steve or divorce. It should always have been about Ros. This mighty woman who had never once not been there for her. She'd just assumed the constancy of Ros like water comes out of a tap and it made Jackie physically wriggle to think about how many times she must have dismissed Ros's problems because they were different to her own. Jackie's longest relationship lay breathing calmly in the bed and Jackie sat and stared and waited for her.

43

Two weeks of hospital visits went by. Always Jackie, but with a rotating cast of others. The Skids took it in turns, Duncan came as often as he could, even Steve popped back in once but left the second Ros woke up from a nap. The most earth-shattering surprise for Jackie was the day Michael walked through the doors.

'What on earth are you doing here?' she gasped, gathering him up into the tightest hug as Leon, David and Freya followed him in.

'I took some holiday. I can't believe Aunty Ros isn't immortal.'

Jackie had cried all over again at Michael's appearance. The divorce of his parents and the death of his grandfather hadn't summoned him, but Ros could.

'I dunno,' he had said, shrugging. 'She's Ros, isn't she? She's a fucking inspiration. I don't know if I'd be doing what I'm doing without her having been around.'

'Language,' Jackie had chided to cover the sound of her heart bursting.

Finally the day came around when Jackie was allowed to remove Ros from the hospital. The world surrounding Ros was universally grateful for this. The patchy memory loss and inability to find the words she wanted were not bringing out the best in her, and Jackie was keen to have her somewhere where they could deal with the frustrations privately. Ros was insisting she could go home to her own place, but Jackie had backbone to spare when it came to nursing and she insisted on moving Ros in with her.

'I swore I should never live in a cul-de-sac,' Ros grumbled.

'You'll be living in a black sack if you don't stop moaning,' Jackie chided, cheerfully, happy to be bickering again.

The second spare room was hastily renovated in two days of back-and-forth trips for Jackie and Jay to Ros's place getting the essentials. Ros and Jackie's lists of essentials had varied hugely but Jackie found herself sighing wearily and packing a DVD of *Con Air* into a box along with the pyjamas and winter socks. In the back of her mind she considered how the house had gone from hollow to bursting in such a short space of time. A positive element to a horrendous situation is never easy to digest and Jackie pushed the thoughts away as she and Jay arranged Ros's personal items and listened to Radio Two.

'How are things at home?' Jackie was trying to make a point of stroking the elephant in the room in an attempt to tame it.

'Oh . . . fine. I barely spoke to Steven anyway, so not much has changed.' A small, puffy laugh pulsed briefly out of Jay as she folded one of Ros's jumpers and put it in the chest of drawers.

'What?' Jackie looked at her.

'It's so stupid, but . . . we were having dinner last week. One of Mum's "Let's Make Everything Normal Again" attempts, and we were midway through when Mum said something about laundry. And, I suddenly put two and two together on why our team is called the Skids. There he was just sitting in front of me at the table, and I could not stop laughing. They thought I'd gone mad. I was so angry and disgusted with both of them, and then realising he was the rolled-up poo pants guy . . . It was like that bit in Harry Potter with the boggart. It just shrank him. So stupid, but every time I think about it, I laugh.' She giggled again and Jackie joined in. They continued pottering about to the soothing sounds of Ken Bruce, occasionally catching each other's eye and laughing all over again until Jackie left to pick Ros up from the hospital.

Ros's memory was an after-photo of a piñata, and Jackie approached her cautiously, knowing she was struggling with not having her quick wits to hand. Ros was sharp, and capable, and a fixer, and Jackie saw how excruciating she found it to be clumsy with her faculties. The doctors were much more worried than Jackie about the results of some of the language tests, but then they didn't know how many phrases Ros had mangled before. Jackie could see the strain in her friend. She at least knew, though, that while Ros might be a terrible patient, she herself was a great nurse and would be there until the end of time if that's what it took.

'Are you ready to go, then?' Jackie smiled at Ros.

Ros frowned back, disliking being sat while people stared up at her. 'I've been ready to go for a week. All this molly-cuddling. I just need to get back to work.'

'You're absolutely not going back to work yet.' Jackie used her stern voice and then smiled at a mini memory of Duncan's positive opinion of her stern voice. She liked how he was starting to creep into her daily memories, not yet replacing Steve but appearing alongside. It was nice. It felt hopeful.

'Then what on earth am I going to do? I always work. I'm a clothes horse for work.'

'A workhorse.' Jackie corrected and then made eye contact with the nurse, who had looked concerned. 'That's normal: don't worry. It'll be fun.' She continued to Ros, 'We'll be like a college house; me, you and Jay.'

Jackie pushed Ros's wheelchair to the car. Hospital policy was that no one use legs unless almost off hospital grounds. For all Ros's annoyance at being patronised, she was seemingly OK with limited physical activity. She was munching on pistachio nuts and filling her pockets with the shells.

'I'm not sleeping downstairs like a nana.'

'I know you're not. You know we've sorted you out the spare room. It's not permanent. Stop being cantankerous.'

'Am I going to have to listen to the two of you shagging all night?' She persisted with looking for a reason for her bad mood.

'No,' Jackie drew on her nursing patience training, 'he doesn't have to stay at all while you're here.'

'He's not moved in?' Ros's voice had the faux innocence of a pageant winner and Jackie was glad she couldn't see her smile.

'No, Ros, I've only been dating him a few months. He just stays over occasionally but he doesn't have to do that while you're staying if it's a problem.'

'He can.' She threw in another handful of shelled nuts. 'I don't mind him.'

Jackie smiled broader. She knew Ros more than didn't mind him. He had beaten her twice in a row at backgammon and Ros was quite taken with his refusal to let her win on the grounds of being ill.

'And I won't have you looking after me twenty-four-seven just because you feel guilty.' Ros twisted in the chair and eyed Jackie, suspiciously.

Jackie dropped her smile and flushed, and their pace slowed. 'What have I got to feel guilty about?' she tested; did Ros want to talk about things?

'Nothing, but it doesn't usually stop you.' Ros shifted back round to look forward and cease eye contact.

Ros hadn't mentioned the initiation argument and as time went on Jackie was finding it harder and harder to broach the subject. There was always half an apology on the tip of her tongue, but she never quite knew how to articulate it. Ros was doing nothing to expedite matters. Jackie rather suspected she was using the virus as the perfect excuse to just put everything to bed without ever needing to talk about it. Ros didn't like mess and faff, and it would be just like her to use a near-death experience to cauterise an unpleasant disagreement without needing to apologise.

Jackie wasn't like Ros. Every word out of her mouth was nearly a 'We need to talk . . .' or 'Listen Ros, shall we just clear up any . . .' but it remained unsaid.

She drove Ros home, with the clinking of pistachio shells only slightly less annoying than Jeremy Vine. Jay was waiting for them on the front step.

'No bunting?' Ros smiled as she gingerly stepped out of the car. She looked tired from even the short drive. Jackie recognised the blusher as a vague attempt at warpaint and decided to try to get Ros into a chair for a rest without her noticing.

'It's inside,' Jay said, smiling, taking Ros's bag from Jackie and holding the front door open. They led Ros into the living room, where Jay had indeed put up balloons and a *Welcome Home* banner: 'Ta da!' she said, waving her hands like a Butlin's Redcoat and beaming at Ros. There'd been a long discussion with the rest of the Skids as to whether they could all be there to celebrate Ros leaving hospital. As Ros sank into the sofa and gave a deep sigh of exhaustion, her eyes flickering shut, Jackie knew she had made the right decision in saying no. She felt a useful, warm pride at being in her best role. She was a caregiver, why fight it? Jackie and Jay stood looking at Ros, unsure what to do next.

Ros opened an eye again. 'Stop standing there like weirdos. It's creepy,' she said, and shut the eye again.

Jay laughed. 'Christ, you two aren't still arguing, are you? I'll make tea.' She disappeared into the kitchen and Jackie watched Ros's eyes peep open a little bit to look at her. It was the first out-loud mention of The Argument from anyone, and Jackie pounced.

'Ros, I'm so sorry.' It tumbled out before Ros could do a fake snore to avoid the subject. 'Open your eyes, I want to talk to you.' Ros opened her eyes narrowly. The scowl looked very funny on someone as pale and weak-looking as she currently was. 'I absolutely took you for granted, and I'm so sorry,' Jackie continued. 'I just had so much on my mind, and I felt pulled in all directions, and somehow, I just forgot that you were complicated too in the middle of it.'

Ros huffed a little and looked at the ceiling. 'Yes, well, look . . . oh I don't know, Jackie, we're good now, aren't we? It's fine. And, sure, I'm also sorry. I was snappy and stuff and I went a bit far.

It was all just a bit much, and I didn't like some of the ways you made me feel, but, I'd rather just forgive you than talk about it, OK? Don't hug me.'

Jackie laughed. Ros's skeleton seemed to be visibly squirming under her skin at the intense displeasure of talking about her feelings. 'I'm going to hug you but I shan't bring it up again.' She nodded at her solemnly. 'Unless you're a total bitch.'

44

'But we showed more than enough use?' Jackie's voice was shrill.

Ros was calmer, bundled in several jumpers and a coat to cheer them on from the sidelines. 'What were the terms they set out in the ultimatum?' she asked.

The woman from the netball league, Meg, sighed and shrugged in a *what can you do* kind of a way. She dealt with Jackie's complaint first: 'I know we did, but even a bunch of us playing netball wasn't more interesting to the council than the money the building company were offering for the land.' She moved her attention on to Ros: 'They're all slippery with it, it was all "maybes" and "will be taken into considerations" rather than a "get X amount and we won't shut them down". They're closing up at Christmas and I think aiming to get started in January.'

Jackie felt crestfallen. She looked across at the Skids, who were, genuinely, warming up. Renee had been unable to make it, and they'd actually had two spares to choose from to take her place; Izzy and Kirsty, two women who'd joined them through Jay's charity work, had agreed to play half of the match each. Jackie had been on such a high at the thought they'd gone from that empty village hall try-out to having spares. Just as coming here was beginning to feel normal, and not just normal but the highlight of her newly normal life, it was all going to end. 'So that's it for the league?'

'Not permanently,' Meg said brightly. 'We're talking to the sports centre to see if there's a way we can book their space regularly. And we're talking to the council to see if we can get a grant now that we're of "special community interest", but

I'm not holding out much hope from them. There's not a lot of spare cash floating about in local government, I don't think. We'll be back somehow, I'm just not sure what it'll look like or when yet. Excuse me.'

She smiled warmly and jogged over to where the other team's captain was waving at her. Meg was refereeing the game between the Skids and their opposition; this was the second time they had faced the dreaded Legal Beagles. Stupid name, Jackie thought, but couldn't say it, for obvious reasons.

Jackie's feet felt leaden making her way over to her starting position. Technically, of course, there were no starting positions as long as you were in your designated section, but Jackie had learned where the women who knew what they were doing started, and it was best not to mess with it. The Skids had had a disastrous game where they'd experimented with 'never being where they expect us to be'. It was true, they were never where the team expected them to be, but they were, as a result, also never between the opposing team and their net. It was up there with one of the worst losses they had had; worse than the one where she and Kath had offered to be the defending duo and had conceded so many penalties for being in the wrong place that the referee had the cheek to ask if they were 'taking the piss'. Laurel had actually stamped her foot like a child. Jackie had been mortified at the time, but then in the Hawk afterwards they had laughed so much she had almost coughed up a lung. It didn't seem to matter how much they were humiliated on the court, it always seemed to send her to bed with a smile on her face.

She looked up to smile at her opposing player for this match and as their eyes met, the smile vanished through the gaping void that was now her stomach. It was the woman from the try-outs. The other pair of hands on the ball. Jackie's mind scrabbled for her name, but nothing was forthcoming; she could feel the heat rising on her old, sagging cheeks as she looked at the athletic woman she would be traipsing around after for the game.

'Oh,' said the woman, recognising Jackie and then glancing around her as if checking she had backup, 'it's you.'

'Jackie,' said Jackie through a clenched throat. 'I am so sorry about my behaviour in the try-out.'

The woman nodded, seemingly making up her mind. 'Libby,' she said finally and the name clicked into place in Jackie's memory. 'Don't worry about it. Mackie explained what you were going through.'

Jackie's bowels turned to hot mush at the thought of Ros having to explain personal details to her staff to cover up for Jackie's temporary insanity. She tightened her stomach muscles and refreshed her smile. 'Yes, it wasn't a good time. But your face looks good.' She prayed there wasn't a bill on its way for facial reconstruction surgery. Why pick a fight with a lawyer?

Libby's face eased its tension a bit with a diluted smile. 'Yes, no long-term damage. I was back to playing within a week. No harm done. Did you manage to get your husband back?'

Jackie flinched at the bluntness and reassembled the thoughts it scattered to try to find a suitable answer. Libby jogged on the spot, trying to keep warm, while the referee sorted out some drama with nails that were a bit too long on the Legal Beagles' centre player.

'No. I didn't,' Jackie murmured, trying not to sound sad about it.

'God, how horrible. I'd hate to be alone at your age.'

Jackie was now beginning to wonder if this woman was thoughtless or just a very casual arsehole. Either way, she decided to just glide past it and be the bigger person. 'I actually have a new boyfriend now, so it's fine. He's extremely handsome. Are you enjoying the league?' she asked, deciding not to bother joining Libby in her on-the-spot jogging. Warming up was a con because as soon as you started playing you were too hot anyway.

'Oh yeah, it's a good blow-out,' Libby said, barely panting. 'I'm looking forward to moving into the sports centre though.'

'Oh really?' Jackie hadn't considered that any of the players would be pleased about the change of course for the league. 'It's going to be quite a lot pricier, I think.'

Libby just shrugged, her eyes focused on the referee, waiting for the whistle. 'Yeah, but actually – I think it'll be good. It'll weed out a lot of the teams who aren't properly committed to it.'

Jackie looked over to where Izzy had just laughed at something Kirsty had said. 'Well, no it won't, it'll weed out the ones who can't afford it and that's not the same thing,' she said, but the game had started and she said it to the gap where Libby had been.

The Legal Beagles scored in under a minute and every one of their victorious high-fives made Jackie's blood boil. Libby strolled back over to where Jackie had remained. The Skids had made an agreement that once it looked pretty certain the opposing team was going to score, it wasn't worth them chasing it and they might as well conserve energy for the next one. It wasn't exactly a winning strategy, but it saved on stitches. Only Laurel still danced around fervently, calling to the others to get into spaces. Jackie didn't really know what Laurel meant by being in spaces, she usually was in a space, but it never seemed to be the right space. What was a space and what was just not really being involved?

'Calms you down when you get the first one under your belt, doesn't it?' Libby said without looking at Jackie, and Jackie made up her mind that Libby was just a traditional bitch. The next three points on the board did nothing to change her decision. The game wasn't even nearly close, but the Skids' usual laughter at their failings failed to materialise. Jackie waited patiently for the endorphins to kick in, but they were off sick and her heavy feet followed her round the court for the full twenty-eight minutes.

As she trudged back to her car at the end of the game the sight of the Legal Beagles in their matching outfits made her feel curiously melancholy. They would be fine with the change of venue; they could afford it. She wasn't sure why she begrudged them that. She could afford it too. But there was something about the new, shiny, expensive hall that felt less . . . less inviting. And not just because of the horrific try-outs. Why did everything have to be so shiny and new?

This would probably spell the end for their team. If other teams had shelled out to play, would they be OK with facing the Skids? Would they feel unwelcome in the league? And what about all the work Jay was doing to find a space for the women coming through the charity? Could they afford it? Probably not, Jackie thought, thinking about the look on Kath's face when she'd heard the potential new fees and mentally factored in them in against Delilah's ballet and Horatio's karate.

It was melodramatic, she knew, but it just felt like there wasn't a place for them. The ones without an easy label: wife, mother, nurse. The ones who wanted a bit of time off from their label: wife, mother, job. Where did they go? She sank into the car and drove the familiar route to the Hawk to drown her sorrows in Ros's company.

45

'That'll be one of our last games, then,' Jackie said the next week, looking sadly into her drink. Meg had confirmed the league was moving to the sports centre, and the prices were astronomical. She'd explained with admirable bright-side-looking all the positives to playing at the sports centre, but all Jackie could do was see a neon 'Michelle' sign over the top of them. Even that made her feel guilty; she found it harder and harder to think negatively about Michelle knowing she was Jay's mum and not just Steve's girlfriend.

'Why?' Ros looked up sharply from her position on the alcove bench between Renee and Kath. Annie, Claire and Jay were stretched out along the other side.

'I just don't know if it sounds right for us when it moves to the sports centre,' Jackie said, and shrugged. 'It sounds a bit elitist, I think.' There was no doubt in her mind that the Skids would be the first team Libby hoped the new prices would squeeze out.

'Oh God, don't make me go back to golf,' Ros groaned and shrank down into her cardigan. She still wasn't back to playing, but that hadn't stopped her being there. She and Duncan were jokingly referring to her at home as his assistant coach. Jackie kept having to pinch herself at how their friendship was developing. Something about him was having a good effect on her through the agony of a slow recovery. She sat nursing an elaborate mocktail and looking jealously at Claire's prosecco. Her first attempts at returning to the arms of alcohol had been rather disastrous alongside the residual memory fuzz from the encephalitis and she and Jackie had embarked on a mission to stay dry until at least the end of the year. Jackie had privately been fairly sure it wouldn't last until *Strictly* started, but Ros had stuck to it. Jackie didn't know if it mostly worried her that Ros was really so shaken that she could stay off it, or it mostly delighted her that deep down Ros did actually take care of herself.

'Yeah, because golf isn't elitist.' Jay laughed.

'There is a women's rugby team at the club I'm a member of . . .' Claire began, but the collective pallor of her team at the suggestion ground her to a halt.

'Anything but that!' Jackie wailed, remembering the force with which rugby players had mashed into each other. Repeatedly.

'What games do they play in Crete?' Kath asked. 'Maybe we can all move into Duncan's place?'

They all laughed at that, and Jackie felt jolted by the unreal memory of Crete and Duncan's villa. How beautifully isolating it had been to be there together. Things had slipped easily into becoming a gentle relationship since they'd got back, but it was undoubtedly different to the absolute seclusion of the villa. She was enjoying his company – more than enjoying; he was beginning to feel integral. But there had been something magical about the way it had been in Crete.

'Just joking.' Kath looked concerned. 'You all right, Jack?'

Jackie snapped out of it. 'Oh God yeah, I was just thinking about being in Crete.'

'The clean version please.' Jay laughingly covered her ears.

'Absolutely not, if I'm having soft drinks I'm not having soft anecdotes.' Ros laughed, and Jackie's heart boomed at the invitation to include Duncan in conversations. It had never been like this with Steve.

'No, I was just thinking . . . when I was in Crete I was so torn.' She hadn't thought any of this through and was alarmed to hear it tumbling out of her mouth. 'I felt like I had this big choice to make between being there or coming back, sticking to the team or wanting a man, and whether I was helping keep the courts and . . . Well, I came back, and we still lost the courts. It feels almost freeing to be powerless. Jesus listen to me, I'm not even drunk.' She laughed but the others didn't join her.

Renee rubbed the back of her hand. 'Not everything is your responsibility, Jack. I know how you feel. You sound like my first five years of being a doctor. Everything felt life and death and sometimes it was, but you have to compartmentalise.'

'I don't think me choosing a holiday or a netball team compares to being a doctor . . .' The attention being on her was starting to make Jackie feel very self-conscious, 'it's just funny, that's all.'

'We all feel like that, I think,' Claire piped up. 'You're the main character in your own story so you feel integral to everything.'

Annie laughed. 'I see myself as an extra: less pressure.'

'Not saying you're not important, Jack,' Claire continued, smiling at Annie's comment. 'I don't know if you and Ros know what you've done with this team, but it's been a big deal.' There were various nods round the table and Jackie could feel a threatening cloud of tears behind her eyes. She held Ros's hand under the table. 'Richard and I had a trial separation,' Claire said, taking a sip of her drink.

'You split up?' Jackie's eyes were wide.

'No,' Claire put her glass back down gently, lining it up neatly on the coaster, 'No, we are staying together. I just . . . we had a break. I was thinking about a lot of the chats we'd been having and I started to wonder if I was disrespecting myself by living the life I was. So we separated and had some frank conversations, but, actually, I realised I wasn't wrong about being happy. I really do like my life. We're carrying on as we were, but everything is just out on the table now. An open relationship. It's interesting. Exciting. But I'm grateful for you ladies, I don't know if I'd have examined it without you.'

There was a silence while they processed.

Jackie looked around the table at all the faces. She'd only known most of them a matter of months, but they felt crucial.

Would they carry on being friends without the team? There was nothing to stop them, obviously, but would life get in the way? There would be new houses on the courts within a year, and new families going about their busy days. Kath's diary would fill up with putting the children first. Jay would get a job and move back to London. It would all disappear back into the woodwork. Jackie's life would carry on too, obviously – she'd probably even take Freya to the new park – and life would go on for everything except the newts.

The women who could afford the sports centre prices would play there and those who couldn't would trickle away. It wasn't fair, but what could she do? She knew she could do nothing, but her mind still chewed over the problem. Resenting the difficulty of finding a space to just be a person, Jackie explored the magnitude of the problem and then let it settle like sediment in swirling water gone still. It was nothing she could fix, and she felt like a coward for wanting to believe that.

She focused back on the warm faces and pub in front of her, where the conversation had moved on to whether it was genuinely possible to be comfortable in a thong. Jay and Claire were putting forward a passionate argument for yes while Kath and Annie extolled the virtues of cotton to a giggling Renee (lace, briefs) and an adamantly commando Ros.

46

'Tea?'

'No.'

'A hot chocolate then?'

'No, I don't want anything.'

'A sandwich?'

'Jackie, if you offer me one more thing to put in my mouth I'm going to scream.'

'You won't be able to scream if I've stuffed something in your mouth,' Jackie replied primly.

Ros was grumpy and it was setting Jackie's teeth on edge. It was their last game at the courts, possibly ever, and Duncan had dropped Jackie off after an early dinner date. Ros had been in a foul mood since she'd arrived with Jay and Jackie was paranoid that it must be down to her date with Duncan. She couldn't see why Ros would suddenly have changed her mind on him, but it didn't stop her assuming. She'd racked her brains to see if there had been pre-game plans with Ros she had forgotten, but nothing came to mind. Duncan had been perfectly pleasant to Ros, but Ros's mood had been musty and cantankerous. Jackie couldn't help but guiltily assume that this sulk was her fault.

'I hate not being able to play,' Ros croaked, jolting Jackie's train of thought off its track.

'You what?' Jackie turned her head to look at Ros; the familiar vertebrae pinged and she decided she really needed to stop getting surprised by things or her neck was never going to last.

'I hate not being able to play.' Ros's eyes stared ahead all glisteny and if Jackie hadn't known her better she'd think she was tearing up. 'I'm not crying. Stop looking at me like that, it's just bitter and the wind is all in my eyes.'

'I thought you hated playing?' Jackie was dumbfounded.

'I do. But I hate not being able to play more. Especially when you lot are all still at it. And it's the last game. And—' She pulled up short. If words were cars there'd be the screeching of brakes.

'And what?' Jackie pushed tentatively.

'And I saw my stupid doctor today and he said it might be best if I don't play again for quite a while. Because of the head bump.'

'It was more than a bump, Ros . . .' Jackie said gently, thinking back to that night in the hospital and the explanation of the head injury Ros had received when she passed out and fell.

'Do you think I don't know it was, Jack? I know. I can't remember half my words, and I'm not allowed to work full time, and I can't run about. He suggested swimming. Swimming? *Have you had a skin fall?* I said back to him. I'm not swimming in a pool with other people, that's disgusting. No. It's all gone and I'm just going to become a useless old bat who can't do anything. No wine. No nothing. I hate it. You should see the way people look at me at work.'

Jackie swallowed her up in a big hug, feeling the slightness of Ros beneath their big winter coats. 'Why didn't you say you were feeling like this?'

A muffled noise came out from under several layers of fleece and Jackie pulled back to allow Ros to speak. 'Because I don't want to be the one who needs help. I want to take care of you. Not the other way round. I hate this. I'd rather be dead.'

'Don't say that, Ros. Don't say that. I'm serious.'

'You're being waved on. Go and play.' Ros pointed to where the match referee was blowing a whistle and waving them over.

'I'll sit this one out with you,' Jackie said quickly. 'If we can't both play then neither of us will.'

'Don't pity me. I hate that more than anything.' Ros was spiky and refusing to look Jackie in the eye. Jackie knew better than to argue.

'All right then. Well, you're assistant coach, remember? Or you can be cheerleader?' Jackie was scrambling and she knew it. 'I'll expect eight sets of rhyming couplets. That can be your job.' Jackie gave Ros's upper arm a rub, but she could get no more response out of her so she made her way over to the court. It was Ros's way to admit insecurity through crankiness, but it did leave it hard to know how to help.

Their final match was as disastrous as most of their others. Jackie was quietly very pleased with herself not to have been called up for any penalties. She considered that practically as good as winning the game. Yes, technically, she had only touched the ball seven times, so there wasn't much opportunity to be called up for errors, but still. Seven clean times is better than none. She scooped a still miserable and monosyllabic Ros off the sideline and whisked her home.

They were foregoing their usual pub trip that night in favour of a fancy team dinner the night after to celebrate the end of the league. The Skids said their goodbyes in the car park and Jay, Ros and Jackie climbed into Jay's car to drive home. A light rain started and Jackie felt the urge to puncture the silence.

She gave the elephant a fond rub on the trunk. 'How's your mum? Are you two OK?'

Jay sighed. 'We're . . . ok.' She put on the indicator and let her shoulders relax. 'We're OK. We've turned a corner, I think.' She took a deep breath. 'I don't think this whole thing changes how I see her as my mum, I just think it's made me think of her differently as a woman.' Jackie digested this, wondering what to say, but Jay carried on talking, staring at the red lights in the traffic ahead of them. 'You love who you love. I get that. But you behave how you behave too, and I think she was shitty. Not as shitty as him. But shitty.'

'Speaking of shitty,' Ros piped up from the back seat, 'You tell her when she gets fed up with his undies she's welcome on the team?'

Jackie laughed. Ros was thawing. 'It's funny you thinking of your mum as a woman.'

'What do you mean?'

'I had a funny chat with Leon a few months ago, and he seemed to find it sort of baffling that me and Steve were just people. I don't know. It depends how people parent, I suppose. I don't think I ever really thought of my parents as normal people either. You're wise beyond your years, Jay.'

Jay laughed. 'I don't know about that. We've just had to spend a lot of time together as adults, so we've existed together outside of parent and child roles, you know? I've seen her be herself instead of my mum.'

Jackie nodded. 'Yes.' Those little labels again. The other woman, mum, just a woman. They arrived home and Ros took herself up to bed, claiming a headache, while Jay and Jackie settled down to half-watch the end of a film.

'Was Ros all right tonight?' Jay asked, pulling the blanket up over her feet.

'Oh . . . she will be. I think. She's all out of sorts with how much she's had to slow down since she was ill. She doesn't like not being in the thick of things. I'm not sure how to help.'

'It must be so hard. She must be feeling so vulnerable.'

'Yes, it might be the first problem she's not had the equipment to just fix. When you're smart, rich, forceful and proactive problems just wilt. But you can't argue with your body.' Jackie's phone buzzed with an incoming phone call from Duncan. 'I'm going to take this and head to bed.' She answered the call and took herself upstairs. She liked these late-night conversations on nights Duncan didn't stay over. They talked for nearly an hour, somehow having a million things to talk about despite having seen each other earlier that day. Jackie fell asleep to the sound of Jay's video game playing through the floorboards, and Ros's snoring coming through the wall, and it felt somewhere near normal.

47

Jackie looked at the clock. 3.42 a.m. The house was silent. Only if she lay incredibly still could she hear the main road in the distance, rumbling occasionally with tyres through standing water.

She thought it could work. This idea that had germinated and woken her without her being totally sure where it had come from. Perhaps this was what convinced people into religion? Ideas just springing up in the night. Good ones too. She lay very still and tried to slow her mind down to think it through. It would certainly make Ros feel wanted, and give her things to do, and in a way that her health could manage while she was recovering. But how to get her to say yes? She wouldn't want charity. Even if this technically would be reverse charity.

Jackie would have to make it seem like it was something for herself. How to do that? Perhaps . . . maybe bartering? What could she offer Ros in exchange? Was there anything she could give Ros that Ros couldn't just get for herself? It all fell into place. Jackie's muscles relaxed into the duvet and she willed her idea to still be good come morning.

48

Jackie slid the papers across the table towards Ros, avoiding the damp patch where she had excitedly slopped latte onto the Formica table.

'I'm proposing a deal,' she said confidently, holding Ros's eye. 'I'll do this for you, and you do something for me.'

Ros looked suspiciously at the papers. 'It's not that I'm begging you to get divorced, Jack, you can take him back if it's what you really want, I'll do a speech at your fortieth anniversary party if it's what you want. And it'll be a crackle too. I was never pushing you to leave him. I just want you to look out for yourself, that's all.'

'I know. I know. And I know I reacted awfully before. But I know you're right.' Jackie kept her tone even, trying to do her best impression of a confident negotiator. 'And I'm willing to do that, strictly for you mind, if you'll do something for me.'

Ros raised an eyebrow, already faintly seeing through Jackie's ruse. 'What's that then?'

'I want you to sponsor the netball league.'

Ros nodded silently, and Jackie went on, 'Your firm has a decent amount of employment law and family law cases and' – she checked the notes Annie had carefully made for her – 'a large percentage of these cases are brought by female clients. So, sponsoring the netball league would be a good way to show the firm's solidarity with the women in our community, as well as exposing you to a large number of new potential clients. There are a lot of women who won't be able to play once the games go into the sports hall, but if you sponsored the league we could keep the cost the same as it currently is for the courts. There'd be a lot of women very grateful to you. They need you.'

She eyed Ros carefully, hoping she wasn't laying it on too thick. Ros blinked at her, doing some mental calculations. 'What sort of sponsoring, banners and the like?'

Jackie pulled her notebook up on to the table and looked at the list of ideas she, Jay and Annie had come up with. 'Banners, yes. Maybe bibs with the firm on too?'

'I like banners. Maybe with my face on?'

'I like banners with your face on. What do you think?' Jackie knew it was going to be a yes.

'Of course I will, you daft old bat, I always would have. I'll have to see how much it'll be, obviously, but it won't be more than the Christmas party and that's always awful so the board will have to say yes. But you don't have to sign these to get me to do it; you only had to ask.'

Jackie looked at the papers lying on the table. 'Well, the thing is, I find it easier to do stuff for myself if I'm pretending it's for other people. So, if you could just pretend you won't possibly sponsor the netball team unless I start divorcing Steve then you'll be doing both of us a favour.'

Ros grinned and rolled her eyes. 'All right, you want my best Scrooge impression, is it? Here goes: Jackie Douglas, you're not getting a Daim bar of my hard-earned dough until you sign those papers and rid yourself of that scurvy knave. Good?'

Jackie laughed heartily and took the lid off her pen, leafing through pages to the first of the sticky tabs Annie had helpfully added. She signed her name on each bare black line and began the process of extricating herself from the man who had been unable to see her in the seat in which she currently sat.

Epilogue

'Never?'

'No. Not once.'

'Right.'

'We're more in it for the . . .' Jackie looked about herself for assistance. 'What are we in it for?'

The rest of the Skids looked at one another, weighing up who might speak. Jay opened her mouth first. 'Well, a variety of reasons but I'd say the one we all have in common is the wine.'

There was a lot of laughter and nodding, and Amanda, their newest recruit, eyed them cautiously. She was short, with a runny nose and wide eyes. She clung to Jay, who had brought her to them via the charity, and was showing her there could be a life after an unexpected pregnancy forces you out of the life you thought you'd have. Jackie smothered her smile down and looked at Amanda seriously. 'If you're wanting to play to win, then we're probably not the team for you.'

'We're definitely not,' Ros chipped in, between bites of Cornetto.

'It's not like we're actively trying not to win though,' Laurel offered, desperate to not seem like a complete loser in front of strangers. 'It is definitely on our to-do list.'

'It is,' Jackie confirmed. 'It most certainly is. We would love to win. Some of us would love to score. It's just sometimes leaving the house is the bigger challenge and once we've done that there's not much energy left to really focus on winning.'

Amanda nodded. She looked tiny and lost. 'Yeah, yeah, OK. You won't mind if I can't play every week?' She glanced over to the corner of the hall to where Duncan was gently rocking her pram back and forth, keeping the baby quiet, 'Things are a bit up in the air.'

'Whatever you need,' Jackie said gently.

'I was so worried about coming in case it went wrong. I don't think I could have coped with another awful thing.' A terrified laugh jolted out of Amanda and was met with understanding smiles from the Skids.

Kath laughed loudly. 'The only thing awful about our netball team is the netball. Everything else is great.'

The game was a failure. A dismal failure. A noble failure. One of their now very traditional failures. An additional downside to playing in the hall was that a fair percentage of the many shots they failed to catch hit the wall and bounced back into the court, taking them by surprise. Claire took a ball to the side of the head that left her ear quite without sound. Jackie missed catches, fell over, and laughed more than she had at any other match. When the final whistle blew they high-fived the disgraceful scoreline and then whooped like gibbons when Annie received player of the match. She took her little mini certificate, sponsored by Mackie and Howard, with a beaming photo of Ros in the top corner, and floated for the rest of the evening. They were so loud in the pub that night that within an hour of sitting down they were the only patrons. Jackie vowed to push away the worry about being obnoxious until another day.

In a matter of months she had gone from being home alone in a creaking, empty house to having almost more people around her than she knew what to do with. At home, the bathroom had a constant queue between her, Duncan, Ros and Jay needing to brush teeth and wash faces and other less fragrant things.

Jay had made her room her own and was showing no signs of feeling like she should move out. Ros was in the second slightly smaller bedroom and by God, she made a noise about being in the smaller room. Jackie knew Ros was probably well enough to go home by now, but Ros was claiming that the money she was making from renting the flat was the only thing keeping the team afloat and Jackie didn't want her to go and so didn't argue. Duncan stayed most nights, meaning every seat on the sofas was full when they all sat down to put the TV on and not watch it. A full house and a full life.

'I'm not staying for ever, though,' Ros warned, waving a biscuit at Jackie and shaking crumbs over Jay's lap. 'Just until I get my noodles straight – that's all.'

Jackie rolled her eyes. 'In that case, you only need to stay until ten years ago. That's the last time I remember you having your shit together.'

'Look at what I can achieve with a busted bonce!' Ros waved a hand at the new sponsored netball bibs for the league. 'You should be truly terrified at what I'd achieve at full capacity. Your divorce would be so eviscerating, do I mean eviscerating? Incinerating? No, I do mean eviscerating. Ha! It would be so eviscerating that Steve would be inventing time travel to go back and stop you meeting me.'

Ros's memory had enormous gaping holes where words should be and the frustration of going from being focused eighteen hours a day to the forced break was a huge weight on her self-esteem. She was trying to learn to relax, and she was taking to it like a duck to concrete.

'You don't think he'd go back and just not cheat on me and leave me?' Jackie asked, feeling a little odd talking about it in front of Duncan but trying to accept that he knew it all anyway and they were adults.

'No,' Ros said quickly. 'The man is ninety-nine per cent pure carat fool.' This made Jay laugh so hard she got hiccups and had to disappear into the kitchen to get some water. When she came back Duncan and Ros were shouting at the poor contestant on the television who had the misfortune to not know an answer they did know.

'Why would you even go on if you couldn't answer something like that?' Duncan stared at the unfortunate individual in disgust.

'Exactly!' cried Ros. 'I bet half of them don't even study for it.'

'Study?' Jackie wailed, but was shushed by a Duncan who wanted to hear the next question. He pressed a hand over her mouth and she giggled and relented.

The next question was also answered wrongly and Ros threw a cushion at the TV in fury.

'Maybe we should apply?' Duncan suggested and Ros had her iPad out before Jackie even processed what he'd said.

'Absolutely. Jay, you're in?'

'Aye aye cap'n,' Jay said from her upside-down position half-drinking, half-spilling her glass of water.

Jackie also nodded her assent and squashed herself deeper into Duncan and the sofa enjoying the anarchy and the noise. This house that had felt like such a mausoleum to her marriage felt alive again. Jackie felt present in a way she hadn't for years, maybe decades. She had it all: Ros, Duncan, Jay and herself. All here under one roof ready to begin the next main bit of her life.

Acknowledgements

I'm not sure what I'm supposed to do with my life now I've managed to finish a novel. I thought it would sit burning a hole in my conscience until at least my eighties. I suppose I should go on holiday or start a new one, but for now, let me string out these 'thank yous' to people you've not heard of.

Firstly, a huge thank you to Kate Hewson and the team at Two Roads for taking a punt on me and letting me write this. The more I think about the huge chance you took on me, the more unbelievable it seems that this book exists. Thank you so much. Thank you for gentle feedback, ego cradling and for liking the world I made. Here's to more of the same.

Thank you to Diana, Andrew and Jo, and to Kate and the UTC team for all the care you've taken with my precious career. I am so grateful to the work that goes on in the background to help me get my silly ideas out into the world.

Thank you to my lovely mum, for letting me draw on her experience having encephalitis to write Ros' story. It's not the most well-known of diseases and I'd never heard of it before that awful week when a bomb went off in our family. I'm really grateful for the opportunity to be able to raise awareness a little bit and hopefully a few more people can catch it early and recover. Thanks for letting me use it mum, I hope I've got it right. I'm so glad we kept you.

A huge thank you to Lucy Dyke at Geoff Productions who many years ago gave me so much faith in Jackie and the team. Thank you, Lucy, for helping me bring Jackie to life so vividly in my mind that she made it to a book.

Thank you to Elle for lending me her law degree notes so I could check I wasn't making Ros the worst lawyer in the world! Thanks to Morwenna and Hattie and Yssy and all the netball girls for starting to play netball in the first place and then for letting me come and watch to get a sense of what the leagues are like. No of course I didn't join in, don't be daft. Oh well, actually I did one time. Remember that pass I intercepted? The one that wasn't a pass but someone trying to toss the ball to the referee? Yuck, awful game.

Always, thank you to my Tom and my Maki for being my home. And finally, thank you to – in the immortal words of every PopMaster player ever – everyone else who knows me.